I0831822

When No One Else Would

M. G. Rolla

ISBN: 978-0-578-22833-4

First Edition

Prologue

Date: Monday, January 6th, 2020

Time: 1510hrs EST

Location: United Nations Headquarters, New York

Temperature: 38 Degrees Fahrenheit

"Please be seated. I now declare open this special session, as requested by the Security Council. On today's agenda is item 71, as presented in the security council's meeting on the 13th of May." United Nations President Álvaro José de Mendonça e Moura, of Portugal, says as the assembly of nations takes their seats in an orderly fashion, "I now turn proceedings over to security council president, Francois Delattre of France, to present item 71."

A tall, average build man with glasses and greying hair soon takes the podium and clears his throat. He understands, fully, that what he is about to propose to the general assembly has never been attempted before nor has it even been considered before a few weeks ago. It will require the collective agreement of every nation currently sitting before him in order to have a chance at working. He clears his throat once more.

"Ladies, Gentleman, representatives, honored and invited guests, I stand here before you to present item 71, The Independent Peacekeeping Initiative. This initiative calls for the creation of an independent and unbiased task force that will investigate, pursue and, if necessary, eliminate any threats to global stability. We, on the Security Council recognize that this will not end the large-scale conflicts that are currently taking place; however, we hope that it will prevent ones from starting in the first place. The exact details of this initiative are present in the folders you were handed upon your arrival this morning. We will reconvene in closed session at 1pm today to debate and vote on this initiative, to maintain the security necessary. Thank you for your time."

With this, the calm ambassador leaves the podium and takes his seat amongst the assembly, glancing around to notice his colleagues flipping through the folder he had mentioned in his speech. The meeting continues for another hour, with proposals being introduced from the various committees that comprise the UN, before being put into recess until the closed session at one o'clock in the afternoon. The representatives carefully avoid talking about item 71 however, choosing only to look at the folder periodically during the lunch break before hurriedly putting it away as cloud of uneasiness begins to fill the building. Many of the press on hand try to ask questions but fail to get anything but the usual response of "we're talking about it in closed session and will be releasing a statement afterwards" leaving them frustrated yet understanding. Freedom of the press is important, but so is secrecy, especially when it comes to the fine details of item 71 and there are some things that are best left unmentioned until details have been finalized.

An announcement goes out over the United Nations P.A. system, stating the representatives should report to the assembly chamber and be seated; one o'clock has come quicker than any of them had expected. Despite the rush, the representative move towards the chamber in the professional calm that depicts their diplomatic role. Side conversations end at the door and a stressful calm falls over the room as everyone takes their seats. The doors are closed, and the outside world is left wondering and waiting as the beginning of debate is signaled, with it soon becoming clear that proceedings were going to take most of the following twenty-four hours. The press leaves for their hotel rooms once blankets are seen being brought in for the representatives; it's going to be a long and largely unproductive night with progress mainly coming in the morning when everyone is awake. Security guards look on, standing at their posts without an unnecessary movement or noise.

Date: Thursday, November 26th, 2020

Time: 0800hrs SST

Location: Midway Base, Former US Minor Outlying Island, Pacific Ocean

Temperature: 77 Degrees Fahrenheit

The morning dew is long gone as a group of six trainees and their trainer arrive at the one-hundred-yard range and begin the morning's target practice. The humid air already forcing their tired bodies to sweat significantly through their shirts due to the trainees running three miles after their 5am workout, with breakfast ending about ten minutes ago. None of the trainees seem to mind however, due to the fact they have been doing this every other weekend for the past few months and this is just another day at the office. As holes begin to appear in the paper targets and dirt splashes from the berm behind them, the trainer approaches the trainee that is closest to the armory.

"I have to say John; your squad is doing well this morning." The trainer says with a clearly deep growly voice, as the trainee he identifies sends another 6.5mm bullet down range to the target.

The trainer stands at six feet five inches tall with no hair and black beard, a muscular build, dark tan skin and a standard American army uniform covering his body. He's a rather intimidating sight that causes most to listen without much of a fuss, except for the squad, though his concerns are rarely leveled towards them.

"They certainly are, though we did promise them a large dinner tonight and half day of training if they put in extra effort this morning." John replies putting his rifle on safe, clearing the chamber, and removing the magazine before picking the rifle up as he stands and placing it on a table next to the trainer.

His squad mates continue firing, causing little plums of dirt to appear in the berm with each corresponding bang.

"You have a point there. All of you have certainly earned it, though I would say you need it more than they do. You look like shit." The trainer says glancing over John's battered and scarred six-foot tall, 210-pound body and dusty brown hair that could desperately use a shower.

"Damn Rob, I don't look that bad, do I?" John says with a laugh, brushing some of the dirt out of his hair and adjusting the tan 1911 mounted in a drop leg holster on his right thigh. "I'll be sure to get a shower before dinner."

Before the conversation continues, a skinny young man with black hair, dressed in a dark camouflage, comes running over to the two men, saluting them before handing John a manila folder, quickly covering his ears when he does so. There's a Ruger Security-9 in a holster on his hip as does Rob. As John quickly pages through the folder his thanks the young man before dismissing him. He returns to a nearby building with "Intelligence Center" written above the main entrance way.

"I guess that shower will have to wait won't it?" Rob says with a disappointed smile on his face, knowing by John's expression that it's going to be a long night.

"That depends on how my next phone call with the Israeli Prime Minister goes." John replies passing the folder to Rob, hoping to get a more experienced second opinion as a couple of his squad mates reload their weapons.

"Well we've known for a while now that he's a bit of a hot head so that's nothing new." Rob postulates as he looks through the folder.

"His words don't concern me. The activity at Ramat David Airforce Base does though." John says simply, turning to watch his squad mates.

Rob instantly turns to the satellite photo that has John concerned. It shows twenty-four F-15I's and eight F-15C's on the taxiway surrounding two of the runways. From the image it is easy to see that all the aircraft have been fitted with external tanks to extend their range miles beyond Israeli air space.

"I'll begin drawing up a strike plan should it be necessary." Rob says heavily as he closes the folder.

"If we reach that point, they will have already lost." John replies confidently and without care how a strike could look, "Give the squad a break till I finish my phone call." He finishes before turning and walking towards the command operations building, as denoted by the letters above the entrance.

"Roger that." Rob agrees before yelling "Cease Fire!" across the firing range, with all gunfire ceasing immediately after.

As the rest of the squad gathers their things, a medium set young woman with curly black hair jogs from the firing range over to Rob. It's John's second in command, Elizabeth.

"Why the sudden break?" She asks curiously on the squad's behalf.

"The Israeli's are acting up again." Rob replies handing her the folder, which she quickly begins to scan through.

"Damn idiots." She mutters under her breath glancing up just in time to catch a glimpse of John walking into the command operations building.

"That depends on their response Liza." Rob replies thinking of what the squad can do to fill the time, "Go get showered, John's going be awhile." He finishes with a sigh and a wave of his hand.

The trainee's do as they're told, heading to their individual houses located near North Beach on the Northern Coast of Sand Island. A storm begins gathering 25 miles to the North, it's not forecast to hit the island though it does create a fantastic light show for those on it.

Chapter One

Date: Wednesday, December 2nd, 2020

Time: 1833hrs EST

Location: Scranton, Pa

Temperature: 34 Degrees Fahrenheit

"The world is still reeling from the suicide of Israeli Prime Minister Benjamin Netanyahu and the destruction Ramat David Airforce Base. The Israeli Government is saying the two incidents are unrelated, however, they are keeping any other details close to their chest. You'll know more when we know more. Back to you Jake." Oren Liebermann explains before the broadcast returns to Jake Tapper.

"Suicide my ass, no wonder these guys get called fake news half the time." A young man scoffs with a thick Russian accent.

"I think the Israeli's don't want what actually happened getting out and I also think you're having a little too much to drink Vladimir." Elizabeth chuckles with her feet in front of her on a couch perpendicular to Vladimir's as she leans back against her boyfriend, Jeremy.

The trio chuckle as John looks on from the balcony above, allowing himself to smile slightly before turning and going into his bedroom, walking through and heading into the bathroom. He takes his tee shirt off revealing several battle scars covering his entire upper body and turns on the shower, making sure to get it nice and warm to help calm down his sore muscles. Before removing the rest of his clothes, he pauses in front of the mirror over the sink, supporting his weight with it in the process. He shakes his head as he glances at himself in the mirror, quickly examining the scars on his forehead and right cheek. They've healed quicker than he was expecting, though he doesn't dare mess with them, just in case.

After taking his clothes off, he turns the shower on to a decently high temperature, not too hot but certainly not to cold. He relaxes as the hot water lands on his scarred, stressed skin. His sore muscles finally releasing the tension that has built up over the course of the day, a small yet welcome reprieve.

On the sink, his phone begins to buzz, displaying a call from Rob as it rattles around harmlessly on the edge of the vanity.

John sighs and blows away some water from his mouth, not wanting to answer the call but knowing he must. Almost annoyed, he jerks the water handle, turning the water off and forcefully accepting the call as he dries his hands and head.

"Go ahead Rob." John says barely containing his annoyance and contempt at being interrupted during his moment of relaxation.

"Sorry for interrupting John, I know it's your nig-." Rob starts but is interrupted by John retorting. "Cut to the chase Rob."

There is short, yet uneasy pause extending for what feels like a few minutes as Rob composes himself after the sudden realization that a twenty-one-year-old is on the road to becoming more battle hardened that a career military man.

"The Dallas has picked up a Russian Yasen class submarine in the Barents Sea. Its mission is unknown, and it was supposed to be in dry dock for at least the next three months." Rob replies after clearing his throat.

"You mean the Krasnoyarsk? That thing wasn't supposed to be launched for another three months." John says as a large screen in the corner of the bedroom comes to life with technical drawings of the Yasen class, a news article and a map of the Barents Sea appearing in rapid succession.

John dresses himself in blue pajama pants and a light grey tee shirt as this takes place, putting the phone on speaker as he does. He's not worried about anyone eavesdropping; anyone who would hear the conversation is a part of the organization to begin with. The thought runs through his head though, as he glances to the still closed bedroom door.

"It's not, it's still in dry dock according to our satellites. According to the sonar operator and Captain on the Dallas it's likely the Kazan. Though we still don't know why it would be there." Rob says as John's eyes focus in on the map of the Barents Sea and the red dot that shows where contact was made.

"Keep me posted, I'll brief the squad in five minutes, make sure Neil and Clara know to expect my phone call." John says, his mind already focused on the mission and pushing forward with formulating any orders that may need to be given.

"While I appreciate your willingness John, how about we wait until morning. You've already had a long week and so has the squad." Rob says derailing John's mind in an instant as tiredness fills his body.

He takes a moment, pondering the time, six fifty-two in the evening. Despite being relatively early the darkness outside makes this time feel much later than it is.

"Okay, I will concede, just…this…once. Have the Dallas tail at a safe distance and have a report sent to me at zero six hundred. I'll brief the squad zero six fifteen if there's anything worth briefing them on, make sure Neil and Clara know to be up." John replies chuckling slightly.

"I'm sure they'll love to hear that. Have a good night John." Rob says with a laughing sigh before hanging up clearly.

John puts down the phone and takes one last look at the computer screen, trying to figure out what could be going through the Russian Defense Minister's mind now. Is it a training exercise? Is it a routine patrol that wasn't shared with the organization? Or is this something more? Maybe it's a show of force to demonstrate that the Russian's are ignoring the squad's threats?

These questions fester in the back of John's mind as he slowly turns the computer off and turns to exit the bedroom. Jeremy is standing at the door, though it doesn't startle John like it would most people, as if he expected him to be there for one reason or another.

"Twenty-One years old and you're worrying about issues that keep President's up at night... and yet, you barely bat an eyelid." He says with a Shakespearean tone that only his British accent can pull off.

"It's easier when you're only running on three hours of sleep a night." John smiles, "What can I do for you Jeremy?"

"Your absence was becoming noticeable and I was nominated to make sure you were still amongst the land of the living." Jeremy says with a subtly sarcastic chuckle.

"I figured it would be at some point; I needed a shower and then Rob called, apparently the Russians might be up to something." John replies

"Well let's just hope they haven't had too much Vodka. Come on downstairs, relax for a bit and grab a bite to eat. Elizabeth is about to pull the ribs out of the oven." Jeremy says with a subtle sigh, patting John on the shoulder to get him to relax; it barely works.

The pair head downstairs after John slips his phone into his pocket, hoping that doesn't go off for the rest of the night so that he can get some semblance of rest and relaxation.

Jeremy let's out a quiet sigh when he observes John's actions, lamenting the fact that John's last "vacation" was three months ago and only lasted 24 hours before the EU decided to cancel Greece's membership, who promptly went to a war footing. A few dignitaries and a few days later, the situation calmed down and Greece could rejoin the European Union.

As the young men arrive downstairs, Elizabeth is already cutting the two racks of ribs into even portions for the squad members to eat. Vladimir finishes another round of Vodka before helping to serve the corn, his Russian fortitude coming in handy as he makes sure to not burn himself.

The group laughs and shares jokes as the four friends get their food drinks and settle down to watch a movie on John's television. They're not expecting to have any classes tomorrow; the snows just started and is coming down at about an inch an hour and is forecast to drop about eight inches by the time the sun comes up.

"So, when are you going to ask Sam out John? You're running out of time here." Elizabeth asks having gotten progressively drunker as the movie played through its run time.

"Possibly never if this job has anything to say about it." John chuckles in good spirits, not even showing any outward signs of sadness to his friends; they know better, however.

Everyone lets out a subtly somber laugh trying to mask how he or she really feels, though happiness returns quickly as the jokes continue to fly left and right. Then… John's phone rings…

Date: Thursday, December 3rd, 2020

Time: 0043hrs WGT

Location: 34,000ft over the North Atlantic Ocean

Temperature: 18 Degrees Fahrenheit

As a matte black Airbus A350-900 streaks across the sky; Jeremy, Elizabeth, and Vladimir are fast asleep trying to get some semblance of rest before they land in London. Each squad member was supposed to have their own special rooms that are very similar to Singapore Airlines Double Suites with a darker color pallet. However, the two squad couples have their own rooms and the two extras were removed and replaced with a larger briefing room. John is currently in that briefing room on a video call with an equally tired Neil, Clara and Rob, all of whom are trying their best to stay awake.

"Someone remind me why I can't just blow the Syrian Prime Minister into the next century." John says frustrated as he pours over the files in front of him.

"Well, you can but chances are you'd destabilize the whole region and kill millions of civilians in the process." Clara replies bluntly, but gently, knowing that John is probably more tired than she is.

"I see… that's a pretty good reason… Can we talk to anyone other than the Russians in order to keep peace in the area?" John asks trying to eliminate the bad choices in his mind.

"Not really. They're the only ones with a controlling stake in the region. The downside is they would likely be in favor of another civil war so they can get a sympathetic leader in power." Rob replies after hiding a yawn.

"Well then we just need to be careful when we do." John says picking a folder up off the mahogany table in front of him.

"Why is that?" Neil asks sound like he missed something; Clara also displays a confused look on her face.

Noticing, John shoots an "I told you so" glare squarely in Rob's direction, who proceeds to quickly explain the situation.

"The Dallas is currently following the Russian submarine Kazan in the Barents Sea. We are still trying to determine the submarine's intentions though it seems to be on a test cruise and nothing more." He says with slight trepidation in his voice, knowing he made a wrong call earlier.

"Meaning we have cards we can't put on the table until we know what's in the deck." John says to hide his slight annoyance about what occurred earlier in the evening before continuing. "Ok so we'll meet you three in London and then we'll have Vladimir speak with Putin when we get to Moscow; he should be sober by then."

"I'll make sure the Captain of the Dallas knows to expect a message from us." Neil says and John nods in approval reorganizing the papers in front of him as Rob gets a quick drink of dark black coffee.

"Have the 1st Carrier and 3rd Cruiser Squadrons on standby alert, we may need them, and I'd rather not have them on their way to the Gulf of Mexico when we do." John say moving the conversation swiftly on, calmly making sure everything is where it should be.

“Copy that.” Clara says, quickly typing out a message that can be heard over the video call.

Rob steps away for a moment to look at something a messenger has brought him. The command and control center behind him come into focus and the pace immediately picks up; something John notices without even looking up as a message has come over the computer in front of him.

“Screw the formalities, I need our planes fueled and hot when we arrive. Make sure there are tankers in the air and have the 1st Carrier Squadron hold station at ready alert in the Persian Gulf.” John says with authority of an Admiral ordering a fleet into battle.

“Roger that.” Neil, Clara, and Rob all reply in sync with one another as an alarm begins ringing throughout the plane, waking up the rest of the squadron members on board the aircraft.

A message flashes up on the screen “*Direct Line Connected*”. John carefully picks up a handheld microphone that’s bungee wired to the desk and presses the talk button.

“Admiral, I need your men at action stations.” John says sternly and calmly as the siren begins blaring across the 1st carrier squadron.

Well-trained men and women begin racing to their posts in a very controlled form of organized chaos. Within minutes a calm falls over the carrier battle group and steady rhythm of plane launches takes place until four flights of four F-18E Super Hornets are in the air conducting a combat air patrol. An uneasy calm descends on the Persian Gulf and the squad will arrive in less than twelve hours.

Date: Thursday, December 3rd, 2020

Time: 1813hrs AST

Location: Persian Gulf, 300 miles southeast of Kuwait

Temperature: 54 Degrees Fahrenheit

As the sun begins to set, the squad arrives over the UNS Kestrel, CVN – 01, and begins a series of final approaches. The only carrier the squadron has available to them due to the limited amount of money granted to them by the United Nations. Already a veteran of numerous combat sorties, the Kestrel was retired and formally decommissioned by the United States in February 2017. Her former designation, CVN – 65 USS Enterprise, comes with a name and a history that weighs heavy on sailors who man her to this day. Her rebuild took many hundreds of hours of labor and manpower, but the UN managed to get her up and running in a record three months; a feat that they do not wish to repeat.

As the F18E's circle overhead, the squad members land their planes carefully and precisely on the deck. Painted a deep dark black their planes stand out against the rest of the aerial fleet with red wolf's heads paint on the tail fins of the each of the aircraft.

Elizabeth, Jeremy, Vladimir, Clara and Neil land in sequence in the Su-33 Flankers. These were obtained from Russia, as they were deemed surplus to requirements and then specially modified by the UN with thrust vectoring engines and a stealth coating. John is the last to land, with the carrier shuttering slightly as he does. His plane is one of a kind, an F-4E Phantom II that was rescued from a boneyard in Arizona. It was quickly modified for carrier operations, fitted with thrust vectoring engines, upgraded single seat avionics, painted with a stealth coating and has an added shark's mouth on the nose. An intimidating presence to be sure, the Vietnam veteran still has plenty of life left in her and has claimed four aircraft kills since becoming John's personal fighter plane.

The ground crew neatly helps the squadron park their planes on the Kestrel's flight deck and set about the task of refueling and arming the aircraft. The other squad members open their planes canopies and climb down, stretching their sore legs and taking a deep breath of natural air.

"Purrs like a kitten and floats like a butterfly Pops; you've done a great job." John says taking his helmet off and turning to an older, slightly overweight gentleman who slight gray hair and a slight beard.

"That's good to hear, I was worried you might try and blow the engines on the way here." Pops replies, wiping some of the grease off his hands with a yellow rag that he puts in the pocket of his blue jumpsuit.

John laughs, as they both know the answer to that question, before he and Pops turn to look across the flight deck as the other members of the squad go over their aircraft with their respective crew chiefs.

"They've handed you an impossible task John, I hope you realize that." Pops says deeply as John unzips the top of his flight suit, letting it hang around his waist and revealing a sweat riddled green tee shirt.

"Yeah, I know, and they know too, trouble is somebody has to do it and no one else wants too." John replies, squinting as the sun blares directly in his eyes.

"Sometimes I wish it didn't have to be you." Pops sullenly responds; John characteristically ignores his concerns.

"I'm going to need Neil and Vladimir's planes loaded with Mavericks; the rest of us will be flying top cover. Mission start time is one thirty hours." He states authoritatively, not wanting to be bothered by sentimentality.

"Roger that." Pops says affirmatively looking down at the feck below him, sighing as he does and realizing what it means for everyone's sleep schedule.

John gives him a pat on the shoulder, shakes his hand and presents him with a half-smile before walking towards the conning tower and meeting up with his friends. Their tired smiles hide the fact that they will likely get very little sleep between now and one thirty in the morning. Upon entering the conning tower, they make their way towards the bridge, every sailor saluting them as they pass. The squad's response is decisively more casual, shaking their hands and greeting them by name. It takes a while, but it's a gesture welcomed by the crewmembers that often hear of the squadron as mythic beings, uncaring about anyone except themselves. Entering the bridge, a medium statured, balding, African American male greets them as he removes his captain's hat.

"Long time, no see Admiral Anderson." Clara says giving him a hug as the rest of the squad swiftly makes their introductions, the old Admiral chuckles and smiles at Clara's remarks.

"Wish it was longer." The battle-hardened captain replies sarcastically, replacing his hat on his head and continuing a smile.

"Unfortunately, we don't have that luxury. Recall all but one of the CAPs. At one thirty hours we will be launching a strike mission against the Russian Aircraft Carrier, Admiral Kuznetsov. The Russians have been launching secret missions to destabilize Afghanistan in the aftermath of our Israeli Operation last month. Our objective will be to blow the carrier to kingdom come." John interjects bringing everyone back down to earth and pulling up a tactical map on the touch screen table in front of everyone.

“Four hundred miles to the east. They’re boxing us in as well. Any chance their operations are just a distraction?” Anderson says looking closer at the map.

“That’s not out of the realm of possibility given that we announced our presence in the region last month.” Neil says looking up at the captain before glancing at John to gauge his response.

“Has the Helena picked anything up on radar?” John asks after hiding a bloody cough from his squad mates.

“Nothing but commercial flights within one hundred miles.” The Kestrels radio operator replies a few seconds later after receiving a reply from the UNS Helena.

“So, there’s a chance they don’t even realize we’re here.” Vladimir says with a slight chuckle, clearly amused by his home country’s possible lack of intelligence, though it could also be his hangover getting the best of him.

“A chance that I don’t know if we’re willing to take just yet.” Elizabeth starts glancing around at the sleep-deprived squadron, “Why don’t we sleep on it for four hours and listen to what the Andromeda brings up?”

She’s noticed the summary provided by the Andromeda’s captain in the upper left-hand corner of the table. John has too.

“I second that, get some rest guys, Captain?” John says looking tiredly up at Captain Anderson, who acknowledges with a slight nod. “Bring us down to ready alert and allow your crew to get a shower. They’re going to need some steak and eggs before we launch.”

“Roger that.” He replies with a smile and the whole room lets out a sigh of relief as the announcement goes out over the ships PA system and the squad begins to leave the room.

John stays behind to catch up with the old Captain and doesn’t notice Elizabeth still standing there, having already kissed Jeremy and told him that she’ll catch up.

“What’s on your mind, Liza?” The Captain asks as a lull manifests in John’s and his conversation.

“Just trying to make sure our fearless leader gets some sleep for once.” She replies giving John a forceful pat on the shoulder with a tired smile on her own face.

John chuckles, she’s done this before and its part of the reason why she is his second in command. She looks after him and even takes care of him when he refuses too. She’s great at keeping high standards and morale up; he knows that the squadron would be in safe hands should he die on a mission.

“I will eventually. I know better than to fly a fighter jet with no sleep.” John says after yawning, only reinforcing Elizabeth’s point.

“You should also know better than to leave a woman hanging John.” Elizabeth replies with a sadistic smile and a punch on the shoulder, which John shrugs off as if it was nothing.

“There’s a time and a place for that Liza and now is not the time nor the place.” John replies coldly forcing Admiral Anderson to step in.

“Both of you need the rest, you’ve had a long day.” He says, the wise tone of his voice immediately calming the situation down.

Without a word Elizabeth and John turn and head below decks to their personal quarters. Most of the crew has already retired for the night, though some of them are still milling about before going to bed. They're so tired that they barely notice their commander and the second in command walking through the hallways. John and Elizabeth don't mind however, it means they can get to their rooms quicker. They reach John's quarters first; he pauses before entering.

"Elizabeth..." He says softly getting her to stop in her tracks, neither one can look at the other, "I'll text Sam tonight if it makes you happy."

"That would." Elizabeth replies softly, wary of what John's reaction will be if he notices her small smile.

"Good. Have a goodnight Liza." John says also trying to hide a small smile before opening the door to his room, "I just don't want her to bear our burden." He finishes softly, the words ringing in Elizabeth's ears more than she expected.

John closes his door, briefly leaving her standing there alone, frozen, before she manages to calm herself down. She wishes things were different but knows this is neither the time nor the place to bring it up any more than she already has. The slow silence is only pierced by the subtitle sound of footsteps coming towards her as she continues to stand there motionless.

"Liza?" Her boyfriend says echoing his concern through the empty hallway; she doesn't immediately respond as he reaches out and gently holds her hand.

"Yeah sorry, just kind of spaced out." She replies finally coming to her senses and trying to ignore what just happened.

Jeremy gives her a concerned look but doesn't say a word as he wraps his tired right arm around his girlfriend, and they walk the short distance to their room. The rest of the squadron is already fast asleep, as the carrier continues to gently roll and pitch in the sea; a soft, unbearable, calm.

A steady hum forms in the background as John changes into his pajamas and stares at his phone. He knows he promised Elizabeth he would text their mutual friend Samantha but a feeling in the back of his mind is preventing him from doing so. It frustrates him; striking deals with presidents, assassinating prime ministers and wiping out warlords and yet he can't even text a girl he might have feelings for. Clenching his fist and gritting his teeth, he finally manages to send a single text:

"*Hey Sam, hope you're doing alright and have a good day tomorrow.*"

Hands shaking, he quickly hits send and locks his phone, throwing it onto the table next to him and rolling into his bed, turning out the light in the same motion. He ignores his phone when it buzzes a few minutes later with a reply, though he is unable to sleep, his mind is wandering way too much. He knows its love, stupid and distracting love, a plague on his mind, nay, a plague on his soul. Does he deserve to experience such a trivial thing as love? Is it even that trivial? Should he even allow himself to feel such an emotion?

These questions cloud his mind, keeping him from seeing something, something right in front of him. He sighs. Getting up, he looks at his phone, only two hours have passed and there is a reply from Sam. He sighs again before sitting back on his bed and holding his head in hands. A short time later, he decides to put on a tee shirt, jeans and sneakers and goes for a walk around the now quiet decks of the Kestrel.

As he passes Jeremy and Elizabeth's room, he pauses slightly, debating whether he should knock on the door. He's certain they're gently asleep in each other's arms; though he also knows they would wake up as soon as he knocked on the door. He decides against it; the presence that fills presidents with dread is not necessary right now.

With only four hours to go until mission time, John makes his way to the hanger without being seen. The small yet dedicated hanger crew is busy rearming and refueling the squad's planes as the main shift sleeps in their racks below, though some didn't make it that far. John remains silent trying to get a handle on the situation and to keep from waking the sailors around him.

"Can't sleep?" A strong calming voice says behind him, breaking the soft silence in the air.

"No Admiral I can't." John replies recognizing the voice but not turning around, "Elizabeth keeps trying to set me up with this one girl back home, but I don't want to drag her into this. It wouldn't be right."

"No, it wouldn't be, but I don't think Elizabeth is worried about Sam." Anderson replies joining the tired commander looking out over the hanger.

"So, she's told you about her." John says barely surprised.

"She did. She can be quite the gossiper, which makes me wonder why you picked her as your second in command. A running mouth can't be good for security." Anderson says with a laugh.

"She can keep her mouth shut when it matters, plus she's the most qualified person I know who can take over if I croak." John replies bowing his head and searching his pocket for something.

"Well, I pray that never happens John, though you could help the cause by getting some sleep for once in your life." Anderson says getting a chuckle out of John as he finds the peace of watermelon gum, he's been looking for and pops it in his mouth.

"Four hours until wheels up. That means waking up in three. Enough time for a nap, don't you think?" John asks with the smile remaining on his face.

"It is, yes, though I'd like to know John. Did you ever text her?" Anderson asks curiously.

John tosses his phone to him; the message has been up on the screen this entire time. The admiral studies the message carefully before reading it aloud to John.

"*Thanks John, I hope you have a good day tomorrow too. Would you want to hang out this weekend?*"

Anderson chuckles before tossing the phone back to John, who quickly puts it back in his pocket.

"Want my advice John?" Anderson eagerly asks, John only nods, "Make sure you hang out with her this weekend."

"That'll depend on the Russians, Admiral." John says in a joking tone.

"Yes, it certainly will, Commander." Anderson replies, noting the change in formality; the informal conversation is over; any talk now is about the mission at hand.

John quickly walks back to his quarters and is just about to climb back into bed before remembering the phone in his pocket. He sighs, pulling it out and unlocking it in one swift motion and stares at the screen. Considering for a second what would happen if he told her the truth, what would happen if he brought her into his world. Instead though, he just replies, "*This weekend sounds great.*" Trying to get the conversation done and over with as quickly as possible. Climbing into bed, he finally manages to put himself to sleep going over the mission details in his head. Launch, fly for an hour, gain air superiority, destroy a Russian Aircraft carrier, and return in time for breakfast. Seems simple enough, though the weary commander is positive that the Russians won't agree with the notion of losing one of their carriers.

Launch, fly, destroy, land; the pattern repeats itself multiple times as John sleeps. This happens every time a mission is about to start; John appreciates it. It means he has every detail down before the mission has a chance to go wrong and something always does.

Chapter Two

Date: Friday, December 4th, 2020

Time: 0035hrs AST

Location: Persian Gulf, 350 miles southeast of Kuwait

Temperature: 53 Degrees Fahrenheit

John and Admiral Anderson are already on the bridge as the rest squad quickly showers and makes their way to the mess to grab a bite to eat. It's a large plate of steak and eggs, a traditional breakfast when a combat mission is about to kickoff. The crew waits anxiously, many of them still waking up in anticipation of the action station alarm sounding, though some are going to get a rude awakening.

"Wonder if John got anything to eat?" Neil says between rapid bites of his breakfast.

"I doubt it. Has anyone even seen him this morning?" Vladimir replies not even breaking his concentration to respond.

"Messenger came down before you woke up Vlad; not everyone was hung-over last night." Elizabeth pipes up, trying to lighten the mood as the entire squad laughs, while trying not to spit their food out.

More tired sailors enter the mess barely noticing the people they treated with such celebrity the day before. Everyone is on edge; the tension is only continuing to build and the only people who seem to be calm are the squadron themselves.

"Alright, I'm going to head up." Elizabeth says suddenly; everyone realizing she's finished her breakfast.

"We'll be right behind-." Jeremy replies, though Clara interrupts saying, "I'll join you."

Before anyone can process what just happened, the two young ladies leave for the bridge, leaving the gentleman staring at each other with confusion and surprise etched on their faces.

As soon as Clara is sure they're out of sight of anyone and largely out of earshot, she speaks.

"Liza, are you feeling alright?" She asks, the concern coming through loud and clear in her voice.

"Yeah, I am Clara, why?" Elizabeth replies, her confusion mixed with concern.

"It's just..." Clara pauses, trying to figure out how to word her thoughts, "It's just the other night, Vladimir told me you finished a whole rack of ribs by yourself and you just ate a thousand calorie breakfast in about five minutes."

"Your point?" Elizabeth says making no effort to hide her annoyance that Clara is bringing this up right now.

"Look, I'm not saying you are, but are you and Jeremy keeping something from the rest of us?" Clara finally says after taking a long breath and getting Elizabeth to stop walking for two seconds.

Elizabeth shakes her head and gives Clara an "*I have no idea what you're implying*" look, gaining a sigh from her squad mate.

"We have a mission starting in less than fifty minutes. Focus on that and wait for the alarm." She says, almost angrily, before storming up a ships ladder towards the bridge, leaving Clara standing alone in the hallway.

Clara checks her watch and heads back to join her squad mates as they finish breakfast. She is careful to hide her frustration at Elizabeth shutting her down and even getting angry with her. She also dodges any questions asked to her, passing it off as a random question and nothing more.

On the bridge, John is waiting for Elizabeth to arrive in order to begin the briefing as the Admiral gets the fleet turned into wind. Already in his flight suit, John is trying to waste as little time as possible once he gives the go ahead. Elizabeth arrives, still fuming slightly from her conversation with Clara mere moments ago, though she composes herself as her commander realizes she's there.

"Good morning Liza." He says with a tired smile as he leans against a railing and crosses his arms.

"Good morning John, Admiral." Elizabeth replies standing across the briefing table and nod to the two men before her before asking, "Did you text her last night?"

John doesn't say a word on the subject, instead unlocking and tossing her his phone before beginning the briefing in earnest.

"An unmanned, stealth, reconnaissance flight landed about thirty minutes ago; their pictures reveal that the Russians are continually launching strikes against rebel targets in Syria. The Andromeda has picked up radio traffic confirming this, and it would appear as though they have no idea that we're here." John says, as he finishes Elizabeth tosses his phone back to him, not even trying to hold back a smile.

"How many ships are in the fleet?" She asks, managing to stay on task despite her happiness that her squad leader is becoming more social.

"One carrier, four cruisers and two destroyers, so antiaircraft fire is going to be a problem if we get spotted." John replies quickly shoving his phone in to his flight suit pocket.

"The fleet is in position Commander and the next CAP is on the flight deck." Admiral Anderson chimes in after consulting with some of his officers around him.

"Send them up Admiral." John orders and less than ten seconds later another flight of F-18 E's are in the air.

"The Helena still hasn't picked anything up but commercial flights within a hundred miles. Looks like we really are in the clear." Elizabeth continues as she looks over a report before handing it to John for his assessment.

Rob appears on a screen next to her barely catching her off guard but still causing her to jump slightly.

"We really need to stop having missions come up in the middle of the night." He says announcing his presence.

"What's the word from the Dallas Rob? We can worry about the time later." John replies still looking through the report Elizabeth handed him, taking care to not miss a single detail.

"All's quiet for the time being, Captain Xi will report back if anything comes up." Rob replies with a tired grumble complementing his voice.

A messenger runs up the stairs, saluting quickly before handing something to John and standing at ease. He's shaking nervously, having never been so close to his commander except for when he graduated from basic training.

“At ease ensign; we’re not in the arctic, at least the last time I checked.” John says with a laugh taking a moment to release the tension in the room; everyone laughs including the sailor.

“Yes sir, certainly sir.” The sailor says, beaming with a smile though his shaking legs are still making him unsteady.

“Certainly. You’re dismissed sailor, thank you.” John finishes calming down though giving off a friendly vibe.

The young man salutes again and heads back downstairs as John hands the note to Elizabeth, who has finally calmed down from her earlier annoyance with Clara.

“Admiral, our planes are ready to go, and our friends are in the process of getting changed. I say it’s time.” John says with a small amount of disappointment is his voice.

Anderson calmly grabs the microphone to the ships announcement system, with a two-tone attention alarm sounding as he takes it off its holder. He takes a deep calming breath and presses the talk button.

“Ladies and Gentlemen. Action stations, action stations, set condition one throughout the fleet.” His commands in a calm and direct tone, sending the fleet into controlled chaos.

John turns to Elizabeth to finish the briefing, as sailors run to their positions around them.

“Vladimir and Neil are going to attack the carrier from the west. You and Jeremy are going to be with them as an initial line of defense while Clara and I fly top cover. Once the carrier is confirmed to be sinking, we will egress and land back on the carrier. Total mission time should be no more than three hours. I’ll meet everyone in the hanger in fifteen minutes and we'll be in the air in thirty." He says calmly and she nods before running back down the stairs to her and Jeremy's room to change.

John turns to Admiral Anderson and the two shake hands.

"See you in under three hours Admiral. Pops will keep you company if you want someone to talk to." John states, glancing over his shoulder.

"See you then Commander. Come back in one piece." The Admiral replies as if he is sending his son into combat.

"We'll certainly try to." John smiles one last time before turning for the door "Don't wait up for us Rob." He finishes by giving a short two-finger salute to the screen as he heads for the hanger deck.

The sleepy calm of a few minutes ago is a distant memory as everyone runs to his or her posts without hesitation or reservation. John is moving at his own deliberate pace towards the hanger deck, navigating the stairs ways and bulkheads with practiced ease. He purposely pulls on his flight suit from around his waist, eases the sleeves up his scarred arm and carefully zips the suit up his chest. He checks his weapon, his tan 1911, loading a 45-caliber round in the chamber and securing it in the holster on his thigh. It's always within John's reach no matter where he goes, just in case he needs it.

Opening walking through a final doorway, John finally makes it to the hanger and puts on the rest of his gear, minus his helmet and oxygen mask. Holding them in his left hand, he calls the squadron over and quiet falls across the hanger deck as everyone turns to face their commander. Everyone bows his or her head, looking at the steel deck below.

"Oh lord, please don't let us fuck this up." John says just loud enough for everyone to hear, before shouting "Hooyah!"

Everyone on the deck responds in kind as the six-squad mates give each other a collective fist bump with the right hands. After this instinctive pre-mission ritual, the pace returns, and the young adult's make their way to their aircraft; their crew chiefs helping with the rehearsed routine.

Pop's helps John get strapped into his plane, giving him a quick handshake before the canopy closes, sealing John inside. The fighter jet shutters, its various digital and analog systems coming online as the tug shoves it to the elevator.

"Radio check, radio check." Vladimir calls out over the radio as his aircraft is placed next to John's, with their engines spooling into life.

"Wolf one checking in." John says calmly.

"Wolf three check." Jeremy joins.

"Wolf four, roger." Clara pipes up.

"Good morning from wolf five." Neil replies, chuckling.

"Wolf two, radio check." Clara says, John and Vladimir clear the elevator and taxi to the forward catapults on the Kestrel's flight deck as the elevator lowers back down to the hanger.

"Wolf six, checking in. Everyone's on frequency commander." Vladimir finishes: Clara and Jeremy appear behind them as the elevator raises back up.

The deck crew quickly sets about connecting the steam catapults to John and Vladimir's aircraft and directs Clara and Jeremy to the offset, amidships catapult. The elevator repeats it's cycle one more time, bringing Neil and Elizabeth to flight deck as the deck crew continues their preparations for the mission to start.

"Wolf one to air boss, comm check. We're all set to go here." John says saluting the catapult officer, signaling he's ready to launch.

"Air boss to wolf one, roger that. On my mark, clock stands at zero one twenty-nine and thirty seconds." The air boss pauses, 'Mark."

On his command, the entire squadron synchronizes the clocks in their heads up displays and take a collective breath. The clock continues to count, a slow and methodical count.

"Alright commander, we've got a good head wind over the deck," The catapult operator bursts over the radio.

Forty-five seconds.

He continues, "Catapult building pressure, eight-five, ninety, ninety-five, one hundred."

Fifty-two seconds.

He finishes, his pace quickening, "We're in the green. Deck crew ready, catapult ready, pilot salute."

John does so; fire walling the throttle and placing his hands-on handles located on the front his canopy.

Fifty-nine, zero, launch.

A shutter rocks the massive fighter jet as it rockets forward toward the end of the deck; jet engines howling in full afterburner. In less than three seconds, the plane accelerates to one hundred and eighty miles an hour and glides easily off the end of the flight deck.

John takes control and skillfully eases the Vietnam veteran into a steady climb, raising the landing gear and attaching his oxygen mask to his helmet as Vladimir follows behind him. With the same practiced rhythm as when they landed, the squadron lifts into the air and turns east towards the Russian aircraft carrier. They climb through a cloud layer in an arrowhead formation, revealing the clear, starry night sky and bright moon above.

"Wolf squadron, this is Sky Eye. We have you on our radar and so far, the scope is clear all the way to your target." A calming South African voice says over the radio.

"Wolf One to Sky Eye. It's good to hear your beautiful voice, I hope you were able to get something to eat before this all got started." John pipes up first.

"Sky Eye to Wolf One, unfortunately my chicken wrap is still sitting here next to me, though at least I remembered it this time." Sky Eye replies with a laugh, the rest of the controllers in the E-2 Hawkeye start laughing as well.

"Wolf Two to Sky Eye, yeah we could hear your wife yelling back in the states." Clara chimes in and everyone practically dies of laughter.

"Sky Eye to Wolf Two, maybe you could talk to her next time. The ship's store is starting to run out of roses." The controller finishes as the squadron settles in for the shorter than normal flight.

All is quiet as the six fighter jets cruise at just below the speed of sound and at an altitude of thirty-five thousand feet. Some minor turbulence is the only thing that causes the planes to deviate from their flight path. Peaceful, maybe too peaceful but it is certainly not unwelcome when compared to the chaos of the Israeli mission two weeks ago. The pilots keep one eye on their radars and the other outside their cockpits: staring out into the starry blackness of night. Everything is proceeding as planned and uneventfully; not a single enemy plane in sight and steering clear of civilian traffic is a breeze.

Halfway through the flight, Elizabeth radios back to the Kestrel, requesting three flights to fly patrols over Syria. The hope is that the flights will distract the Russians and keep them from interfering in the squadron's operation against their carrier, though how well it will work remains to be seen.

"Wolf Four to Wolf Two, good call." Clara calls out trying to mend the fence she feels she dented earlier.

"Wolf Two to Wolf Four, figured we didn't need our party interrupted." Elizabeth replies joyfully, giving Clara some hope.

"Wolf Three to Wolf Two, I thought it would have been fun, the more the merrier." Jeremy chimes in with a laugh, which the rest of the squadron joins in on, except for John.

"Wolf Six to Wolf Three, are you hinting at something Jeremy?" Vladimir interjects, getting John to smile slightly under his oxygen mask.

"Wolf Three to Wolf Six, what on earth could you mean?" Jeremy replies playing the dimwitted boyfriend perfectly.

"Wolf Five to Wolf Three, I think you know exactly what he means you sneaky bastard. You're not fooling anyone." Neil joins in, egging on Jeremy and causing Elizabeth to blush slightly, making her extremely glad no one can see her at the moment.

"Wolf Three to Wolf Five, I have no idea what you're talking about." Jeremy continues.

Maybe it's true, maybe it's just a rumor; either way, John will know the truth as he receives update medical records for the main squadron members

"Sky Eye to Wolf One, you're keeping awfully quiet, care to share something with the rest of us?" Awacs calls in, trying to bait John into the conversation.

"Wolf One to Sky Eye, I'm keeping my mouth shut on this one." John replies and an audible gulp can be heard from Jeremy and Elizabeth.

They both know that John knows, they were just hoping it would take a little while longer for Elizabeth's physical to reach his files. The radio falls silent as everyone regains their composure and manages refocus on the mission at hand.

"Sky Eye to Wolf One, roger that. You're thirty minutes from the mission target. Let's get ready to wake them up." Awacs responds, as the mood intensifies.

John and Clara break formation and climb to thirty thousand feet while the rest of the squadron decreases their altitude to just two thousand feet above the ocean below. They have gone lower before, during several training flights over the squadron's base at Midway Island, however, it wasn't necessary to do so for this mission.

"Wolf One to Wolf Squadron, maintain radio silence until we are within striking range of the target. Even if the Russians are drunk, they're still awake and I don't need any of you spoiling the surprise party." John calls out, glancing at the mission clock in his cockpit and subsequently at his radar.

"Hey!... I heard that." He says, a little quieter than expected as he tries to get rid of a pounding headache.

With that last message, the radio waves fall silent as the squadron continues to close in on the Russian aircraft carrier; leaving everyone to their own thoughts until they are ten miles away.

Clara uses the time to reflect on how Elizabeth reacted to her question before the mission took off. She knows that she did cross a line that she most definitely shouldn't have, but it was out of concern for her one of best friends, so surely that makes it okay, right? She sighs; impatiently wishing she could apologize to Elizabeth just to get this massive weight off of her chest. She was just trying to look out for her friend... seems that some of John's mentality has rubbed off on her. She smiles, recalling a training incident where John threw himself between her and a pyro charge the trainers had set off to make the exercise more realistic. The scars from the blast are still visible on John back and left shoulder; afterwards John only said, "*It's worth it, so long as my friends are ok.*" That singular sentence has stuck with Clara ever since then.

Elizabeth is also thinking about what Clara said earlier; the more she thinks about it the more she realizes how harshly she brushed aside her friends concerns. It only made the earlier moment even more awkward for the twenty-one-year-old and she doesn't even want to think about what John is going to say when the return to the carrier later this morning. She knows the same goes for Jeremy; wondering how either one of them could have thought that this was a good idea. Did they honestly think that John wasn't going to find out, or was it out of a vain hope that he would simply overlook it with everything else going on? How will all of this affect things to come, not just for her and her boyfriend, but for everyone else, especially Clara and Neil.

Elizabeth knows how John reacts could change the squadron forever, or it could not change a damn thing. Though she also knows she shouldn't be thinking about this right now; it's just impossible to keep them away completely. She takes a breath and a moment to clear her mind; deciding that she needs to apologize to Clara when the squad returns to the carrier and finally refocusing on the task at hand; something that Vladimir is still struggling with.

It's not because of the hangover that he's finally getting over; it's the action of killing upwards of 1600 fellow Russians in the name of saving the world. It's something he's been quietly struggling with ever since this mission came to fruition. However, he has his orders and he knows that he must follow them; even though he is Russian, that allegiance officially died when he accepted John's offer to join the squadron. Patriotism in one's former nation means nothing when your allegiance is to the world as a whole, no matter who is in front of the barrel of your gun. Vladimir knows he'll have to pull the trigger and he's already accepted the fact that he's going to, but it doesn't mean he doesn't want to.

"Wolf flight, ten miles out, you are weapons free." Sky eye calls out after what feels like only seconds and the squadron takes a collective breath, releasing the safeties on their cannons and missiles. Vladimir and Neil instantly gain a lock tone from their anti-ship missiles and rapidly ripple fire them with eight trails of light screaming into the distance. The four-plane flight quickly raises their altitude to a safe level.

John observes the missile paths on his radar, keeping a careful eye out for any response from the Russian task force below. Predictably, CIWS fire lights up the dark, early morning sky and five of the eight missiles are shot down as a result, but they can't hit all of them. Three missiles strike the Kuznetsov, one at the bow, one amidships, and one in the stern. The carrier lurches under the ferocity of such fire power and slowly drifts to a halt, flooding and on fire.

Several fighters, mainly MIG-29K's who had sortied to Syria and were returning to the Kuznetsov, begin swarming around the ship. Running low on fuel, they are torn between flying to land and trying to find those responsible for destroying their home. Several of them cross right in front of the consolidating Wolf Squadron, easy targets. Heat seeking missile lock tones growl in John's headset, he takes a breath and pulls the trigger; four Aim-9X sidewinder missiles streak into the night sky. Four massive explosions light up the sky like a Fourth of July fireworks display.

"Wolf Two, Wolf Three, cover Wolf Five and Wolf Six and escort them back to the Kestrel. Wolf Four, form up with me. We'll take up the rear guard and make sure we aren't followed." John calls out over the radio, his adrenaline levels rising with each passing moment.

"Roger that Wolf One." Elizabeth replies instantaneously as the squadron falls back from the chaos in the ocean below.

As soon as the flight turns around, a radar lock alarm blasts through John and Clara's headset. Instinctively, they snap their heads over their shoulders and break hard to the left in an effort to shake the unsettling lock on tone. Staying in the turn, John and Clara eyes snap between the skies and their radars, searching for anything that could give them a hint as to who is trying to fire on them. Their radars reveal nothing to them, and the lock tone stubbornly refuses to go away; the two pilots remain calm however, anticipating a missile launch at any moment.

Despite the stealth coatings on their fighters, the squadron knows that their aircraft can be spotted by certain radar frequencies when they launch missiles. It's a troubling weakness, but one that is unavoidable when your resources are relatively limited by the United Nations. Suddenly, for a brief instant, a small blip appears on the two pilots radar screens before disappearing just as quickly; a missile lock warning begins sounding off replacing radar lock from earlier.

"Wolf One, Wolf Four, Raptor at zero seven zero, range is zero seven miles and closing." Sky Eye yells out, using the E-2's more powerful radar system to peer through the darkness.

"Roger that Sky Eye." Clara calls out as two missiles streak past her canopy without exploding; at the last second, they've lost the radar lock they had on the two fighters.

"Wolf Four, I'm out of heat seekers and switching to the cannon." John commands: Clara reverses her turn in a well-rehearsed maneuver where she briefly makes herself the bait for an enemy pilot so John can blow it out of the sky.

The Raptor takes the bait and reveals himself against the dark night sky as he launches another radar guided missile. John pulls back on the stick, initiating a 12G pull to come in line with approaching stealth fighter. The missile loses guidance again and disappears off into the distance as Clara pulls another 12G's to back up John's attack should he not be able to bring it down. John swiftly selects the 20mm Vulcan Cannon as his primary weapon, lines up the gunsight with where he predicts the Raptor will be, takes a breath, and squeezes the trigger. Over a four second burst, four hundred rounds streak across the sky and slam into the F-22 Raptor head on. It instantly bursts into flames and disintegrates as John and Clara scream past the wreckage at nearly the speed of sound.

The earlier calm returns as the squadron resumes their formation and proceeds to egress the combat zone as the Russian fleet below is still reeling from the lethal blow. Rescue operations begin immediately as countless Russian sailors plunge into the ocean trying to escape the flames.

Chapter Three

Date: Friday, December 4th, 2020

Time: 0427hrs AST

Location: Persian Gulf, 375 miles southeast of Kuwait

Temperature: 65 Degrees Fahrenheit

"Wolf Two, final landing checks are complete, you're cleared to land." The landing signal officer radios as Elizabeth lines up with the carriers landing strip.

"Roger that LSO. Wolf Two cleared to land." Elizabeth replies as her squadron members planes are carefully parked on the deck of the Kestrel; her commander is still in a holding pattern above her.

"Wolf Two, meet me at my quarters after the debriefing, bring Jeremy as well." John says catching her completely off guard; he hasn't mentioned anything until now.

"Roger that... Wolf One." Elizabeth replies, her nervousness rapidly overtaking the earlier calm in her voice.

Elizabeth carefully sets her plane down on the deck of the carrier and the crew rapidly begins clearing her out of the way so John can land. Despite her nervousness, Elizabeth manages to calm down as she shuts down her planes systems and opens the canopy, getting a view of her boyfriend as she does. He's always been a calming presence for her, someone she can tell anything and everything too. Climbing down from the cockpit, she quickly tells her crew chief what needs to be done before calmly runs over to him as he finishes talking things over with his own crew chief.

"Have an enjoyable flight sweetheart?" Jeremy asks softly as the two embrace each other softly.

“It was pretty boring on my end, if I am honest.” Elizabeth replies with a smile, closing her eyes and resting her head on her boyfriend's chest.

The piercing sound of John’s fighter can soon be heard and the carrier shutters under its weight as it touches down on the deck. The ground crew rushes in and swiftly guides John to his on-deck parking space, and he shuts down his plane’s engines seconds later. The rest of the squadron heads towards the pilots briefing room in order to relax for a moment before discussing what was ultimately achieved during this mission.

“John needs to see us.” Elizabeth says softly to Jeremy; no one else hears her though he takes the news better than she did.

“Everything will be alright.” He replies simply with a slight smile on his face as he gently places his arm around his girlfriend.

She glances at him as they walk inside the control tower and head for the briefing room. She wishes she could be as confident as he is right now, especially with the situation looming over their heads.

Meanwhile, John opens his canopy, leans back in his seat slightly, and takes a long, slow, deep breath to calm his tired nerves. The 12G turn he pulled to come in line with the Raptor took more out of him than he was expecting. It’s the most amount of force he’s put on his body, yet he’s done it before, and he’s never felt like this afterwards. He coughs, spitting up a bit of blood on to his flight suit as an iron taste fills his mouth. He brushes his brief concern aside as Pops calls up to and he does his best to hide it as he climbs down from his fighter.

“You made it back on time. Someone should make sure that this is recorded for posterity's sake.” Pops says jokingly, managing to get a tired laugh out of John.

"Duly noted Pops. Check her over for me; nothing's wrong but I pulled a tight turn and I don't need the wings falling off." John says patting the side of his airplane's fuselage.

"Sure thing Commander. Was there anything out there that will keep me up at night?" Pops ask quickly wiping the sweat off his forehead with a yellow rag.

"There was a Raptor in the airspace that I had to shoot down. I have no idea whether or not they were supporting the Russians, though in all likelihood it was only watching them when it stumbled into us." John replies trying to keep the worst-case scenario in the back of his mind, where it belongs.

"Let's hope that's all it is." Pops replies, placing his hand on John's shoulder, "You're second mission and everyone came back, let's focus on that."

"Yeah, that's probably for the best. Thanks Pops." John replies, doing his utmost to keep from falling asleep right there on the deck.

After this short exchange John makes his way inside and towards the briefing room where his equally tired squad mates are waiting. The sailors around him are running on autopilot, performing their duties with such practiced focus that they don't even notice their commander walking past them. John doesn't mind, he's barely noticing them as well as his eyes and mind are spaced out, focusing on a random point right in front of him. Unsurprisingly though, he manages to make his way to the briefing room without getting lost in the carrier's numerous corridors and passageways. He takes a breath, places his tired hand on the door and pushes it open; his talkative squad mates instantly falls silent and looks of concern replace their tired yet jovial expressions.

"John... are you okay?" Vladimir asks as John continues staring off into space, not even acknowledging Vladimir's question.

"John?!?" Clara asks, the concern in her voice unmistakable though clearly inaudible to John at the moment.

"John, you're scaring us!" Jeremy joins in and yet there is still no response from the usually fearless commander.

John can't see anything at this point, his vision is blurred, and spiking pain is piercing its way through chest. He coughs, producing a sizable stain of blood on the floor in front of him, gaining a clear gasp from his friends. He falls back from the pain, leaning against the wall to support himself as blood slowly runs out of his mouth and drips onto the floor. He friends rush to his side as he finally passes out and loses the strength in his legs as they take his weight and yell for a medic. One rushes into the room mere seconds later and immediate begins cutting John's flight suit off of his body as his friends both assist in the treatment and look on in horror of what might be happening.

Date: Friday, December 4th, 2020

Time: 0445hrs MST

Location: 700 Miles North of Arkhangelsk, Barents Sea, Depth of 250 feet.

Temperature: 8 Degrees Fahrenheit Air, 35 Degrees Fahrenheit Water

"*No change in aspect of contact sierra two. Course is zero three zero at eight knots.*" The message is written on a small note in the hand of Captain Xi on the UNS - Dallas.

The message is only five minutes old and was written down by sonar technician Jamal Turke as silently as possible in order to not give away their position. Despite being in the Kazan's baffles, any noise at this moment would almost certainly give away the fact that the Dallas is tailing the Russians at four thousand yards. The entire crew is either resting or trying to take very shallow breaths at their combat stations. None of them know what the Russians are planning; this could just be a short cruise from port, or it could be something more sinister.

The last encoded transmission from the Kestrel came in five minutes ago. It relayed what had happened during the mission against the Kuznetsov and keeping the captain informed on John's condition. The young commander had developed an ulcer in his stomach caused by a bacterium, this ulcer burst when pulled a 12 G turn and caused him to cough up blood and pass out. His prognosis is good but it's still a worrying situation for the thirty-year-old Chinese captain.

Another note comes to the Captains attention by way of the XO, the Russians have changed course to starboard in an effort to clear their baffles and ward off any followers. Captain Xi silently orders an "all stop" to the propeller of the former Virginia Class nuclear submarine; it coasts silent to a stop and begins drifting with the slight ocean current. The crew waits, hoping the Russian submarine doesn't notice the giant submarine sized hole in the water behind their stern.

"PING!"

The sudden noise rocks the Dallas and nearly deafens Jamal before he is able to rip off his headset. Carefully, placing it back on his head, being sure to have only one ear covered, he listens intently for what the Russians are going to do next: his heart drops.

"Con, Sonar, Torpedo in the water, bearing zero three seven, range four five thousand." He calls out, releasing the ship from ultra-quiet.

"All ahead flank cavitate, planes thirty degrees down bubble, rudder thirty to port." Captain Xi commands quickly and the practiced sailors respond before he even finishes his sentence.

The submarine lurches to life, responding dutifully to the commands the sailors have asked it to do, though it is slow to respond.

"Countermeasure launch on my mark. Fire control gain a solution!" Captain Xi calls out, holding on to the railing above him with a death grip as the submarine dives steeply downward.

"Roger." The sailors respond instinctively, carrying out their orders with a rehearsed perfection.

Several tense seconds pass as the torpedo gains a sonar lock on the Dallas and begins pinging away with its active sonar. The Kazan continues to turn to starboard, lining up for another firing solution on the diving Dallas.

"Mark!" Captain Xi shouts and the countermeasures launch instantly, making as much noise as possible in order to confuse the incoming torpedo. It works and the torpedo loses track of the Dallas and passes harmlessly overhead, commencing a snake search pattern as it swims off into the distance.

"Con, Fire Control, we have a solution for tube one." The fire control station shouts as the Dallas begins reversing its turn.

"Ahead one third, Weapon Ready?" Captain Xi calls out as the sub begins slowing down to five knots.

"Ready." Is the response.

"Ship Ready?" Captain Xi continues urgently, expecting the Russians fire at any moment.

"Ready." The XO replies instantly.

"Shoot Tube One." Xi orders knowing that he has run out of options.

"Shoot tube one, aye." The fire control station responds, and the torpedo launches from the torpedo tube instantly.

The torpedoes active sonar activates instantly and begins pinging away as it searches for the Russian submarine. It finds it and begins homing in on the target, pinging quicker and quicker as it gets closer and closer.

"Con, fire control we've lost the wire." The fire control station calls out, signaling that the Dallas can no longer control the torpedo.

The torpedo continues tracking towards its target as the Russian submarine begins cavitating as it increases to flank speed. They launch countermeasures of their own, however the torpedo is too close and slams into the stern of the Kazan, exploding on impact. The Kazan slows to a stop and begins sinking slowly to the bottom of the Barents Sea. Captain Xi makes the executive decision to not stick around and leaves the area skirting the bottom at twenty knots. The pressure at the deeper depth is preventing any cavitation though any ship within a few miles will have heard the torpedo explosion and be coming to investigate.

Everyone on the submarine breathes a silent sigh of relief, though they know that they are not entirely in the clear yet. Adding to their slight trouble is the fact that they will need to go to periscope depth and signal the Kestrel with an after-action report. Captain Xi decides to worry about the report later and has the Dallas continues at the present depth, course and speed. If all goes to plan, they'll be in friendlier waters by nine in morning and Captain Xi will send the report then.

Date: Friday, December 4th, 2020

Time: 0632hrs AST

Location: Persian Gulf, 400 miles southeast of Kuwait

Temperature: 71 Degrees Fahrenheit

The squadron is quietly huddled around Johns bed in his room, nervously waiting for him to wake up. Clara and Elizabeth are resting in their boyfriend's arms as Vladimir sits in the corner, nodding off from time to time as tiredness overtakes the young adults. The doctor came in about fifteen minutes ago to check John's vitals and to reassure the squad that their commander is going to be alright, though it provided little comfort. No one is talking, they're too tired to do so, though the silence is doing nothing to diffuse the tension. Elizabeth takes a quick drink from the water bottle she's holding in her hand, clearing her throat when she's finished.

"Clara." She whispers as she notices Neil napping and she doesn't want to wake him with something that doesn't concern him.

"Huh." Clara replies tiredly as she glances over her shoulder at Elizabeth, doing her best to not wake up her boyfriend.

"I'm sorry about earlier, I was too defensive and I'm sorry." Elizabeth says as quietly as possible, continuing in her efforts to not wake anyone up.

"It's okay Liza, I understand, especially when it comes to things like that." Clara replies with a quiet smile.

Elizabeth only smiles in response; she doesn't want to risk talking to much longer and preventing her friends from getting some much-needed rest. The door opens softly and Admiral Anderson steps through silently as Clara nods off to sleep joining her four squad mates. Elizabeth glances up at him, as the only one awake and gently receives the piece of paper he is holding in his hand. He tips his hat forward slightly before silently exiting the room and closing the door gingerly behind him. Elizabeth unfolds the note in her hand and begins to read it; it's an intelligence report from the Andromeda.

"*Russians are withdrawing from the Arabian Sea, reporting that the United States fired on the Kuznetsov. The United States is holding Russia responsible for the loss of the Raptor. Syria is no longer burning. Tensions are high, yet stable for the time being.*"

Elizabeth sighs when she finishes reading the note, partly out of relief and partly out of concern. She's glad things have stabilized though she's worried about what could happen if anymore incidents occur between the United States and Russia. Should things escalate, the squadron is going to have to put themselves in the middle of the two strongest armies on the planet; a prospect no one would find ideal let alone sane.

Elizabeth begins thinking of who is going to meet with the American and Russian governments and if they should do so publicly or in secret in order to keep the two superpowers in their corners. The thought that she is in charge while John is passed out is the least of her concerns, as well as the thought of what John will think of her personal situation when he wakes up.

Pulling out her phone, she silently sends a message to Captain Anderson and Rob, asking them to have the squad's resources keep an eye and an ear on what the Russian and American governments are saying about and to each other. She knows both of them are likely heading to bed at this point however, in order to catch up on some of the sleep they've lost during this mission. As a result, it doesn't surprise her when neither one of them reply immediately as she slides her phone carefully back into her pocket. She looks over at John, he's barely moved a muscle ever since the medical personnel placed him on his bed and pulled the blanket over him after injecting something into his stomach. Due to her tiredness, Elizabeth is still wondering what exactly it was they injected into his stomach. All she knows, and can remember, is that the medics told them John had a burst ulcer in his stomach caused by a bacterium.

A moment later, a heavy set, black gentleman enters the room wearing a white lab coat over light blue scrubs and black shoes. Dr. Keller is embroidered on the left breast pocket of the lab coat.

"Nice to see that you're all resting for once." He says to Elizabeth in a soft yet booming and calming voice.

"Wish I could say the same for you Doc. Sorry for waking you up at this hour." Elizabeth says standing up and shaking his hand; she's still fighting to keep her eyes open.

"No need to apologize, I'm just glad that this time it's something relatively minor and certainly easy to treat." He responds sitting down next to John and taking his plus; it's unsurprisingly calm.

"An ulcer is easy to treat?" Elizabeth asks curiously, she's never had one nor seen one treated before now.

"The one John has is at least. Did it burst? Yes. But it's relatively small and the medicine the medics injected earlier should help it shrink until it disappears completely." Dr. Keller responds calmly, moving on to listening to John heartbeat with his stethoscope; just like his pulse, it is predictably calm, steady, and unwavering.

"Is there anything I need to be aware of going forward doctor?" Elizabeth asks, quickly realizing that everyone around them is sound asleep.

"Well, your commander is only sleeping right now, though he may need help injecting the medicine himself over the next week or so. It should be once a day right after he eats breakfast. Besides that? He's stubbornly healthy and will be perfectly fine once the ulcer heals." Dr. Keller says calmly, reassuring Elizabeth as she continues to struggle to keep her eyes open.

"Roger that doc." Elizabeth replies simply as she begins nodding off again and falls back into her boyfriend's sleeping arms.

"Get some rest Elizabeth, it's not like your body is going to give you another option." Doctor Keller responds with a reassuring smile as he stands and heads silently out of the room.

Elizabeth finally allows herself to fall asleep, curling up in her boyfriend's arms and resting her head gently on his chest. She can make out his steady heartbeat over the background noise of the carrier; it helps her drift off into a deep sleep just like it did during the lead up to the mission.

As the squadron sleeps, the carrier battle group steps back from its combat alert as the most recent combat air patrol comes into land and the cruisers Helena and Andromeda scan the skies, depths and airways for any possible threats. A shift change takes place at seven in the morning and several members of the crew head off for some much-needed rest, while others grab a quick bite to eat before also heading to bed. A welcome calm has quickly replaced the controlled chaos of the previous mission, only the second in the united nations special forces short yet violent history.

Date: Friday, December 4th, 2020

Time: 0900hrs MST

Location: 850 Miles Northwest of Arkhangelsk, Barents Sea, Depth of 400 feet.

Temperature: 17 Degrees Fahrenheit Air, 35 Degrees Fahrenheit Water

An uneasy calm has fallen over the crew of the Dallas they continue directly west at twenty knots; only occasionally slowing down to make sure they aren't being pursued by warships of any nation. Captain Xi made his way to the captain's quarters about an hour ago, leaving the XO in charge in the control room. He's trying to figure out how to proceed, both with reporting what happened to the commander and how to monitor the Russian reaction. One thing at a time however and he quickly writes a short message down and heads out of his room towards the radio operator in the control room.

"Commander on deck." The XO calls out when the Captain reaches the control room, doing his best to hide the fact that he is in a rush.

"At ease gentlemen." Captain Xi quickly responds sending everyone back to their duties as soon as humanly possible, "Radioman Jones, when we reach periscope send this message to the Kestrel. Dive bring us to periscope depth and make turns for five knots. Bring us up nice and slow."

The sailors follow his commands to the letter and soon, the submarine is only fifty feet below the waves.

"Scope is clear captain, nothing in visual range." The XO says as the periscope drops back down to its stowed position.

"Roger that XO, raise the radio mast." Captain Xi calmly commands and mere seconds later the radio mast is raised, and Radioman Jones is sending the message written down in front of him as fast as he can.

"Message sent Captain." Jones calls out a couple of seconds later, though it felt like fifteen minutes.

"Roger that Jones, XO lower the radio mast and dive make your depth four five zero feet and make turns for twenty knots." Captain Xi orders calmly and once again the sailors around him carry those orders out to a tee.

"Radio mast stowed for dive." The XO calls out and the Dallas creeks slight as it descends back to the cold depths of the Barents Sea.

"Con, Dive, making turns for two zero knots and depth is four five zero feet." The dive station calls out as the submarine finishing level out and everyone goes back to standing normally.

"Excellent." Captain Xi replies relieved, though maintaining his calm demeanor in front of his crew.

He quickly debates whether or not to head back to his quarters deciding against in order to maintain the sense of calm amongst his crew. Normal operations quickly resume, and emotional order is restored to the Dallas; they're still exiting the area at twenty knots, but the anxiety of battle has finally passed.

Chapter Four

Date: Friday, December 4th, 2020

Time: 0902hrs AST

Location: Persian Gulf, 425 miles southeast of Kuwait

Temperature: 78 Degrees Fahrenheit

Jeremy is woken up by the sound of a messenger rushing into the room, by some miracle not waking the other five members of the squadron up in the process. He clears his eyes and reveals the young Indian sailor in front of him, saluting and holding out a piece of paper.

"My apologies for the intrusion sir, a message was received from the Dallas." He whispers, his accent barely hiding his nervousness; he knows he shouldn't have barged like he did.

"It's alright sailor, at ease." Jeremy replies after yawning, taking the note gently from his hand, unfolding it carefully in front of him; careful to avoid waking his girlfriend who is still sleeping soundly in his arms.

Quickly he realizes that it is an after-action summary of what happened between the Dallas and Kazan. A pit forms in the bottom of his stomach as he knows that he is going to have to wake up his girlfriend because of this. He calmly dismisses the sailor back to his duties and wonders how he is going to wake Elizabeth up without startling her. The sailor gently closes the door behind him, and Jeremy decides that it's better to get it over with rather than waiting any longer.

"Elizabeth, sweetheart." He says, gently moving her slightly with his free hand; she moans slightly, clearly not wanting to wake up.

"Elizabeth, I need you wake up now." He continues softly, nudging her a little and she finally begins to open her eyes slightly.

Slowly, but surely, the tired young woman comes to her senses though it takes a moment for the grogginess to disappear from her body. Taking a breath to gain her composure, she looks up at her boyfriend and takes his head in her hands and kisses him on the lips. The move comes as no surprise to Jeremy, it's something she's done ever since they started dating, but eventually they need to get to the business at hand.

"Do you two need a room?" A voice asks catching them completely off guard and ending the kissing instantly.

"John? You're awake?!" Elizabeth says with a start, jumping to her feet and turning to face John's bed; everyone instantly snaps awake, startled by Elizabeth's tone and volume.

"Yes, I am. Don't tell me you were already deciding on what my tombstone would say." John says sitting up, revealing a white tee-shirt and green flannel pajamas that the medical personnel changed him into after cutting his flight suit from his body.

No one immediately responds to John's remarks, still processing the surprise that their commander is awake so soon after receiving treatment for a bleeding ulcer in his stomach. An uncomfortable silence falls over the room as the young adult's struggle to find the words to convey their emotions. Jeremy finally and calmly breaks the silence.

"A report has come in from the Dallas about three minutes ago." He says calmly handing John the slightly crumpled piece of paper.

John looks it over calmly; no one is able to get a read on what he is thinking, as he skillfully hides his thoughts with his usual level of calm and professionalism. With bated breath, his colleagues impatiently wait for what he has to say; wondering why it's taking so long for him to respond.

“Stand down people, everything is going to be alright. Have the Dallas continue on its course and keep a close eye on the Russians. Nuclear war won’t start today, maybe tomorrow or the next day, but not today.” John eventually says calmly, crumpling the note in his hand and taking a deep calming breath before he speaks.

“Roger that commander.” Elizabeth promptly says with a shaky smile, still stunned the John is awake, let alone sitting up and giving orders; the rest of the squadron is still grasping for words.

“Are you up for this John?” Vladimir finally utters though immediately wishing he could take back what she said, John doesn’t mind; however, he expected this line of questioning to occur.

“I’m awake, aren’t I?” John replies smoothly and calmly, though not overtly trying to dismiss his squad mates’ concerns.

“Yes sir.” Neil says, his smile widening as the squadron members begin heading for the door.

“Elizabeth, Jeremy, hang on a sec.” John says just as the other squadron members make their way through the door; his warm words cut through their ears like ice as they freeze in place as he continues saying, “I think you know what I am going to ask you about.”

“Yeah... we do.” Elizabeth says exacerbated, unable to turn around and face her still sitting commander even though her boyfriend is able to; albeit barely.

She does eventually turn around but not after long awkward pause and subsequent silence. She’s completely worried about her leader’s reaction to what they are about to talk about; unsure if she will even be a part of the squadron after the next few minutes take place.

Her boyfriend is almost as calm as John, though his general demeanor gives away the fact that he is at least slightly nervous.

"First things first, I'm not going to kick you out of the squadron." John says, as calmly as he could while remaining seated on his bed; he takes a breath, "And I need both of you to know that I will give you whatever support you need during the coming months and years."

John's calm and controlled response catches the couple completely off guard and disarms any defensive response they may have had.

"Thank you... thank you John." Elizabeth says bowing her head, trying to hide the tears building in her eyes; Jeremy puts his arm around her, trying to comfort her.

"But I also need you to know that this is going to be a lot more difficult from here on in. Not right now but in a couple of months I am going to have to ground both of you from combat ops. I hope you understand that it's-" John pause composing his thoughts as he stands, "It's for your family's sake."

"We understand John." Jeremy says, his emotions finally manifesting on his face in the form of tears as he holds his girlfriend tighter and tighter; not that she minds as she's doing the same thing to him as she continues to hide her face.

"Come here you two." John says fighting off the sudden onset of dizziness he is experiencing in order to hug his friends, who gladly accept his embrace as he jokingly finishes by saying, "Now, I just need you two to get married."

Jeremy and Elizabeth laugh as soon as the words leave his mouth, tears still rolling down their cheeks. The truth is however, neither one of them entirely know how to respond to the comment just made by their commander.

"We'll have to get back to you on that. First things first." Elizabeth eventually manages to blurt out before shyly burying her face in her boyfriend's chest.

"Alright. Both of you need to take easy at some point, but right now we need to fly back to the states to make sure they don't do anything stupid." John says quietly and the mood shift back to the business at hand.

"Roger that commander." Jeremy replies and he and his girlfriend finally leave the room leaving John alone.

He manages to quickly stretch before turning to the small locker in his room, muttering "*I made a promise*" under his breath before opening it to reveal five more flight suits. Changing into green flight suit, he picks up his phone dials Captain Anderson's number; when he answers, John asks him to add Rob to the call so he can stay up to date on the squadron's whereabouts.

"I'm here John, what's the plan?" Rob asks upon picking up the phone from one of his assistants.

"We're going to return to the United States for a few days. So far as I can tell the Russians are still sitting on their asses and I don't need congress or the president to change that." John replies zipping up his flight suit and refreshing the squadrons specialized news feed on his computer.

"We copy that John, but are you up for another long flight so soon?" Rob asks as John can hear Anderson typing away on his own computer.

“If we don’t tell my doctor for the next thirty minutes I will be. Have the Dallas meet up with Supply Squadron one off the coast of the Falkland Islands, I’m sure Captain Xi’s crew could use the break. Captain Anderson I want your battle group to join them.” John says swiftly and characteristically moving the conversation along from his health.

“I’m sure our crew will appreciate the break from the heat, we’ll begin launch preparations on our end.” Anderson says, unable to keep his happiness from infecting his voice.

“We’ll get the tankers up on our end and I am going to head to the Falklands to meet up with the Dallas when it arrives.” Rob continues managing to maintain his composure a little better than the old captain.

“Sounds like we have a plan. Rob let me know when you meet up with the Dallas; we’ll end up in the area next Friday to discuss our options going forward.” John says, placing his 1911 in its holster on his thigh once more.

“Roger that commander and safe flight.” Rob replies swiftly.

“Safe flight commander.” Captain Anderson finishes, still not able to hide his excitement at the fact that the fleet is going somewhere that isn’t the Middle East.

The phone call ends without another word being said as John takes a deep breath. Despite the calm he is able to put up for those around him, he fears that two hornets’ nests have just woken up and both are waiting for the other to make a move. John just doesn’t want to end up in the middle, that’s not the squadrons job. No, their job is to make sure the middle never appears and that the hornets know their place in society. The thought causes John to remember what he texted to Sam yesterday before the mission even kicked off; does he really want to bring her into this life? The question causes him to punch the desk below his right fist, it hurts but then again, it's supposed to. Barely pushing the thought to one side, he rushes out of the room: it's 925 hrs. in the morning and the squad leaves in twenty minutes for the thirteen-hour flight back to Scranton. If all goes to plan, they will be landing at 1545 hrs. in the afternoon, eastern standard time.

The crew prepares for the squadron to leave; well rested after getting a few hours of sleep and not being at combat alert. Their joy at leaving the sauna of the middle east is also blatantly apparent, it's all they've seen for the last month and a half and they haven't been able to go ashore during that time.

Admiral Anderson looks over his small fleet of ships, including the carrier Kestrel, the St. Louis Class Light Cruisers Helena and Andromeda, the Atlanta Class Destroyer Juneau, and two support vessels. The pride he has for what the squadron is trying to accomplish is strongly affixed to his battle-hardened face for all to see. He orders the carrier to turn into the wind as the squadron's planes appear on the flight deck and the sound of screaming jet engines soon echoes across the nearby airspace.

The six squadron members soon launch in sequence and disappear off into the distance as they climb to their cruising altitude of thirty thousand feet and cruising speed of five hundred and eighty-five miles per hour. Breaking through the cloud layer, the flight of six fighter jets turns North East and sets their autopilots for the Scranton Airport, allowing the pilots to sit back and relax until the reach the first refueling tanker.

"Vladimir." John says over the radio gaining his attention, "It has occurred to me that I never said sorry for having to sink the Kuznetsov."

"It's alright John, we're all going to have to fight our own countries at some point." Vladimir responds appreciating the apology though feeling it's not entirely necessary.

Due to this being a ferry flight, the squadron is refraining from using their individual callsigns; it allows them to keep things necessarily informal.

"How are you feeling John?" Clara asks after missing her opportunity to do so before they left the Kestrel.

"I'm doing just fine." John replies simply and dismissively, heavily wishing that people would stop asking him how he is feeling.

In actuality, the pain in John's stomach is close to unbearable anytime he shifts around in the cockpit of his fighter jet. This fact makes him glad that this isn't a combat mission otherwise he might become an easy target should someone manage to get close enough.

"John?" Clara says breaking the brief moment of silence, "Do you have any plans over the next week apart from possibly threatening congress." Her tone giving away the fact that she's worried about John's reaction; she doesn't want John to be angry with her because of her curiosity; though he doesn't get a chance to answer.

"Of course he does." Elizabeth blurts out, completely failing to hold in her sarcastic and teasing tone gaining a slight chuckle from her colleagues.

"No need to blow this out of proportion Liza." John says waiting a second for his friends to calm down, "To answer your question Clara, I do have plans to hang out with Sam at some point during this weekend."

A gentle silence falls over the squadron; Elizabeth and Admiral Anderson already knew about John's plan, but the rest of the squad didn't, so they need a moment to process what John has just said.

"Glad to see you're being social for once in your life." Neil finally states sarcastically knowing what his commander's response is going to be.

"What are you talking about Neil? I'm perfectly social when I want to be." John jokingly retorts, allowing his friends to do the same from here on in without the fear that their commander is going to be upset with them.

The jokes continue as the flight settles into monotonous routine of simply making sure the flight of six fighter jets doesn't encounter any civilian or military air traffic. Humor allows the time to pass quickly and soon the pilots reach the first of several KC-46 aircraft that are stationed along their flight path. Time though, is not going quickly enough as the squadron still has a long flight ahead of them and they can't go much faster as they will run out of fuel quicker than they can afford to. With the autopilots engaged, they take turns taking half hour naps as they rocket across the sky, though John refuses to take his turn and passes it to Elizabeth. No matter what his friends say, he's going to make sure he's awake for the rest of the flight.

Date: Friday, December 4th, 2020

Time: 1704hrs EST

Location: Scranton, Pa

Temperature: 32 Degrees Fahrenheit

John has been crashed out on his couch for about the last hour or so, ever since arriving from the airport and after changing out of his flight suit and into black tee-shirt and jeans. His squad mates have gone to their houses for the night, which are scattered across Scranton, but none are more than two minutes away from each other for mutual support, just in case. This is the farthest thing from John's mind at the moment as he is really wishing that he had gotten more sleep, both before the mission and before the flight back home. His phone vibrates on the coffee table next to him, though it's not a message from any of his squad mates or anyone affiliated with the squadron; it's Samantha. John reluctantly picks up the phone and proceeds to read Sam's text message after swiftly unlocking it with his right index finger.

"Hey John, just wondering if you're home and if I could come over for dinner or something." The message reads and quickly John decides to respond instead postponing; knowing how happy it would make Elizabeth and Sam depending on the circumstance.

"Sure thing Sam, I'm home so you come over anytime." He responds, hitting send the instant he finishes the message, picking up the television remote and turning the television on mere seconds later with the channel set to CNN.

As John tosses the remote on to the couch, he decides to he over to the kitchen to get something to drink. His stomach is still causing him a great deal of discomfort, though not as much as it was at the beginning of the ferry flight to get here. Grabbing a Coke-Cola can out of the fridge, he sits back down on the couch and takes a small tin of pills out of his pocket, medicine that the squad's doctor insisted he take after he refused the injectable version. He carefully places two pills on to the palm of his right hand and downs them with a quick drink from the Coke-Cola can in his left. The tanginess of the soda helps to mask the terrible taste of the pills and John needs the caffeine the soda provides in order to remain awake for the next few hours.

His phone buzzes again, another message from Samantha appears on the screen as John picks it and unlocks it. The message reads: *"Sounds good, I'll be right over."* John doesn't feel the need to respond; he doesn't need Sam texting and driving on her way over to his house. She certainly knows the way to his house, she's been there before, but it's not a risk John wants her or anyone taking; it's simply not worth it.

John makes note of the fact that CNN is only covering domestic issues at the moment with the usual anti-president sentiment ever since he was re-elected just over a month ago. They're quiet on what the Russians might be doing or thinking, either meaning they don't care, or, more likely, the Russians are still formulating their response to the sinking of the Kazan. This doesn't surprise John though he was expecting that they would have already sent a response out stating that the submarine had sunk. Maybe they're too embarrassed that one of their latest submarines had been bested in battle. After a couple of minutes, John changes the channel to something a little more relaxing than the evening news, HGTV where reruns of Property Brothers are showing.

The medicine begins to kick in, numbing the pain slightly though not making it go away completely like John hoped. His stomach growls as well, he's desperately hungry, having not eaten since breakfast before the mission started; the doctor told him to not have anything solid food, fearing it would make the ulcer worse. John is still debating whether or not to obey the doctor's orders when there is a soft knock on his front door.

John sighs, he lost track of how long it had been since Samantha had texted him and he knew it doesn't take her long to get from her house to his. Getting off of the couch, he gingerly makes his way to the door, doing his best to hide the lingering pain in his abdomen. He doesn't want Samantha to worry about him, especially when the squadron is already worried about him more than he wants them to be. With a slight level of apprehension, he gently places his hand on the doorknob, turns it and pulls the door towards him as the cold outside air rushes into the warm house.

Standing before him is a light skinned young woman with light green eyes, standing at five and a half feet tall and her black hair back in a ponytail. She's wearing thick pink sweatshirt over a light blue tee shirt along with blue jeans and short heeled, brown ankle boots with a zipper on the side. Both of them can barely hide shy smiles from each other as Samantha Adams steps through the threshold and John closes the door behind her.

"Feels like it's going to snow soon." She says quietly still trying to keep John from seeing her smile, failing, but still trying.

"Yeah it does." John replies realizing that hiding his smile is a hopeless cause and promptly giving up on it, "It's good to see you Sam."

"It's good to see you too, John." She replies, finally giving up on trying to hide her smile as well.

"So what brings you over?" John asks as the two young adults head for the couches in John living room.

"My parents are out of town for the next week and I just needed someone to hang out with to avoid getting bored." She replies with her characteristic honesty.

"Ah, that's understandable. I haven't had dinner yet; do you want to go out and get something?" John asks recognizing that it is a slightly silly question since they just sat down, though Sam doesn't seem to mind.

"Yeah, where were you thinking?" She asks, her tone revealing to John that she was hoping he was going to ask her to go out to dinner, catching him slightly off guard.

"How about the Backyard Ale House? Might be slightly crowded but maybe the weather will keep people away." John suggests after taking a moment to think about the nearby options.

"Sounds good to me." Sam replies joyfully, preparing to jump up and head outside.

"Alright, I'll drive." John says and the pair get from the couches and head outside towards John's red Jeep Gladiator Rubicon after John grab's his own sweatshirt off of a nearby coat rack; Sam's car is parked behind it, a white Ford Escape.

Normally, Sam would playfully argue with John, saying that she should drive, but she's too tired tonight to put up any form of resistance. Additionally, John is a lot better at driving and carrying a conversation than she is, a fact she has freely admitted to him numerous times over the last four years that she has been able to drive. During this time, her parents have also grown to like John and trust him with their daughter to the point that she is able to stay at his house if she is too tired to come home after hanging out with him; with some conditions that John has strictly abided by.

After starting the mid-size pickup truck, John carefully guides it out onto the road and pair head towards the restaurant with the radio tuned to the local country station. It doesn't take long for Sam to notice that something isn't right with John, seeing right through his effort to hide the pain in his stomach.

"You're hurting." She says the concern in her voice plain and concise.

"It's that obvious, huh." John replies still trying to hide the stubborn pain in his stomach and maintain his concentration on the road in front of him.

"What happened?" Sam says, her concentration firmly planted on the young man next to her forcing John to be mostly honest with her.

"I had an ulcer burst in my stomach earlier this morning, don't worry a doctor has already looked at it and I took the medicine he told me too." John replies keeping calm and only saying the what and not the why, with regards to the injury; not lying but not telling the whole truth either.

John's words go a long way to alleviating Sam's concern, but she still can't help but wonder why the ulcer burst and how it got there in the first place. Knowing how John is, however, she decides not to ask him direct questions about the injury as she doesn't want him to be annoyed with her.

"Are you able to eat?" She asks kindly trying to make sure that both of them are going to enjoy dinner and not just her.

"Yeah I am, the worst of it has passed." John replies with a reassuring tone and a relaxing grin; the decision to ignore his doctor, coming easier in the moment than it did when he actually had to think about it.

Samantha takes him at his word, though makes a mental note to keep a closer eye on John during dinner. She was able to pick up on his pain so easily as she's seen it before, within the last six months in fact, though she never received a direct answer. Realizing that she's not likely to get one now, she decides to change the subject to something else before they arrive at the restaurant in a couple of minutes.

"So, are you seeing anyone John?" She asks cautiously yet curiously as she never really thought to ask John this particular question before.

John pauses for a moment before answering, though he knows where this likely going to lead.

"No, I'm not." John says simply, "How are things between you and Richard?" He asks, seemingly already knowing the answer; Samantha sighs, the disappointment washing over her.

"No... he broke up with me two days ago." Sam finally admits, she knew she would have to tell him at some point, she only hoped it wouldn't be so soon.

"I'm sorry to hear that." John states softly, "You deserved better than him Sam, I hope you know that." He's trying to be reassuring.

"Yeah, I know, just hurts right now." She replies on the verge of tears, though managing to hold them back for the time being.

John doesn't say a word, simply placing his right hand on her left and holding it gently. A reassuring warmth passes through Sam's body, dissipating her watery eyes and allowing her to take a deep breath and her emotions to pass.

"Everything is going to be alright." John reassures her with his typical half smile and calming tone; noticing that traffic is lighter than usual.

“Yeah, it will be.” She replies allowing herself to smile once more and letting go of John’s hand after holding for a few more seconds than he was expecting.

The light amount of traffic allows John and Sam to quickly arrive at the Backyard Ale House, parking along the mostly empty street in front of the restaurant and across from the Lackawanna County Courthouse. The pair’s hope that the weather would keep most people home is well founded as the local bar/restaurant is mostly empty, though not entirely. A couple of patrons are seated at the bar while others are seated at the tables dotted around the open floor space. Sam suggests sitting at a two-seat table that isn’t near many of the patrons and John follows her, not putting up any objections because he’s focused on trying to keep Sam in a good mood. A waitress heads over as soon as they are seated, handing them menus and asking if they want anything to drink; John asks for a Mike’s Hard Lemonade and Sam asks for a glass of Pinot Grigio, both handing the waitress their licenses as proof that they’re at least twenty-one. The waitress kindly hands their licenses back to them and tells them that she’ll be back in a minute with their drinks. John puts down the menu, already knowing what he wants and how he wants it.

“You’re too quick.” Sam remarks still looking at the menu for what she is in the mood to eat, unable to make up her mind.

“It’s not my fault I already know what I want.” John retorts with a smirk and a laugh.

“When are you going to try something new for a change?” Sam continues to joke.

“When it’s carefully planned out with back up plans.” John says, playing along to keep Sam smiling, though he can’t say he doesn’t enjoy it.

The waitress returns with their drinks and asks if they are ready to order. John and Sam thank her for the drinks and place their order, a cowboy burger and a plain cheeseburger respectively; they're doing their best to try and keep things easy for the tired waitress.

"I meant to ask earlier, where are your parents for the weekend?" John asks curiously, taking a small sip from his drink as Sam takes a sip from hers.

"They're down in D.C. for some political fundraiser. A congressman's re-election campaign, I think." Sam replies, knowing she didn't really pay attention to what her parents said as they walked out the door.

"I guess it's never too early to start campaigning." John remarks remembering that that the election was just a few days ago.

"I guess not." Sam starts with a smile; that soon changes as she gathers her thoughts, "Would it be alright if I stayed at your house tonight? I don't want to b-."

John cuts her off.

"You know you're always welcome at my house, no need to explain it to me." He says softly as if he already knew she was going to ask; again trying to keep Sam's spirits up, "Just make sure you text your parents and let them know."

Sam smiles, she doesn't want to be alone, not tonight.

"Thank you, John, and I will." She says simply, "You've always been nice to me."

"We're friends, it's my job." John replies shortly though avoiding sounding dismissive at the same time.

"It's more than that though, isn't it?" Sam asks, sincerely hoping that she's right though trying not to reveal that to John.

"Sam... This is how a guy is supposed to treat you." He pauses knowing his bluntness has caught Sam off guard, "Not as a thing or a servant, but as a person with feelings, wants and needs. I am simply trying to show you that Richard was doing the former and not the latter."

Sam takes a moment to compose herself and process what John has just told her; deep down she knows he's right, but simply can't believe him right away. She wants to believe, she knows she should believe him, yet she can't seem to bring herself to believe him; it's simply too soon to do so. Before she can respond however, John catches her off guard again, realizing what she's thinking.

"I'm not asking you to believe me Sam, just know I am speaking the truth." He says as she looks away from him, still trying to make sense of everything, "Chin up Sam, one day I am going to need you. Just like you need me right now."

His words softly even out Sam's roller coaster of emotions as she turns back to him, gently looking into his eyes and allowing a reassuring warmth to wash over her.

"If it's ok with you, I am probably going to have more than one glass of wine." Sam says finally allowing herself to forget her atrocious ex-boyfriend for the first time tonight.

"I was already planning on driving." John replies allowing his smile to go wider as he notices the waitress is on her way over with their food.

"Thank you, John, you're the best." Sam says as the waitress arrives and sets out their burgers in front of them.

The pair thanks her at the same time and in response she asks if they want anything else. John asks for a Pepsi to replace the Mike's Hard Lemonade he had while same asks for another glass of wine as she planned. The waitress walks off to get the drinks, her spirits lifting that she has nice customers for once at this time on a Friday.

John and Sam continue about their meal, catching up and taking their time as a small crowd makes its way into the restaurant. The crowd, however, is not its usual summertime size and by no means makes the bar crowded. After an hour a steady hum has fallen over the bar and Sam and John have managed to finish their meals after Sam finishes drinking her third glass of wine. She's certainly feeling the effects as she can't stop giggling and keeps leaning from side to side in her seat; her condition signaling to John that it's time for him to get her home. The waitress notices his signal for her to bring the check over which she does so with a little more energy than when the night began.

"I can pay." Sam suddenly pipes up, her words barely coherent while remaining slightly understandable.

"It's ok I got it." John replies, putting his UN Visa Debit Card in the card slot of the receipt holder; it looks the same as a normal Visa, it's just tied to John's UN bank account so he can use his money anywhere on the planet.

"You always pay John, let me pay for once." Sam continues barely able to keep her eyes open as John shakes his head.

“Next time Sam, alright?” John says knowing full well that he’s not going to let her pay whenever he is treating her to dinner.

Sam begrudgingly, mainly due to her drunkenness, agrees and allows John to pay for dinner before they leave the restaurant and climb into John’s Jeep Gladiator. As John starts the midsize pickup, Sam almost instantly falls asleep, moaning something that is neither English nor a noise that a human usually makes. John decides to let her sleep, even though the drive back to his house is going to take only a few minutes, any amount of rest is going to help right now. He turns the radio down and is careful to avoid as many potholes as he legally can in a successful effort to keep Sam comfortable on the way to his house.

Pulling into his driveway, he soon realizes that he’s probably going to have to carry Sam into his house; she is sleeping so soundly that not much beyond an explosion would be able to wake her up. Turning the car off, he gets out and heads for the passenger side door where Sam is seated; when he opens the door, she slumps into his arms resting against his chest and the seat belt. John carefully reaches around her to undo the seat belt and lifts her out of the truck closing the door with his back as he easily carries Sam’s one hundred and thirty-five-pound frame in front of him. She moans slightly again, resting her head against his and draping her arms around him, letting them limply hang over his back as her legs hang in the air. John carefully maneuvers both of them into the house and heads upstairs towards the spare bedroom, barely straining to hold Sam’s weight for this amount of time.

Once in the spare bedroom, John gently sets Sam down on the bed, setting her down slowly so he doesn’t drop her. As he does, he feels her hold on a little more than he was expecting, as if she was trying to hug him or get him to lay in the bed with her.

"You still have a pair of pajamas in the dresser from the last time you were here." John says softly whispering into Sam's ear.

"Can you get my shoes?" Sam asks, fully aware of what she's asking though too tired to do it herself.

"Sure thing." John replies after a silent moment, unzipping her boots and setting them on the floor by the foot of the bed.

"Thanks John, you're the best." Sam says here words fading to silence as she falls completely right there on the bed, street clothes and all.

John smirks as he glances over Sam as she sleeps soundly on the queen-sized bed; he figured the evening would turn out like this as soon as she told him about the breakup.

"Sweet dreams Sam, sleep tight." He whispers as he pulls the comforter over her and tucks her in for the night.

He leaves the room, quietly closing the door behind him so he doesn't cause Sam to wake up; she's needs to sleep otherwise she'll regret it in the morning. It's almost 2100 hrs. in the evening, as John heads back downstairs and sits on the couch wanting check the news one last time before heading to bed. After turning the television on and making sure the volume is low enough that it won't wake Samantha up, he sends a quick text message to Elizabeth explaining how the night went. He knows that she'll be curious and not let him go to bed before telling her every single detail; additionally he needs to ask her if she's heard anything regarding the United States or Russian Government. Of course, his second in command focuses on the more personal issue at hand rather than the more important one.

"I'm glad you two had a good night together, though I can't say I am sorry her ex. boyfriend broke up with her. He was an idiot and she deserved better. She deserved you, I hope you know that."

The last part of Sam's message is what changes John's mood from one of annoyance to one of embarrassment. He partly wishes she hadn't said it and is mostly dismissive of her remark, feeling that it's not matter her deserving him, but of him deserving her, feeling certain that he doesn't. He sighs, noticing CNN is still complaining about something random that the president did, and replying with:

" We'll talk about that later Liza. Have you seen or heard anything?"

He's able to keep annoyance mostly contained due to the person he's texting with being Elizabeth, if it was anyone else, he would have likely yelled at them and possibly shot them by now if the yelling didn't get them to stop. He changes the channel to MSNBC, deciding that CNN is likely going to hold any breaking news to a time when people are actually watching. Elizabeth soon replies to his earlier message, keeping to task as she knows she was getting close to a line she shouldn't cross, at least not yet.

"All seems to be quiet for the time being, Vladimir's Russian contacts say closed room meetings took place, but they ended hours ago."

John figured this might happen; while neither country likes each other at this point, they also don't want to admit to losing some of their most valuable military assets. It would cause a public relations disaster for both countries and neither would know how to respond. John knows how to respond to Elizabeth though.

"Alright, get some sleep. I'll be going to bed soon after one last check of the networks. I'm sorry for my shortness earlier, I'm just trying to keep Sam happy and it's been a long day."

John slightly regrets the way he worded his second message to Elizabeth, though he understands why he said what he said, and this will be the only apology for it. Not because John is trying to be mean to Elizabeth, but because the reason he gave is the only reason he wants her to know and worry about. Luckily for John, Sam also understands where he is coming from; she had to make the same thirteen-hour flight he did and only got slightly more sleep than he did along with the fact that he had an ulcer burst soon thereafter.

"It's okay John, I understand. We hope you have a goodnight and aren't into much pain from earlier."

Sam finally replies, referring both to her boyfriend and too the ulcer in John's stomach that he managed to forget about after taking the medication he was given before Sam arrived.

John returns his phone to his pocket and spends the next half hour flipping between MSNBC, CNN and FOX, none of whom have deviated from their usual messaging or programming. He relaxes as he turns the television off, knowing that the certain chaos isn't going to happen tonight, and he may just be able to sleep for a full eight hours.

Heading back upstairs, he pauses outside the spare bedroom door; debating whether or not he should check on how she's doing. In his heart, he knows tonight was about much more than one friend taking care of another. However his mind "knows" what will happen if he ever reveals what he does for a living to her.

Realizing that he's just standing there in front of the door, he moves to his bedroom, and rapidly changes into his pajamas, almost jumping into his queen size bed when he's finished. As soon as he turns the light off, he falls asleep, failing to notice that he's left his door slightly open; he's just that tired.

Chapter Five

Date: Saturday, December 5th, 2020

Time: 0325hrs EST

Location: Scranton, Pa

Temperature: 26 Degrees Fahrenheit

Sam begins tossing and turning, becoming restless and wakeful in the process. Jolting awake, she props herself up against the headboard of the bed, taking a couple of deep breaths to calm herself down although it barely works as her heart rate remains elevated. She wipes her face with her hands before placing her face in her palms and bursting into tears. She tries to keep the tears from running down her face but it's no use; she can't stop crying, not on her own anyway.

Eventually, she decides to head to the bathroom to splash some water on her face, hoping that it helps rather than knowing. She only makes one stop before heading out of the room and that's to change out of her street clothes and into the pink flannel pajamas she left here a couple of weeks ago. When she finally reaches the bathroom and turns on the light, she finds the streams of tears on her face and the redness surrounding her eyes. Shakingly, she turns the faucet on, making sure the water is ice cold; with her hands shaking she's barely able to splash water on to her emotional and tired face. After a few minutes pass, she finally feels better enough to head back to the spare bedroom, though she's far from completely better.

As she shuffles her now bare feet along the soft carpeted hallway, she notices that the door to John's room is partially open. She stands in front of the spare bedroom door, just staring at John's room as the tears from earlier return to her eyes and cheeks. She can't stop staring, the shaking in her hands and legs increasing to a point where she can't stand and has to drop to her knees. Breathing heavily, she soon finds that she can barely breathe to begin with, unsure what she should, or can, do next.

"John." She says, her words barely audible between the shakiness in her voice and her overall tiredness.

"John." She repeats, hoping that he hears her, though she knows that it's unlikely given the hour.

She tries to say his name a third time but fails and just starts sobbing, leaning against the spare bedroom door that she is unable to stand up and walk through. Little does she know, John did hear her just as she started crying, in fact it's what finally woke him up.

"What's the matter, Sam?" John asks softly, wrapping his arms around her and resting her against his chest.

She only continues to cry, barely able to hear what John's saying and unable to see him as her eyes are pinned shut with her emotions. Frozen with a shaking fear, she can't move nor return the fact that John's hugging her; underneath the outburst of emotion however, she appreciates that he's there holding her, providing her with a level of warmth that she desperately needs right now. Slowly but surely, the shakiness in her body begins to die down as John continually reassures her that he's there for her and everything is going to be alright.

"He... He..." Sam quivers trying to speak but failing in the process, though slightly relieved she was able to say anything resembling a word.

"Just breathe Sam, just breathe." John replies softly, rubbing Sam's back as he holds her to help her calm down.

"He didn't break up with me John. I broke up with him after he... after he..." Sam continues and instantly John realizes the severity of what Sam is trying to tell him.

"Sam..." John sighs softly

"He raped me John... he... raped me." Sam finally mutters burying her face in John's chest as she speaks, her cries increasing in intensity.

"Oh Sam..." John says holding tighter and thinking of what to say, "Everything is going to be ok. Everything is going to be alright."

Sam doesn't immediately respond; she just sits there cradled in John's arms with her head buried in John's chest as her tears begin to dampen his tee-shirt. He doesn't mind; however, he's only focused on her right now.

"I'm sorry for lying earlier, I just couldn't face the truth and I still feel like I can't." Sam says though John barely hears her.

"Don't worry about that right now. I'm here and I'm not going to let anything happen to you and you don't have to face the truth alone Sam. I will always be beside you and in front; always beside you and in front." He says just as quietly.

The pair sit quietly as Sam finally manages to start calming down though her tears show no sign of stopping or slowing down. John begins rocking her back and forth slightly, hoping it helps and knowing that the only way to get Sam to stop crying is to get her to fall asleep. He contemplates texting her parents and letting them know what happened, but it doesn't take him long to decide that isn't an option, especially if she hasn't told them already.

"John... if it's not too much trouble... can I stay with you tonight?" Sam finally asks feeling the onset of exhaustion brought on by her emotions.

"Sure." John replies gently, only hesitating for a mere moment before responding.

The pair slowly get off of the floor as John supports most of Sam's weight but doesn't carry her like he did earlier. He keeps his arm around her as she wraps her arms around his stomach with her face still buried against his chest. He guides her into his bedroom, closing the door behind them as Sam proceeds to lay down on his bed. After scooting herself underneath the comforter, she holds it up for John so he can slide underneath it a little easier. John smiles, appreciating the effort as he slides underneath the comforter and positions himself so that Sam can rest her head on the right side of his chest, and he can wrap his right arm around her.

"Thank you, John, for everything." Sam says, her tears finally beginning to slow as she drifts off to sleep.

"Anytime Sam. I'm here for you." John replies as exhaustion finally overtakes his body.

He doesn't mind that he lost almost an hour of sleep because of Sam, he'd rather lose sleep than see her hurting. He wants her to be happy, he's always wanted for her to be happy; he just doesn't know if he's the right person to make her happy. Helping her like he is at the moment simply feels right to him but making her happy for the rest of their lives is something that he doesn't know if she even wants and that's without knowing what he does for a living.

Before the issue makes him as restless as Sam was, he decides that he needs to tell her; that he needs to be honest with her. He's always been honest with her except for this one instance and the issue is going to eat away at him until he addresses it. He knows the risk, that it could end with neither of them talking to each other ever again, but it's something that he's starting to feel that he owes it to her. She trusted him enough to ask to sleep with him two nights after something unthinkable happened to her, the least he could do is trust her with the one secret he's kept from her.

John's mind finally manages to begin falling asleep once this final thought moves to the back of his mind. He can feel Sam's heartbeat and breathing against his chest as he drifts off; both have finally settled down from their earlier concerning pace. He smiles, glad that what he did actually helped Sam rather than bringing up anymore bad memories from her previous relationship. Just before John completely falls asleep, he takes one last glance at Samantha; thinking something to himself, he falls asleep in peace for the first time in a long while.

Date: Saturday, December 5th, 2020

Time: 0748hrs EST

Location: Scranton, Pa

Temperature: 27 Degrees Fahrenheit

The early morning sun peaks its way through the curtains in John's bedroom, slowly and gently waking up the two tired young adults from their restful slumber. Their positions haven't changed much since falling asleep in each other's arms around three hours ago. Both of them slowly and reluctantly begin to open their eyes as the emotions of a few hours ago rapidly become a distant memory.

"How'd you sleep?" John asks smiling at Sam as she looks up at him, returning his smile with her own.

"That's the best I've slept in a long while. You?" She replies, forcing herself to sit up on the bed and yawning as she stretches her slightly stiff arms and legs.

"Same here." John replies simply, still smiling as he looks into his friend's light green eyes.

It soon becomes apparent to both of them that the other is debating what they should do next; their hearts telling them one thing, their minds telling them another. John sits up on the bed, across from Sam, still looking into her eyes as he remembers that he needs to tell her something. Before he can speak however, Sam smiles wider than he's ever seen her smile and falls into his arms and wraps her arms around his chest, giggling to no end. John, not knowing what to say or where to start, simply rest his arms around Sam, trying to figure how to transition the moment from the welcome and comforting hug, to telling her about what his job is.

"Thank you, John, I know I've said it a lot, but thank you." Sam says softly not wanting to let go of him.

"You're welcome Sam." He starts seeing a small opportunity, "Listen, there's something I need to tell you."

"What's up?" She replies looking up into his eyes as her looks down into hers, causing John to hesitate as he sees a beauty he hadn't noticed before.

"I haven't been completely honest with you Sam. There's one thing I've kept from you and I'm sure you've noticed my lack of responsiveness from the last few times you've asked me." John says looking away, almost ashamed and disappointed in himself; sure enough Sam did notice.

"When I ask what you do for work..." She says quietly after a short pause, looking down at the bed they're sitting on.

John slides off of the bed without saying a word and walks over to the computer desk on the other side of the relatively large bedroom. Setting his index finger on a fingerprint sensor hidden on the desktop, the computer unlocks, and the desktop image appears on the wall behind the desk. Sam positions herself at the edge of the bed, facing the screen as she rests her feet on the soft carpeted floor, curious as to what John is going to show her. Suddenly, she's caught off guard when John speaks after typing a couple of words on the extremely clicky keyboard.

"Security Clearance Code, Zero Zero Zero Zero One, Commander John Hilderbrand." He says with a commanding tone; as soon as he finishes a document appears on the wall, Unit Nations Security Council Resolution 71.

He steps to one side, turning to face Sam whose eyes are fixated on the document displayed before her. It's captivating her attention so much that it forces her to stand up and walk towards the desk as she tries to process what she's reading and what just said to access the file.

"Commander... John Hilderbrand." She mutters to herself, her eyes not deviating from the wall for even a split second.

"You trusted me last night, I felt I needed to trust you with this." John says still trying to wake up and read Sam's reaction at the same time.

"Forgive me if this sounds stupid, what does all of this mean?" Sam asks after another short pause.

"It means that most of the scars on my body aren't self-inflicted. Do you remember when the Israeli Prime Minister died?" John says leading Sam to the conclusion that she was eventually going to come to.

"Yeah I do... He committed suici-..." She replies, stuttering slightly through her sentence before cutting herself off before she finishes her sentence.

"He was killed by a six-point five-millimeter bullet fired from one thousand yards away. The Israeli's were saving face to avoid a public relations disaster." John states moving back to the bed, sitting down in order to not come across as overbearing.

Sam is staring blankly at a random point in the air in front of here, though she's able guide herself back to the bed and sit down next to John who puts his arm around her.

"The ulcer... Are you ok?" She asks finally looking him in the eye once again; John's surprised but also amused.

"Yes, I'm fine Sam, it just burst when I took a tight turn in my fighter jet, that's all." John replies, seemingly relieved that he can finally talk to her about what he does.

Sam is still processing what she read, the limited information that John has just given her has certainly helped but overall, she still doesn't fully understand what John is trying to tell her. Despite this however, she does appreciate that John has finally been honest with her about what he does instead of trying to hide it again, like he has been doing for the last six months or so.

"What do you want me to make of all this?" She asks, though her tone is not one of anger or sadness, but one of curiosity and a longing to know more.

"That's for you to decide Sam. I'm only trusting you with highly classified information that could get you killed if you tell anybody." John responds, not trying to scare her, just make sure she knows the reality of the situation.

"I'm guessing Elizabeth, Jeremy, Neil, Clara and Vladimir are a part of this." She states, finally coming back to her senses.

"Not just them, thousands of people are. From support staff to special operations personnel. You name it we probably have it." John says, his joy feeding its way into its into his voice without him even realizing.

"I see..." Sam pauses, "Do you want me to be a part of this?"

Sam's question doesn't catch John off guard, he was expecting to have to answer it sooner or later.

"Only you can decide that and if I'm honest, I don't want you making the decision right now. You're too emotional after what happened a couple of days ago and your parents aren't here to talk it over with you. Speaking of, if they knew about last night, they'd probably take my head off so let's keep it between us, ok?" John answers softly, not wanting Sam to rush into this like he did when he joined the squadron.

"Alright." Sam says letting out a smile that causes her to close her eyes in the process, John smiles as well, finally relaxing now this has gone well.

John feels a warmth rush over him, very similar to what he felt earlier this morning when Sam made herself comfortable against his chest as they fell asleep. His mind races with how he should deal with this feeling, yet his heart remains surprisingly steady; beating as if he was about to shoot the Israeli Prime Minister again. This response was trained into him almost five months ago when he was training with snipers from Seal Team 6 and the British SAS, all of whom made sure he knew the value of keeping his heart rate down and to react on instinct alone.

"You're feeling the same thing I am, aren't you?" Sam asks easily noticing John's indecision.

"Yeah I guess I am." John responds after taking a moment to have the words make their way through his muddled mind and out of his mouth.

Sam chuckles and plays with her hair with her left hand as she looks down at the floor for a moment. She finally looks back up at John and reaches out with her right hand, gently holding his head as he places his left hand on her right. Then, with only a slight moment of hesitation, she kisses him softly on his lips before pulling back with a wide smile.

"I'm going to get a shower." She says softly, gently pulling her hand back and letting go of John's head, who's both stunned and grateful with what just transpired.

"Alright, the towels are in the same spot and I'll get breakfast ready." John replies with a chuckle of disbelief.

With this final exchange, Sam gets up from the bed and heads for the bathroom by the spare bedroom, patting John on the shoulder as she passes. John heads downstairs and begins preparing an eggs benedict recipe that he has perfected over the last couple of years. He turns on the television to find that the situation in both the United States and Russia hasn't changed since last night, a small relief given what's happened in the few hours since then. He hears Sam start the shower just as he gets a large pot of water to a rolling boil and begins cooking the eggs for the eggs benedict. During the few seconds he has while the eggs are cooking, he sends a quick message to Elizabeth explaining most of what has happened since he last messaged her, though he conveniently leaves out the earlier kiss.

He knows if he even hints at that moment, Elizabeth won't focus on anything else for the rest of the week and right now he needs her and the rest of the squadron to keep their eyes on two opposing superpowers. However, he does tell Elizabeth that he revealed the squadron to Sam, fully expecting to get yelled at as soon as he hits send on the text message. To his surprise, the expected and probably warranted yelling, fails to materialize.

"*How did she take the news?*"Sam responds, ignoring the security breach for the time being.

*"Surprisingly well, though I don't know if she'll be willing to join us and even if she was, there's still the obstacle of her parents."*John replies, being as honest as he can be about the situation; it doesn't take long for Elizabeth to respond.

*"That's understandable. I guess we'll find out in due time. Slightly off topic, but have you heard from Vladimir at all? I texted him last night, but still hasn't gotten back to me."*Her messages reads, sending a slight chill through John's spin as he scoops the eggs out of the rolling boil.

*"I haven't heard anything from him since we landed yesterday. I can check his tracker if you think it's necessary."*He texts back to her, wondering what could possibly be going on.

The tracker John mentions was a compromise between the squadron and the United Nations. The United Nations wanted to be able to locate any member of the squadron with a GPS implant and John was able to get them to back down on their requirements. It's still present, but instead of being an implant, it's on their phones and any use of it has to be done with John's explicit supervision and presence. It's never been used before and John's hoping that this instance won't be the first as he finishes assembling the two servings of eggs benedict for Sam and himself, placing ham on top of four English muffins.

"Let's hold off on that. Part of me feels that his probably still asleep and I don't think we need to trigger a full-scale war to find him. If I don't hear from by noon, then Jeremy and I will go knock on his door." Elizabeth writes, allowing John to return his relaxed state as he hears the water turn off upstairs.

"Keep me posted." John replies before swiftly finishing cooking and preparing breakfast as he can hear Sam getting ready for the day on the floor above.

Just as he begins to plate the dish, he feels the pain in his stomach return and return sharply. He's able to weather it long enough to finish plating breakfast but not much beyond that as he almost falls to a knee, using the countertop to support himself as he reaches for the medicine bottle, he left in the kitchen last night. Sliding two pills into his hand, he quickly washes them down with a small glass of tap water. Just before he finishes the drink however, Sam comes down the stairs barefoot, wearing a pink tee shirt and blue jeans that John recognizes from the fact that she left them here three weeks ago along with the pajamas. Her smile almost makes him forget the piercing pain still present in the stomach; almost making it easier to hide, almost.

"You alright?" Sam asks gently moving over to him and place her left arm around him and holding his left hand with her right he puts his left arm around her after putting the glass down on the counter.

"Yeah... I'm ok now." He replies smiling, grateful that Sam asked as the warm feeling once again washes over his body.

"You need to take it easy, John. I don't know what I'd do if you weren't here." She says softly, her words lingering in John's ears as if the world was moving in slow motion, forcing him to pause before responding.

"Unfortunately I don't have that option most of the time... But I will always be there for you Sam, no matter what." John says just as softly, thinking of his words just before they leave his mouth.

Sam sighs, knowing John's words are unfortunately true, but she's also glad that he said what he did. It brings her a level of comfort that she hasn't felt in years because of her former boyfriend.

"I know" She pauses for a moment, still smiling, "Come on, I'm sure breakfast is getting cold."

Sam leads John by the hand as the pair take the plates of eggs benedict from the counter to the dining table, where Sam proceeds to surprise John, sitting down next to him at the table. Up until now, she's always sat across from him at the other end of the rectangular dining table, but the simple act of moving closer to him tells John something has changed between them. He only hopes that it's the right kind of change and that it's for the right reasons so he doesn't have to make any promises he can't keep. The two eat breakfast in silence; not uncomfortable or stifling, they're simply enjoying each other's company in a way that they weren't able to while Sam was dating the asshole who raped her three days ago. That's all he is now to John, an asshole. An asshole who signed his death warrant the instant he laid his hands-on Samantha that day. Knowing that thinking about what happened will only get him riled up, he keeps his thoughts to himself and continues presenting an outward calm and happiness.

When the pair finish breakfast, they don't immediately get up from the table; staying there giggling and smiling at each other as they clean up from the meal. When they finally stand up and take their dishes to the kitchen sink, John checks his phone, seeing if there has been any update from Elizabeth about Vladimir; no notifications have popped up since his last conversation with her. For the moment he takes it as a relief, though he knows they're going to come up on Elizabeth's noon deadline in no time. Luckily, he manages to keep his confusion hidden as he once again turns to Samantha, wanting to see what she wants to do during the course of the day.

"I guess I better get my shower now, right?" He says as Samantha gives him yet another hug, making her the person who has hugged him the most since his parents passed away a couple of years ago.

"Yeah, but one second." Sam replies, looking up at him and kissing him on the lips one more time, longer than she did earlier this morning.

"You really like doing that don't you?" John says, a wide smile forming across his face after their lips part.

"Yeah... it helps." She replies simply, trying to hide the fact that she's blushing by burying her face against John's chest.

John laughs slightly, knowing exactly what Sam is doing and finding it rather cute; a word he's never really used or associated with anyone before now.

"You're not going to let go, are you?" He says still laughing slightly; not that he wants the hugging to stop.

"Nope. Though you do need to shower." Sam says, also not wanting the hugging to stop either but realizing that John also needs to get his day going so they can actually leave the house and do something enjoyable before John's work gets in the way.

"Yeah I do." John replies though making no effort to get Sam to stop hugging him.

It takes a further few minutes for Sam to release John, though she does follow him back upstairs, asking him if she can read a little more about what he does for a living. John hesitates slightly when she asks, both surprised that she wants to know and unsure if he should let her fall down the rabbit hole of the squadrons policies and procedures. Eventually, and after some prodding from Samantha, John relents and says yes, unlocking the computer in his room once more.

"You will have access to all of our files, but remember, this information is highly classified. Not even Presidents get to see it." John warns, wanting to make sure that Samantha is well aware of the need for secrecy with what she might find while he is getting his shower.

"I understand." Sam replies, her tone instantly telling John that she does in fact understand and is not annoyed that he warned her.

After this short exchange, John heads into the master bathroom as Sam sits at the desk and begins sifting through the various files that she can find. Training reports, personnel files, fleet status reports, and even more that she doesn't fully understand. Going back through the personnel files, one catches in particular catches her eye, it's John's file. Opening the PDF file, a total of ten pages load on to the screen, with John's picture taking up a quarter of the first page. Most of the details she finds on the first couple of pages she already, such as John's age and personal history, but then she finds John's training and mission report from the first mission he was a part of, the assassination of Israeli Prime Minister.

Initially, the information she sees doesn't concern her, even though she barely knows what the reports are actually saying. However, she then finds the medical report from the squadrons doctor regarding injuries that John sustained during the training missions. Abject horror doesn't even come close to describing her reaction; nearly vomiting as she scrolls through the exhaustive list of bruised and fractured bones, numerous stitched up scars and multiple shrapnel wounds. She wants to look away, but her eyes are glued to the screen, hanging on every injury listed with a date next to it. She comes to realize that he was hanging out with her the day after some of the most severe injuries occurred. Her mind races through these moments, searching for anything that she may have missed that may have given away the fact that John was in a severe amount of pain. She fixates on a memory from four months ago, when the two of them went to the movies with her parents while her now ex. boyfriend was out of town.

Between the teasing from her parents about how John was her actual boyfriend and the movie, Sam remembers that John almost fell asleep at numerous points during the film. He was also moving stiffer than normal for some reason, but he passed it off as a long day lifting heavy objects at work, though she knows now that he wasn't telling her the whole truth at the time. Scrolling to the exact date in John's personnel file, Sam is able to figure out what had happened to John the few days prior to going to the movies.

John was on a training mission with Vladimir, taking out African Warlords in Nigeria with members of the British SAS. The squad of eight began taking fire after some of the warlord's soldiers stumbled upon them while marching from one base to another. The ensuing firefight killed one of British Soldiers and wounded two more in addition to John being shot twice in the left shoulder and sustaining four broken ribs from rocket propelled grenade blast that occurred twenty feet in front of him. The mission report goes on to state that had John not held his ground before the RPG went off, the two wounded British soldiers would have likely been killed. According to the included pastor's report, the death of the first British soldier stayed with John, likely to this very day. The reason he was stiff and tired when he went to the movies with Sam and her parents is because of the bandages around his chest and shoulder and the painkillers his doctors insisted he take.

Unable to read any further, Sam closes the file and sets back in the chair, trying to calm down and collect herself before John gets out of the shower. Her emotions are one large mass of confusion as on the one hand she's happy that John has finally let her into his world, and she is finally getting answers to some of her questions. On the other hand, she's horrified that John has been through and suffered so much that he's never told her about; mainly because he couldn't. As this last thought makes its way through her mind, she makes the decision that she has to join the squadron; she owes it to John to be there for him just as he's been there for her. She knows that he is likely going to argue that she doesn't owe him anything, but she doesn't care; her mind is made up and that's that.

"I'm guessing you found my personnel file." John says, startlingly Sam almost out of the chair and causing her heart to jump, almost out of her chest.

Sam turns gently, finding John wearing and pair of blue jeans and in the process of putting on a green tee shirt. Glancing over his upper body, she easily finds the scars of the two bullet wounds on his left shoulder along with numerous scars from various shrapnel wounds across his chest and arms. Given what she sees on John's chest; she's certain that a similar number of scars on his back that are obscured from view. She continues staring as John efficiently slides the shirt on, confirming his suspicions that Sam did indeed find the file and her reaction doesn't surprise him one bit.

"I know telling you that I'm okay is a moot point, so I just need you to know that I am healing and that any injuries I receive are an occupational hazard that I can't do much to diminish." He says calmly moving to the desk side of the bed and sitting down, keeping eye contact with Sam the entire time.

"I know." She replies softly, barely knowing what to do with what she's seen or what she's been told.

"That being said, I don't care how hurt I get, I will always be there for you no matter what." John reiterates, calmly placing his hand on her shoulder and doing his best to cheer her up.

Sam smiles as John's comforting gesture begins to take effect, though she still wishes he wouldn't get hurt in the first place.

"Everything is going to be alright." John says softly, only slightly unsure of how true his statement is going to be, given that he's in uncharted territory with regards to his personal life.

Before Sam can respond beyond continuing to smile at John, his phone buzzes to life with a phone call from Elizabeth. Quickly checking the time, John knows that the news can't be good.

Chapter Six

Date: Saturday, December 5th, 2020

Time: 1045hrs EST

Location: Scranton, Pa

Temperature: 38 Degrees Fahrenheit

"I don't have the full details yet John. All I know is the Richard showed up at Vladimir's house and Vladimir knocked him out." Elizabeth says, her tone clearly conveying the uncertainty of the situation.

John is driving his Jeep Gladiator with Sam in the passenger seat; his phone is on speaker phone while being located in a center console cup holder.

"Not meaning to be harsh but I want to stop hearing that answer Elizabeth." John replies clearly upset yet focused on the task at hand.

"I'll update you when you get here." She replies before hanging up, not taking any offense to John's words; she heard them all before.

John flicks up the armrest and reaches into the storage compartment for something that Samantha doesn't immediately see, though isn't entirely surprised when he finally pulls it out.

"Put this on your right thigh." John says, his tone noticeably more serious than earlier this morning as he hands Samantha a black thigh holster.

Secured in the holster is John's standard issue Ruger Security-9 and a spare magazine; he may not carry it often, but he makes sure it's around just in case he needs it. Sam does as she's told, quickly undoing her seatbelt just long enough to secure the holster both to her belt and around her thigh. Strangely she doesn't feel nervous, despite thinking that she certainly should be. She wonders if it's because of John being there with her or, at the very least, knowing what he is capable of. Though she is curious about one thing.

"What about you John?" She asks calmly referring to the fact she has a firearm and he doesn't.

"Open the glove box." He replies and she does so, soon finding John's Tan M1911 also in a thigh holster, "Can't go anywhere without it, I'll need you to toss it to me when we get to Vladimir's house." He finishes, Sam nods in response.

They're only going slightly above the speed limit, in line with the normal traffic pattern so they don't arouse the suspicion of the local authorities, not that it would matter if they tried to interfere. Thankfully, it doesn't take much longer for them to arrive at Vladimir's house with John carefully parking the Jeep Gladiator behind Jeremy's Ford Ranger, Clara's Ford Focus RS and Vladimir's Ram Rebel. Both of them jump out of the midsize truck as John swiftly attaches the forty-five-caliber handgun and its holster to his belt and thigh. Walking over to his squad mates, he glances at Sam who is a step or two behind him; she's acting tough, but he can tell that she's nervous.

"What do we have Vladimir?" John asks wanting to get right down to business after he and Sam greet everyone; they're all wondering why John allowed Sam to join them for this, but they keep their thoughts to themselves.

"A drunk asshole who thought my house was hers." Vladimir replies, doing his best to reduce the abrasiveness in his voice, which thankfully works.

"Alright, Jeremy and Neil, drag him out here. We're going to have a word with him and then figure out what to do from there. Vladimir and Clara, I need you to keep Sam company for a moment while I talk with Elizabeth" John says placing his hands on his waist.

"Roger that." Everyone responds, except for Sam who's slightly confused at what is happening still trying to focus on keeping her composure.

Before speaking with Elizabeth, John takes Sam to one side, hoping to help her calm down.

"Look, you're about to see a side of me that isn't pleasant, so I completely understand if you want to look away. You don't have to prove anything to me. Clara and Vladimir can help with that if you want." He says softly so that only she can hear him.

"I should be alright but thank you. Please be careful." She replies, trying to keep her emotions from boiling over.

After this short exchange, Sam sneakingly gives John a hug and kisses him on the cheek, taking great care that his squad mates don't notice before he walks off towards his truck with Elizabeth. Sam stands there staring before beginning a conversation with Clara and Vladimir, though she can't help but glance in John and Elizabeth's direction.

"What's up?" Elizabeth asks as soon as she and John get out of earshot of the other squadron members.

"I need you to get ahold of Sam's parents and get them back up here as soon as possible. She's insisting on going down a path that I don't think she's ready for, but I also know none of us are qualified to convince her otherwise. Is it my fault? Yes. But I didn't think she would take this situation as well as she is." He says his concerned tone surprising Elizabeth as she's never really heard it before.

"Roger that John. Are you okay? You're acting stranger than usual." Elizabeth says knowing the risk of asking John such a question.

John takes a moment to collect his thoughts and catch his breath, for the first time in a long while his heart is racing.

"I hope so, otherwise, no one is going to like what they see today." He replies ignoring the fact that painkillers are preventing his stomach from bothering him at the moment.

He turns towards the house just in time to see Jeremy and Neil dragging a shorter and heavier statured young man with jet black hair and deeply tanned skin out on the lawn. The movement has woken him and he's not happy about it, anger causing him to stumble to his feet and shout "where's the whore" repeatedly as he staggers from side to side. Sam takes a few steps back as Clara and Vladimir put themselves between her and Richard. John is the only one to move towards him as he falls on the ground again, clearly not in control of his faculties or senses. He places his hand on his 1911 though doesn't draw it, not wanting too unless absolutely necessary. The move forces Richard to realize that he's in a lot more trouble that he initially thought as he freezes for a moment.

"Yo... you can't sho... shoot me, I have... ri... rights." He manages to stammer as he begins crawling backwards along the ground.

"Richard, when I'm around, the only rights you have are the ones I say you do." John responds, his voice harsh and deeper than anyone present has heard before.

"I kn... know you..." Richard continues to stammer, running out of space to back up as he runs into the front door of Vladimir's house.

"Yes you do Richard, and right now I am your worst nightmare. I warned you that if you did anything to Sam, the wrath of God would feel pedestrian compared to what I was going to do you and now, here we are." John replies, the sinister tone of voice growing darker and more menacing with every word.

Just as John pulls Richards two-hundred-and-fifty-pound frame off the ground by his shirt collar, Clara has Sam turn her head; then the screaming starts.

"You don't have to watch this." Clara whispers to Sam, finding the bloody scene almost too hard watch herself.

"I know, it's just... I want to see him suffer. The same way he made me suffer. Is that normal?" Sam replies, trying to figure out her own emotions.

Clara simply nods in response before the pair turn back to the gruesome scene being presented in front of them. Richard is a near lifeless heap on the ground, blood pouring out of his mouth and nose as John stands over him taking a few deep breaths to bring his nerves under control. Vladimir walks over with a towel that John uses to wipe off the blood covering his right hand, revealing his bruised knuckles.

"Feel better?" Vladimir whispers as he takes the towel back and John takes a particularly deep breath.

"Yeah, I do." John gasps, his words barely audible as he stares down at what's left of Richard on the ground.

“Let’s go before someone shows up. Is it ok if I crash at your place?” Vladimir asks as the pair turns back towards their friends; he only gets a nod in reply.

Just as John reaches Sam, who gives him a quick once over while making sure his hand is ok, Richard’s distinct inability to keep his mouth shut catches up with him.

“Not going to shoot me. Big mistake asshole!” He shouts spitting blood into the grass in front of him.

John stops in his tracks, still facing away from Richard as the rest of his squad mates turn to face the senseless asshole. Sam is still looking at John, concerned for his wellbeing and for what’s going to happen next. Without a word, John proceeds to put foam ear plugs in his ears, signaling to the rest of the squad to do the same as he hands a pair to Sam. He then places her right hand on the Security 9 in the holster on her thigh, as if to tell her what’s going to happen next.

“You know what Richard, now that you mention it.” John starts, turning back towards Sam’s ex. boyfriend, making sure his footing is stable before continuing his statement, “No, we’re not going to shoot you.”

“Just as I thought, you’re too soft.” Richard spits sealing his fate.

“No Richard, I misspoke. What I meant to say was that I’m not going to shoot you. She is.” He replies barely holding back a laugh and pointing to Sam, who systematically draws the handgun from the holster.

“Wait, what? Sam, plea-.” Richard starts, trying to plead his case, but he’s too late.

“Bang... Bang Bang.”

Three shots ring out in short succession before Sam places the Ruger back in the holster and takes a breath. Richard, crumples over lifeless without making another sound or saying another word, having suffered two gunshot wounds to the head and a single gunshot wound to the groin.

"Everyone regroup at my house. We need to update Rob and make sure that World War three isn't about to start." John says before any one is able to get over the shock of what has occurred; pulling out his hearing protection as he speaks.

Everyone heads back to the vehicles they arrived in, leaving Richards body with a note stating that he was killed due threatening a member of the squadron. These kinds of notes keep local law enforcement off of their backs while they conduct their operations, though they don't keep the squadron members from getting a speeding or parking ticket.

It doesn't take long for John to notice that Sam is shaking in the passenger seat; given it's the first time she's fired a gun in anger, he's not surprised and can sympathize with the experience. He takes her hand gently in his own and soon Sam is leaning against his right shoulder.

"You did well Sam. I know it doesn't feel like it now, but you did well." John says softly, the menacing tone that was present in his voice earlier is now completely absent as he speaks, thankfully replaced with the same caring tone that he's been using since last night.

Sam knows he's right and it felt good to pull the trigger, yet she can't shake the abnormal feeling that it's given her. It felt good but it doesn't feel right.

"John... what was it like when you first killed someone?" She asks wondering if he's ever experienced the same feeling; her question doesn't surprise John.

"It wasn't an easy feeling, if that's what you're asking. Yes, the person deserved to die according to the squadron's standards, just like Richard did, but it still wasn't easy to get over." John replies, his soft tone only getting softer.

"I know what you mean." Sam says quietly, gaining some comfort from the fact that John felt the same way as she is now.

"Just remember, I'm here for anything you need Sam." John continues, gently squeezing Sam's left hand.

"Always beside me and in front." Sam whispers to herself remembering John's words from earlier this morning and recalls where John was positioned when she shot her ex. boyfriend.

Sam sits there quietly as the pair drive back to John's house, wondering if this is what John goes through during his mission as she leans against his shoulder. Her mind though, soon turns to another thought. If John treated her so well, and better than her ex-boyfriend did, just as a friend; what would it be like if they were together as a couple? Will he treat her even better than he does now, or would things remain roughly the same? She knows for certain however, that he will treat her right, no matter what.

Date: Saturday, December 5th, 2020

Time: 1138hrs EST

Location: Scranton, Pa

Temperature: 38 Degrees Fahrenheit

"So let me get this straight. You had your friend kill her ex. boyfriend because he raped her. In the process, you revealed all of the squadrons secrets to that friend because you finally wanted to be honest with her as a result of you thinking that you like her!? Do I have that straight John?" Rob yells over the phone recounting what his commander has just told him as the rest of the squadron waits outside John's closed bedroom door; Samantha is downstairs waiting for them to return.

"I don't know why you're upset Rob. I was well within my authority to do what I did." John replies, brushing Rob's obvious concern aside as he looks at status updates from the Kestrel and the Dallas.

"I will concede that you're correct on that John, it just doesn't seem like you to make rash decisions like this. Why did you do it, if you don't mind me asking?" Rob says, calming down slightly as he tries to regain control of his temper, slightly surprised that John hasn't raised his voice at all during the conversation.

"One of life's great mysteries Rob. One you'll find out when I feel you're ready too. Plus I know I have five pairs of ears listening in on this conversation from outside my room." John says, finding tennis ball on his desk and throwing it with a fair amount of force at the bedroom door; several of his squad mates respond to the gesture with an "ouch".

"Alright, just make sure you know what you're doing John and I'll keep you updated on my end. See you in a couple of days." Rob says completely calming down and regaining his composure.

"Will do; see you in a couple of days." John replies, hanging up the speaker phone call and tossing his phone in his right jeans pocket before heading for the door.

Upon opening it, he finds that Neil and Elizabeth are rubbing their foreheads in an effort to dull the pain, while Jeremy, Vladimir and Clara chuckle uncontrollably.

"I was worried you were going to chew Rob out for insubordination." Clara says finally bringing her near laughter under control.

"Someday I will, but today, it wasn't necessary. Elizabeth, I will need you Jeremy and Vladimir to head down to the Falklands to meet up with Rob. Neil, Clara and I will stay here with Samantha until tomorrow evening so that we can talk with her parents. We will then join you in the Falklands, yes I know this is cutting our time home short but with one of our houses compromised staying here for the next week or two is too much of a risk." He says knowing the disappointment that it will cause despite safety concerns.

"So much for a small break." Jeremy says sarcastically, getting John to chuckle.

"Yeah, I know, and I am sorry about it and will make it up to you guys somehow, but for the time being this is what needs to happen. We'll all grab lunch before you guys leave." John says as the group heads down the stairs and Sam perks up upon seeing them; she hasn't heard much of what's happened and is just happy to see a few friendly faces.

"We're going to go get lunch, is there any place you'd want to go?" Elizabeth asks Sam kindly, allowing her to pick where they go for lunch.

"Does Mansour's Cafe sound good to everyone? I haven't been there in a while." Sam asks shyly, still trying to make sure everyone is okay with her choice even though she's surprised that they let her pick to begin with.

"Neither have we. Let's go." Jeremy says with a laugh as everyone heads for the door, with Sam hanging back slightly so she can walk next to John.

As everyone gets in their respective vehicles, Sam notices that John is being unusually quiet as he starts his Jeep Gladiator for the third time today. She gently grabs his right hand to get his attention, hearing him sigh and gently swallow when she does.

"Elizabeth, Jeremy and Vladimir are flying down to the Falklands after lunch." He starts, figuring the best course of action is to not hide what is happening, "Neil, Clara and I are flying down tomorrow evening after we have a conversation with your parents, who are flying back here tonight. What we tell them is largely going to depend on what you want."

Sam takes a moment to process what John just said, though her reaction certainly surprises him.

"Tell them the truth John, because I am going to tell them that I want to be with you. I feel safe with you, and you've taken care of me more in the last twenty-four hours than Richard ever did." She says with a soft sternness and level of certainty John hasn't seen from her in a long time.

"Are you sure you want that Sam?" He sighs, desperately wanting her to think about this more than she seems to be, no matter how much he likes her, "You've just been through two dramatic events in the last week and you still have a lot to learn about what I do for a living. I'm not saying you shouldn't come with me, but I at least want you to be sure about this."

Sam pauses: she understands why he's saying that because this is a huge step for both of them and it's all happening so quickly that she really hasn't had time to stop and think rationally about it. She needs to decide whether or not she is acting rationally or emotionally, and she doesn't have a lot of time to make this decision as this conversation is happening tomorrow. However, she knows that her heart has already made up its mind and that her gut is telling her to go with it.

"I know enough to be sure that I want to be with you, John." She says eventually looking over at John as he guides the truck through a couple of turns.

"You're sounding like me. Alright, if you're sure that's what you want then I will make sure we communicate that to your parents." He chuckles as Samantha's response is incredibly similar to one, he would sometimes give during his training, though he leaves out the fact that he's also wanted to be with her for the last year.

With Sam on board with joining the squadron, John's focus shifts to how he is going to convince Sam's parents that her decision is a good idea. This isn't something that John and his squad mates had to deal with as their parents had passed away by the time they were living on their own and going through college. The circumstances differ for each squad member, but none of them had to ask for permission in order to join the United Nations initiative. On the contrary, other members of the yet to be named United Nations initiative, such as combat and support personnel, simply brought their families with them to avoid the awkwardness of being unable to talk about what they do with their families. This is the first time that an initiative member's family, might not involve in what the squadron or the initiative does. Additionally, this whole situation could ruin Samantha's relationship with them if they don't want her to be a part of the United Nations initiative and John's command squadron.

Yes, Samantha is legally old enough to make her own decisions and to override her parents if they go against what she wants. By the same token, her parents could disown her for going against their wishes, which would put the entire initiative at risk depending on how much John tells them. It's a risk that John is going to have to take in order to advocate for what Samantha wants; he only hopes that it isn't going to escalate beyond a simple conversation. His heart pounds as the thought crosses his mind though it doesn't increase from its calm and orderly beat. He only hopes that Sam understands the consequences of what is about to happen and leaves it at that; this is one situation he can't deal with preemptively.

Date: Sunday, December 6th, 2020

Time: 0303hrs FKST

Location: Stanley, Falkland Islands

Temperature: 43 Degrees Fahrenheit

"Sorry to cut your vacation short." Rob says calmly, as Jeremy, Elizabeth and Vladimir approach him after climbing down from their SU-33s.

"It's alright, wasn't turning out to be much of a vacation to begin with." Jeremy responds shaking Rob's hand, with Elizabeth and Vladimir soon following suit.

"Unfortunately, you're going to have to get used to it." Rob replies as the four soldiers climb into a nearby silver Land Rover; something that blends in with the local traffic and doesn't bring attention to the squadron.

“How far out are the Dallas and the Kestrel?” Elizabeth asks curiously as she climbs into the front passenger seat, while Jeremy and Vladimir make their way to the backseat; their small duffle bags are placed in the cargo area by a member of the support staff.

“The Dallas is still three days out as is the Kestrel battle group. However, we called in the Georgia’s battle group and they’ll be here by Tuesday. Cruiser squadrons one and two are returning to Midway Base.” Rob replies as they make their way down the quiet streets of Stanley, towards The Waterfront Hotel.

“Do you think that amount of fire power is going to be necessary?” Vladimir asks knowing the punch the UNS - Georgia can pack should something be unlucky enough to be in its crosshairs.

“I certainly hope not Vladimir, but it’s always better to have a can of whoop ass in times like these.” Rob replies trying to lighten the mood; it likely would have worked better if the three young adults in the car with him weren’t half asleep.

The four finally arrive at the hotel, quickly checking in and heading up to their second-floor suites; Jeremy and Elizabeth are sharing one while Vladimir and Rob get their own. All say goodnight before heading inside, knowing that having any further conversations will be practically impossible without a good night's sleep. As Jeremy and Elizabeth change into their pajamas, they reflect on John’s reaction to the news that they’re pregnant and the strange amount of leeway that his is allowing to take place. They certainly appreciate his reaction; it just feels strange to them.

“You feeling alright?” Jeremy asks after he and Elizabeth change into their pajamas and they slide into bed to snuggle together.

"Yeah, I am. Just wondering why John has been acting strangely calm the last couple of days." She replies, resting her head on Jeremy's chest and using her hand to check her slightly larger stomach as Jeremy turns out the rest of the lights in the room; the only remaining illumination coming from the stars and moon.

"I wish I knew the answer, but then again, things were always different with him when Sam was around. He's more open and slightly calmer, as if he feels safe around her." He replies, beginning to drift off to sleep as he gently pulls his girlfriend closer.

His words don't immediately dawn on Elizabeth due to her tiredness, but after repeating what he said in her mind three or four times; she realizes why that's the case. She smiles when she figures it out, drifting off to sleep after snuggling closer to Jeremy and unable to stay awake any longer thanks to the long flight and slight amount of jet lag.

Date: Sunday, December 6th, 2020

Time: 0231hrs EST

Location: Scranton, Pa

Temperature: 25 Degrees Fahrenheit

Josiah and Abigail Adams are just getting off of their late flight at Scranton International Airport, after being told that they need to come home immediately. Their dress clothes are the same ones they wore to dinner earlier that night as they didn't have time to change between the fundraiser and getting on the plane.

"Thank you for cutting your weekend short Mr. and Mrs. Adams." A familiar voice says as they collect their luggage from the baggage claim.

"It's quite alright John, though I wonder why you couldn't have waited a day or two." Josiah says, his voice deep and calming as he turns to face the young man as his wife grabs her bag from the baggage carousel.

Josiah's slightly short yet proportioned frame, goes well with the tuxedo he is wearing and his slightly greying, black hair. His wife is wearing a long, sparkly black gown that matches her black stilettos, jeweled earrings, pearl necklace and brown hair. They both work the National Parks Service at the Steamtown National Historic Site and a former superintendent of the site was elected to congress. They went to the dinner to show their support and wanted to explore Washington D.C. afterwards, though, clearly one of those won't be happening now.

"Unfortunately, this couldn't wait... Dad... Mom." Sam replies before John can say a word, revealing herself from behind John in order to stand next to him; she's tired but she needed to be here.

"Sam?!" Abigail says shocked that her daughter is there, expecting her to be back at John's house asleep.

She glances at John, before running over to her parents, falling into her mother's arms as she bursts into tears. Josiah glances back towards John as he takes his wife and daughter into his arms; John only stands there, stoic and unflinching.

Chapter Seven

Date: Sunday, December 6th, 2020

Time: 0330hrs EST

Location: Scranton, Pa

Temperature: 25 Degrees Fahrenheit

Sam is talking with her parents on the couches in John's living room as he stays in the kitchen with Clara and Neil drinking Coke Cola. He wishes he could be next to Sam right now as she recounts what happened to her a few days ago, but she requested that she handle this on her own. She's leaving the squadron and what ultimately happened to Richard out of the conversation, saving those topics for when everyone has had a chance to sleep.

"You seem nervous John." Clara whispers so that only he and Neil can hear her, her comment snapping John out of his slightly tired daze.

"Yeah... sorry, I just haven't... I just don't... I just want to be with her right now." John says just as quietly as Clara did, though his tiredness and inability to process what he is feeling causing him to stutter.

"It's alright John, it's alright." Clara replies as she and Neil gently place their hands-on John's shoulders and back in an effort to help keep him calm.

Josiah glances over noticing the gesture from John's friends and instantly understanding how he is feeling. It brings him a certain level of comfort to know that John was there to help his daughter when she was unwilling to go to them for help. It does hurt him slightly that she didn't tell him and her mom first, but if there was anyone, he'd rather she go to, it's John. He excuses himself, saying he needs to get something to drink, his ulterior motive being that he wants to make sure John is doing alright and have a word with him about all of this. He's also clearly able to see the same uncertainty and emotions that Clara and Neil are, though John isn't exactly trying to hide it. Clara and Neil move slightly out of the way when Josiah approaches; they've only met him a couple of times before tonight, but they can already tell that they're not the ones he wants to talk to.

"How are you holding up?" He asks warmly, opening the fridge and grabbing a bottle of Coke Cola, hiding it slightly so he doesn't get an earful from his wife.

"I'm pretty tired if I am honest Mr. Adams." John responds after turning back from glancing at Neil and Clara as they moved away.

"Please John, call me Josiah. We've known each other long enough." Josiah responds with a smile and a chuckle.

"I'll remember that Mr. Adams." John says, his politeness knowing no bounds even though he can barely tell what words are leaving his mouth, Neil and Clara chuckle slightly at the reply.

"So what do you make of what happened?" Josiah says turning to stand next to John and look back over at his wife and daughter to get an idea of what he is missing.

"Beyond being sad? I'm glad she's not with that asshole anymore. Pardon my French." John states, the tiredness clearly removing any filter he would usually have when talking with Sam's parents.

"It's alright John, I thought he was an asshole too. I'm just upset that I couldn't kill him myself." Josiah says, a slight chill going through John's spine.

“I didn’t think she was going to tell you about that.” John replies simply.

“She did and I appreciate that you allowed her to do it. I obviously have questions, but I am sure we’ll address those later.” Josiah says calmly, looking back towards John.

“Yes Mr. Adams, we certainly will.” John replies simply, not wanting to say anything more while he is this tired.

“Abi and I are going to head home here soon since we’re all pretty tired. Sam told us she wanted to stay here with you for the night. I’m guessing that’s alright with you?” Josiah continues.

John only nods in response, not having the wherewithal to do much else.

“I figured as much. You’re a good guy John, we’ll talk more later, and I look forward to hearing about this initiative you and your friends are a part of.” Josiah says before walking back over to his wife and daughter, his words hanging in John’s ears, blocking out any other noises.

John walks over a couple of seconds later, placing his hand on Sam’s shoulder as her father says that he and her mother need to head home so they can get some semblance of sleep. John asks if they would want to get lunch later that day and they graciously accept knowing that they were going to have meet up to continue this conversation to begin with. John and Sam walk Josiah and Abi to the door, waving goodbye to them as they get in their Audi A4 and drive down the road to their house. Closing the door, they turn back to Neil and Clara who are just as tired as they are.

"You're welcome to stay in the guest room if you want." John says unable to hold back a yawn as he speaks.

"Thanks John. We'll see you in the morning." Neil says, soon after, he and Clara head upstairs, not even thinking about where Samantha is going to sleep, though John doesn't forget.

"Do you want to sleep with me again?" He asks wanting to make sure, though he already knows the answer.

"Yeah." Sam replies the tiredness in her voice is unmistakable and inescapable.

John places his right arm around Sam and the pair head upstairs to his bedroom. After closing the door and changing into their pajamas, Sam turns off the lights and they slide into John's queen-sized bed as he pulls the warming comforter over them and pulls Sam gently into his arms. Instinctively, she rests her head on his chest and makes herself comfortable while also making sure John is comfortable as well, though even if he wasn't, he wouldn't say.

"John?" She says softly, knowing how tired both her and John are and not wanting to prevent them from getting any rest.

"Yeah?" He replies, keeping his eyes closed.

"I want this." She continues just as softly as before, certain in her feelings and convictions.

"I do too." He says, finally opening his eyes as he feels Sam looking up at him.

"Yeah?" She asks as a smile falls across her tired face and she hugs John a little tighter.

“Yeah.” He replies smiling and unable to take his eyes off of Sam; his heart is pounding again despite staying at the same steady beat.

No further words are exchanged as the pair begin to drift off, however, before they both close their eyes, Sam pulls herself up and kisses John on the lips. The kiss lasts longer than any of the others that she’s given him up until now. After a minute or so, she carefully repositions herself against John’s chest and allows her eyes to close as he does the same. The pair finally allow themselves to fall asleep, safe in the knowledge that what limited rest they will get will likely be the most comfortable night’s sleep that they have ever had.

Date: Sunday, December 6th, 2020

Time: 1030hrs FKST

Location: Stanley, Falkland Islands

Temperature: 50 Degrees Fahrenheit

Jeremy and Elizabeth look out over the small bay outside The Waterfront Hotel, waiting for Vladimir and Rob to join them as they enjoy a small breakfast of bacon and eggs.

“It’s not often we get any sort of peace anymore.” Elizabeth says, breaking the calm silence of the morning as adjust her black tee shirt and blue jeans.

“Which is why we should enjoy it when we can. Do you want my leftovers?” Jeremy offers noticing that his girlfriend’s plate is practically clean.

“Yeah. Sorry, I was really hungry for some reason.” She replies turning to look at her boyfriend and seeing Vladimir in the background.

"Well you are pregnant so I would expect you'd be hungrier than normal." Jeremy says with a chuckle as he shuffles what's left of his bacon and eggs on to Elizabeth's plate as he too notices Vladimir approaching them from the hotel, surprised that he's awake before Rob is.

"Oh... yeah." Elizabeth says, seemingly having forgotten the fact that she has to effectively feed another human being in addition to herself.

"I'm surprised that you two are up so early." Vladimir says finally arriving where Elizabeth and Jeremy are sitting.

"We're surprised you're up before Rob." Elizabeth retorts, getting her boyfriend to laugh and Vladimir to smile.

"Yeah I guess getting up early has its perks." Vladimir says noticing the lack of food present on Elizabeth and Jeremy's plates, especially after Elizabeth finishes the little bit of breakfast that Jeremy gave her.

Vladimir sits down on a nearby chair and a short while later, Rob appears from the hotel, wearing his characteristic skintight, dark blue shirt, green army pants and black boots. Something that not only shows off his massive biceps and triceps, but also seems to go well with his bald head.

"Isn't it a little cold for your Rock impersonation Rob?" Jeremy says jokingly once Rob walks within ear shot.

"Bitch, I am the Rock." Rob replies starkly, following along with Jeremy's joke and getting Elizabeth and Vladimir to laugh at his expense.

"What's the game plan?" Elizabeth asks, knowing that she's the one in charge while John isn't around.

"Well until the Georgia gets here, the name of the game is intelligence gathering. Russia and the United States aren't the only countries at odds with each other at the moment, Iran is trying to get under the United Kingdom's skin again. They seized another oil tanker last night, their first in just over a year." Rob says handing a manila folder to Samantha who passes it to Vladimir after looking through it.

"I'm guessing we have some phone calls to make." Jeremy says as Vladimir passes him the folder and turns his attention back to Rob.

"We only have to call the Iranians thankfully. The British Prime Minister has graciously decided to meet with us later today when he arrives for a tour of the Falkland Islands." Rob says, mostly sarcastically, alluding to the squadrons usual threatening tactics.

"What'd you say this time? That'd you chop his balls off if he didn't free up fifteen minutes in his schedule for a bathroom break?" Elizabeth asks, knowing has Rob usually threatens world leaders.

"No, this time I told him it would be in his best interest if he asked for thirty minutes of free time, otherwise he would find his dinner to be rather unpleasant." Rob says using a mocking British accent that Jeremy easily laughs at, spitting out his drink in the process.

"Either way, you're persuasive as usual Rob." Vladimir says as Jeremy recovers from the discomfort caused by spitting out his drink of water.

"I try." He replies with a smile and turning towards the bay in front of him and enjoying the slight sea breeze that is keeping the relatively low temperature comfortable by increasing the humidity.

"I'll get a briefing together for when John, Clara and Neil wake up in a couple of hours. Though I say we handle this one largely ourselves, just in case Russia or America does something stupid and John has to keep his focus on that." Elizabeth says after checking to make sure her boyfriend is alright and handing him her glass of water to help him clear his throat.

"Sounds like a plan, I'll handle the Iranian's if that's alright with everyone." Vladimir volunteers, receiving nods of approval in response.

"I guess that means I'll have to handle the British Prime Minister." Jeremy says, his voice slightly hoarse from the earlier drink incident, though quickly getting better.

"I guess that's our plan complete then. I'll have some of our special forces teams finish things up in Syria and keep everyone in the loop over the next couple of days." Rob says confirming everything and recalling the small cleanup effort necessary after the regional instability the Russian bombing caused in Syria; thankfully, most of the people in power survived and are unwilling to cause trouble.

For the time being, the long-term goal is to make sure middle eastern nations such as Israel and Syria can coexist peacefully. Not getting along by any means but staying within their own borders and making sure they're able to provide for their people. This wasn't able to be done in Israel with the former Prime Minister, so he was removed from power, but the initiative does feel that it is possible with the current leadership present in Syria. Rest assured however, should that leadership step out of line, then they will be dealt with swiftly and decisively.

Date: Sunday, December 6th, 2020

Time: 1102hrs EST

Location: Scranton, Pa

Temperature: 34 Degrees Fahrenheit

Neil and Clara are already downstairs cooking a small omelet breakfast as Samantha makes her way down from John's bedroom. All of them are still wearing their pajamas and woke up within the last fifteen minutes or so, with John still waking up. They have time to get ready however, with their lunch meeting with Sam's parents taking place in under two hours so none of them are in any rush, nor do they have to be.

"Sleep alright?" Clara asks softly as her boyfriend continues making omelets for everyone.

"I did. I'm guessing you guys did too." Sam replies, sitting at the kitchen island as Clara places a glass of orange juice down in front of her.

"Yeah, we did." Clara replies with a slight chuckle, knowing that Sam slept well for roughly the same reason she and her boyfriend did, "So what do you think of what we're trying to do here." Clara continues to keep the conversation going, while being genuinely curious about what Samantha thinks of the squadron and the initiative, they're a part of.

"I think you're doing a job that needs to be done and that I want to be a part of it despite the occupational hazards." Samantha replies confidently after taking a drink from the glass.

"That's strange." Clara says quietly to herself but loud enough for Samantha to hear.

"What do you mean?" She asks curiously.

"Nothing, it's just... that's what we all thought when we were told about the initiative and what we would be doing." She replies looking down at the countertop with a smile of disbelief of on her face, looking back up at Samantha after a couple of seconds.

"I see... Do you ever think that it's too much pressure?" Samantha asks curiously, recalling what she saw in John's personnel file.

"Sometimes yes, but it does have its perks and means we can have a direct impact on world events rather than simply standing by and watching them happen." Clara responds as Neil begins plating the four omelets and footsteps can be heard coming from the second floor.

Sam knows she experienced one of those "perks" yesterday when she shot and killed her ex. boyfriend for raping her; a license to kill anyone who has been deemed too much of a threat. The footsteps from the second floor grow slightly louder as they get closer and closer to the staircase, gaining Samantha and Clara's attention while Neil finishes plating the omelets. When he does finish the task, he allows himself to look towards the stairs just in time to see his commander walking slowly down them. Clearly still trying to wake up despite being awake enough to walk.

"Good morning commander. I hope you slept well." He says with a mocking accent and tone that nearly causes Samantha to spit out her drink and requires his girlfriend to support herself against the island as she laughs.

"You should know better than to patronize me Neil but thank you. I did in fact sleep well." John replies ignoring the laughter, placing a gentle hand on Sam's shoulder as she manages to finally swallow her drink.

"That's good to hear. You made it just in time for breakfast." Clara says also recovering from her fits of laughter and handing omelets to both Sam and John.

John then proceeds to sit down next to Samantha at the kitchen island as Neil finishes putting the pan he used in the sink and joins his girlfriend on the other side of the island. As the four enjoy their small yet tasty breakfast, John checks his phone and finds the report sent by Elizabeth, updating him on the Syrian situation. Also mentioned is the impending phone call with the Iranians and the impending meeting with the British Prime Minister. He then quickly runs through his news feed to see if the United States and Russians have managed to keep calm while he was asleep last night. He manages to find a Pentagon press release stating that an F-22 was lost during a training exercise, while the Russians blame the loss of their aircraft carrier on a spark igniting one of the jet fuel storage tanks. Thankfully, neither side is blaming the incidents on each other, if they even realize that the other was in the same area; however, John has an uneasy feeling about the whole situation.

He wasn't expecting either country to handle things this well and knows that something isn't right. Sure enough John's gut is telling the truth as he continues scrolling through the squadron's custom-made news feed and finds that the United States has moved two carrier battle groups, the Ford and the Truman battle groups, into the Sea of Japan. For the time being, they're staying in South Korean territorial waters, but the move could cause the North Koreans to cancel the upcoming nuclear summit between themselves, China, Russia, the United States, Japan and South Korea.

Upon discovering the news, John can't help but put his face in his palm and sigh; while he knows the United States is merely posturing, the North Koreans don't, and they've tested missiles with less provocation. Sam, Neil and Clara immediately notice the shift in John's mood as he pushes his plate away and begins texting commanders in the field to keep an eye on the developing situation.

"So much for being able to take a break." Clara says softly, recognizing what is happening immediately and causing Neil to pull out his phone so that he can get in touch with Rob and view the same articles that John found.

"Unfortunately, you're correct Clara." John say reluctantly as notification bells begin going off on all three of their phones while Samantha sits there having finished her breakfast, confused as to what is actually happening.

"What's going on?" She finally asks placing her hand gently on John's back in order to get his attention.

"North Korea might start world war three in response to the United States moving two carrier battle groups into the Sea of Japan. This is a response to the loss of their own fighter jet and the Russian's only aircraft carrier." John explains quickly, hoping that it will satisfy her curiosity until he is able to get more information.

"Oh, that doesn't sound good." Is the only thing that Samantha can think to say in response to what she's been told; she's still confused, but glad that she has a vague idea of what is going on.

"It does have the potential to be incredibly bad yes, though Russia and the United States don't want another war; at least not yet. Which is likely why they are covering up how the fighter jet went down and how the aircraft carrier sank." Clara replies trying to alleviate Samantha's concerns, though soon realizes that her statement had no effect.

“It still means that we’re probably going to have to head to South Korea at some point in order to intervene.” Neil says, interjecting before making his way towards the stairs.

“Exactly, I give it a week before we have to be there, possibly less.” John says making the quick calculation in his head, knowing that they can’t do anything until they leave later this evening and noticing that there is no press release for the loss of the Kazan.

This realization fills him with more dread than anything he’s read so far, as he knows that the Russians aren’t likely to hold back on a second incident that’s largely as bad as the first. He becomes upset with himself for not noticing the issue sooner and instantly begins formulating a plan as Neil makes his way upstairs to change and shower.

“Head on up and shower, Sam. I’ll get mine when you’re done.” John says suddenly and with a strange calmness, avoiding eye contact as a result of his realization.

“Okay. Is everything alright John?” She says quietly as she turns to him, getting him to glance up at her; Clara looks at both of them though they don’t notice her gaze.

“Yeah... Everything is going to be fine.” He lies, speaking softly hoping that Sam doesn’t notice his uncertainty.

“Okay.” Sam replies, seeing right through John’s lie and giving him a quick kiss on the lips before heading up stairs; Clara has to cover her mouth in order to keep herself from screaming with happiness upon seeing the romantic gesture.

“Not a word Clara, not a word.” John says sternly once Samantha is out of earshot.

"But... but John..." Clara stammers, knowing that John lied, and that Sam saw right through it, but only trying to get over the surprise caused by the short kiss.

"I know you're happy right now Clara, but I need you focused, and I don't need you telling anyone else." He continues, keeping the stern tone to ensure that Clara gets the message.

"Roger that commander." Clara eventually says reluctantly vowing to herself to tell Neil as soon as she gets the opportunity and to inform Elizabeth when they meet up with her tomorrow morning.

"I need you to get in touch with our Russian contacts. They haven't announced the sinking of the Kazan yet and that has me worried." John says moving the conversation along before Clara can get any more ideas in her sometimes easily distracted mind.

"Do you think they know and are holding back or that they haven't found out yet?" Clara asks trying to get a read on John's thought process and she begins messaging the Russian contacts that John was referring too.

"Right now I am doubting that it's the first one and hoping it's the second. Neither option is good though given they just lost their navy's flagship and they're likely going to try and refocus the public's backlash." He replies, finally putting his phone down and trying to wipe the sand out of his still slightly tired eyes.

"Makes you wonder if we should have even sunk the aircraft carrier rather than just intercepting their attacks." Clara says off hand, quickly wanting to take back her remark.

"That was an option, but we didn't have the time or manpower to pull it off. It was quicker and easier to sink the carrier and deal with the consequences. The wrench in the plan occurred when the Dallas was discovered and had to fire back." John replies with his characteristic calmness.

"I see, so it was both the best and worst plan available to us." She remarks in an understanding tone.

"Exactly, and we weren't entirely in control of what happened. That's the name of the game though, sometimes you have to be proactive and other times you have to be reactive. Unfortunately, sometimes you don't get to choose which." He says, rising from his seat to collect the remaining dirty, empty plates and place them in the sink; the sharp pain in his stomach returns as he reaches for each of the plates causing him to sigh.

"You okay?" Clara asks, immediately noticing John's discomfort and unable to keep her concern to herself.

"Yeah, I'll be fine." John states reluctantly, knowing that he's going to have to have another round of foul-tasting medicine before they meet Sam's parents for lunch.

Clara passes him the medicine bottle and quickly removes two pills and swallows them with a quick swig of water. It pains her to see her commander in such a painful condition, though she knows that there's nothing she can do about it. It's not the worst shape she's seen John in, that occurred after the training mission Sam managed to find in his personnel file. He was stuck in a hospital for a week and no one was allowed to stay with him at night, forcing him to suffer instead of sleeping while the rest of the squadron was kept away since they weren't family. This unfortunate policy was changed soon thereafter in order to prevent any other squadron members from having to go through what John did. Unfortunately, the emotional damage had already been done with the even scars on John's arms being the physical manifestation of his grief and loneliness.

"Have Elizabeth keep me posted throughout the day with how their meetings are going. I don't need the British deciding that Iran needs to be wiped off the planet, as much as it would probably save us the trouble of doing it." John says once he gets past the terrible taste of the medicine and taking another drink of water to prevent his mouth from drying out.

"You certainly have a strange sense of humor John, has anyone told you that before?" Clara says, making a mental note of what she needs to tell Elizabeth.

"People usually don't say it to my face." He replies, resisting the urge to smile as he hears the showers turn off upstairs.

"In fairness, you have the ability to kill them three times over before they even finish the statement." Clara responds as John begins heading for the staircase.

John only smiles as Clara also heads for the staircase; she is right though John can usually think of a better reason to kill someone than them saying he isn't funny. The two soldiers head upstairs to their respective bedrooms, with Clara entering as soon as she reaches the door, though John pauses. Realizing that he can't just barge into his own bedroom with Samantha still getting dressed. He chuckles at the thought; he and Samantha have slept in the same bed the last two nights and yet he is hesitant to open the door. Eventually, he gently knocks three times against the solid wood door, pausing slightly between each one.

"Come in." Samantha says, her voice mostly muffled by the door that John soon opens to find her putting on a pink tee shirt to go with her tan pants and the same brown boots she's had the entire time she's been at John's house; he only catches a glimpse of the beige bra as she was pulling the shirt down.

"I'm going to get a shower and then we'll head out and get lunch with your parents and then we'll go from there." He says softly, trying to ignore what he had just seen and move on with the plan of the day.

"Sounds like a plan." Sam replies with a smile and tilting her head slightly, managing to hide her nervousness at what lies ahead of her.

John returns the smile, he's nervous too though it's for drastically different reasons. He's still worried that Samantha isn't thinking things through like she should and that her judgement has been clouded by the events of the past few days; he knows his would be. He's also worried about how her parents are going to react to the news that their daughter wants to be with an orphan who happens to command enough firepower to destroy multiple capital cities at once. Samantha notices this slight hesitation on John's part and moves closer to him, hanging her arms around the back of his neck.

"Everything is going to be alright John. I want to be a part of the initiative and I want to be with you. Nothing is going to change my mind, nothing." She says as if she knows what John's thinking.

"I know, and I know that no matter what I try, I'm not going to be able to talk you out of it." He replies, finally accepting the fact that Samantha is certain in her convictions.

Sam chuckles at John's remark and continues smiling at him, seemingly forgetting that he still needs to shower and get his day started. John doesn't seem to mind for the moment, he's happy to be lost in Sam's eyes with his arms around her and hers around him.

"You need to shower, don't you?" Sam says finally remembering the plan for the day.

"Yeah I do." John says, still smiling though he doesn't want this moment to end.

"Go on, let's get today over with." Sam replies, acknowledging that today has the potential to be incredibly unpleasant.

John doesn't need to be reminded twice and heads into the bathroom to take his pajamas off and get a hot shower. The short exchange with Sam has put his mind mostly at ease though he can't avoid his concerns entirely. As the steam fills the bathroom, he can't help but feel relieved for the first time in a while, as if having Samantha's assurances has lifted a weight off of his shoulders. He's still not sure if having Samantha join the squadron is the correct move, with that becoming the focus of this worry, but Sam isn't giving him another option, so he doesn't have a choice. Another good choice that is and John isn't about to let the alternative even work its way into his mind.

Chapter Eight

Date: Sunday, December 6th, 2020

Time: 1332hrs EST

Location: Scranton University, Scranton, Pa

Temperature: 37 Degrees Fahrenheit

John, Sam, Neil and Clara are already seated inside the Mall at Steamtown's food court, waiting for Sam's parents to arrive. The cold, and the lack of rail excursions from the nearby national historic site have kept most people away from the mall. It's sad to say that the scene has become more common place over the last few years, owing to lower tourism and the decline in mall popularity as a whole. This place was picked so that Sam's parents didn't feel as though John, or his squad mates were being overbearing when the meeting occurs in just a few minutes.

John is wearing a grey zip up hoodie, green tee-shirt to go with his blue jeans and black sneakers. Clara is wearing dark green, khaki pants, blue sneakers and a purple sweater, with Neil wearing dark blue jeans, black sneakers and a grey long sleeve shirt. They're making sure to enjoy their time in civilian clothing given that they're likely going to wear nothing but flight suits for the next couple of days.

"Crap, how's Sam going to come with us? Our airbus is in the Falklands at the moment." Clara realizes as she puts the lemonade in her hand down on the table in front of her; her sudden words catching everyone off guard as they weren't expecting them.

"That's a good point and none of our fighters are two seaters." Neil adds in as John continues taking a long drink from his Coke Cola.

Samantha glances around, again confused at what Neil and Clara are saying or implying.

"You forget Neil; my Phantom has a back seat." John finally says as Neil and Clara fail to explain their thoughts to a confused Samantha.

"Oh yeah, it does. We'll just need to get her a flight suit, helmet and mask, and I'm sure we have some in storage." Clara says as it takes her boyfriend a little longer to process what John has said, though it's done nothing to clarify things for Samantha.

"Make the call." John says and Clara quickly pulls out her cell phone and walks a short distance away so that she can't be disturbed, her boyfriend finally realizing what John said.

"What's going on?" Sam finally asks softly, after being unable to form her question effectively.

"We're getting you flight gear for later today. Our usual private jet won't get here in time so you're going to have to fly as my back seater." John replies knowing that it's going to be an adjust me for Sam, given that she's never had to wear a flight suit or an oxygen mask before; just another first that has to take place for today to go smoothly.

"I'm guessing we won't be flying first class, then." She says with a small smirk on her face.

"No, unfortunately that's going to have to wait." John replying seeing Sam's parents in the distance, arriving right on time as expected and with both wearing business casual attire.

As he and Neil rise from the table, Sam jogs over to them and hugs them, fully aware that she probably isn't going to see them for a while. She then guides them over to the table where John and Neil are standing, Clara joins them seconds later after finishing her phone call to their staff at the Scranton International Airport.

"Glad to see you when you're actually awake." Josiah says softly as he shakes John's hand while his wife shakes Clara's; Sam is standing behind John, her hand gently placed on his back.

"Likewise Mr. Adams." John replies before shaking Abigail Adams and the six adults sitting down at the table; Sam is between Clara and John, while Neil is sitting next to her parents.

The tension manages to stay at a low level as more pleasantries are exchanged, though John moves the conversation along quickly knowing that he can't belabor telling Sam's parents about the initiative. He knows that they want to learn as much as possible about the initiative, but he also knows that he's going to need more than a couple of hours to do it. Sam can sense John's impatience, though she knows that it's about to be over matched by her parent's impatience.

"Right, I think we need to talk about what we actually came here to talk about." She says suddenly, catching her mother off guard with her frankness and directness.

"Yes, my apologies Mr. and Mrs. Adams, we shouldn't be dodging the subject." John says softly before anyone else can respond, Samantha grabbing his left hand gently under the table so no one else can see, or so she thinks.

"Well, your candor is certainly appreciated John." Josiah replies as his wife takes a couple of seconds to regroup.

"Then I'll get right to it. Neil, Clara and I are a part of the United Nations Initiative, the same goes for Vladimir, Elizabeth and Jeremy. This you knew from last night, but it's a lot more complicated than that. Back in January, the United Nation Security Council proposed the formation of a small fighting force in order to deal with international incidents when doing so would be too risky for any one nation. This force would receive resources from all members of the United Nations and would have the independence to do whatever their commander deemed necessary to ensure the stability of the world." John starts, stopping to take a drink to satiate his dry mouth; his words causing Sam to squeeze his hand a little tighter.

"So, if there was a terrorist attack in London, you would go after those responsible?" Abigail asks, though her husband already knows the answer.

"That is correct, though it's not all that we do. Do you remember when an Israeli air force base exploded, and their prime minister supposedly committed suicide?" Clara joins in as her commander is still taking a drink.

"Yeah, we remember." Josiah says softly recalling the wall-to-wall news coverage the event received for three days.

"That was an air strike conducted by Clara, Elizabeth, Neil and Jeremy and an assassination mission conducted by me and Vladimir. It was concluded that Israel was about to conduct an airstrike against the Iranian government and allowing them to do so was going to plunge the region into chaos with millions of civilians caught in the middle. This, of course, is all classified information, though I am guessing you already knew that." John says, putting down his drink as Josiah covers his mouth with his hand as his wife looks at him in shock; Sam is staring blankly into the distance, waiting for her parent's reaction.

"Yeah, I had a hunch." Josiah says softly still trying to process what John has just told him.

"You said it was a small force, but to pull that... mission... off you probably needed support personnel." Abigail says softly, taking the news a lot harder than her husband is.

"We have ten thousand combat personnel with a further forty thousand support personnel. On top of that, there are around eight thousand children under the age of eighteen that are affiliated with the initiative. This is done to maintain the secrecy of the initiative but also to keep families together. Meaning when we recruit someone for the initiative, we take in their family as well. The children are kept away from any form of combat until they are eighteen." Neil says after a quick glance at John to make sure he's allowed to answer, John only nods.

Josiah and Abigail don't immediately respond, the information hitting them like a ton of bricks along with the realization of what their daughter wants to be involved with. It verges on too much for them to handle, something that John knew could happen as he's seen other family's reactions when one of their family members was recruited by the initiative.

"Sam, you want to be a part of this?" Her mother asks, snapping her out of her daze; she had been hoping she wouldn't have to talk much and wanted this meeting to be over with as soon as possible.

"I do mom." She replies simply and shortly, not wanting to speak for any longer than she has to; her answer doesn't go over well.

"Are you aware of what that would mean for our family? The risk you are bestowing upon all of us?" Her mother replies almost snapping at her for the first time in years.

Josiah looks to John as he tries to keep his wife from yelling and attracting attention to the table, not that there's anyone around to hear them. John glances to Josiah, the look on his face letting Sam's father know that this decision is out of his hands and can only be made by Samantha.

"I know what it means mom, I've thought about this every waking moment since John told me about it." Sam responds still trying to avoid an argument as her emotions build and she squeezes John's hand even tighter.

John checks his watch, fourteen hundred hours, two hours until they need to leave for the Falkland's. He notices Josiah's gaze, knowing that he can tell that Samantha is clutching his hand due to her nervousness. Josiah can also tell that John already made sure that this is what Samantha wants, multiple times over.

"Tell me something John, who is the commander of this initiative?" Josiah asks, interrupting his wife and calming the situation down instantly.

Clara and Neil look to John, wondering if he is actually going to reveal himself as commander of the United Nations Force.

"I am Mr. Adams. Commander John Hilderbrand, callsign Wolf One." He says softly, with a hint of the commanding tone that Samantha heard when he first revealed the initiative to her.

"I could have guessed." Josiah says allowing himself to emit a satisfied grin as he leans back in his chair.

"What do you mean Jed?" His wife asks clearly confused, something that is shared by Samantha, Clara and Neil.

"Surely, no one else would have been allowed to share so much about this initiative except for the initiative's own commander." Josiah replies with a laugh as John smiles and Samantha relaxes her grip on his hand without letting go of it.

"That is certainly the intention Mr. Adams, good read." John says finally relaxing, the tension being released from his shoulders and neck.

"I've been around the block a time or two." He replies, a strong smile placing itself across his experienced face.

Everyone else is still slightly confused as to what is going on, though they can feel the tension drop away from the conversation. John notices but doesn't seem to care as he takes a sip of his Coke Cola and collects his thoughts.

"Mr. Adams, would you care to join us at the airport before we leave. Our Airbus will be here early tomorrow morning to fly you to our main base. I'm not going to tell you where it is, though it will be fairly obvious once you get there." John says placing his drink back on the table; his calm demeanor putting his squad mates and Mrs. Adams at ease, while Samantha is still slightly confused.

"It would be our pleasure Mr. Hilderbrand, lead the way." Mr. Adams replies, as everyone stands, and he shakes John's hand and motions towards the door everyone came in.

Sam continues holding John's hand as they head for the door, Neil and Clara following close behind them and her parents just a few feet behind them. John knows that Sam's gesture is going to gain him even more teasing and pestering from his friends, much like the kiss will, though it's the furthest thing from his mind. What is at the forefront of his thoughts, is how he going to handle Samantha's tidal wave of questions that she is likely to unleash upon him when they climb into his truck. Sure enough, John's hunch is spot on and as soon as the doors to his truck close, Sam begins to speak.

"What just happened and how?" She asks trying to get over her confusion.

"What happened? Your father took your side in this situation and that meant your mother was out voted. How? I appealed to your father's curiosity while your mother was still processing what was going on." John answers bluntly though with a welcoming tone, inviting Sam to ask as many questions as she needs to.

"But you never told me that whole families had to be a part of the squadron. Why leave that out?" Sam asks wondering, albeit only slightly, if John set her up.

"Because I wanted this to be your decision Sam. I knew once I told you about the initiative, I wouldn't be able to stop you from being a part of it. However, I also knew that I would need to convince your parents to support your decision, so I omitted some information to ensure that would happen." He replies, answering her questions with his characteristic reassuring and calm tone without breaking a sweat.

"You knew all of this would happen?" Sam asks, now wondering if John is some kind of prophet though the answer, she gets is much less religious.

"Mostly. What happened with Richard was a bit of a curveball, but I've known you and your parents since we were both kids. I've learned to read how the three of you respond to certain situations, cues I can pick up on and use to guide a situation." John says, guiding the Gladiator out on to the main street in the direction of the airport, his squad mates and Sam's parents following close behind.

"I see." Sam says softly, her questions answered so quickly that she wasn't expecting to move on to another subject.

“Don’t worry Sam, this is going to work out. From here on in though, I need you to read everything you see. In fighter pilot speak, I need you to keep your eyes outside the cockpit.” John says taking her hand gently and further softening his tone.

“Keep my eyes outside the cockpit.” Sam whispers to herself, doing what she can to understand those six words.

It doesn’t take long for the three-car convoy to reach the airport, though John doesn’t lead it to the normal arrivals and departures area. Instead, he guides them down a back road towards the east side of the airport, on the other side of runway 4/22 where an unmarked hanger is located. It wasn’t there six months ago; however it was built in a matter of weeks under the guise of the navy needing a maintenance hangar. Surprisingly, and with the United States Navy’s cooperation, the ruse worked, and no one has questioned it since, giving the squadron a small base near their homes. The drive does little to calm Sam’s mother down, though she has at least been able to breathe since leaving the mall despite not saying a word to her husband.

Josiah parks his car beside Clara’s, which is in turn parked alongside John’s along the southern side of the hangar. A nineteen-year-old mechanics apprentice runs over to greet them as they exit their vehicles, stopping and saluting in front of John.

“What’s the word specialist?” John asks returning the salute and shaking the young man’s hand.

“Birds are fueled up and ready to go on your order, sir.” The specialist replies: despite being only two years younger than John, the difference in their tones is stark.

“Excellent, thank you specialist. I want to introduce you to Samantha Adams; you’ll be seeing her a little more from here on in.”

John says turning to “present” Samantha to the young mechanic as she shakes his hand.

“Good afternoon Ma’am. We have your flight gear ready if you wish to try it on before your flight.” The specialist replies bowing his head slightly before releasing Sam’s hand; his words sending a slight shiver down her spine.

“I think that’s a good idea specialist, please show Sam to the locker room. Clara, if you could give her a hand as well?” John says turning to Clara and soon the specialist is leading her and a still stunned Samantha to the locker room at the back of the hanger.

“Don’t worry, it took me a while to get used to it too.” Clara whispers in Sam’s ear, recalling the first time she was ma’amed.

“I see what you mean.” She replies doing her best to keep the specialist from hearing as a regional jet lands on the runway behind them.

As Samantha and Clara disappear behind the outer door of the locker room. John and Neil begin heading towards another exterior door that leads into the main hangar. Josiah and Abigail follow swiftly behind wanting to get out of the cold, though Mrs. Adams is still unsure about the whole endeavor. Another mechanic’s apprentice opens the door, saluting as John, Neil and their guests walk past with John and Neil salute in return as they cross through the threshold and into the vast hangar. Their black fighter jets are lined up neatly in a single row, wing tip to wing tip, facing the door of the hangar. Josiah and Abigail are in awe as they stand beside John and Neil, gazing over equipment they’ve only seen in pictures and museums.

The jets are fully loaded with three external fuel tanks each, in addition to a full complement of four heat seeking, four radar guided missiles and cannon ammunition.

"Welcome back commander." A dark-skinned mechanic says shaking John's hand, sweat dripping from his forehead down onto his green jumpsuit.

"Chief Logan, I hope you were able to spend sometimes with your wife and daughter over the last couple of days." He replies softly.

"Only a few hours sir, though it was greatly appreciated by the misses." Chief Logan replies handing John the clipboard that was in his hand that holds the maintenance log for all of the jets in the squadron.

"Well, be sure to send her my best." John says quickly looking the log over and signing off on the work that has been done, "Remind me, how old is your daughter now?"

"Nine months sir and she keeps getting bigger anytime I see her." Chief Logan replies, pulling out a picture of his daughter as John hands the clipboard back to him.

"She's certainly got your hair Chief." John says looking at the picture as Neil begins looking over his plane and Josiah and Abigail begin walking around the hangar.

"Yes she does sir. If you don't mind me asking, sir, who are they?" Chief Logan asks gently not wanting to barge in where he isn't welcome.

"They're our newest members parents' chief, she's getting changed at the moment to make sure her new gear fits correctly." John answers, not minding Chief Logan's question.

“I see, sir. I hope she finds it comfortable.” Chief replies placing the picture of his daughter in his back pocket and positioning the clipboard under his arm to make it easier to carry; he then heads back to the maintenance area so John can conduct his preflight checks.

“So this is your plane?” Abigail asks, momentarily distracting John from the task at hand, though it only takes him a second to refocus.

“Yeah, this is my plane.” he replies, climbing up the staircase platform next to his plane and crouching down to look into the cockpit and make sure the back seat is ready for Samantha.

“Where’d you find her?” Josiah asks giving John the impression that another wave of questions is incoming.

“A boneyard in Arizona. She had been there for twenty-six years before which she was used as a drone and flew in Vietnam.” John replies after adjusting the rear seats harness.

“So she has some history under her wings.” Abigail remarks, closely examining the underside of the Phantom’s left wing.

“That she does, Mrs. Adams, that she does.” John says quieter as he climbs out of the rear seat and into the front seat to look things over.

“My bird is good to go commander.” Neil calls out gaining, Mr. and Mrs. Adams attention though John barely bats an eyelid.

“Roger that Neil, everything checks out with mine as well. Go ahead and get changed. We’ll take off around fifteen hundred hours.” John replies, his voice easily carrying through the hangar as Neil climbs down his cockpit ladder to the concrete floor.

“Roger that commander.” Neil says before heading off to the internal door of the locker room, passing Clara and Samantha as they make their way out of the locker room and into the hangar.

Clara silently tells Sam that she's going to look her plane over, and that Sam should head over to John. Sam nods, though she is clearly not used to wearing a full flight suit with her hair back in a ponytail as she turns and walks towards her parents, holding her plain white flight helmet and oxygen mask in her right hand. John clambers down the flight steps upon seeing her. Her parents are surprised at how well the flight suit fits their daughter, as if it was tailor made for her.

"I guess we now know how you would have looked if you went into the air force." Her mother says, giving her a gentle hug.

"Yeah we do, though I didn't think it would be this uncomfortable." Sam replies quietly, as she releases the hug from her mother.

"I have to admit, that flight suit looks good on you, Sam." John says, his voice causing Sam and her parents to turn to him. "It will soften up after you wear and wash it a few times."

"That's good to hear at least." Sam replies walking towards John and looking up at the massive fighter to her right, it's sheer presence finally having an impact. "The last time I saw one of these was when we went to the Air and Space museum in D.C."

"Now you're actually going to be able to fly in one." John says turning to look back at his plane and placing his right arm around Sam's shoulders.

"My plane is ready to fly commander." Clara says, walking over from her fighter jet, reading more into John's gesture than Sam's parents are.

"Roger that Clara. Show Sam's parents to the briefing room, while I go over bail out procedures with her."

As Sam makes her way up the flight staircase, John notices the look of concern forming on Sam's mothers face.

"Don't worry, we're not going to leave without you knowing. We'll be joining you for the full mission brief in a few minutes."

John's words manage to provide a fleeting level of comfort to Mrs. Adams as Clara leads her and her husband to the small briefing room, located next to the squadron's locker room. Sam's father keeps his emotions largely hidden; he's certainly nervous, but he's grown to trust John over the last few years and seemingly knows that he won't let anything happen to his daughter.

"I'm going to have to say goodbye, soon aren't I?" Sam asks once her parents are out of earshot as she examines the seat where she will be sitting for almost thirteen hours.

"Not goodbye Sam. We'll be flying them to our pacific base and we'll likely be there in a week or so." John replies climbing up the staircase behind her as a muffled roar from a landing jet makes its way through the hangar door and echoing in the hangar itself.

"That's a relief." She says with a deep breath while John gently places his hand on her shoulder and crouches down next to her.

"I'm sure it is Sam. Here, hand me your helmet and have a seat." He says knowing that he has to move the safety briefing along.

Sam does as she's told, passing John her flight helmet and oxygen mask and carefully guiding herself onto the Phantom's rear seat and making sure not to impale herself on the control stick as it comes up between her legs. She places her arms through the seats harness though doesn't fasten and proceeds to make herself as comfortable as she can.

"Now, we will be putting you through a more intense flight

training program when we arrive in the Falklands, so I will only be going over what you need for this flight ok?" John begins, making sure Sam is paying attention and ready for the safety briefing.

Sam nods.

"Alright. I'm not going to sugar coat this, but if you have to use any of what I am telling you during this flight, it means something has gone extremely wrong and we need to get out of the aircraft as soon as possible. If that is the case, I will call out the phrase, *bail out bail out bail out.* On the third bail out, I need you to grab the black and yellow handle between your legs and pull them as hard as you can while keeping your head back against the headrest. What happens next will be incredibly jarring and violent, but it beats the alternative. The canopy will blow off and you'll feel an incredibly strong gust of wind before being launched out of the aircraft. A few seconds later, the parachute attached to your seat will deploy and everything will calm down again." John says, guiding Samantha through the procedure as he speaks.

"Just you describing it is making me nauseous." Sam says with a giggle as she walks through the procedure in her head and John leans against the side of the cockpit.

"Well you won't be able to puke until you reach the ground or the ocean; the sudden rush of adrenaline will guarantee that. Speaking of, when you reach either the ground or ocean, though especially with the ocean scenario, be sure to cut away your parachute as quickly as possible. Surviving the ejection but drowning afterwards, defeats the main purpose of ejecting to begin with." He says, doing his best to not scare Samantha, yet telling her the truth at the same time.

“That’s comforting.” She replies, snapping at John with the sarcasm and surprise in her voice making her feelings known loud and clear.

“I know, I know, but you need to know in case this does happen, though thankfully that’s the only scary part to this endeavor.” John says, bowing his head slightly in shame.

“I’m sorry, I didn’t mean to snap at you. Please continue John.” Sam says after a few moments of rather uncomfortable silence, lifting John’s head up with her left hand to look into his eyes.

“It’s alright, this is an emotional day for you so it’s natural that you would be reactive to certain things. The last thing you need to be aware of for the flight is to not touch the throttle lever on your left or the control stick between your legs. I need to have complete control of the plane at all times.” John continues, forgiving Sam for the attitude she gave him, but still clearly rattled as he points out the controls to her; taking his eyes off of her though she doesn’t take her eyes off of him.

It annoys him slightly that Sam’s attitude shift is getting to him so much. It usually wouldn’t, but for a reason beyond his vast comprehension, it is.

“I understand John, I understand.” Sam says wrapping her arm around the back of John’s neck and using the leverage to hug him; he slowly wraps his right arm around her after setting her helmet on the platform.

“I do too Sam.” He says, embracing the calm feeling that the hug is providing, snapping him out of his dazed state and once again allowing him to completely focus on the task at hand.

Sam feels herself being compelled to say a certain phrase as she doesn't want to let go of John, though she is still hesitating to speak. Not knowing how John would react to her saying the phrase in question is scaring her slightly and she decides to keep the phrase to herself for the time being.

"Come on, let's head to the briefing room." John says softly, helping Samantha out of the cockpit of his Phantom.

"Okay." Sam replies softly once she's standing on the platform with John, kissing him on the cheek before walking down the stairs to the hangar floor.

John smiles, sliding down the stairs using his forearms to glide along the railings with practiced ease. Neil appears from the locker room just as Sam and John begin walking towards the briefing room door, John motions towards the door letting Neil know where he needs to go. Neil only nods in response, opening the door and holding it for John who pauses after Samantha walks through and hugs her parents.

"Are you sure about this commander?" Neil asks gently, keeping the conversation between him and John.

"Honestly... I'm not... but I know that she is." John says, motioning to Sam as he struggles to get the words to come out of his mouth.

"Well that's a slight comfort at least. Everything is set and ready to go commander and Elizabeth messaged me to remind you that the British Ambassador is arriving in an hour." Neil says moving on to the business that is going to take place while they're in the air.

"Roger that Neil. Let's not delay this any longer." John replies patting Neil on the shoulder and finally entering the briefing room with Neil closing the door behind him.

The room instantly falls silent once everyone sees John standing at the front of the room, Neil and Clara have a seat in one of the ten desks located in the middle of the room.

"Right, I know this is happening quickly, but we really don't have the time. Earlier this week, Sam's ex. boyfriend was killed to prevent further harm to Samantha and, by association, the squadron. This comes in the wake of the sinking of Russia's only aircraft carrier and the downing of a US Airforce stealth fighter to prevent further harm to the Syrian people. This is in addition to the self-defense sinking of a Russian submarine by the UNS Dallas, which will be regrouping with the majority of our fleet at the end of next week. On top of that, the British and Iranians are acting up yet again, and the cleanup in Syria is going to take away about half of our special force's squadrons. I'm going to be frank; we're spread pretty thin here." John begins, the commanding tone returning to his voice as he leans against the wall behind him and crosses his arms.

Sam's parents are only slightly shocked to hear what John has to say, given Sam had told them most of it earlier in the morning. However, it's still startling, and they are visibly shaken as John finishes speaking. Neil and Clara show no emotion as John continues the briefing after taking a moment to catch his breath and survey the room.

"Yesterday, Wolf Two, Three, and Six headed to the Falkland Islands to coordinate the regrouping effort with Rob and to deal with the British and the Iranians. Today, Wolf One, Four, Five and Samantha will be joining them, while Samantha's parents are picked up early tomorrow morning and taken to our main base. Wolf One through Six and Samantha will join them a week from now. Are there any questions?" John finishes, still speaking in the third person as this briefing is for himself as well, despite the fact that he also has to deliver the briefing to begin with.

No one says anything after John asks his question, they're either used to this or to consumed by the events of the day to even ask.

"Alright, seeing no questions, I'm going to change and then we'll get our flight underway. Hooyah, Wolf Squadron." John calls out, his voice swelling as he finishes his sentence.

"Hooyah!" Neil and Clara respond with Sam saying it quietly and her parents not saying a word as John heads for the door.

He stops to let everyone out of the briefing room and then quickly turns towards the locker room before anyone can say anything to him. He's not trying to be rude, though it's certainly coming across that way. He just knows that Sam needs to have a heart to heart with her parents about what is going to be happening and, more importantly, to say goodbye to them until a week from now when the squadron regroups at their primary base. It's an unpleasant feeling that he's grown used to over the relatively few months he's been commander, though he will never truly get used to it.

He closes the door to the locker room behind him and easily finds his flight locker in the far-left corner. Taking off his warmer street clothes, he soon has his flight suit over his legs and resting around his waist and is grabbing a long sleeve green tee shirt out of the locker. He hears the door to the locker room open and close just as he is pulling it over his chest and grabbing the single dog tag off of his lockers shelf.

"I guess this is it, isn't it?" Josiah asks as John places his dog tag loosely around his neck and tucks it underneath his shirt.

“It is Mr. Adams.” John replies, pulling the rest of the flight suit up over his arms and shoulders and then zipping it up.

“Please John, how many times am I going to have to ask you to call me Jed. I’ve known you since you were in first grade.” Josiah says, not annoyed just joking.

“That’s exactly why, Mr. Adams.” He says frankly pulling his flight harness out the locker and adjusting it over his back and chest.

“I should have guessed as much. Anyway, I wanted to thank you for all you’ve done for Sam, especially over the last couple of days. I know it wasn’t easy for you, seeing her with that... well with that asshole... If it’s any consolation, Abigail and I hated him too, though we respected our daughter’s decision.” Josiah continues causing John to wonder where he is going with all of this as he puts on his thigh holster and places his 1911 in it.

“No need to thank me, Mr. Adams, just doing my job, both as a member of this squadron and as a friend.” John replies, frankly, giving his gear a once over to make sure everything is comfortable and secured to his body.

“I think it’s safe to say my daughter and you are more than just friends. Right John?” Josiah says in a slightly sarcastic tone, though his message makes it clear to John that he saw Sam holding his hand earlier.

“You’d have to ask her that Mr. Adams, though I want you to know I will do everything in my power to take care of her and keep her safe.” John replies after a brief pause so he could grab his black, with red and blue stripes flight helmet and oxygen mask before turning to face Josiah.

"Good answer John. Have a safe flight and try to make sure Sam doesn't lose her lunch." Josiah responds shaking John's hand firmly and grabbing his bicep.

"Roger that Mr. Adams." John says smiling and the pair walk out of the locker room together to find the hangar door is open and Sam is standing by John's plane next to her mother.

Neil and Clara are doing one final walk around of their aircraft, double checking the checks they performed before the briefing began. Josiah walks over to his wife, who shares a more detailed "be careful" list with John, especially when compared with the relatively short list her husband gave him mere moments ago. The moment gets Sam to chuckle, unconsciously wrapping her arms around John's left arm. It only takes him a moment to realize what is happening, though he doesn't pull away as there is no point in trying to hide the relationship anymore.

"You two be careful alright?" Samantha's mother finally finishes after what feels like forever, with her getting every concern off of her chest.

"Don't worry Mrs. Adams, she's in safe hands." Clara calls out from her cockpit before she puts her helmet and oxygen mask on.

John chuckles trying to avoid blushing at Clara's remark, though he's only mildly successful.

"We'll be alright mom and we'll see you soon okay?" Sam replies, noticing John isn't able to talk.

"See you soon Sam. Remember, we love you." Her father says shaking her hand before shaking John's hand one last time as Samantha hugs her mother and then heads up the flight steps to the rear seat of John's Phantom.

John shake's Abigail's hand before they step back as Neil and Clara's planes are towed out of the hanger. John quickly climbs the flight steps and helps Sam strap into the ejection seat as well as gently helping her put her helmet on and making sure the oxygen mask is placed where it should be. Once everything is sorted, he gives her a thumbs up which she returns in kind, indicating that she is comfortable and ready to go. A second later, John jumps into the front seat of the old war bird and straps himself in, getting his own helmet and face mask on as the steps are pulled away and a tow tractor hooks up to the plane's undercarriage.

"Wolf one, comm check. Wolf one, comm check." John says over the radio as the canopy closes and the cockpit fills with daylight.

"Wolf four reading you loud and clear wolf one." Clara responds almost immediately as the dull roar of six jet engines fills the afternoon sky.

"Wolf five also reading you loud and clear wolf one." Neil says checking in as the three tow tractors disconnect from the fighters.

"I hear you." Sam says softly, finally remembering where the radio switch is in the back seat.

"Roger that, wolf one to wolf flight. Comm check complete, proceed to runway four once clearance is received from the tower." John replies to everyone as his plane shutters while is its engines spool up, forcing Sam to gasp and take a deep breath.

"I'm okay." She says softly doing her best to calm down, knowing she doesn't need to be nervous; they're not even in the air yet after all.

"It's okay to be nervous Sam, you're not used to this." John states in a calming tone, flicking the radio channel to the control tower, "Tower, this is Wolf flight requesting taxi clearance to runway four for IFR flight to PSY."

"Wolf flight, this is the tower, taxi clearance granted to runway four for IFR flight to PSY. You may taxi when ready. Stop and hold short for in bound American Airlines flight." The air traffic controller responds, she's an initiative member stationed at Scranton International Airport.

"Roger that tower, wolf flight proceeding to taxi to runway four. Will stop and hold short for American Airlines flight." John responds and the mighty phantom lurches forwards as he leads towards the runway threshold.

"Seems like it's a good day to go flying." Sam's says, breaking the brief moment of silence, though the jet engines are stretching the definition of the word silence.

"It should be with clear skies and minimal turbulence." John replies as he performs his takeoff checks.

The three-plane formation stops just short of the runway as an American Airlines MD80 finally comes into view on final approach to the airport.

"Wolf flight to tower, we're stopped and holding short of runway four. Have visual of American Airlines traffic. Traffic is on final approach, about three miles out." John says relaxing with nothing to do until the MD80 clears the pattern.

"Tower to Wolf flight, copy. You are stopped and holding short of runway four and have visual on American Airlines traffic." The controller responds efficiently and precisely.

"Sam?" John says gently, leaning back in his ejection seat and closing his eyes as he takes a few gentle breaths.

"Yeah John?" Sam replies, her gaze firmly fixed on the MD80 coming in for a landing, now two miles out.

"Were you going to say something earlier? After the safety briefing?" John asks, double checking that he isn't broadcasting their conversation to the tower or the rest of the squadron.

"I was but it didn't feel like the right time." Sam says is a surprisingly unflinching tone, doing her best to remain calm.

"I understand." He replies, still curious to what she was going to say but accepting her answer for the time being.

The American Airlines flight glides overhead and to a perfect landing on runway four, the engines roaring in as the pilot reverses the thrust and slams on the brakes to slow the jetliner before turning on to the main taxiway.

"Tower to Wolf flight, proceed to runway four. You are cleared for takeoff. Turn to heading one four five after reaching three thousand feet. Safe flight and good hunting." The controller radios and the butterflies begin fluttering in Sam's stomach.

"Solid copy tower. Wolf flight proceeding to runway four with takeoff clearance. Will turn to one four five at three thousand feet. Enjoy your vacation." John replies and the phantom once again shutters as he increases thrust to taxi speed with Clara and Neil following close behind.

Stopping at the end of the runway, John makes one final check of his control surfaces before the flight officially begins and sets the brakes while he waits for Clara and Neil to do the same.

"We'll be pulling some G's on takeoff Sam, so just lean back and try to enjoy the ride okay?" John says looking over his shoulder to check on his wingmen, getting a thumbs up from both of them.

"Roger." Sam says taking a nervous gulp as she takes one last look at the hangar, unable to see her parents.

"Alright, wolf four, wolf five, we're set to go." John calls out over the radio as Sam's nervousness continues to rise.

"Roger wolf one, we got your six." Neil replies and everything briefly falls silent as Sam takes one final, calm breath.

John firewalls the throttle, sending the two modified J79 engines into full afterburner and causing the F-4E to shutter under the force of seventy thousand pounds of thrust. It shakes and rattles violently as it strains against the brakes holding it back. After a second or two passes, John releases those brakes and the fighter lurches forward, rapidly accelerating down the runway, fifty knots, one hundred knots, one hundred and fifty knots and so on. John pulls back on the stick as the jet engines continue to scream, causing the nose wheel to lift into the air. Sam fights to move her body even slightly, but it's no use, she's pinned to her seat and is merely along for the ride. At two hundred knots, the mighty phantom lifts into the sky as if gravity itself has insulted it and begins climbing at two thousand feet per minute.

Clara and Neil have managed to follow the same takeoff pattern, forming up on John's left and right wings respectively as three fighters climb to the turning point at three thousand feet. They throttle back to half throttle just before executing the turn and Sam is finally able to breathe normally again, taking a couple of deep breaths as she glances down at the ground below them. John makes sure to take the turn to heading one four five, a little gentler than he would normally; not wanting to force Sam to pull more G's than she can handle at the moment. Once on heading, he relaxes and sets the autopilot to maintain a gentle climb to their cruising altitude of the forty thousand feet.

"Well you didn't barf, so I call that a successful take off." He says jokingly as Sam continues to catch her breath.

She only chuckles in reply.

Chapter Nine

Date: Sunday, December 6th, 2020

Time: 1700hrs FKST

Location: Stanley, Falkland Islands

Temperature: 57 Degrees Fahrenheit

"The British Prime Minister has arrived, and John, Clara and Neil are in the air. Our Airbus has also left for Scranton to pick up Sam's parents." Jeremy says to Elizabeth after placing his cell phone in his pocket as they wait patiently in their hotel room.

"Okay. Vladimir is still on the phone with the Iranians. Rob checked in with him about an hour ago and apparently things were getting contentious." Elizabeth replies. resting her hands on her stomach as she lies on the bed and looks out the window at the bay.

"I would have suspected. Do you want to stay here, or would you like to join me for the meeting?" Jeremy asks, sitting down next to his girlfriend and cradling her in his arms.

"I'll join you; the pregnancy hasn't made me that tired yet." Elizabeth answers with a smile before kissing Jeremy on the lips and getting off of the bed.

Jeremy only smiles as the two exit the room, instantly hearing the Iranian President yelling at Vladimir as they enter the hallway. They only pause for a moment before quickly walking away as they don't want to get dragged into a verbal war with the Iranian President and knowing that Vladimir has it handled. Walking out of the hotel, they meet up with Rob, who has just returned from seeing off the squadrons private jet.

"You don't want to go in there." Jeremy says jokingly, looking into the distance trying to see the British Prime Minister's convoy.

"That bad huh." Rob says seemingly done with the events of the day; though with world leaders acting like children, it's not that surprising.

"Yeah, though it buys us some time with the British Prime Minister. If he's willing to give it to us." Elizabeth replies finally spotting the convoy and pointing it out to her boyfriend.

"Well he hasn't had anything to drink yet and he's wearing a suit so that's a start." Rob replies as the convoy of black Land Rover's draws closer.

"Yeah it certainly is." Jeremy says with a sigh as he thinks back to the last time he had to meet with Boris Johnson about the effects Britain leaving the EU had on the world's economy; the night ended with both of them drunk and singing drinking songs; it wasn't his finest moment.

"Wonder how Sam is holding up? It's her first time flying in a fighter jet." Elizabeth says shifting the conversation in order to ease the mood.

"I'm not sure honestly, John said she wasn't talking much after takeoff." Rob says softly with a slight smile, knowing what Jeremy or Elizabeth is likely to say.

"Well with John flying I'm not surprised, that Phantom can be a beast even in level flight." Jeremy says with a laugh, which Rob and Elizabeth return in kind.

"She does have a few hours to get used to it though, so hopefully she'll perk up by the time they arrive." Elizabeth finishes just in time for the British convoy to roll up in front of them at the hotel and the Prime Ministers guards quickly exit the SUVs before they even come to a complete stop.

The move would intimidate lesser human beings but no such luck when it comes to the squadron, they've seen it all before during the initial round of meetings when the force was first formed. After the small force of guards stand to their posts, Boris Johnson exits the middle Range Rover, adjusting his suit but doing nothing to straighten his messy blonde hair as he and two of his guard's approach Jeremy, Elizabeth and Rob.

"Thank you for making the time Prime Minister." Elizabeth says politely shaking the eccentric Prime Ministers hand as his guards place their hands on their Glock handguns, barely hidden under their suit jackets.

"I wasn't given much choice, but you are quite welcome madam." Boris replies with his characteristic charming tone as he shakes Rob and Jeremy's hand; clearly not recognizing the young man who met with him mere months ago.

"This way Mr. Prime Minister." Jeremy says, taking control of the meeting and motioning back towards the hotel, keeping a slight eye on the Prime Ministers guards, who still have their hands on their weapons.

"Yes, quite right. Say you wouldn't happen to have any martini's? You see, they wouldn't let me have a drink on the flight down here and I am quite parched." Boris continues, walking with Jeremy as Rob and Elizabeth follow a short distance behind them, with the guards a little further back.

"That can certainly be arranged Mr. Prime Minister. Would your guards care to partake in the consumption of a beverage or two?" Jeremy asks, slightly imitating a posher version of his own accent, though it's subtle enough that only Elizabeth notices and has to resist the urge to chuckle.

"Wonderful and I'm sure they would greatly appreciate it. Right gentlemen?" Boris continues briefly face the two guards at the back of the line and receiving a smiling nod from both.

"Excellent, right this way." Jeremy says, continuing with the slightly mocking accent and motioning to the porch as waiter arrives to take everyone's drink order.

The friendly beginning to the meeting is a common tactic the squadron tries to use whenever possible as it disarms any hostility and allows the meeting to go quicker. It also endears the squadron to world leaders, which can help when the squadron needs the leader to do something that they otherwise wouldn't do. It doesn't always work however, and that's ultimately why the Israeli Prime Minister had to be killed after a continual refusal to back down. Luckily for the British Prime Minister, he can be persuaded with less forceful tactics such as a good drink.

Date: Sunday, December 6th, 2020

Time: 1510hrs EST

Location: 40,000FT above Washington D.C.

Temperature: 34 Degrees Fahrenheit

"How are you holding up Sam?" Clara asks over the radio just as the squadron begins to pass to the east of Washington D.C.

“I’m doing okay, I think. Haven’t thrown up yet, so that’s good at least.” She replies softly after taking a moment to find the radio talk button.

“Well that’s better than I did when I first got into a cockpit. Lost my entire lunch when I landed.” Neil chimes in, doing his best to keep the conversation light.

“You weren’t only one Neil most of us lost our lunch that day.” His girlfriend replies after taking a moment to laugh.

“Did you throw up when you first went flying John?” Sam asks noticing that he hadn’t joined the conversation yet.

“No, I didn’t. I was smart enough to skip breakfast that day.” John replies simply, clearly preoccupied with something else as he speaks.

Neil and Clara instantly chuckle while Sam picks up on the distracted tone in John’s voice.

“What’s on your mind?” Sam asks making sure she doesn’t broadcast to the whole flight, that way John is thc only one who hears her.

“It’s nothing.” John replies simply, though his dismissiveness only makes Sam even more curious.

“You know I can tell when you’re lying, even without seeing your face.” Sam replies with a slight chuckle.

“Am I really that easy to read?” John asks also chuckling, though he already knows exactly what Sam is going to say.

"Only to me John, only to me. Now are you going to tell me what's on your mind or am I going to have to annoy it out of you?" She responds, her joking tone decreasing the harshness of her words.

John shakes his head slightly; his prediction was spot on.

"It's just... I feel bad for turning your life upside down over the course of the last two days. I know you said you wanted this but it's not stopping this sickening feeling I have in the pit of my stomach." John says eventually as a small break in the clouds reveals the Washington Monument.

"Are you sure it's not the ulcer is acting up?" Sam asks, half-jokingly while she tries to formulate an actual response to John's concerns.

"Yeah I'm sure." John replies, quickly checking his gauges before taking a glance down at the ground.

"Well I'm not going to lie John; it was certainly a shock when you showed me what you do for a living and then allowed me to murder my ex. because he raped me. As shaken and surprised as I am, however, all of this feels strangely right, especially because I'm with you. Besides, if I didn't want to come with you, I wouldn't be in this seat right now." She finally says, giving John the full answer he was originally expecting when she mentioned the ulcer in his stomach.

"I appreciate your honesty." John says smiling underneath his oxygen mask and letting out a slight sigh of relief.

"Certainly is a pretty view down there." Clara pipes up after bringing her earlier laughter under control.

"Yeah it is." John replies as a thought crosses his mind "Want a better look Sam?" He eventually asks.

"Sure." She replies simply and before she even knows how to react, John gets the Phantom to gently perform a half barrel roll; replacing the sky with the ground as Sam feels herself pushed into the straps of her seats harness.

"How's that?" John asks, though he's not expecting a response, Sam still has a lot to learn and even simply maneuver like this can prevent a normal person from speaking.

"It'...lik...aaa.... roll..." Sam manages to get out before laughing herself into a coughing fit and John completes the maneuver, returning the old fighter to straight and level flight.

Sam instantly feels lightheaded and queasy when John finishes the roll, with the blood flow in her body rushing down from her head and slowly returning to normal. She closes her eyes and leans back in the seat, taking deep slow breaths as she does her best to keep her lunch from making an unwelcome appearance.

"Careful John, I don't think you want her lunch on the back of your head for the next twelve hours." Neil says, though his words are barely audible to John's air sick passenger.

"You okay back there?" John asks gently as Sam finally brings her breathing under control though she still feels nauseous.

"Yeah, I should be fine." She eventually says, gasping slightly for breath from her oxygen mask.

"John will teach you how to fight that feeling. It's normal to feel sick your first couple of times flying upside down." Clara says seemingly sensing how Sam is feeling.

"That's good to hear because I don't know if I can handle much more of that." Sam says, exacerbated at this point and wanting to fall asleep despite the ejection seat not making the most comfortable bed.

"Get some rest, no need to worry about it right now." John says, shutting down the training conversation as if he's not looking forward to it, though that's only partially true.

"Roger that." Sam says, keeping her eyes closed and doing her best to make herself comfortable.

The flight soon turns south by south east, on a direct heading towards the Falkland Islands. Neil checks in, letting John know that the private plane has taken off and is heading north and that the meeting with the British Prime Minister has just started its second drink. He chuckles upon hearing the news; he figured drinks would be involved and wholeheartedly expects that it will take more than two to convince him to cooperate with the squadron. However, it is worth noting that the British Prime Minister has been one of the more cooperative world leaders when compared to his compatriots from other nations. The least cooperative being the Russian president, the former Israeli Prime Minister, and the Iranian Supreme Leader and President, with the South Korean President and Chinese President pulling up a close second. Despite the media attention, the United States President has been largely cooperative with the initiative, as has the North Korean Supreme leader, though that could change at any given moment for any of them. Lastly, most of the EU is largely indifferent towards the initiative as while they don't openly oppose it, they also don't openly support it either.

Date: Sunday, December 6th, 2020

Time: 1730hrs FKST

Location: Stanley, Falkland Islands

Temperature: 52 Degrees Fahrenheit

"Mr. President, Mr. Supreme leader, if you would just let me speak for a moment." Vladimir struggles to say after not being able to say a word for the last half hour; the Iranian President and Supreme Leader don't hear him.

Elizabeth walks in as quietly as possible so the Iranian leaders don't know that she's in the room.

"That bad huh?" She says quietly as the yelling from the leaders continues unabated.

"You don't know the half of it. I'm five minutes away from suggesting that we allow the British to wipe them off the face of the earth." Vladimir replies, being careful the cover the microphone of his cellphone to prevent the two leaders from hearing him.

"Well the fact that you're even willing to suggest it is scaring me, although doesn't come as a surprise. These two have always been hot heads, even before we came along." Elizabeth says, slightly disappointed that the situation has come to this in less than an hour.

"I can't help but wonder if John would handle this better, but part of me also thinks they would have been dead by now." Vladimir continues, chuckling slightly to keep his own spirits up.

"Possibly. To that end, if they haven't calmed down in ten minutes politely inform them that the British have been given authorization to use whatever force they deem necessary to protect their interests." Elizabeth states, sighing before she speaks as she knows the far-reaching consequences of allowing the British to bomb Iran, especially with the instability still present in Israel.

"Roger that. Let your boyfriend know that you guys need to save some drinks for me." Vladimir replies still keeping the conversation light.

"Will do." Elizabeth says with a smile before turning and leaving the room.

She heads back outside to the porch where the meeting with the British Prime Minister is still taking place with Rob already drunk and her boyfriend and the Prime Minister himself not far behind. Due to the pregnancy, Elizabeth has been strictly keeping to soda, making her the evenings designated squadron member. The two bodyguards that followed the group earlier, have passed out asleep on two chairs behind the meeting.

"Mr. Prime Minister, while it has been a lovely evening so far, I fear we may have to cut it short so you can make a phone call." Elizabeth says as she rejoins the group.

"Why would that be Miss Elizabeth?" He replies, clearly tipsy and shooting a look to Jeremy who doesn't notice.

"The Iranians are being uncooperative, even with us. They have nine minutes to calm down otherwise we are giving your government permission to bomb military targets." She replies, sitting in her boyfriend's lap as Rob leans back in his chair and begins pointing randomly at the sky.

"I see." Boris says, almost immediately sobering up as does Jeremy, seemingly shocked but not surprised at what Elizabeth has said,

“What does the boss have to say about all of this?” He asks after another sip of his drink.

“Given that Commander Hilderbrand was more than willing to wipe one middle eastern leader off the face of the Earth, I’m sure he won’t mind if you eliminate a different one for us. Though I will obviously confirm this with him in nine minutes.” Elizabeth replies as her boyfriend puts down his drink and quickly switches to drinking a glass of water.

“Then I guess we’ll find out in nine minutes then won’t we.” Boris replies, his gratitude fading in a buzzed haze, though it is still appreciated by the acting commander.

Date: Sunday, December 6th, 2020

Time: 1540hrs EST

Location: 40,000FT above and 75 miles Southwest of Washington D.C.

Temperature: 34 Degrees Fahrenheit

“Wolf five to Wolf One, incoming transmission from Wolf Two on the ground.” Neil calls out, breaking the silence that has been hanging over the formation; Samantha is still asleep in the back seat of the Phantom.

“Roger that Wolf five, patch it through.” John replies calmly, adjusting in his chair slightly to keep his limbs from going numb.

“Wolf two to Wolf one, come in commander.” Elizabeth says a few seconds later, breaking in over the satellite communication network that has been seamlessly integrated into the squadrons communication systems.

"Wolf one to Wolf two, reading you loud and clear Elizabeth, what can I do for you?" John asks keeping his tone as friendly as his oxygen mask will allow.

"Roger that commander, we are having issues with the Iranian leadership and the British Prime Minister has been extremely cooperative. I am going to give them permission to proceed with the bombing of military targets given that the Iranians have yet to let Vladimir have a bathroom break, let alone speak. However, I wanted to run it by you before I said anything official to the British." Elizabeth says after a couple second delay due to the distance the message has to travel.

"I trust your judgement Elizabeth, just remember to look at the whole board when you tell the British to proceed." John replies upon hearing the message, laughing slightly upon hearing about how the Iranian President and Supreme Leader are treating Vladimir.

"Thank you, commander. On a separate note, how is the flight going?" Elizabeth asks kindly as she writes the affirmative message down on a piece of paper and hands it to Jeremy to give to the British Prime Minister.

"Uneventful so far though we got a nice view of D.C. before turning southwest. My passenger has been asleep since then. She didn't feel good when I did a barrel roll." John says, performing a quick check of his instruments.

"I would have expected as much; Rob is asleep though it is for different reasons." Elizabeth says smiling slightly though definitely tired.

"Did he have too much to drink?" Clara pipes in curiously as John finishes his checks and stretches his shoulders.

"Yeah he did, though he doesn't do it often, so I think we'll only have to deal with his hangover tomorrow rather than him drinking even more." Elizabeth says calmly, yawning before she speaks.

"Shame, I would have asked to join him." Neil says with a chuckle though he only broadcasts his message to the formation as he doesn't want to risk upsetting Elizabeth.

"Sounds like all of you are having a nice vacation, though make sure you take care of Vladimir. He's had to process a lot over the last couple of days and I need him in the right state of mind in case we have to launch a combat mission." John states, knowing what it took for him to fire those missiles earlier in the week.

"Will do commander, we've saved him a couple of drinks like he asked, and I'll keep an eye on him until you arrive." Elizabeth replies, having no trouble seeing John's point; it can be troubling when firing on one's own country.

"Thank you, Elizabeth, I hope you are holding up alright and be sure to get some rest. I know we will be when we land." John continues, doing his best to avoid yawning as he talks but it's no use.

"Thank you John and we will." Elizabeth says before hanging up the line and Neil disconnects it on the formations end.

Through the entire conversation, Samantha has managed to remain asleep; not even moving slightly upon hearing Elizabeth's voice. John doesn't mind, Neil and Clara have always been good at keeping him company and entertained on long flights across large bodies of water and long stretches of land.

"Wish we could sleep as soundly as Sam right now." Neil says after glancing over at the phantoms rear seat.

"An advantage of being uninitiated." Clara says as John glances back to make sure his passenger is still asleep, "Been meaning to ask. Do you two consider yourselves a couple?" Clara continues, treading softly.

"You're asking the wrong person to determine that Clara." John replies warmly, leaving the relationship in Samantha's hands, honestly believing that it's not up to him.

"Stoic as always commander." Neil replies, not wanting to push the issue any further.

"Maybe, but I want her to decide where our relationship goes from here, especially given what's happened to her over the last couple of days." John replies settling back into the long flight.

"Plus you need to focus on making sure the world doesn't explode." Clara joins in, somewhat sadly.

"Exactly wolf four, exactly." John says simply and with a slight sigh, giving his instruments one more check before leaning back in his seat.

Little does John know; Sam wasn't completely asleep while the conversation was taking place. In fact, she heard every word the formation said with John words providing a kind of warmth in the inconsistently cold cockpit. She smiles, unable to respond as she falls back asleep; her stomach finally feeling better and heart rate back to a steady norm.

Chapter Ten

Date: Monday, December 7th, 2020

Time: 0500hrs FKST

Location: Stanley, Falkland Islands

Temperature: 46 Degrees Fahrenheit

John carefully guides the Phantom to stop on the aircraft ramp at Stanley's airport after using most of the four thousand five-hundred-foot runway to land even though it was lengthened by two thousand feet when the initiative came into existence. John's parking job places the phantom neatly at the head of the line of the squadron's aircraft; all in one row on the ramp and all in order. Two small aircraft ladders are placed on the right-hand side of the cockpit just as Neil and Clara make their way over from their Su-33's after handing them over to the ground crew for a check over.

"You must be glad they lengthened the runway for you." Neil says, unzipping his flight suit, letting it hang around his waist and revealing a long sleeve grey tee shirt.

"It almost wasn't long enough." John replies taking his helmet off, setting it in his lap and wiping the sweat out of his hair.

"I thought it was pretty smooth all things considered." Sam says having woken a few hours before hand and finally figuring out how to undo her oxygen mask.

"Compared to the controlled crash of a carrier landing, but... I was standing on the brakes for that entire landing roll." John replies clearly exhausted from the flight as he pauses for a short moment on the ladder before sliding down to the asphalt below.

Sam looks slightly perplexed as she works through John's statement in her head as he tosses his helmet to a member of the ground crew and climbs up the ladder by her seat.

"Need a hand?" He asks softly, referring to the helmet still on her as she continues to try and unstrap it from her head.

"Yeah. Sorry, not used to taking this thing on and off." Sam replies allowing John to undo her helmet for her.

"Don't be too hard on yourself. It takes practice plus it's a new helmet, so the snaps are a little tight." John replies, giving a quick yet strong tug on the chin strap forcing it to come undone.

Sam only smiles though despite her nap; the hour is still causing her to be tired. When she and John finally get her helmet off, John tosses it to the same crew member he tossed his helmet too and helps her climb out of her seat and guides her on to the ladder.

"Took you guys long enough." Elizabeth says, appearing in the distance wearing Jeremy's green sweatshirt over her light blue pajamas and sneakers; Jeremy is standing next to her, in a hastily put on black tee shirt and jeans.

"You didn't have to wait up for us. I hope both of you were able to get some sleep." John says helping Sam unzip her flight suit before unzipping his own revealing their green long sleeve shirts.

"We weren't the only ones." Elizabeth replies, taking John's slight joke in stride and motioning behind her to the British Prime Minister and his security detail.

"Now that is surprising." John says quietly looking over to the tired Prime Minister, who clearly is not used to being up this early in the morning.

“Is that who I think it is?” Sam says quietly, as she finally gets a good look at the Prime Minister.

“Yeah, it is. I’ll be right back.” John says calmly and reassuringly before walking towards Boris Johnson.

He gives Jeremy and Elizabeth a high five as he passes them as they head towards Samantha, Neil and Clara who have begun assessing how Sam’s first flight went.

“Fancy seeing you here Prime Minister, I would have thought you’d be on your way back home by now.” John says shaking Mr. Johnson’s hand firmly and doing his best to hide is relative tiredness and longing for a bed.

“Our tour ran long commander. Mainly because of the Iranians, though I am sure you already knew that.” Boris replies as John shakes the hand of the head of the prime minister’s security detail.

“I had a hunch yeah. My number two was running point on that operation.” He replies taking a towel from one of the maintenance personnel and wiping the sweat off of his face.

“She did well I feel, though from what I’ve heard, the Iranians were less than cooperative.” Boris replies softly, yawning as soon as the sentence leaves his mouth with John following suit.

“More like they wanted to hear their own voices for hours on end Mr. Prime Minister.” John says as Boris gives a look of acknowledgement, “If you’ll excuse me Mr. Prime Minister, I've had a long day and would like to get a shower and make friends with a bed.”

“That makes two of us Commander, have a goodnight.” Boris says shaking John’s hand once more.

"You too Mr. Prime Minister. Goodnight guys." John says releasing Boris's hand and waving to the guards behind him, all of whom have their hands on their weapons and only relax as the young commander walks away and returns to his squad mates.

The Prime Minister and his security detail return to their Land Rover's and head back into Stanley as the small ground crew begins work on the squadron's jets, refueling and checking them over.

"What'd he want?" Clara asks softly as Elizabeth, Jeremy and Neil continue talking with Sam about the flight.

"Nothing really. Just wanted to say hello." John replies, quickly stretching his sore shoulders and looking over to Sam as she chats away.

"Figured but was still curious." She says turning to look in Sam's direction as well, "She's taking this extremely well."

"Yeah, she is, at least publicly. Bad experiences still become bad memories unfortunately and it's going to take her awhile to get over what she's been through." He replies softly, yawning once again as his body desperately wants him to lie down.

Clara doesn't reply, she doesn't need to. For one, she's just as tired John is right now and secondly, she knows the painful truth of John's words from watching him go through it after the training mission that killed a British Soldier. It wasn't pleasant then and she knows that it likely won't be pleasant now, even without knowing every detail.

"We should probably get back to the hotel." Jeremy eventually states after checking the time on his phone and realizing how little sleep John, Sam, Clara and Neil have gotten when compared to how long they've been awake.

Sam initially looks confused when Jeremy says this, though she goes along with it as the squadron walks towards their waiting Land Rovers. John quickly receives a small piece of paper before climbing into the passenger seat of the front most Land Rover with Jeremy driving and Sam jumping in the back seat behind John. He gently hands it back to Sam so she can read it and leans back in the comfortable, leather seat as Jeremy gently guides the Land Rover off of the airport's property.

"We'll be seeing them in a week Sam, though you'll be able to call them when they wake up." John says after Sam quietly hands the paper back to him.

"Fine by me." Sam replies with yawn as Elizabeth pulls the second Land Rover in line with them and follows a short distance behind.

"I thought it would be." John replies with a smile, glancing out the window at the small harbor as the small capital of Stanley begins surrounding the short convoy.

"John, remind me I have something to ask you when you wake up." Jeremy says suddenly though Sam fails to notice; John instinctively knows what Jeremy is referring to.

"I will Jeremy, don't worry." John states simply, tiredness quickly overtaking his aching body.

"Thanks and you ought to know that the incident involving the F-22 has been on the House Armed Services Committees agenda for this afternoon." Jeremy continues remembering the note Rob handed him before he went to bed a few hours ago.

"I see. We'll deal with it when the time comes. Shouldn't need much more than a phone call or two to limit the discussion and keep it off of the house floor." John replies, the incident rapidly becoming the furthest thing on his mind right now.

"Roger that. The Russians are keeping their losses close to their chests for the time being. Any ideas why?" Jeremy ponders as the two SUV's pull up in front of the hotel.

"Haven't a clue Jeremy and right now I am just hoping they're drinking too much vodka to care." John replies, easing his sore body out of the SUV and holds the door for Sam who laughs lightly upon hearing his remark.

"That's a little disconcerting, but I guess it's the best we can hope for." Jeremy replies shaking John's hand as Clara and Neil make their way inside the hotel.

"Well, knowing that will at least allow me to sleep until noon if that's alright with you two." John replies as Jeremy's girlfriend joins them.

"That's fine by us. We'll have the watch until you wake up." Elizabeth says after giving a quick glance to her boyfriend.

"Alright, have a good morning and I'll see you then. Oh and before I forget, can you take her shopping in the morning? I don't think she wants to wear military clothes the whole time." John says softly motioning to Sam who has unwittingly leaned on his shoulder.

"Not a problem, have a goodnight you two." Elizabeth says just as softly, noticing Sam's gesture but chooses to not mention it.

"We'll try." Sam says finally speaking though barely getting over her own exhaustion to get the phrase to leave her mouth, it's hard to tell if she even knows what John said.

With that, Elizabeth and Jeremy return to the Land Rovers in order to park them in a more sensible location and Sam and John head into the hotel. The room they eventually stop at has a view of the bay, much like Jeremy and Elizabeth's. However, the furniture has been changed around style wise, including a modern style kitchen and bathroom with warm colors, and the room is physically larger than the other rooms.

After entering the room, John and Sam find two black duffle bags on the queen-sized bed contain, each containing a couple pairs of jeans, green tee shirts, grey flannel pajamas and under garments. Sam's duffle bag also contains a pair of white and black sneakers and both bags also contain standard toiletry items.

"It's a small advanced package we put together when we don't have the opportunity to pack ahead of time." John explains, noticing Sam's slightly confused look though she's more tired than anything.

"You guys certainly plan for everything." She says quietly, fighting through another yawn as she lays out the pajamas in front of her.

"We try to." John replies, sitting down on the bed, resisting the urge to lay back and fall asleep in his flight suit.

"What's going on with the world?" She asks suddenly, picking up the pajamas and looking down at them for a moment.

"Well, the Syrian President tried to continue the civil war in the region. We were going to talk to the Russians, but they started attacking the rebels, forcing us to step in. We're waiting on them to make their next move, while keeping an eye on the United States after one of their jets engaged us while observing the sinking Russian Carrier." John begins knowing that this is going to be a longer than normal explanation, "Branching off of that, the Iranians seized another British Oil Tanker and refused, at length, to release the crew. Initially, we were going to broker a peaceful solution, but they wouldn't let Vladimir talk so we're going to allow the British to hit a few military targets to try and get the Iranians to budge. In the meantime, some of our ground forces are helping with the cleanup in Syria, with the possibility of removing the president should he start on his war path again."

"The way you say it makes it sound like an average day." Sam says, sitting down next to him, leaning against his chest and closing her eyes.

"For us, it is, but if you're asking if the world is going to end, you can rest assured that it's not going to end today." John replies softly.

"That's good to hear." Sam says, smiling and turning to look into Johns tired eyes once more.

"Yeah." He says simply, smiling in return as he continues to fight the mounting urge to fall asleep in his flight suit.

"I'm going to get changed and then we're going to bed." Sam says softly and with a gentle tone, contrary to the commanding nature of her sentence, as she gets up and heads for the bathroom.

"Says the person who napped for four hours on the flight down here." John says jokingly as he begins changing out of his flight suit and removing his shirt, while Sam chuckles and closes the bathroom door.

It takes John a little longer than normal to change, the three long flights leaving him sore and just wanting to lie down for a whole day; not that he could even if he wanted to. He's stomach has largely stopped bothering him, though he knows the issue could return if he doesn't continue with the medicine the squadrons doctor gave him.

It bothers him slightly that his body is starting to give out barely six months after joining the initiative. Sure, he's suffered some horrific injuries in that time, caused by everything from bullets to shrapnel, but he hoped that he would be able to hold out longer than two combat missions. After changing, he lies down on the bed, doing his best to lie still, relax his sore muscles and close his eyes as he lets exhaustion take hold. He makes no effort to position himself under the comforter or to keep himself from sprawling across the bed.

"You look comfortable." Sam says opening the door and taking a moment to observe the scene before speaking.

"I am." John replies barely moving to see the beautiful young woman approach him and sit on the bed by his stomach.

"You're kind of cute when you're tired." Sam says after taking another moment to play with her hair.

"Now I know that's a lie." John replies with a laugh, only able to imagine how he looks right now and knowing he won't look into a mirror until it's time to shower later in the morning.

Sam only chuckles as John slowly sits up next to her and makes his way over to the light switch in the room, flicking it off and instantly flooding the room with darkness. Sam slides underneath the comforter as he carefully makes his way back to the bed, unable to see much in the inky early morning darkness. When he gets close enough, Sam takes his hand and guides him on to the bed and under the comforter; she wraps her arms around him and pulls him closer.

"You know..." She starts in a long, slightly sarcastic tone as John closes his eyes, "it's up to you too, if we're in a relationship or not."

“I didn’t realize you heard that conversation.” John replies softly after taking a breath.

“Only that part.” Sam responds just as softly, finally closing her eyes and resting her head against his chest as he takes a moment.

“It’s really not up to me Sam, not truly. You know why?” He finally asks, doing his best to get his statements out before he falls asleep.

“Why?” She replies curiously and just as tiredly.

“Because I know I would be happy with you, Sam. That’s why it’s up to you.” He says, his voice trailing off as exhaustion takes over.

Sam doesn’t respond, not wanting to keep John awake any longer than his body will allow. Instead she smiles as John’s words and steady heart rate continues to provide the comfort she’d been longing for since she started dating Richard over two years ago. Ironically, that’s around the same time that John fell for her but decided to keep his feelings to himself out of reluctant respect for her decision. She knows how lucky she is that they remained good friends during that time.

Meanwhile, Elizabeth and Jeremy return to the airport where Rob is overseeing the maintenance being done to the three fighter jets that just arrived. Vladimir is there participating in the maintenance of his own jet, after remembering a slightly concerning power stutter on the flight down to the Falklands.

“Think I found the cause.” Vladimir finally says calling the three initiative members over to his plane.

“Is it what you thought it was?” Elizabeth asks, looking up at the area Vladimir is working on, underneath the starboard engine.

"The fuel pump. Yeah. There seems to be some build up restricting the fuel flow." He replies, his voice muffled as he struggles to remove the stubborn part, finally getting loose and handing it to a nearby mechanic as he lowers himself down from the ladder he was standing on.

Rob's phone rings and he answers it almost immediately.

"Hold on Lieutenant... You're on speaker." He says quickly holding out his phone and the three, tired squadron members gather around.

"Sir, we have bogeys incoming bearings two seven zero and two eight five at three hundred miles and closing. They are unresponsive to hails on all channels." The nervous air traffic controller says surprisingly calmly.

"Two seven zero to two eight five, that's from Argentina." Jeremy says, quickly working out the bogey's country of origin.

"That means they're not coming for us; they're coming for the prime minister." Elizabeth says glancing at her boyfriend and Vladimir before the three of them run to the nearest hanger to change.

"Alright Lieutenant, we're on it. Make sure the Prime Minister knows that he needs to leave as soon as possible." Robs says before quickly hanging up the phone and directing a small army of mechanics to Vladimir's plane to replace the now missing fuel pump.

Within minutes, the air raid siren is piercing through the early morning sky, soon joined by the sound of four jet engines roaring to life. Jeremy and Elizabeth take to the sky with a frustrated Vladimir stuck on the ground keeping an eye on the situation from his cockpit.

"How long will it be before John, Neil and Clara join?" He asks half-jokingly, knowing none of them were fully able to get to sleep.

"I give it five, maybe ten minutes at most." Rob replies as the mechanics finally get the new fuel pump installed and begin closing up the fuselage.

"Sounds about right." Vladimir barely manages to reply before he gets the go ahead from the chief mechanic and closes his canopy.

Within thirty seconds, Vladimir's plane roars into life with ease and a further thirty seconds later, he is in the air forming up with his two comrades. Meanwhile the airfield calms down and the panicked personnel take a few seconds to catch whatever rest they can. They know their jobs are done for the time being and one way or another, they are spectators for a rapidly approaching air battle.

"Wolf Two to Wolf Three and Six, I have the bogey's on radar. Eight of them. I'll take four, you guys split the rest." Elizabeth calls out over the radio as Rob arrives in the control tower.

"Roger that Wolf Two. Thanks for leaving us the scraps." Vladimir replies doing the quick math in his head of the remaining targets.

"Behave you three, don't take any unnecessary risks." Rob chimes in knowing that the squadron members can get ahead of themselves on occasion.

"Roger Tower, we'll come back in one piece." Jeremy replies as he scans the purple horizon for any sign of the approaching threat.

Rob notices a fast-moving vehicle approaching the control tower and a quick pang of dread races down his spine. He had been hoping that John would stay asleep for once, not for any personal reason but just for the fact the he desperately needs to rest. It only takes a few moments for him, Clara, and Neil to come rushing into the control tower, flight suits and all.

"I decide to lay down for a couple hours and Argentina decides to start a goddamn war with England." He says slamming a folder on a desk as he hurriedly adjusts his holster and flight vest.

"The prime minister is on his way-out commander and the other half of the squadron is in the air." Rob replies simply, doing his best to weather his commanders sleep deprived attitude.

"Remind me to shoot the Argentinian President when this is all said and done." John says rushing down the stairs before anyone gets a chance to respond.

"Please tell me Sam is still asleep." Rob says catching Neil and Clara before they rush after their commander.

"Thankfully, she's a heavy sleeper though you'll have to deal with her if she wakes up before we get back." Clara says candidly as she and her boyfriend rush down the stairs after John, who's already on the ramp and climbing into his fighter jet.

"Damn kids." Robs mutters to himself as the sound of two modified J79 jet engines echo across the airfield, soon joined by four Russian engines.

They howl against the early morning sky as the three-fighters taxi to the runway and hold short for a few seconds.

"Wolf Two this is Wolf One, we're ten minutes behind you." John calls out over the radio catching Elizabeth, Jeremy and Vladimir off guard; none of them wanted him to wake up, knowing he needs to rest.

"Roger that Wolf One. Bogeys are still closing fast; we should have a visual in roughly ten minutes." Elizabeth replies managing to bottle up her surprise for the time being.

"Roger that Wolf Two." John replies, firewalling the throttle of his F-4E, sending the engines into full afterburner and rocketing the fighter down the runway.

Clara and Neil take off, side by side behind him, struggling to keep up with their commander as they chase his burner plumes.

Date: Monday, December 7th, 2020

Time: 0615hrs FKST

Location: 30,000 ft above and 200 miles NW of Stanley, Falkland Islands

Temperature: 48 Degrees Fahrenheit

The eight Argentine fighters, aging IAI Nesher's (Dassault Mirage 5s) handed down from the Israeli air force, form up having reached their attack vector after taking off from two different air bases.

"Target is fifteen minutes out." The lead pilot says in his characteristically Spanish voice and language.

"Roger." The co-pilots reply in sequence, seeing nothing on their radars and leaning back in their seats, doing what they can to relax before they need to line up for the attack run on the British Prime Minister.

Suddenly, the leftmost plane explodes in a massive fireball and is soon consumed by the morning sun. The Argentine pilots scatter, looking over their shoulders as they frantically break formation, turning and burning to try and visualize where the attack is coming from. A missile lock tone rings out in the flight leads cockpit forcing him to call out to his wingmen to see if they can do anything, but to no avail. An AIM - 120D radar guided missile slams into the planes mid-section and explodes, igniting the fuel tank and forcing the wreckage to burn and buckle down to the ocean below, leaving the pilot no chance to eject. The second in command assumes the role of flight lead and manages to get his fellow pilots to regroup into a loose formation as he takes a moment to assess the situation.

"Control, this is Viper Two. We've lost two, requesting a contingency plan." He calls out, impatiently waiting for a response as the radar operators frantically try to regain the formation and what is attacking them.

"Viper Two, this is control. Nega-." The controller attempts to respond but another AIM - 120D comes out of the sky and slams into the cockpit of the Nesher, killing the pilot instantly.

The formation scatters once more; now leaderless for a second time, none of them know what to do next due to their collective inexperience, this was their first combat operation after all. In a way, the scattering postpones their slaughter for a little while as Elizabeth, Jeremy, and Vladimir lose radar lock on any of the Argentine fighters and forces them to pull back and wait for an opening.

"Wolf Two to Wolf One, three fighters down. Identity confirmed as Argentine Nesher's. Rest have scattered. Holding fire for the moment." Elizabeth says as the three-plane formation gently circles five miles from the struggling Argentinians.

"Copy that Wolf Two. We're seconds out, my gun is hot, and the safety is off." John replies, his engines screaming in full burner, "I'll see if I can straighten them up for you."

"Roger Wolf One, we'll keep an eye on them." Elizabeth responds following her commanders' line of thinking as Rob continues listening from the airport, another figure catching his vision on the aircraft ramp.

He quickly runs down to the tarmac, leaving one of his staffers in contact with the squadron for the time being. Quickly exiting the control tower, he walks over to the figure in question, the early morning light soon revealing it to be an incredibly sleep deprived Sam.

"Can't sleep?" He asks, his warm voice catching Sam off guard and causing her to jump slightly upon hearing it.

"Unfortunately no, my new boyfriend got dragged away and without someone to hold, I just couldn't sleep." Sam replies with a small chuckle and a yawn as Rob motions for her to join him in the heated control tower that he just exited, forgetting how cold it was.

"I'm sorry to say but that was partly my fault. The Argentinians are trying to assassinate the British Prime Minister who is due to take off at any moment, thankfully." Rob says trying to keep Sam's spirit up while also telling her the truth; a delicate balance that he is still trying to master.

"Still hard to believe that there's a group that deals with incidents like this." Sam replies as the pair work their way upstairs to the main level of the control tower; the British Prime Minister's Airbus begins taxiing towards the runway.

"Well it's a job no one wanted to do, and someone needed to do it, so it got dropped in the United Nations lap." Rob replies simply, putting his headset back on and listening in on the squadrons radio traffic.

"Wolf Two, this Wolf One, we're ten clicks behind you and closing at four hundred knots." John calls out catching a glimpse of the flights exhaust.

"Roger Wolf One, though you're going awfully quick aren't you?" Elizabeth replies glancing over her shoulder.

"Wolf flight be advised. British Prime Minister is airborne." Rob says, breaking up the conversation and instantly changing the tactical situation.

"Roger control, Wolf Five, Wolf Six, fall back to Stanley and cover the prime minister." John replies as Neil and Vladimir break away from the formation and proceed back to the Falklands.

The Argentine pilots have finally started to regroup, trying to maintain a small semblance of order as they decide whether or not to continue the attack. John takes the lead of the now four fighter formation and gazes down at the Argentine fighters below, deciding how to line up an attack run that keeps them away from the British Prime Minister.

"Wolf flight, this is Wolf One, I'm rolling in hot to make a single pass. You clean them up from there." John says finally spotting the opening he's been looking for.

"Roger Wolf One, we have your back." Elizabeth replies as the massive F-4 snaps into a left hand, downward barrel roll, leveling off at Mach 1.2 and a mile behind the five Nesher's.

Keeping the throttle pinned to the firewall and rapidly closing the distance, John takes careful aim with his gun sight, doing his best to keep the lead fighter centered. He takes a breath and gently squeezes the trigger on his control column. The 20mm Vulcan cannon storms into life with a quick two second burst, peppering the lead Nesher and quickly igniting the fuel tank. John pulls back on the stick, soon avoiding the ejecting Argentinian pilot. His wingman gains a faint radar lock on John's F-4 as it passes over head and lets two missiles fly. Both instantly lose lock and arc towards the southeast.

"Wolf flight, you're cleared weapons hot. Happy hunting." John says, after taking a moment to chuckle at the vain attempts of the Argentine pilots.

"Wilco Wolf One." Jeremy replies with an unavoidable smile on his face as the three fighters roll in, coating the area in missiles.

It doesn't take long for the four remaining fighters to fall to the ocean below, all told costing Argentina eight Nesher's and five pilots, with the three remaining pilots floating aimlessly in the South Atlantic Ocean. Meanwhile, Vladimir and Neil finally reach the British Prime Ministers plane, forming up on each wing as an escort while they make radio contact with the British pilot.

"Commander, we'll be escorting you away from the Falklands airspace." Vladimir says, keeping his tone as upbeat as possible.

"Roger that Wolf Six, we appreciate the..." The British Commander begins before an alarm rings out in the cockpit of the Airbus forcing him to finish his thought frantically, "Wolf Six, we have incoming."

Before Vladimir can respond, he catches a glimpse of the missile trails off of his left wing and instinctively breaks into them, releasing chaff in an effort to get the missiles to break their lock. The first missile sails harmlessly over head as the lumbering Airbus dives for the deck, however the second momentarily picks up Vladimir's SU-33 after losing contact with the larger commercial jet. It slams into the Russian fighter's cockpit, scattering the pieces below as the rest of Wolf flight listens to incident over the radio. Their hearts sinking along with the wreckage of Vladimir's plane.

"Wolf Six, Wolf Six, come in Wolf six. Come in Vlad." Neil screams over the radio trying desperately to get a response.

"Wolf Fi..." Elizabeth tries to interject while also trying to hold her own tears back for the time being.

"Wolf Six?!" Neil says one last time, cutting Elizabeth off before bursting into tears.

Sam looks around trying to gauge the reaction in the control tower, however Rob remains reluctantly quiet until he is forced to speak, betraying how he really feels.

"Wolf flight... return... return to base." He says choking up as he speaks, and a single tear falls from his cheek to the floor below.

Chapter Eleven

Date: Monday, December 7th, 2020

Time: 0712 FKST

Location: Stanley, Falkland Islands

Temperature: 49 Degrees Fahrenheit

The mood has been sullen ever since the five remaining members of the squadron landed back at Stanley five minutes ago. Neil and Clara have headed back to the hotel as Elizabeth and Jeremy stayed behind to keep an eye on John and to oversee the maintenance on their planes. Rob has been keeping Sam at a distance, knowing that the young adults in the squadron need their space at the moment.

"Just give them time Sam." He says gently as she asks to head over to them one last time.

"Alright." She says softly, feeling the pain that her new friends are going through, though she notices that John has disappeared into the nearby hanger before asking, "Is this the first time?"

"Unfortunately... yes." Rob replies signing off on some paperwork from the mechanics as Elizabeth and Jeremy embrace and slowly walk over.

"We're going to head back to the hotel. Keep us in the loop if anything comes up." Elizabeth says to Rob before receiving a hug from Samantha.

"Will do. Take it easy." Rob replies gently as he also hugs Elizabeth, as Sam does the same for Jeremy.

"We will... Sam... John's in the locker room on the left side of the hanger. You may want t... he could use a friendly face right now."

Elizabeth manages to say softly, though she struggles to get a coherent sentence out of her mouth.

"Okay." Sam says quietly before jogging over to hanger as quickly as she can, as Rob guides Jeremy and Elizabeth to a nearby Land Rover.

Entering the hanger, Sam quickly finds the locker room on the left-hand side as an eerie quiet falls over the vast space. It's completely empty, the news of Vladimir's death has hit the entire organization hard and no one is willing to talk or even be seen.

"John?" She says softly as she opens the door to the well-lit locker room, though she doesn't immediately see John, though she can hear the sound of running water emanating from the back of the room.

She gently walks towards the only noise in the room, careful to make only the slightest of sounds as she doesn't want to startle her new boyfriend.

"John?" She gently repeats finally reaching the source of the noise as she turns and passes the dividing wall between the restrooms and changing area of the locker room.

She finds the young commander motionless, supporting himself with both arms on a sink and with his head held incredibly low; ice cold water slowly dripping from his face. The upper part of his flight is draped around his waist as he continues to just stand there. As he continues to just stand there.

"John?" Sam repeats softly for a third time, not wanting to approach her boyfriend too quickly; she soon discovers that she has a good reason to hesitate.

Without any semblance of a warning, John pulls his right fist back and slams it into the bathroom mirror, breaking it into thousands of tiny shards and bursting into tears in the process. Sam stands there for a moment, gasping at the sight she's just witnessed and keeping her hands over her mouth to keep from losing too much air at once. A brief moment of silence follows, only broken by the muffled cries coming from John's soul and the intermittent dripping of tears from his heart.

"Why couldn't I see that?... How could I not see that?..." John finally utters, the words only intensifying his sorrow.

Blood begins to pool in the sink from the shards of mirror still embedded in his right hand; the gentle flow of tap water beautifully washing it down the drain. He spits into the pool, disgusted by his failure yet unable to contain his emotions much further.

"There was no way for you to know what was going to happen John. You're not a prophet." Sam eventually says, doing her best to remain calm as a warm ruby red begins covering her boyfriend's hand; she doesn't dare get any closer than she is right now.

John tries to compose himself, yet quickly discovers that he can't. At this moment, he is no longer the commander of the United Nations Initiative. He's just a twenty-one-year-old who's lost one of his best friends; unable to speak or even comprehend.

"Everyone... everyone is expecting..." He stammers, trying to articulate a coherent sentence.

"John no one is expecting anything of you. Not now." She says, finally approaching closer and gently resting her hand on John's shoulder, "No one is expecting anything of you."

John remains silent.

"Do you remember when I first got my license and I got arrested when the police thought I was driving drunk even though I was simply nervous?" Sam asks kindly and gently as she begins to tend to the open wounds on John's hand.

"Yeah, I remember." John replies simply, his voice barely audible.

"My parents were at work and could've gotten me, but I called you. You were there within minutes... I can only imagine what was going through your mind at that point, but there you were, not judging me in the slightest..." Sam continues, softly recounting the story.

"I also remember you wanting to hug me before they even took the handcuffs off of you." John says allowing himself a slight chuckle as Sam carefully pulls the small pieces of mirror of his hand.

"Yeah." Sam laughs, "For that whole day... You didn't expect anything of me... I was worried that you were mad at me or worse, but you weren't... I remember... I remember asking why you were being so nice to me and... and you told me it was because you weren't expecting anything of me because of how emotional I was... So I'm telling you John... no one is expecting anything of you..." Her words softly fill Johns ears and force him to gently put his left arm around Sam's shoulders.

"You know... I don't like when people quote me to myself." He eventually says as Sam takes the last piece of mirror out of his hand.

"I know, but sometimes you need to hear yourself." Sam states simply and directly as she looks the wound over, now having a better view of it after washing the blood away, "Let's get you patched up and John?"

"hmm?"

"I'm sorry for your loss." She says hugging him tightly.

John pauses for a moment as they begin walking.

"Thank you, Sam." He says quietly as they turn to leave the locker room, arm in arm.

Upon exiting the hanger, Samantha is the one to call for a nearby medic, snapping her out of the daze she's been in since hearing the news. She leads them over to a nearby medical tent where she proceeds to gingerly wrap John's hand in gauze after disinfecting it. The whole process agitates the cuts in John's hand, causing them to sting immensely with the only thing taking his mind off of the pain being the loving gaze he is sharing with Sam right now. This should have happened a long time ago, but they're both glad that it finally did.

"Do you two need a room?" The medic finally asks with a slight South African accent as the sun finally makes an appearance.

"We already have one ensign, but thanks for asking." John replies as an unavoidable smile falls across his face and Sam's cheeks turn bright red; the ensign also allows herself to smile.

"If you don't mind me asking, sir, what happens now?" The young medic asks, finishing the relatively skinny bandage on John's hand.

"Well the first thing will be the funeral tomorrow morning, once the Georgia arrives. After that, will be either be an angry phone call to Argentinian President, or taking a day to pay him a visit in person. Beyond that, just a trip back to base and we'll go from there." John states after taking a moment to ponder his answer.

"Be sure to give him hell commander." The ensign replies, the serious tone returning to her voice as the three of them stand up from the folding chairs they had been sitting on.

"Lord knows he deserves it ensign. Thanks for patching me up." John says gently as the young medic salutes and he returns it with the best salute possible given the condition of his right hand.

After leaving the small medical station, the couple pauses for a moment outside and gazes off into the rising sun, briefly mesmerized at the stunning beauty of the coming morning.

"You know, the British are going to bill you for that mirror." A familiar warm voice says from the vehicle staging area.

"Cracking jokes or is that the ice beneath your feet Rob?" John replies smartly, turning to face the squadrons advisor as Samantha does the same, a second behind him.

"Very funny commander." Rob replies with a smirk adjusting a clipboard he has in his hands and taking a final glance of a post it note, "Elizabeth asked me to remind both of you that despite the circumstances, you need to sleep."

"Makes you wonder if she's actually my second in command or my mother." John replies as Samantha closes her eyes and rests her head against his chest, "We're on our way. Wake me if there is any news regarding anything and tell the Argentinian President to expect a phone call at some point in the next twenty-four hours."

"Roger that commander, I know it might be hard, but try to sleep well." Rob says as he pats John on the shoulder and shakes him a little bit before motioning for the tired commander and his girlfriend to leave.

Without another word, the couple heads for one of the Land Rovers though when John heads for the driver's side door, his girlfriend cuts him off and puts her hand in front of him.

"You're a good driver John, but with your hand hurt it might be best if I drive." Samantha says softly yet confidently, on top of being incredibly tired from little to no sleep.

"Alright, it's a short drive, but the first time you swerve, and we switch, okay?" He replies, waving his left index finger slightly before heading over to the passenger side of the vehicle.

Luckily for the two of them, Sam's driving is good enough to get them back to the hotel and they're soon back at their original hotel room. It takes but a moment for them to change back into the pajamas that they left on the floor before the fight with the Argentinians and crawl into bed and into each other's arms. Not long after, Sam notices John's still tiredly gazing at her as they both begin to bear the full brunt of exhaustion.

"Get some sleep, sweetie." She says, chuckling slightly and poking him in the nose.

"I will. It's just hard when I have the perfect view." He says with a whisper and soft smile, causing Sam to blush and try to hide her face.

Sam pulls herself closer to him, making sure that there is barely any distance between them and that they're still comfortable. She closes her eyes, rests her head on his chest one more time and sighs deeply.

"I love you, John." She finally says after taking another moment, her words hanging in the air like falling flower petals in an autumn breeze.

John also takes a moment to sigh, relieved to finally hear the words he's longed to hear for years. The words, he's always wanted to say to Samantha and now he finally can. The feeling of relief being equivalent to that of a large boulder being lifted off of his tired and scarred shoulders.

"I love you too, Sam." He replies before kissing her gently on the lips, closing his eyes and resting his head gently on her own.

Date: Monday, December 7th, 2020

Time: 1215hrs FKST

Location: Stanley, Falkland Islands

Temperature: 51 Degrees Fahrenheit

"Mister President, I am warning you now. The next conversation you have is not going to be with me and is going to be even less pleasant. So I suggest you calm down and talk with me because it's the only way I can guarantee that you're going to remain alive for the next twenty hours." Elizabeth says yelling into her cell phone at the Argentinian President, who has chosen this exact moment to turn into a massive asshole.

Jeremy holds his girlfriend's hand gently, hoping that the Argentinian President calms down enough, so Elizabeth can keep her emotions in check. Emotions are still running hot from Vladimir's death, and the fact that the Argentinian President was partly responsible isn't helping one bit.

"Mister President, and please know that I am saying this with all due respect, you're a son of a bitch." Elizabeth says, angrily, a few seconds later before hanging up the phone and having to resist the urge to chuck it at a nearby wall.

"I know sweetheart, I know." Jeremy says taking the phone from his girlfriend's hand and doing his best to gently restrain her from punching him or anything else within striking distance.

"How does John do it?" She asks, doing her best to calm herself down and falling into her boyfriend's chest.

"He doesn't, he just hides it well." Jeremy replies rocking Elizabeth back and forth after draping his arms around her, "Rob left a note as you were taking the call, apparently John had to have his right hand bandaged earlier this morning and the airport is sticking us with the bill for a shattered mirror. Sam was there, she saw the whole thing and eventually got him to bed."

"I see..." Elizabeth says upon hearing the news, "at least the two of them can rest for a while now, though we both know that John is going to be itching for a fight when he wakes up."

"I know, we just need to remind him to not use the nuclear option just yet and to talk with the Argentinian President before putting a bullet in his skull." Jeremy says knowingly, doing his best to be the calmest voice around, though the truth is that he wants blood just as much as John does.

"He's going to need more than a reminder." Clara says approaching the couple from behind, Neil following along not far behind her; all are dressed in various forms of casual clothing.

"I'm surprised you two are even up." Jeremy says turning and shaking their hands before his girlfriend does the same.

"We couldn't sleep, at least not well." Neil says quietly, the pain of what transpired this morning still fresh in his mind.

"That's understandable." Elizabeth replies, just as softly if not softer than Neil's original statement.

"Where do we go from here?" Clara sighs gently, pulling a chair over and sitting down next to Elizabeth as she looks longingly at the rest of the group.

"I don't know Clara, I don't know." Elizabeth replies, taking her hand gently in her own as she develops a thousand-yard stare.

"There's Sam." Neil says quietly staring into the ground over his girlfriend's right shoulder.

"Yeah, but what plane does she fly? We don't have any spares available, heck we don't even have spare planes in case ours go down for maintenance." Jeremy pipes up after doing a quick count of what is available back at Midway.

"Damn, you're right, not even the Kestrel has extra fighters." Clara says resting her head in her hand.

"You're mostly right." The experienced voice of Rob says as he appears behind the four squadron members, who immediately turn around to face him. "I just got a note from Midway Base." He finishes, passing a small piece of paper to Elizabeth.

"Next hundred special forces soldiers are ready to deploy. Samantha's Parents are a few hours away. John's spare plane was completed yesterday at seventeen hundred local time." She reads aloud for all to hear, stopping abruptly after stating the news regarding John's spare plane.

"Do you think he'll go for it?" Jeremy asks cautiously after taking a moment.

"Usually I'd say no, but John's been a little... softer... than usual. Ever since Samantha came on board the other day. Not that's a bad thing, I like seeing him relax a little." Clara says recounting several moments over the last week.

"We'll run it by him when he wakes up and I definitely second the statement about him relaxing." Elizabeth says as she pats Clara gently on the back and lets a small smile form across her face.

"Sounds like a plan. Just so everyone knows, the Georgia is due in at zero six thirty tomorrow. She's going to be escorted by the destroyers Johnston and Samuel B. Roberts. Lastly, when John wakes up, make sure he gets on the phone to Argentinian President before he goes off the rails again." Rob finishes, knowing that it's going to be hard for the squadron to keep going at a time like this.

"Roger that, thanks Rob." Elizabeth replies before Rob returns to the airport and continues to monitor the Initiatives forces around the globe from the top floor of the control tower.

"If only all problems were that easy to solve." Neil sighs, sitting down behind his girlfriend and gently rubbing her back.

"The Argentinian President knows to expect us, and the British Prime Minister is on his way back home. So, that's something at the very least." Elizabeth says gently as she gazes over the bay, "We'll solve it the way we usually do, one step at a time."

"One step at a time." Clara quietly repeats as she leans against her boyfriend, noticing two figures moving towards the group.

“Well, isn’t this a motley crew.” John says, sparing a chuckle and a smile as he and Sam finally come to a stop a few feet away from the four squadron members; the bandage on his hand freshly changed after getting a shower.

“Commander... we thought you were sleeping.” Jeremy says, startled and turning around to face his leader as Clara, Neil and Elizabeth stand just as quickly.

“It’s alright, we got plenty of rest. The company certainly helps, as I am sure all of you know.” He replies frankly as he scratches his head with his right hand and the altitude returning to his voice; Sam laughs as she wraps her arms around his left arm.

“Amen to that commander. Just so you’re aware, the Argentinian President is expecting us, we got off the phone with him about fifteen minutes ago.” Elizabeth says, approaching and checking on John’s hand.

“Leave it alone mother, Sam did the bandage before we came over here.” John says half-jokingly and getting Elizabeth to back off slightly as Sam blushes.

“You did a good job.” Elizabeth whispers to Samantha as she backs away and retakes her seat.

“Look... this isn’t easy... Vladimir... Vladimir was an integral part of this... of this family... Not only was he my spotter, but he was... he was... our brother and our friend... I definitely feel it’s an understatement to say that he’s going to be missed... There’s a gaping hole in my heart where he used to be and I’m sure it’s the same for you... I pray that he has made good friends with the lord above and that he continues to look over us as we go forward as best we can... I know this isn’t the best eulogy... But it's the best I can do at the moment...” John says, choking up more and more as he continues speaking, eventually finishing his statement, almost in tears.

"It's ok John." Sam whispers kindly into his ear, though the squadron overhears her and joins the response with a nod.

"Thanks..." John sighs, "Talk to me about options. The Argentinian President is expecting us, and we need to decide what's going to happen to him." John finishes finally taking a seat.

"There's really only two options commander, there's the talking option and the assassination option. Now it's worth noting that the President is willing to talk and has agreed to suspend any attack plans until we meet with him in person." Elizabeth starts, reluctantly agreeing that the business of the world still needs come first, despite the previous tragedy.

"You really don't want to know how much I want to put a bullet in that man's head, which leaves the talking option. Okay. What are our goals coming out of this meeting?" John asks, struggling to contain how he truly feels.

"Well for the time being, it'll be to keep the Falklands out of Argentinian hands, but I think we need to find a way to keep them from attacking the islands ever again." Jeremy says, he's not the only one who's had the idea.

"So long as the islands remain a British territory they'll remain a target and we don't have the manpower at the moment to keep a permanent guard force in place." Neil joins in, running through the options as quick as he can in his head.

“The British aren’t going to give up the islands. They went to war over this territory.” John follows up, running through the same options in his head.

“Which brings us full circle commander. If we go with the talking option then we have to convince the Argentinian President to give up on the Falklands, something that the Argentinian people are not likely willing to do.” Elizabeth says, managing to sum up the last two minutes with a well thought out phrase.

John takes a moment to think, trying to put the pieces together in his mind before he says them out loud.

“What’s your take Sam?” He finally asks, needing a fresh view of the situation.

“I’m really not sure John. On one hand it doesn’t seem like you’ll ever get the Argentinian people to back down. On the other is a need for retribution and a peace deal that normally takes years to negotiate.” Sam replies slightly startled at how practiced and educated she sounded without even thinking about it.

“You’re not wrong. Okay, after the Georgia arrives tomorrow, Clara, Neil and myself will head for the Argentine capital to speak with the President. What happens after that is up to him.” John says, bringing the conversation on the topic to a close.

“Sounds like a plan commander.” Elizabeth says quietly, trying to decide what to talk about next in order to keep the conversation going, so no one can get lost in their own thoughts.

“Sam, would you want to go shopping? I know you still need some clothes given that you didn’t have time to pack.” Clara states before Elizabeth is able to get her thoughts together.

“That would be great, thanks. Would you want to join Elizabeth? Make it a girl’s trip?” Sam asks, doing her best to perk up in spite of the depressing mood.

“You don’t need to ask me twice.” Elizabeth replies with a smile and after exchanging hugs with their respective boyfriends, they head off into town to take their minds off of things for a few hours; leaving the guys to their own devices in the process.

Chapter Twelve

Date: Monday, December 7th, 2020

Time: 1534 FKST

Location: Stanley, Falkland Islands

Temperature: 50 Degrees Fahrenheit

"How long does it take for women to go shopping, I mean seriously." Neil says with a laugh as the three male squad members prepare to have a round of drinks at the local bar.

"As long as they want it too Neil, the sooner you realize that the better." Jeremy replies taking a sip of his beer.

"Look who's talking, just wait until you have a kid Jeremy. As soon as they arrive, you're done making decisions." John speaks up putting down his bottle of Mike's Hard Lemonade, revealing that he's already finished a third of its contents.

Neil's mouth drops in shock; it's the first time he's hearing the news.

"Sir, I think you just gave Neil a heart attack." Jeremy whispers to John, remembering that he and his girlfriend haven't had a chance to tell Neil or Clara ever since the news came across John's desk.

"In fairness Jeremy, I wouldn't count out Neil's heart. He's a strong young man after all. Though if he keeps his mouth open, then someone is going to think its a tunnel." John replies, taking a quick glance before downing another third of his beverage in one go.

"Very funny commander, but in all seriousness... Jeremy? You and Elizabeth are having a kid?!" Neil finally replies after getting his jaw realigned and turning to Jeremy who has finally made it halfway through his beer.

"Yeah, we are Neil. We're two months pregnant at the moment. We've been meaning to tell you and Clara, but we haven't had the time." Jeremy finally admits as he puts the beer back on the bar counter.

"That's great man, congratulations to you both." Neil says more joyfully than he's said most things over the last six months as he pats Jeremy sternly on the shoulder.

"Thanks Neil." Jeremy replies, smiling nervously and glancing towards John who only smirks as he ignores Jeremy's gaze while he finishes his bottle of Mike's Hard Lemonade.

Jeremy doesn't entirely know how he feels about his commander outing him like he did on the issue of he and his girlfriend's pregnancy. On the one hand, they were going to have to tell the other squadron members eventually, but it annoys him that they didn't get to do it on their own terms. Then he gets the shock of his life.

"Elizabeth texted me about a half hour ago, telling me to get you to admit to the pregnancy. She told Clara and Sam while they were dress shopping." John whispers to Jeremy after ordering a second Mike's Hard Lemonade; his usual drink limit.

Jeremy is dumb founded but also understanding, now stuck halfway between being mad at his commander and glad that his girlfriend gave him some cover to actually tell Neil about the situation. While thinking on this however, another thought begins to form in his mind, a question he's been meaning to ask John for the last three weeks.

“John, can we talk outside? Privately?” Jeremy asks softly, doing his best to keep any form of nervousness or annoyance out of his voice, both of which John immediately picks up on.

“Yeah, we can. Neil, give us five minute and pick up the tab for us, I’ll pay you back later.” John replies taking the bottle of Mike’s Hard Lemonade with him as he turns around and stands.

“Roger that, John.” Neil replies faithfully, picking up on Jeremy’s earlier tone and seemingly knowing what he is going to ask given the unfortunate absence of Elizabeth’s parents.

Jeremy and John move softly outside the bar and look out over the minimal amount of traffic taking place by the bay. No one is close enough to hear what they are saying.

“I’ve been meaning to ask you this for a while and it has to be you, because unfortunately Sam’s parents aren’t here and...” Jeremy begins rushing through his words as nerves overtake his emotions before John cuts him off.

“Jeremy, calm down and breathe. Ask me what you want to ask me, there is no need to make a big to-do about this, at least not yet.” John says resting his left hand on Jeremy’s shoulder and forcing him to take a deep controlled breath.

“I want to ask Elizabeth if she’ll marry me and I want your blessing to ask her.” Jeremy finally blurts out, cutting straight to the question.

John pats him twice on the shoulder before putting his hand in his jeans pocket and taking a quick sip from the bottle in his right hand. The moment seems entirely too long for Jeremy’s liking.

“Commander?” He asks, doing his best to not sound impatient.

"I'm flattered you hold me with such high regard Jeremy, but if you want to marry Elizabeth, I am not the one you should be asking. If you know what I mean." John says gently and warmly after turning back to Jeremy and looking him square in the eye.

"Yes sir, I believe I do." Jeremy replies quietly, a nervous and hesitant smile falling across his face.

"Well, I guess we need to get to a jeweler before we leave for Midway. Don't worry about the cost, I'll take care of it." John says with a chuckle as Neil finally joins them on the patio of the bar after paying for the drinks; he's clearly confused as to what is happening.

"What's happening Chief?" Neil asks curiously, wanting to catch up on what has happened in the last few minutes.

"Come Neil, we're putting on an engagement and wedding. This is men's work." John says exuberantly, faking a pompess accent as he throws the now empty bottle in the trash.

"You're enjoying this way too much commander." Jeremy says as John puts his arms around the shoulders of his subordinates and laughs.

"Yes I am and guess what?" John starts, smiling wider than he has for a while, "You're going to enjoy every single minute of it."

"Yes, I'm sure I am commander." Jeremy says extremely sarcastically as Neil joins in John's laughter at Jeremy's expense.

Date: Monday, December 7th, 2020

Time: 1603 FKST

Location: Stanley, Falkland Islands

Temperature: 49 Degrees Fahrenheit

“Wonder what the men are getting up to?” Sam asks as the three of them continue looking through a local clothing store at various dresses and shoes, deciding what they want to purchase.

“They’re probably having a drink or at the airport working on their planes.” Elizabeth replies, taking a particular interest in a pair of strappy, white heels.

“Probably... Those would go well with a wedding dress.” Clara says taking notice of what Elizabeth is looking at, having glanced at a message from Neil a few minutes ago.

“They would but I’m not getting married anytime soon.” Elizabeth says, slightly disappointed at the mere thought of having a kid before getting married.

“Get them, you never know, maybe you could wear them some other time.” Sam says also taking note of what Elizabeth is looking at, having been shown Neil's message by Clara soon after she received it.

“You two are going to make this an expensive trip.” Elizabeth replies with a laugh, picking up the heels and adding them to the small pile of long sleeve dresses and a couple of sweater coats.

Clara and Sam chuckle, having only picked out an outfit each, a red sweater, jeans and black sneakers for Clara and a skintight, long sleeve, black shirt, skinny dark blue jeans and a pair of short, black bootie heels for Samantha. Neither one of them can compare to the amount clothes Elizabeth has grabbed though it is worth noting that half of her clothing pile is because of her pregnancy.

After checking out, the three of them put everything into a Land Rover and continue debating with each other on where to go next. It’s been awhile since the three of them have been this happy and even longer since any of them have had any girl time. A welcome break from the issues that their normal lives have presented them over the last few weeks.

Date: Monday, December 7th, 2020

Time: 1618 FKST

Location: Stanley, Falkland Islands

Temperature: 49 Degrees Fahrenheit

"You don't think it's too much?" Jeremy asks in a whisper as he gazes down at a silver and gold flower petal setting with a single, one carat diamond in the center.

"Not by a long shot Jeremy, she'll love it." Neil replies reassuring his fellow squadron member with a warm tone of amazement and awe.

"What's your take John?" Jeremy asks softly, showing his otherwise occupied commander the beautiful ring.

"I think it's stunning Jeremy, I really do, but you have to feel right about it. It's up to you if you feel right about it or not and either way, my opinion doesn't matter too much." John replies in a way that negates the normally sad tone of his sentence.

"Trust me commander, it feels so incredibly right." He replies, the joy in his voice confounding the uplifting mood.

"Then that's all you need to know Jeremy." John says patting him on the back as Jeremy looks back to the jeweler.

“This one.” He says as a massive smile falls across his face as he hands the ring back to him and the jeweler returns a respectful nod before placing the ring in a box.

John moves over to the cash register before Jeremy can collect his thoughts or even think about money, though Neil makes sure to break up Jeremy’s sight line before any money is actually exchanged. Soon after, the trio is heading back outside as Jeremy slips the small black box into his jeans pocket, making sure it’s secure for what he has planned later this evening.

The trio continue walking, heading towards the hotel in order to change for the night’s festivities, though “change” is a massive overstatement. The three of them don’t even take their jeans off, instead choosing to replace their tee-shirts with button up formal shirts of varying shades of blue and white.

Before meeting up with Neil and Jeremy, John makes a quick stop by the airport to check the maintenance progress on the squadron’s planes.

“Commander, forgive me, I didn’t expect you to be up.” Rob says finally noticing that John has arrived and is looking over his plane.

“Putting on an engagement and wedding for a friend; wouldn’t miss it for the world.” John replies smiling, shaking Rob’s hand.

“Ah, men’s work.” Rob replies proudly, getting his commander to laugh, “If there is anything I can do to help, you know I’ll be there.”

“Thanks Rob; be by the bay in about two hours.” John replies, still smiling and shaking Rob’s hand.

“Sounds like a plan commander.” Rob replies as a thought enters his mind, “What about you commander?”

"I've waited so long already, that a short time to get it right won't be so bad." He replies simply before walking away.

Date: Monday, December 7th, 2020

Time: 1706 FKST

Location: Stanley, Falkland Islands

Temperature: 48 Degrees Fahrenheit

"Alright John, we'll make sure she's there." Samantha says quietly before hanging up the phone, keeping a careful eye on Elizabeth while keeping her distance from her.

"What'd the commander want?" Clara asks softly, having noticed the phone call as soon as Samantha answered the phone five minutes ago.

"He asked us to make sure that Elizabeth was down by the bay, in front of the hotel, around six fifteen. Jeremy has something to ask her." Sam replies, after taking a short moment to realize who Clara is talking about, but also maintaining a small element of surprise by not revealing the entire situation.

"Wonder what he wants to ask her." Clara says curiously, quickly getting distracted by several of the paintings and trying to decide which one she wants in her and Neil's house back at Midway Base.

"Beats me." Samantha says quietly to herself, being extra careful to not allow her tone to betray Jeremy's true intentions.

"How are things going between you and John if you don't mind me asking?" Clara continues a short time later as the trio regroup and continue looking reverently at various paintings that catch their fancy.

"Pretty... pretty well." Sam replies hesitating slightly as she doesn't know what she wants to share yet.

"You sure?" Elizabeth asks gently, having immediately noticed the slight hesitation though not wanting the prod more than she has too.

"Yeah... I am... it's just, the nightmares haven't stopped entirely, though he's the only one who's been able to help me control them." Sam continues clarifying her earlier hesitation though slightly zoning out as the mere thought of the nightmare's she's been having sends shivers down her spine. "I know it can be hard to believe at times but he's just so gentle and warm, like a thick blanket." She finishes barely realizing that she's speaking.

"Don't worry, we know. Behind that tough as nails exterior and shoot first attitude is a genuinely kind human being who genuinely wants to help. You're not the only one who has noticed Sam though it's good that you finally did." Elizabeth speaks softly, her words floating through the air.

"What do you mean?" Sam asks, confused by the last part of Elizabeth's statement.

"You'll know when the time is right. As for the nightmare's, continue letting John help you. It'll take time, but they'll go away." Clara interjects steering the conversation as they move to another part of the store, merely to look as they don't want to spend all of their money.

Sam only smiles, managing to regain her concentration and get back to enjoying herself and her friends' company. She also takes comfort in the fact he she finally has the friends and boyfriend that she's not only needed, but deserved, and they are here for her from here on in and she can't wait to see what happens in just over an hour.

Date: Monday, December 7th, 2020

Time: 1813 FKST

Location: Stanley, Falkland Islands

Temperature: 46 Degrees Fahrenheit

"John, is it normal to be nervous like this?" Jeremy asks almost overcome with anxiety, shaking almost constantly as he paces back and forth in front of his stoic commander.

"I wouldn't know Jeremy, but I would imagine that this is normal." John replies with a satisfied chuckle to mask the fact that he hopes to feel the same way at some point in the near future.

"Very funny commander." Jeremy replies shortly as Neil rejoins the pair by the water; the sun continues to set, glistening brilliantly against the salty ocean.

"The women should be here any minute." He says standing next to John, as Jeremy continues to pace, sweat slowly building on his button up shirt, "Has he thrown up yet?"

"Only three times in the last hour." John replies quietly as Neil laughs at Jeremy's expense, though the moment is unfortunately interrupted by John's phone ringing.

Pulling it out of his pocket, he sighs, knowing that whoever is on the other end is not going to tell him something good.

"I need to take this. Good luck Jeremy, you're going to be great." He says quietly and quickly as he shakes Jeremy's hand before walking back towards the control tower, a couple football fields away.

A couple of minutes later, Elizabeth, Clara and Samantha arrive, with the latter failing to completely contain their excitement with what is about to transpire while Elizabeth remains clueless.

"Where's John?" Samantha asks, her excitement turning to concern as she realizes he's not there.

"Had to take a phone call. He'll be back at some point." Neil replies calmly and softly as Sam starts for the control tower, "He'd want you to stay here. If it was important enough for him to take, it usually means it's not good."

Sam stays put, knowing that Neil is likely to be right even though she would want to be there with him to help keep him calm, though that might be ideal given the circumstances. The group begins unpacking the Land Rover that the girls arrived in, taking out several blankets and picnic baskets containing everything from selections of cheese to lunch sandwiches. Nothing hot or heavy, no one would be able to stomach a full meal at this point.

After sitting down next to his girlfriend, Jeremy has managed to calm down slightly though it's clear to everyone except Elizabeth that the prospect of proposing is keeping his mind and emotions wandering aimlessly. They have to resist the urge to chuckle while Elizabeth slowly begins to realize that something is up, though she's still not sure what.

"Everything okay sweetheart? You're shaking." She finally says after taking a few minutes to analyze the situation; John still has not returned from the control tower and there is no sign of Rob.

"Yeah... I'm fine..." He replies with a smile, his attention snapping back to him as he turns to face his girlfriend, quickly realizing that he's not going to get a much better moment than now to ask her.

The other squad members begin taking out their phones to secretly snap pictures of the special moment.

"Elizabeth... can I ask you something?" Jeremy finally says quietly, after a few tense moments; the squad members can't hide their smiles though with her gaze fixed on her boyfriend, Elizabeth doesn't notice.

"What is it sweetie?" Elizabeth says, half expecting something bad to happen in the next few seconds even though Jeremy hadn't indicated anything like that.

Jeremy takes a deep breath, briefly glancing down at the blanket beneath them before looking back into Elizabeth's eyes.

"With everything going on I know it may not be the best time, but...but..." Jeremy begins before hesitating and chuckling trying to alleviate some of the tension building up inside him and the other squad members.

His hand is now resting inside his pants pocket, on top of the small black box containing the ring he picked out just for this moment. John's continued absence is quickly becoming a distant thought in everyone's mind.

"But what?" Elizabeth says, finally catching on to what is happening and trying to ease Jeremy through it; a wide smile is permanently affixed on her face.

Jeremy takes another breath, realizing that if he doesn't he'll likely pass out at any moment, before finally asking what he's been so desperately trying to ask.

"Elizabeth Foster... Liza... Will you marry me?" Jeremy asks softly, gulping and gasping as he does, unable to contain his emotions any longer as he pulls the small black box out of his pocket and reveals the ring inside.

Elizabeth's heart jumps into her throat, briefly jumping to her feet and turning once before sitting back down and falling into Jeremy's free arm as tears of joy stream down her cheeks. She keeps nodding, almost uncontrollably before finally speaking again.

"Yes... yes... yes..." She repeats continually, the word barely audible to everyone except Jeremy, who can hear it loud and clear.

Neil, Clara and Samantha have already taken at least a hundred pictures between them and the count continues to increase as Jeremy takes the ring out of the small box. He's shaking, Elizabeth is shaking, which makes the process of putting the ring on the correct finger incredibly humorous for those who witness and experience it. Finally, the ring is in its place, on Elizabeth's left ring finger as a mountain of hugs arrive from the three other squad members. Yet, there's still no sign of Commander John Hildebrand and his absence is becoming conspicuous just as quickly as it became an afterthought.

Chapter Thirteen

Date: Monday, December 7th, 2020

Time: 1830 FKST

Location: Stanley, Falkland Islands

Temperature: 46 Degrees Fahrenheit

"How long do we have before this completely kicks off?" John asks pouring over the satellite photos on the table in front of him.

"Five days to a week at most." Rob replies working the phones with other intelligence gathering staff as the pace reaches a fever pitch.

"Alright, it's a two-hour flight to Buenos Aires, an hour to meet with the Argentine Prime Minister and then two hours back, that writes off the whole day tomorrow. Leaving us four days to deal with the situation." John continues doing the math in his head as he begins to realize just how thinly the squadron is stretched at the moment.

"Four days to reposition everything we have in case a rescue and bomb defusal operation needs to take place in the middle of Hong Kong. That's simply not possible." Rob says, double checking the map in front of them before speaking.

"There's only one way this gets done Rob and we both know what it is." John replies solemnly wishing that the only option, wasn't.

"As much as I don't like it, you've all trained for it and all of you are ready for it." Rob says sighing as he hangs up the phone and turns to his commander who is continuing to stare at the pictures in front of him.

"Not all of us Rob. Not all of us." He replies simply as the staff around them realize the weight of what is going to have to happen.

John then turns for the door, to deliver the unwelcome news to his squad mates; wishing that it didn't have to be delivered now. Rob looks on, knowing that five young men and women are going to have to go on a suicide mission to keep stolen nuclear weapons from leveling Hong Kong. John pauses after exiting the control tower, needing a moment to collect his thoughts and decide how he's going to tell his friends about the upcoming mission. They've had one tragedy occur already and now he is about to ruin the largest moment of happiness, many of them have ever had. The world is forcing his hand and he hates, no, he despises it; but at the moment, there is nothing the young commander can do about it.

As he begins walking over to the spot where is friends are located, he catches sight of them celebrating and embracing, forcing the uneasy feeling in his stomach to grow. He doesn't want to take this away from them, not now when it's quite possibly the only joyous feeling they have. The entire time this thought is present in his mind, he continues walking, eventually reaching his friends.

"John, he asked! He finally...asked..." Elizabeth starts joyously upon seeing him, but her tone trails off as she, almost, hugs him, finally noticing his expression.

"John, what's the matter?" Jeremy asks as the mood grows quickly grim and the five young adults gather around the still silent commander.

"John? Sweetheart?" Sam says approaching slowly and gently placing her hand on John's shoulder; he instinctively rests his left hand on hers as he stares blankly at the ground.

"A few minutes ago, the Russian President called to inform us that terrorists have stolen a warhead from a missile silo in Ukraine...

The Russian Government has received demands from the terrorists to give Iran the bomb or they will set the warhead off... in Hong Kong." John says, clearly struggling with the words as he fights the urge to keep them to himself.

"How long do we have?" Clara asks softly, despite not wanting to be the first one to speak.

"Till the end of Saturday." John replies not wanting to say anything more despite expecting questions.

The squadron takes a moment to comprehend what they've just been told.

"Have the Chinese been told?" Neil finally asks realizing just how big the powder keg is.

"As we speak, meaning we'll see it on CNN International within the hour." John replies finally snapping out of his daze and wiping the sweat off his forehead with his still free, bandaged, right hand.

"That's sure to keep the panic to a minimum." Jeremy says sarcastically as the group instinctively starts walking towards the control tower, even though there's nothing they can do until tomorrow.

"It actually might. The Russians seem to think that the Chinese are going to force as many people out of Hong Kong as possible and then quarantine the city." John replies remembering the earlier conversation.

"Is that even possible?" Samantha asks, barely keeping pace with her boyfriend as she hangs on to his arm.

"It'll be a public relations disaster for the Chinese but yes, it's theoretically possible." John replies frankly as the group reaches the control tower.

After making this latest remark, John turns on the spot and wraps his arms around both Jeremy and Elizabeth, catching both of them off guard and nearly choking them. Eventually they wrap their arms around him and sigh as the others stand there in uncomfortable silence.

"I am so happy for the two of you and I am so sorry that I had to ruin today for you." He says softly, tears flowing from his eyes.

"It's okay John. Really. It's okay." Elizabeth says completely understanding that even though the situation wasn't John's fault, he's going to feel as though it is no matter what they say.

"Congratulations. I am so happy for both of you, I really am." John continues as the three of them touch heads and continue to pause for a moment, clinging to the last moments of happiness before having to go back to work.

"We know." Jeremy says smiling and patting John on the back, placing his left arm tightly around his fiancé's waist.

John chuckles, getting Elizabeth and Jeremy to do the same as they finally and gently end the embrace before the entire squadron enters the control tower. Sam takes John's hand as the pace quickens, smiling as he glances at her and allows himself to smirk slightly.

Date: Monday, December 7th, 2020

Time: 1909 FKST

Location: Stanley, Falkland Islands

Temperature: 45 Degrees Fahrenheit

“Let’s run through the next five days one more time.” John says walking around the planning table; normally his statement would annoy everyone in the room, however, everyone is determined to get this plan right.

“Tomorrow, after the Georgia’s arrival and the funeral; we’ll fly to Buenos Aires to meet with the Argentine President.” Elizabeth starts, almost immediately after John finishes his sentence.

“Wednesday, we fly to Midway base to rearm and rest up before taking our private jet to Hong Kong on Thursday.” Neil continues the thought as John continues going around the room.

“That leaves us Friday and Saturday to find the bomb and defuse it.” Clara continues as Jeremy returns to the table with Rob after meeting with the Chinese and Russian leadership via conference call.

“Latest intel suggests that the bomb is going to be placed in the city's financial district; we’ll pick up radiation detectors at Midway Base.” Jeremy states as Samantha begins to feel slightly left out before Elizabeth places a reassuring hand on her shoulder.

“The markets will crash when the news breaks so the financial effects will outweigh the physical. However, if we don’t stop the bomb then neither will ever recover.” Elizabeth continues as John keeps his thoughts to himself.

“What resistance should we expect?” John asks breaking his silence.

“Thirty guys at most, all are former Russian military and KGB wanting to see the world burn. The typical Russian bad guys.” Neil says, the condescension in his voice, blatantly apparent.

“Either way, I want as much information as we can get on these men. Who they’ve slept with? What their favorite ice cream flavor is? You get the picture.” John continues picking up the pace of the conversation.

“Roger that commander.” Jeremy replies sending the intelligence gathering team into a frenzy in order complete their commanders order.

“Well, the world is either going to burn in five days or live to see the sixth and we all know which one I would rather have happen.” John says commandingly after a few moments of processing the information, hitting the table with his fist before he speaks.

“Nothing to it commander?” Jeremy says with a smirk, knowing that they need every ounce of morale they can get right now.

“Right, nothing to it.” John replies exiting the room swiftly as everyone in the room looks on, mostly with looks of admiration, though Sam looks on in confusion, wondering where her boyfriend is going.

She motions back to the other members of the squadron, wondering if she should follow him or not; finally receiving a response from Elizabeth telling her to go after John. Instantly, she runs out of the room in an effort to catch up to him, all the while he is walking with purpose. Out of breath, she catches him as he reaches the halfway point between the control tower and the hanger. He stops when she touches his arm and takes a deep breath before allowing them to embrace, still not entirely used to having someone to share a moment like this with.

“Nothing to it?” Sam asks quietly, not even trying to hide the concern in her voice, “This doesn’t sound like nothing, John.”

"It's not... but we don't have a choice in the matter." John replies barely able to look his girlfriend in the eye, the memories of those lost flooding back into the forefront of his mind.

"Is this the first time?" Sam asks, still trying to get a decent view of her boyfriend's eyes but he's fighting her on it.

"Yes." He replies simply, his emotions overflowing but still desperately keeping them internal, not wanting to scare Sam more than she already is.

"John, please... I don't want to lose you." Sam says, tears coming to her eyes, the happiness of the earlier engagement becoming a distant memory.

"You won't, Sam, you won't." John replies after taking a moment to hold his girlfriend closer to him, comforting her as much as she is his comforting him right now.

"Is that a promise?" She asks, wanting a guarantee, something she knows to be true and unbreakable.

John sighs, he knows he can't promise her anything right now, including his own safety on this mission.

"Here... come with me." He says taking his concerned girlfriend by the hand and leading her towards the hanger.

Only a couple of maintenance personnel are around, and they don't pay the couple any mind; some of them have seen John in this mood before. A pre-mission ritual he's repeated before every single planned mission from the first training one to the mission to destroy the Admiral Kuznetsov. A solemn and solitary ritual that he is finally allowing himself to share with someone else and with someone who has meant so much to him for so long.

They finally reach John's plane, which has just been refueled and is now peacefully resting before it's next flight. John gently releases Sam's hand and places his own on the side of the fuselage just below the cockpit, slowly examining the aging warbird.

"This plane has gotten me to and from plenty of battles, having fought in many of them herself. In all that time however, through all that loss and triumph, she's never let me down." John starts softly, walking gently down the fuselage and along the leading edge of the left wing as Sam looks on, hanging on every word. "That's the connection between a plane and her pilot. An unending trust right up until the very end."

"Sounds a lot like love." Sam says, breaking her silence with the gently hanging sentence.

"It is." John chuckles, as he moves around to the trailing edge of the wing with Sam in tow, "It is a lot like love, which is why a lot of pilots give their plane a name."

"A name?" Sam asks.

"Yeah, a name. Like Memphis Belle, or Old Crow. Just to name a couple."

"Did you name yours?"

"I did."

The conversation being soft and fast paced only showing the connection and trust that Sam and John share. Building to something, though Sam doesn't know what.

"What did you name...her?" Sam finally asks chuckling and getting used to the fact that John referred to his plane as a female.

"Funny you should ask." John replies not even resisting the smile that is falling across his face as he moves out of the way to reveal a single, italic word just before the burner shield at the rear of the phantom.

Sam moves closer to get a better look, what she sees is both expected and catches her completely by surprise.

"*Samantha*"

"How long has that been there?" She asks, keeping her voice down as she slightly gasps for breath and allows herself to rest in John's arms.

"I put it there five months ago after my first solo flight. She... you, have brought me luck ever since." John replies rubbing Sam's back.

"You... you are... hopelessly hopeful sometimes." Sam states with a laugh, brushing her hair out of her face slightly.

John only laughs, it's not the first time he's heard that though it wasn't from Sam. It was from Elizabeth, five months ago when he hand painted Sam's name on his plane.

"I still have nightmares, they're not as bad but I still have them." Sam continues softly, trying not to dampen the mood but needing to get this off of her chest.

"I know." John states, "I still get them too, every night."

"How do you deal with them?" She asks, making sure she's comfortable in John's arms.

"You can't get rid of them. You can only live with them. Though cuddling helps a lot." He replies with a chuckle, leaning on the experience of the past few nights.

"Yeah it does." Sam says returning the chuckle, "The kissing doesn't hurt either."

"That's true." John says, bowing his head and sneaking a glance of his feet before looking back into his girlfriend's eyes, "In all honesty Sam. Time and having the right people around you helps the most. That's how I managed when you were with Richard; I still had the squadron to fall back on for support."

"But that leaves months where you had no one." Sam replies, separating from John slightly.

John bows his head again, trying to figure out how he is going to word his next sentence without overtly upsetting his girlfriend.

"Yeah, I suppose it does, but that's the past. I choose to enjoy what I have now, and I will forever be grateful for it... for you." John replies as he and Sam subconsciously step closer to one another.

"After everything you've gone through; you're still a big softy underneath that scarred exterior. I'm simply grateful to finally have someone who actually cares about me in my life... for you." Sam replies trying not to tear up as she continues to approach her boyfriend.

John smiles, barely realizing that he is doing so as Sam finally jumps back into his arms, hugging him tightly.

"You better come back you stubborn bastard, I'll kick your ass if you don't." She says, her voice muffled by his shirt.

"Roger that, Sam." He replies simply before kissing her on the forehead and returning her hug.

It's not often that John takes orders from someone else. Presidents and Dictators have been known to tremble in his presence and yet, this is different. Samantha has always managed to work her way through John's armor, put up due to years of loneliness. She's managed to get John to show a side of him that few have seen since he was a kid. She's gotten him to open up and let his guard down for once in his life and he welcomes it. As a result, her words become more a required request from a loved one than an order from an equal or superior.

The couple soon leaves the hangar; walking back towards the control tower where the rest of the squadron is waiting outside.

"Ready Commander?" Elizabeth asks shaking his hand.

"Born ready Wolf Two, but just so you know; you and your fiancé are grounded for this mission." John replies, strutting the line between sarcasm and seriousness as the group walks to the waiting Land Rovers.

"Commander... are you sure?" Jeremy asks trying to figure out if John intends on follow through on his words.

"If it helps Jeremy, consider it an order. I don't want to risk more members than I have to. Besides, we have a family to worry about now." John says as Sam takes his arm; John doesn't even turn around as he speaks as Elizabeth and Jeremy glance at each other with Neil and Clara chuckling at them, "Alright, let's pay the devil a visit and kick his ass."

John's last words perfectly capture guiding principles of the initiative. To kick in the door to hell, save people who need to be saved, when no one else will lift a finger to help them. The ultimate safety net for a world bent on destroying itself.

Chapter Fourteen

Date: Tuesday, December 8th, 2020

Time: 0700 FKST

Location: Stanley, Falkland Islands

Temperature: 48 Degrees Fahrenheit

The slowly rising sun provides the perfect silhouette for the UNS - Georgia and her six, 18-inch, 48 caliber guns as she sails a mile off the coast of Port Stanley. Flanking her are UNS - Johnston and UNS - Samuel B. Roberts; both, former Arleigh Burke class destroyers and both having the honor of being the most modern ships in the United Nations fleet. The UNS - Georgia, BBN - 01, was formerly BB - 62, USS New Jersey, until the United States sold her to the United Nations in the same arms package as the former USS Enterprise. Her three old, triple sixteen-inch gun turrets were removed along with her steam turbines and replaced with three new, dual 18-inch gun turrets and a modern nuclear reactor. All of the crew members are on the decks of their respective ships, standing at attention in respect to their fallen leader.

At the airfield, the maintenance personnel are standing in two evenly spaced rows leading out to the water. All standing at attention in their dress uniforms as the two rows make an even picture frame for the Georgia and her destroyer escorts.

Not long after the Georgia arrives on the scene, the five remaining squadron members appear in various tee shirts and jeans, joined by Rob, as they carry a small wooden boat towards the water. Samantha follows close behind, though keeping a careful distance as she never had the opportunity to get to know Vladimir before he was killed.

There's no music, no tears, as everyone looks on while the squadron gently places the small wooden boat in the water. Elizabeth, Jeremy, Clara, Neil and Rob all pull back from the scene, leaving John kneeling at the edge of the water, holding the boat against the shore as he stares at the portrait of Vladimir laying against a wreath in the center of the boat.

"See you soon, old friend." John whispers before shoving the boat out to sea and stepping back to join his squad mates.

A couple of minutes later, the tide has carried the small boat out to sea as the squadron looks on. The front turret on the Georgia takes aim before unleashing a single, 18-inch, armor piercing shell with a thunderous boom and the small boat disappears in a geyser of saltwater. The spray gently rains down on the squadron as everyone else recoils in an effort to shield themselves, though they soon come to their senses and their blood pressure returns to normal.

John takes a breath, causing a small vapor cloud in front of his face; this all happened way sooner than it should have.

"Alright, Wolf Four, Wolf Five, let's move out." He states, defiantly staring down the events that are about to unfold.

The entire squadron turns and heads for the hanger as uneasy calm falls over the airfield, soon punctuated by the sound of six screaming jet engines as John's F-4 and two SU-33s shutter into life.

Date: Tuesday, December 8th, 2020

Time: 1045hrs ART

Location: Buenos Aires, Argentina

Temperature: 73 Degrees Fahrenheit

Wolf One, Four and Five landed at Ministro Pistarini International Airport around ten minutes ago, although, the crowd that had gathered to watch is only just dispersing as the black fighter jets disappear from view. The Argentine Army is keeping their distance, not wanting to invoke the squadrons wrath despite being unaware that one of their comrades died yesterday. The local police have closed down the roads leading from the airport to Casa Rosada, the Argentine President's office; the resulting travel time being cut down from a half hour to just over fifteen minutes.

"They rolled out the red carpet for us." Clara says breaking the tension as the three squadron members exit their SUV.

John only scoffs in response as the three enter Casa Rosada and are soon escorted by one of the president's guards.

All three squadron members quickly changed back at the airport into black tee shirts, jeans, black sneakers and have their respective sidearms in holsters on their right thighs. A move that certainly has the guard escorting them on a knife's edge.

Upon arriving outside the President's office door, the guard knocks before opening it and stepping to one side, allowing the squadron to enter as he rests his hand on his sidearm.

"You're causing me a great deal of trouble Mauricio and you know I don't like it when people cause me trouble." John says sternly shaking the President's hand as the four adults sit down across from each other.

John, Clara and Neil are perfectly relaxed, a stark contrast to Mauricio's slight tepidness and perspiring skin.

"Those islands are rightfully ours commander, there is no reason for them to be un-." He begins, trying to mask he nervousness with a stern attitude but John cuts him off.

"First Mr. President, disabuse yourself of the notion that this is a negotiation among equals. Second, the last time your country went to war over those islands, it was embarrassed into overthrowing it's military government. Third, I'm in an incredibly sour mood due to the situation in Hong Kong so please take all necessary consideration when I tell you that I am in no mood to fuck around." John replies instantly seizing control of the conversation and putting the Argentine President under an increasing amount of stress.

Clara and Neil stay in the background of the conversation, allowing John to lead with his "take no shit" attitude that has endeared him to many world leaders.

"I understand commander." Mauricio replies taking a big gulp of water from a nearby glass as he continues to sweat, "Want do you need from me?"

"Me? Well if it didn't start an international crisis, I'd shoot you right now, but luckily for you I'm not going to do that. No. Instead, I am I going to tell you that those islands are off limits to all Argentinians. If you so much as flinch in their direction again, I'll be sure to send some eighteen-inch reminders via express delivery. Do I make myself perfectly clear Mr. President?" John says, his voice containing an underlying growl.

"Geez John. He's going to need to change his pants after that." Elizabeth says over the small earpiece in the squadron commanders ear; having heard every word.

“Yes, I understand commander.” Mauricio replies tepidly, his voice wavering as much as his body is; Neil and Clara masterfully hide their own impulses to start laughing.

“Excellent Mauricio, glad we could come to an understanding.” John says, brilliantly masking the sarcasm in his voice as muffled laughter bursts out over the radio.

“Yes commander.” The shaken Argentine President says as the four adults stand and exchange handshakes once more before the squad members leave the room.

As they walk out, Neil and Clara calmly pull out their sidearms and shoot the four guards standing outside the Presidential Office. All die having not fired a single shot from their own, drawn, weapons. The three squadron members calmly walk out the front door and back to the Land Rover, paying no mind to the traffic around them.

“Commander, Georgia has three contacts about sixty miles out. No sign of them being hostile.” Elizabeth calls in as John jumps into the front passenger seat while Neil takes the wheel and Clara sits behind him.

“Allow the Georgia to investigate. We’ll observe from the air since we have some extra time.” John replies calmly.

“Roger that. I’m sure that will make Captain Evans happy.” Elizabeth responds with a slight chuckle as she sends Rob to relay the message.

“Yeah it will. It’ll also send a clearer message to Mauricio.” John sighs as he tilts his head back against the seats headrest, his shoulder muscles tightening.

Date: Tuesday, December 8th, 2020

Time: 1215hrs FKST

Location: 60 Miles Northwest of Stanley, Falkland Islands

Temperature: 53 Degrees Fahrenheit

"Confirmed, three Argentine Destroyers. Bearing three-two-zero. Range is two, two, miles. All guns report ready to fire, Captain." Gunnery Officer Jenson shouts over the general quarters alarm rigging throughout the massive battleship.

The young, twenty-year-old almost jumping out of his seat with excitement, almost losing his helmet in fact.

"Roger Jenson." Captain Evans says, his thick Louisianan accent perfectly matching his booming character and frame.

While his reaction is more measured than that of his sailors, his excitement is causing him to shake slightly, yet noticeably.

"Keep the guns trained on the lead destroyer. Currently awaiting permission to fire." The Captain orders as the alarm finally falls silent, signaling that everyone is at their post.

"Roger Captain." The CIC personnel, including Jenson, respond; continuing to look at the screens in front of them.

A few tense minutes later, the Captain receives a range update from Jenson.

"Range now one nine miles Captain." His says, his voice shaking though nowhere near the excited yell it was a moment ago.

The captain acknowledges his sailors statement as he continues to view the tactical situation forming around them.

The Johnston and Samuel B. Roberts are keeping a tight formation on either side of the battleship, providing an extremely effective missile shield with their CIWS systems. The three Argentine destroyers are still maintaining their course, coming towards the squadron from just off the Georgia's port bow. No one has fired a shot, yet, and currently the Georgia would only be able to fire with her two, forward, eighteen-inch turrets.

"One seven miles, Captain." Jenson calls out and Captain Evans seizes the moment, quickly and decisively.

"Starboard twenty." He calls out and the massive ships lists as the turn is executed with the two destroyers following suit.

"Weapons Ready?" He continues.

"Ready." Jenson replies.

"Ship Ready?" Evans calls out.

"Ready." The XO returns, calling over the intercom from the bridge of the Georgia.

"Fire." Evans orders confidently.

"Fire." Jenson replies.

Mere moments later, six simultaneous and massive explosions rock the battleship back into the water as six, three thousand-pound, high explosive shells, rocket towards the lead Argentinian destroyer. A sharp whistling leaves the small ship and her crew, mere seconds to react before they... simply cease to exist. Disappearing in a cloud of water, metal and detonating high explosives.

The other two destroyers hesitate, wondering how their lead ship could disappear without any warning of a shot being fired: a gruesome advantage of using unguided shells rather than missiles.

The crew of the Georgia trains its main battery on the right most destroyer; range, sixteen miles.

The following seconds seem to run in slow motion as the crews of both Argentine destroyers stare in awe at the spot where their comrades vanished.

"Guns will be loaded in fifteen seconds." Jenson calls out over the intercom, as the crew on the massive battleship recovers from firing a full broadside.

A steady supply of adrenaline courses through the ship as her crew braces for the second broadside; terrified by the amount of firepower their ship possesses.

"Five... Four... Three... Two... One... Guns loaded... Weapons ready." Jenson calls out.

"Roger Jenson. Ship Ready?" Captain Evans quickly asks his XO, who winces, knowing what's coming.

"Ready, Captain." He replies, almost ducking below his console on the bridge.

Captain Evans takes a breath.

"Fire." He orders.

"Fire." Jenson repeats.

The whole ship shutters violently as six more, three thousand-pound shells head towards their targets across the Atlantic.

The sharp whistling returns to the small Argentine fleet with a second destroyer disappearing in a cloud of smoke and water seconds later.

With two destroyers lost, the captain of the third immediately orders his ship to turn around and head back to Argentina, if only it were that easy. Captain Evans and his crew are out for blood, slowly growing to like the taste as their bodies become saturated with adrenaline. They barely notice the rumbling of six jet engines overhead as John, Clara and Neil survey the destruction.

"Fuck me." Clara gasps, barely able to look at the two oil patches where the Argentine ships used to be.

Just as she glances one more time however, the final salvo of six shells, disintegrates the final Argentine destroyer. None of the six hundred sailors survived the one-sided massacre.

Both Clara and Neil glance at their commanders aircraft, knowing he won't respond yet hoping he'll say something. Something to admit he's feeling the same dread they are upon witnessing the capabilities of the Georgia's guns. To their dismay, he remains stubbornly silent.

Date: Tuesday, December 8th, 2020

Time: 1300hrs FKST

Location: Stanley, Falkland Islands

Temperature: 54 Degrees Fahrenheit

John, Clara and Neil jump down from their fighters as maintenance personnel swarm the three jets to get them rearmed and refueled before they leave for Midway.

"Our special forces squadrons have almost finished in Syria and the Kestrel will arrive tomorrow morning. It'll be staying for a week to support the Georgia." Rob says handing John a folder as Sam, Elizabeth, and Jeremy join them.

"What about the Iranians?" He asks without skipping a beat while reading through the documents he's just been handed.

"They've calmed down for now, but our intelligence agents are keeping an eye on them." Elizabeth joins in as Rob coughs.

"What's the turnaround time on our fighters?" John continues, not even minding that Elizabeth filled in while Sam struggles to keep up with the squadron.

"They'll be ready to fly by fourteen hundred hours and your flight time to midway is twelve and a half hours, cruising at one point zero five mach." Rob replies giving Elizabeth an appreciative glance.

"So we'll be landing four hours after we take off, that's definitely not going to screw up our sleep cycles." John says sarcastically as he unzips the upper part of his flight suit and lets it hang around his waist once more; there's no point in taking it off.

"I thought we were leaving tomorrow?" Sam asks curiously, just trying to follow the ever-quickening pace.

"Due to the time zone adjustment, it's better if we leave today that way we have a day to rest before going on another mission. Plus we need the extra time for our support crews to fly from here to Midway." Clara replies kindly, indicating the entire squadrons feeling that they don't mind her question at all; Sam is going to have to learn all of this anyway.

"Oh... makes sense." Sam says mulling the thought over for a moment.

"Plus it's another day you get to spend with your parents, who landed at Midway a little while ago." John adds happily, though he barely looks up from the folder in his hand.

Sam considers the thought, admitting to herself that she had forgotten her parents had been flown to Midway Base soon after she arrived in the Falkland Islands. She smiles, remembering how much she misses them and wants to see them.

"How are they adjusting?" Sam asks not even realizing that she's speaking until the sentence leaves her mouth; lost in the thought of seeing her parents.

"From what the base commander tells me, they're adjusting just fine, though it will take a while for them to get used to living on a military base." John replies, snapping Sam out of her trance without skipping a beat and handing the folder back to Rob.

"That's good to hear." She says softly.

"Alright everyone, wheels up in fifty minutes and not a moment later." John continues, ignoring the slightly confused looks of his squad mates; with his voice returning to the commanding tone that was present earlier.

"Roger that." Most of the squadron members reply before walking over to their respective aircraft; Jeremy, Sam and Elizabeth follow John to his phantom, though it seems that John expected this to happen.

"What do you need Liza?" John asks almost sternly as he begins checking his planes control surfaces and Sam gently places her hand on his back.

"Nothing commander, are you feeling alright?" Liza asks, slightly caught off guard by the suddenness of John's remarks.

"I'm feeling perfectly fine Liza, thanks for asking." He replies almost with a sigh in his voice, "Remind me to transfer my spare plane to Sam when we arrive."

"Are you comfortable with not having a spare plane John?" Jeremy asks, not questioning his leaders actions but wondering if he wants to take the risk.

"We've been flying without spare planes ever since this started. I think I'll be able to manage." He replies, his tone suggesting he knows about the earlier conversation his squad mates had.

Sam is slightly surprised though not shocked; given what's happened over the last few days.

"Sounds like a plan John, sorry for the questions." Elizabeth says affirmatively, about to walk away with Jeremy, but John responds before she leaves.

"It's okay Liza, I don't mind." He says, revealing a tired smile as she turns to face him, which allows her to be more comfortable with his softer side.

She smiles before she and Jeremy head to their respective planes, leaving John and Sam to have a private moment to themselves. The air continues to thicken as the Georgia's battlegroup regroups off the coast of Stanley with the Kestrel's battlegroup finally coming into radar range and making radio contact with Rob in the control tower.

With their naval forces taking a well-deserved shore leave in the Falkland's, the coming fight is solely going to be a ground war for the young adults. Not that it matters much to them, it's all the same hell anyway.

Chapter Fifteen

Date: Tuesday, December 8th, 2020

Time: 1830hrs SST

Location: Midway Base, Former US Minor Outlying Island, Pacific Ocean

Temperature: 30 Degrees Fahrenheit

"We really need to stop flying so far, so often." Clara says sarcastically as the squad slowly regroups on the tarmac, stretching their incredibly stiff limbs.

"We also need to stop changing time zones while we're at it." Neil says as several support personnel hand the tired pilots their leather bomber jackets.

"Here. Before you catch a cold." John says quietly to Sam, helping her put on his bomber jacket as they haven't had time to make her one.

"Thanks." Sam says on the verge of shivering before the warming effect of the coat fully takes effect.

The squadron forms up on the ground as the maintenance personnel surround the fighter jets. In the distance, a small crowd of the most recent recruits have begun to gather in the hope of catching a glimpse of the squadron they've learned so much about.

"We have just over a day for some R and R. Use it. Spend it together, spend it with your family. On Thursday, we get to work." John says calmly and tiredly..

"Roger that commander. Is dinner at the usual time?" Neil asks tiredly, glancing at his watch.

“Dinner will be at nineteen thirty hours; I hear that chef Fangio has something special planned.” John replies smiling and noticing two familiar faces in the crowd behind Neil.

“I wonder why.” Jeremy says sarcastically as he and Elizabeth chuckle slightly before kissing in front of everyone.

“So do we.” John quips getting the whole squadron to laugh as he subtly waves the familiar faces over before continuing his thought, “Alright, see you guys in an hour. Squadron dismissed.”

“Thanks John. See you in an hour.” The squadron replies in varying forms and at varying times as they head to their respective houses.

Though, not before realizing who the two familiar faces are and saying hello as they pass.

“Mom! Dad!” Sam yells excitedly, realizing who the two people approaching are as the crowd begins to disperse.

She runs from John’s side and straight into the arms of her waiting parents; excited to see them despite having done so a couple days prior. John hangs back, not wanting to ruin the perfect moment by encroaching. He unzips his flight suit, a result of overheating despite the colder temperature and revealing a grey long sleeve shirt underneath.

A messenger arrives a few seconds later with the latest intelligence on the evolving situation in Hong Kong. Half of the population has been relocated to refugee camps in China, Japan and South Korea. A general unrest has become common as more and more people make their way to the outskirts of the city, trying to clear the potential blast zone. The intelligence packet also reveals that the bomb is relatively small, though it can still level Exchange Square if placed in the right spot. The nuclear fallout, while limited, would make the whole financial district uninhabitable for at least the next hundred years. The news gives the young commander mixed feelings, in some ways things are better than he expected and in others, they're worse.

John thanks the messenger before sending him on his way and placing the small intelligence packet in the left thigh pocket of his flight suit. As he completes the task, he notices Sam's Dad waving him over as his wife and daughter proceed to catch up on the events of the last couple of days. John obliges the request, despite his tendency to ignore his own orders when it comes to resting before a mission.

"How are you holding up?" Josiah asks, echoing the same question he asked a couple of days ago and shaking John's hand as the pair step to one side.

"Apart from the tight muscles in my back, I'm doing ok." John replies simply, trying to be frank with himself and, consequently, with Sam's father.

"Carrying the weight of the world on your shoulders can do that after a while." He replies, placing a warm fatherly hand on John's shoulder as the two continue to watch the conversation between Sam and her mother.

"Well no one else would do it and someone has too." John says, mesmerized by the way Sam looks against the setting sun.

"I must confess, I wish it didn't have to be you. Now more than ever. And yet... I'm almost glad that it is." Josiah continues, the warm tone in his voice nearly warming John's body as he considers zipping his flight suit back up to block the wind.

He chuckles, flattered by Josiah's remark as Sam and Abigail continue their conversation as if they haven't seen each other in years.

"If I may, I am sorry about Vladimir, John. I know both of you were close." Josiah finally says; John almost expected his comment despite his mind wandering slightly as he wonders if now is the time.

"Thank you Mr. Adams... that means a lot." John says quietly, silently deciding that now is not the time and allowing himself a brief moment of vulnerability.

"Anytime John and be sure to take care of yourself. It doesn't take a brain surgeon to see that Sam needs you." Josiah says calmly, almost implying that he knows what John was thinking.

"With all due respect Mr. Adams, but I need her just as much." He says instinctively, his thoughts following his words as if he was being dragged along by them.

Josiah smiles and pats John on the shoulder as the women finally remember that their significant others are still around.

"John, you're going to catch a cold." Sam says as soon as she notices the flight suit draped around his waist; she hurriedly tries to remove the bomber jacket though John cuts her off.

"Sweetheart I appreciate the concern, but I'm okay." John says, helping her put it back on as she shyly leans against his chest.

Sam's parents chuckle slightly at the sight, forcing her to blush; the whole scene reminding them of how they were when they first started dating.

"How's your hand doing?" Sam asks a moment later, after catching a glimpse of the bandage still around John's right hand.

“It’s okay, feeling better.” John replies almost whispering.

“That’s good to hear.” She replies, the blushing smile only getting wider on her face, “Is it ok if my parents join us for dinner?”

“Certainly.” John says returning the smile as Sam’s parents continue to take in the whole scene, not that John or Sam immediately notice.

Eventually the four walk towards John’s base home, in order to rest for a little while and change into something drastically more comfortable.

Date: Tuesday, December 8th, 2020

Time: 1933hrs SST

Location: Midway Base, Former US Minor Outlying Island, Pacific Ocean

Temperature: 28 Degrees Fahrenheit

Elizabeth, Jeremy and Clara are seated around the squadrons usual table in the middle of the base restaurant, though calling it that is a bit of a stretch. The vertical wood paneling, darker paint, vinyl floor and country style decorations give the place more a saloon or bar vibe rather than that of a restaurant. Their civilian clothes allowing them to relax more than their flight suits ever would.

“Neil is on his way. He’s sorry for oversleeping.” Clara eventually says after getting a text message on her phone; he had laid down for a quick nap.

"Can't say I blame him; we've all been operating on compromised sleep schedules lately." Elizabeth says calmly, as she begins to wonder where John, Sam and Sam's parents are.

"Ain't that the truth, I'm surprised John hasn't arrived yet. He's usually very prompt." Jeremy says sensing what his fiancé is thinking.

Elizabeth and Clara chuckle at his remark though his point is perfectly valid given what their commander has become known for over the last few months. Neil arrives a couple of minutes later and his girlfriend instantly falls into his arms as soon as he sits down. Mild exhaustion over taking her body as it did with Neil an hour earlier. Ten minutes after Neil's arrival, John, Sam, Josiah and Abigail finally arrive at the restaurant. All of them are tired but in good spirits as they sit down at the table with their squadron mates.

"Sorry for being late, we lost track of time." Samantha says, seemingly not wanting to give away too much and luckily the squadron is too tired to follow up.

John has managed to change into a heavy black sweatshirt, jeans and black sneakers, while Sam is wearing the long sleeve black shirt, dark jeans and the black bootie heels that she bought in the Falkland Islands.

A waiter soon arrives, interrupting the light conversation that had developed and wearing the typical initiative combat uniform as are many of personnel present in the restaurant. Everyone gets some form of alcoholic beverage, though also ordering a water or soda.

"Are you sure you should be having that?" Clara jokes with Elizabeth as she takes a sip from a bottle of beer in front of her.

“It’s fine for now.” Elizabeth says sarcastically and laughing as she puts the bottle back on the table; more base personnel come off shift and begin filling the establishment.

Jeremy chuckles at this slight exchange though as the conversation wears on, it’s abundantly clear that the entire squadron is in desperate need of a good night's sleep. Exhaustion is forcing everyone, except Sam’s parents, to act slightly drunk despite barely making their way through their beverages by the time the waiter returns to take their orders.

“The usual commander?” The waiter asks confidently, alluding to John’s usual order of tomato soup and grilled cheese, while snapping him out of a slight daze caused by the Mike’s Hard Lemonade in front of him.

“Yes, thank you ensign.” John replies with a slight smile, handing him the menu as Sam leans back against him.

“Tired?” She asks quietly.

“Yeah, a bit.” He reluctantly admits, almost annoyed that his seemingly superhuman endurance has finally started to fail him.

“Want to go to bed early tonight?” She asks, placing John’s right arm around her chest.

“That’s up to you.” John says looking down at his girlfriend and squeezing her comfortably with his arm.

Sam smiles, hugging John’s arm before holding his hand as the two of them return to the group conversation about how John threatened the Argentine President into changing his pants. Both of them are blissfully unaware that their brief, albeit, cute exchange was noticed by Josiah. They also fail to notice the tired smile that had formed across his face upon seeing the scene as memories of his youth begin flashing through his mind.

“So what’s it like meeting with world leaders?” Abigail asks curiously, her question getting the squadron to think as none of them gave it much thought.

“Well, it usually depends on what they’ve been doing.” Elizabeth starts after John invites her to speak; wanting to hear what his squad mates have to say, “If they’ve been cooperating and keeping in line then we’re usually pretty relaxed with them.”

“Meaning Elizabeth usually takes the lead.” Neil chimes in as the other squad members nod in agreement.

“Exactly.” Elizabeth continues, briefly pointing in Neil’s direction, “However, if they’ve been causing trouble, John takes the lead.”

“Which usually causes the leader to shit themselves.” John adds before taking another sip from the Mike’s Hard Lemonade.

“With good reason.” Clara says, taking over for Elizabeth, “Word has gotten around that if they don’t behave, they have a habit of dying.”

“Those are certainly high stakes.” Abigail says with a chuckle, taking a sip from the glass of red wine in front of her to mask her own intimidation at what the squadron is capable of.

“They certainly are, but there’s no one else we’d trust with them ma’am.” The waiter says returning with everyone’s order, causing everyone to briefly celebrate.

As the food is being handed out, the restaurant begins to liven up as yet more soldiers and personnel arrive for their evening meals. All of whom want to at least catch a glimpse of their leaders before settling down at a table or the bar. The whole scene jogs John's memory and he places his hand in his pocket, remembering that there is something he needs to give Sam. Pulling out a small coin, only about an inch and a half in diameter, he places it to his right hand and whispers in Sam's ear.

"There's something I want you to have."

"What is it?" She asks curiously as John takes Sam's left hand with his right, which is still cradled around her chest, and carefully hands her the coin.

"It's the squadrons challenge coin. Only members of wolf squadron have it, making it exceptionally rare, so please don't lose it." John replies, softly chuckling as Sam turns the antiqued bronze coin over in her hand.

On one face is the wolf's head symbol present on all of the squadrons planes with the words "Wolf Squadron" embellished underneath. On the other is a simple phrase, " *When No One Else Would*". A phrase that nearly shakes Sam to her core as she realizes the weight those words carry. Her sudden dose of fear is quickly quelled however, as she also realizes the promise John is making to her by giving her his own, personal coin.

"Thank you John." She says softly kissing him on the cheek.

"You're welcome Sam." He replies just as softly before gently returning the kiss to Sam's cheek.

Once again the slight exchange doesn't go unnoticed with both the waiter and Josiah seeing gesture as Sam and John begin eating, still in each other's arms.

"It seems we have a challenge ladies and gentlemen." The waiter calls out causing a huge cheer to move through the bar as the squadron laughs and Sam looks around, slightly confused.

One by one, everyone in the bar presents their respective challenge coin, with most people presenting a coin with the seal of the initiative on both sides, including Josiah and Abigail. The other members of the squadron present their coins as Sam looks down at the one in her hand before looking back into John's eyes.

"Looks like the first round is on me ensign." John finally says with a laugh and raising his bottle of Mike's Hard Lemonade before finishing it off as the entire restaurant erupts in a massive cheer.

Someone starts the jukebox and a lively atmosphere fills the small space. Drinks are shared, stories are told, and dances are performed. Everyone is having a great time, including John, though he is losing his battle with exhaustion.

"I'm going to step outside. I'll be back in a minute." He says to Sam around eight thirty at night; he's hoping the cold air will help keep him awake.

Sam asks him if she should come with him, but he politely says no; wanting her to enjoy the party and stay warm for the time being. She reluctantly agrees and let's go of John's arm as he heads outside into the bitterly cold air. His hope of the air helping him wake up was well founded as it instantly snaps him awake as he quickly checks his phone for any updates from Rob. Much to his surprise, the only update that Rob has sent is a single text saying, "All is quiet for now, enjoy the night." He chuckles before putting his phone back in his pocket and looking out over the moonlight base, placing his cold hands in the pockets of his sweatshirt with the sleeves riding up his palms slightly.

"You've never liked crowds." A familiar, father like voice says from the door of the restaurant.

"True, though this time I think I just needed some air." John replies turning to face Josiah as he joins him by the porch railing.

"We all do from time to time." Josiah returns, taking in the same sight John is as waves continue to crash against the shore, "It seems like there is something eating away at you, John."

John chuckles, trying to buy time for his mind to formulate a semi coherent thought.

"The funny thing is, we don't have a psychiatrist on staff. If we did, the whole squadron would be grounded for months. Yet, you're able to read me like a book." John says chuckling.

Josiah continues to listen carefully as John continues to let his thoughts spill out, "No wonder it was so easy for Sam to read what I'm feeling."

"In fairness, I think I've learned it from her rather than the other way around." Josiah says as John pauses to collect his thoughts, "Ask me what you want to ask me John." He finishes softly causing John to softly gasp for breath.

"Are you sure it's not too soon?" John asks, his voice continuing to choke up as he glances away for a moment and an unnoticed tear falls down his cheek.

Josiah chuckles.

"John, you've been around her for the last eleven years and having sleepovers for the last six; too soon would have been five years ago." He says patting John gently on the shoulder who finally let's himself smile slightly as Josiah continues “Honestly John, it’s surprising you didn’t ask sooner.”

“It just never felt like the right time.” He says instinctively.

“It never is.” Josiah replies, knowing all too well the range of emotions John is going through right now.

“I promise I’ll take care of her.” He says holding out his right hand, running on pure instinct as his mind fails to keep up.

“I know you will.” Josiah says, a warm smile falling across his face as he shakes John’s hand firmly before asking, "You already have a ring don't you?"

"Only for the last three years."

Josiah smiles: he figured as much given how heartbroken John seemed to be when Sam started dating Richard two years ago. While not under the best of circumstances, he finds it reassuring that his daughter and John are finally able to be together.

The pair re-enter the restaurant after spending a few more minutes outside in silence, taking in the cold air and ocean tide. Inside they find that the party's just beginning despite most of the squadron having finished their meals and the empty plates are slowly being gathered from in front of them. Josiah sits back down next to his wife, giving her a slight nod when she glances in his direction; she only replies with a sigh and a grateful smile. Sam falls back into John’s arms when he sits down, blissfully unaware of the conversation he had with her father, having been distracted by Elizabeth and Jeremy discussing names for their child.

It doesn’t take long for the rowdy atmosphere to turn to an alcohol induced sing along as someone, no one quite knows who, puts a quarter in the jukebox at the end of the bar. The first song played is Elton John's, Saturday Night is Alright for Fighting and absolutely everyone joins in, including the bartender.

Date: Tuesday, December 8th, 2020

Time: 2145hrs SST

Location: Midway Base, Former US Minor Outlying Island, Pacific Ocean

Temperature: 26 Degrees Fahrenheit

John and Sam finally return to John's on base home; a simple, thousand square foot affair. Sam is completely and totally drunk, stumbling from side to side and giggling constantly, forcing John to carry her out of fear of her falling and hurting herself; not that he minds. He takes her back to the bedroom, lays her down gently on the queen-sized bed and helps her take off her shoes while handing her the pajamas she brought with her from the Falklands.

"Do you want to make out?' She asks, still giggling constantly as both of them struggle to get changed, though for vastly different reasons.

"Not when you're drunk sweetie, okay? We both need to rest." John replies softly, knowing the emotional swings Sam can go through when she's drunk.

"You sure?" She persists cutely, rubbing his back gently after she finishes changing.

"I'm sure." He replies finally laying down, smiling as he pulls the comforter over both of them and cradles Sam gently in his arms.

"Okay." She says after yawning, continuing to smile before sharing a long tender kiss with John that neither one of them seem to want to end.

Apart from the kissing and sleeping in the same bed, it's a scene vaguely similar to those of the last six years, with John realizing exactly what Sam's father meant during their earlier conversation. It's almost as though this was meant to be and was always going to be, regardless of the circumstances. He finds comfort in this thought as the two of them share a second kiss before drifting off to sleep like a raft on the ocean.

Chapter Sixteen

Date: Wednesday, December 9th, 2020

Time: 0715hrs SST

Location: Midway Base, Former US Minor Outlying Island, Pacific Ocean

Temperature: 28 Degrees Fahrenheit

Elizabeth and Clara begin making breakfast at Elizabeth and Jeremy's base home as their respective significant others finish cleaning themselves up from their early morning runs. There's been no sign or communication from Samantha or John, though the squadron decides not to bother them; mainly out of a longing for John to rest.

"How are the eggs coming?" Elizabeth asks as four more pieces of toast pop out of the toaster; only lightly toasted as that's what the squadron prefers.

"Almost done. Hope the boys get down here soon or they're going to get cold." Clara replies, smiling as she tends to the scrambled eggs.

"Or there will be more for us." Elizabeth interjects, getting both of them to chuckle; she's starting to feel the effects of being pregnant.

Neil is the first to come downstairs, having finally gotten dressed after catching a quick shower in Jeremy and Elizabeth's spare bathroom. After hugging his girlfriend, he begins setting the kitchen island for six with dutiful ease. Jeremy finally comes down a short while later, just in time to share a kiss with his fiancé and starts pouring orange juice in the six glasses that Neil set out. The eggs are now finished and being plated by Clara when there is finally a knock on the door and John enters with Sam following close behind. Everyone is wearing various forms of tee shirts and jeans in an effort to enjoy their brief time off.

“Finally decided to show up.” Neil jokes, shaking his commanders hand as everyone gathers around, taking a seat behind each place setting.

“It’s not often I get to enjoy more than four hours of sleep.” John quips, pulling a chair out so Sam can sit down before sitting down himself.

“Ain’t that the truth.” Elizabeth jokingly scoffs, knowing how hard it is to get John to even sleep for those four hours.

After this remark, Sam leans against John’s chest, wanting to laugh at Elizabeth’s remark though her mouth is already full of scrambled eggs, forcing her to settle for a wide smile. This short moment is interrupted when John’s phone, with the full weight of ironic timing, buzzes with a message from Rob; asking him to check in at the intelligence center immediately for an update on the Hong Kong situation. The entire squadron sighs upon hearing the news, though they eventually switch to looks of understanding as he kisses Sam on the forehead before walking out the front door.

“He never gets a complete break does he.” Sam says quietly, still glancing slightly at the door.

“Unfortunately. While we joke about the lack of sleep, when John’s phone rings it’s usually for a good reason.” Jeremy says, putting down his glass of orange juice, having just finished taking a sip.

“I’m guessing the world really doesn’t care about giving him a break.” Sam says softly, knowing what she signed up for but unable to help herself.

"No they don't." Clara says, a tang of dread in her voice, "We're lucky that he takes most of the heat though. While John might be tired, he tries to make sure we get plenty of sleep just in case things escalate."

"Amen to that." Neil adds, as his girlfriend takes a drink from her glass.

Sam pauses, finally realizing the full extent of the weight that is on her boyfriend's shoulders, even when compared to the rest of the squadron.

"That's why we're all glad you're here Sam. John needed you." Elizabeth says kindly, snapping Sam out of her brief daze and getting her to smile; she already knew as much.

Date: Wednesday, December 9th, 2020

Time: 0730hrs SST

Location: Midway Base, Former US Minor Outlying Island, Pacific Ocean

Temperature: 29 Degrees Fahrenheit

"This had better be good Rob. I was in the middle of breakfast, which is not something I get to enjoy too often." John snaps upon entering the intelligence center while Rob stands patiently on the screen at the far end of the room as a map of Hong Kong appears on the digital table in the middle of the room.

The intelligence staff briefly pauses upon hearing this remark before returning to work, not wanting to be next in their commanders crosshairs.

"My apologies commander. If I could have waited, I would have." Rob replies after sighing in disappointment, "The evacuation of the financial district will be complete in the next few hours. There was a slight delay as pro-democracy protests blocked some of the evacuation routes."

"Casualties?" John asks looking down at the table as the locations in question are marked with red circles.

"No deaths, only minor injuries ranging from bruises to a broken arm. Thankfully, resistance was minimal, especially when compared to last year's protests." Rob replies directly, his earlier hesitation becoming a distant memory.

"What about the Truman and Ford battle groups? I haven't heard anything from them in a while." John continues, looking at the bigger picture.

"They're keeping their distance for now, but the United States has offered their assistance should the Chinese want it. The North Korean government is also holding back for the time being. For the moment all is quiet and we can focus on Hong Kong." Rob replies giving John only the necessary information.

"I guess Kim doesn't want to be blamed for the actions of rogue Russian agents." John chuckles as a red perimeter, with a mile radius, appears around Exchange Square, "Think it's far enough?"

"Due to the buildings, terrain and harbor, structural damage will be kept to a minimum. However, the projected fall out is expected to spread five miles in all directions, effectively cutting the city in half." Rob replies as Pops appears behind him with a coffee mug in his hand.

“Something isn’t adding up.” John says quietly to himself, “Usually terrorists go for maximum damage and casualties, but with the evacuation proceeding as planned all they’re going to succeed in doing is causing a brief, albeit, bad recession.”

Rob gives John the time to think as he continues to mull things over, trying to see the terrorists endgame.

“Plus with the city evacuated, surely we would have picked up some sign of them by now... Rob?” John finally asks, seemingly on to something.

“Yes commander?” Rob says, curious as to what John is thinking.

“What did you say the North Koreans were doing?” John asks, switching the map on the table from Hong Kong to Pyongyang.

“They’re holding back, keeping quiet for the most part. Why?” Rob replies, now nervously following his commanders line of thinking.

John thinks, scanning the most recent satellite images of the North Korean capital city for anything that might confirm what he is thinking, though he continues to hope that he’s wrong.

“Fucking pieces of shit.” John says quietly to himself, before continuing for all to hear, “The attack isn’t directed at Hong Kong.”

“What do you mean commander?” Pops says, finally announcing his presence, not that John cares very much right now.

“Neil said that the Russians who stole the warhead were former KGB and Russian Military. They’re not going after China; they’re going after the United States.” John replies, zooming in on a known missile launch site located in the mountains to the south of the coastal town of Wonsan.

“Son of a bitch.” Pops says, nearly spitting out his coffee, as it finally begins to dawn on everyone that the core mission has massively changed.

“Rob.” John says directly, knowing how quickly they are going to have to move in order to keep the situation under control, “How much does this change our timeline?”

‘Thankfully it doesn’t, but it certainly changes the risks involved.” Rob says, doing his best to quickly get over the shock of this most recent revelation.

“Of course it does, we just went from having to face thirty guys to the entire North Korean army.” John says solemnly, wiping his hair out of his face.

An uncomfortable hush falls over the room as John walks the razor thin line between reluctant acceptance and absolute, unbridled rage. He places his left elbow on the table and rests his head in his left hand as he runs through as many scenarios as possible; most of them not turning out well and giving him a headache.

“Alright, I want two battle plans, one for a ground assault and one for an air assault. I’ll be back in one hour for an update.” John finally says quietly, an underlying growl accompanying the “fed-up” tone of his voice.

“Roger that commander.” Rob replies, before John practically storms out of the room, having to heavily resist the urge to put his fist through someone’s head.

“Poor kid.” Pops says quietly to Rob as the room swiftly begins working on the two plans as ordered by their commander, “Things are finally slipping through the cracks.”

“He’s barely holding the world together and it doesn’t want to be held.” Rob replies, as he too begins working on the two plans: collaborating with many of the staff at Midway base from the Kestrel’s CIC.

Pops remains silent after this remark, having nothing further to add despite wishing there was a way he could help more.

Date: Wednesday, December 9th, 2020

Time: 0755hrs SST

Location: Midway Base, Former US Minor Outlying Island, Pacific Ocean

Temperature: 29 Degrees Fahrenheit

Sam approaches patiently as John looks out over the water with the sun continuing to rise over the ocean. The rest of the squadron is a few feet behind her; all having just heard the news regarding the change in mission. Sam announces her presence by placing her left hand gently on John’s back, simultaneously not wanting him to go on this mission but knowing there is no way to stop him.

“Sorry, I just needed a minute.” John says softly upon feeling Sam’s gentle touch.

“I know.” She says quietly, wrapping her left arm around her boyfriend and looking out over the water.

“I’m not going to hide it. Whichever option we go with is likely to be a suicide mission.” He chuckles, having an easier time holding back his emotions than he did earlier.

“I know.” She replies simply, resting her head on his shoulder.

John remains silent, not entirely knowing what to say next. Luckily Sam continues speaking, removing that small weight from his shoulders.

"I know you're coming back. Don't ask me how I know, but I know you're coming back. You've been through too much to die now; you still have a whole life to live." She says warmly, as if she's draping thick blanket over his cold, worn out body.

"I appreciate the confidence sweetie." John says quietly, kissing his girlfriend on the head after he speaks.

"You're welcome." She replies with a wide smile falling across her face as they look into each other's eyes before sharing a short kiss.

Finally turning around, John faces his squad mates, all of whom are happily enjoying the scene and brimming with confidence. All of them are ready for a fight, almost too ready in the case of Jeremy and Elizabeth.

"Looks like we have work to do commander." Elizabeth states confidently, seemingly forgetting the fact that her and her fiancé are grounded from this mission.

"That we do Elizabeth. I want you and Jeremy in the intelligence center; they're going to need all the help they can get over the next half hour. Neil and Clara, you're with me, we need to get in some range time." Their commander replies, his confidence finally returning to his voice.

"Roger that commander." Neil replies before he and Clara run off, heading for the armory as Jeremy and Elizabeth head for the Intelligence Center.

"Where should I go?" Sam asks curiously.

"Spend some time with your parents. They should have the next two days off from their initiation and I have a feeling that they would like to spend some time with you. We'll begin your official training when I get back from this mission." John replies still smiling as he looks down at his girlfriend.

"Alright." She says, ever so slightly disappointed before asking, "Is there any chance we could join you at the range?"

"It has been a while hasn't it?" He replies sighing, knowing how much Sam enjoyed going to the range with him in the past.

"Yeah... it has..." She says, her tone trying even harder to convince John to say yes.

"Alright, give me a call around nine o'clock and we'll get you on the range." John relents deciding to allow himself some level of enjoyment on this workday.

"You're the best John." Sam says kissing him on the lips before running off towards her parents on base house as John looks on.

"I try." He says, briefly looking on before heading over to the armory.

Date: Wednesday, December 9th, 2020

Time: 0845hrs SST

Location: Midway Base, Former US Minor Outlying Island, Pacific Ocean

Temperature: 31 Degrees Fahrenheit

"Alright, time's up." John says announcing his presence as he struts into the Intelligence Center, rifle slung in front of him.

Neil and Clara follow behind with their own weapons; Neil holding an M27 IAR while his girlfriend is holding a modernized M4 assault rifle. Both firearms take the same ammunition as well as the same magazine; a hallmark of the majority of the initiatives weapons other than those used by John himself.

It's worth noting that no one bats an eyelid upon seeing the extra firepower, given that everyone has their own sidearms on their upper thighs.

"We had to completely right off the air strike option commander." Elizabeth starts as Rob is taking a drink, "It simply wasn't practical when the resources needed to pull it off were compared to those that are currently available."

"Not to mention it's not guaranteed to completely remove the threat thanks to the terrain." Jeremy adds as Rob finally finishes his drink and composes himself on screen.

"Meaning we have to move forward with the ground assault, which, ironically, starts with a HALO jump from forty thousand feet." Rob begins as he disappears from the screen and a digital map of the missile base takes his place.

As Rob takes the squadron through the mission, the map updates in real time, illustrating exactly what he is saying.

"John, Neil and Clara will start from one of our C-17 transport aircraft, taking off at eighteen hundred hours exactly on the evening of the 11th. With a nine-hour flight time, this will put you over the target at twenty-three hundred hours local time. Jumping from forty thousand feet, you will fall for approximately three and a half minutes before deploying your parachutes at two thousand feet. Boots on the ground will occur at twenty-three zero seven hours local time." Rob starts before catching his breath as everyone remains silent, staring at the screen.

"When you land, you will regroup behind this abandoned building on the southern side of the complex. From our current intel, this area is only patrolled in day light and is unimportant to the North Koreans." Rob continues, a large warehouse highlighting itself in bright blue on the map as he continues at a brisk pace, "Once you regroup, the assault on the base will begin at twenty-three ten hours. Estimated strength varies at this point but our best estimate puts the number of North Korean and Russian soldiers at one hundred. It is unlikely you'll run into any armored resistance."

Rob takes another drink from the water bottle in front of him; the brief pause giving him a chance to rest his voice and catch his breath. Though, he soon has to continue before the silence in the room becomes uncomfortable.

"We believe that the warhead is stored in this building here."

A small nondescript building illuminates in blue on the eastern side of the base.

"This will be confirmed by the radiation detectors currently being integrated into your eye protection's augmented displays. Once the warhead is found, you will need to remove the nuclear detonator before attaching your own explosives and retreating to a safe distance. Here."

A spot behind a nearby building appears as a blue dot.

"Even though we are destroying the warhead, there won't be any nuclear fallout since the detonator will be removed. Time estimates range from twenty to forty minutes for this stage of the mission."

Everyone runs through the math in their heads working out that it will likely be anywhere from thirty to ten minutes to midnight local time by the time the warhead blows.

"After the detonation, you will make your way to the nearby river where a V-22 Osprey, based out of Japan, will be waiting for you. They will only take off once the warhead is destroyed. Special Forces Team Three will be on board in case you run into any resistance. Total mission time from drop off to pick up will be no more than three and a half hours." Rob finishes, taking another drink to soothe his now dry throat.

"What's the anti-air threat?" John asks.

"Minimal. Best we can tell is you'll be dealing with tripod mounted PKM's." Jeremy says uncrossing his arms and turning to face his commander.

"Aftermath?" John continues, the map returning to the table and Rob returning to the screen.

"North Korea could think the United States launched a covert operation against the base, which will be considered an act of war. Anything we say will be considered an effort to cover up what the North Koreans think actually happened." Elizabeth says giving her boyfriend and Rob a longer break than they expected.

"Meaning, we have to make the whole thing look like an accident or the act of defectors." John muses, now staring at the briefing table with his arms crossed.

"Yes commander." Elizabeth says quietly as the air falls still as John thinks over everything he's been told, running through every scenario he possibly can.

He clears his throat.

"Do you want to hear the odds commander?" Rob asks, just trying to break the silence in the room as it was making everyone uneasy.

"No." John replies directly, almost annoyed that Rob would interrupt his thought process though too distracted to mention as much, "That won't be necessary Rob." He finishes instinctively to ease the tension in the room.

Knowing the odds of success won't change anything. Not now. The North Koreans saw to that as soon as the rogue Russian soldiers made contact.

"Alright, we have a plan. Neil. Clara. First mission run through will be at eleven hundred hours, we'll break for lunch and do a second run through at thirteen hundred hours. Let's get this right everyone." John finally says after several agonizing moments.

"Roger Commander." Everyone says before they leave the room.

The mood quickly shifts from a tense uneasiness to an excited eagerness as everyone on the base prepares for the coming battle.

Date: Wednesday, December 9th, 2020

Time: 0900hrs SST

Location: Midway Base, Former US Minor Outlying Island, Pacific Ocean

Temperature: 32 Degrees Fahrenheit

"If you value your hearing, you're going to want these." Sam says jokingly, handing her parents each a large headset that blocks loud noises and amplifies softer ones.

John is nearby, loading one of his rifle magazines at one of the ranges ten shooting benches; Neil and Clara are also reloading several magazines before they ensure the perfect function of their firearms.

"So this is what you two would get up to after class sometimes." Sam's mother says after putting the headset on and getting over her initial surprise at how well it accomplishes its intended purpose.

"More or less." Sam replies before putting on her own headset and the three of them head over to John's shooting bench.

John doesn't say much beyond hello as the three of them approach, he's focused on the mission despite being thankful for this brief amusement. He has Sam show her parents how the rifle works, how to load it, and how to fire it. She handles the whole task like she's done it before; almost as if she's held and operated that exact rifle before. John smiles as he watches the scene, slowly becoming more comfortable with the decision he made a few days ago.

Chapter Seventeen

Date: Wednesday, December 9th, 2020

Time: 1300hrs SST

Location: Midway Base, Former US Minor Outlying Island, Pacific Ocean

Temperature: 34 Degrees Fahrenheit

Lunch is a distant memory as John, Clara and Neil set up to make a second run through of the mission; the first run this morning going almost exactly to plan. Sam and her parents have joined Jeremy and Elizabeth in the intelligence center in order to watch from the safest angle. Abigail's hair is still slightly messed up from the five rounds she fired earlier this morning, while her husband felt comfortable enough to send a full fifteen round magazine down range.

"Everyone in position?" Elizabeth asks over the radio.

"We're all set Elizabeth. Ready when you are." John replies, his voice cracking due to electrical interference from the bases power system.

The television displays three separate video feeds from cameras mounted on the three squadron members eye protection; their vital signs are also displayed, taken from biometric sensors mounted in the arms of the glasses.

"Roger commander. Begin training exercise fifteen point zero two in three...two...one... now." Elizabeth responds with a certain authority masked by her usual light and friendly personality.

With that, John, Clara and Neil begin running through how the ground operations will go; using a makeshift mockup of the base and warhead, both made as close to the actual thing as possible. Making their way through the complex with relative ease, their bodies take in every movement, every twitch and every action possible, a byproduct of their initial training. Several targets are dotted around the makeshift complex in an effort to approximate the likely positions of enemy troops during the mission. The positions have changed slightly from this morning though it hardly throws the practiced squad members off.

Fifteen minutes into the training session, several of the targets have been shot and the three squad members have the makeshift building in their sights as they perform a quick ammunition check from the safety of cover. Their heavy breathing slowly subsiding as they compose themselves for the practice assault.

"Just another walk in the park." Clara chuckles between breaths.

"Don't get cocky yet sweetheart, we still have to pull this off for real." Neil says, chuckling as well.

"Would you two stop flirting and get a room already." John chimes in, taking quick aim at another target in the distance, taking it out; the entire Intelligence Center struggles to keep from bursting into uncontrolled laughter.

"Not a bad idea commander." Neil quips, still chuckling every so often as the three squadron members calm down and prepare to kick in the door of the structure containing the mockup warhead.

As they stack up on the door, John uses his hand to count down from three; kicking in the door and immediately getting out of Clara's way when the count reaches zero. Neil follows swiftly after her and John brings up the rear as the three decisively take out five targets that had been placed inside. They're right on schedule as the mission clock reaches twenty minutes and counting.

Date: Wednesday, December 9th, 2020

Time: 1600hrs SST

Location: Midway Base, Former US Minor Outlying Island, Pacific Ocean

Temperature: 32 Degrees Fahrenheit

John, Neil and Clara wipe the sweat from their foreheads, having just completed the fourth run through with no breaks in between in order to increase their stress level. This most recent run through was their last until they complete two more under the cover of darkness in order to replicate the actual mission conditions.

Sam, Abigail and Josiah, who had been watching on, slowly approach the tired young adults; closely followed by Elizabeth and Jeremy. They're keep their distance however, not out of fear or reluctance, but to give Sam the moment she is going to need with her boyfriend. Especially after getting a taste of what he is willing to put himself through in order to get something done. John stands up from the boulder he is sitting on upon seeing her, handing his rifle and ammunition to Neil as he and Clara head for the armory. His sweat soaked clothes nearly radiate heat against the cold air as his molten breath causes a slight layer of steam to appear in front of him with every breath.

"So that was the tough part?" Sam asks, messing with his hair before pushing it to one side to get a better view of his eyes.

"Not exactly. The tough part comes on Friday when we have to do it for real." He replies softly, once again being as honest as he possibly can be.

"Practice makes perfect, right?" She returns, wrapping her arms around him as he returns the favor by resting his arms around her.

"That's the theory at least." John says with a reassuring sigh before kissing her on the head; the gesture being noticed by her parents.

Both of them are enjoying the fact that their daughter finally has someone who cares for her as much as she cares for them. Elizabeth and Jeremy are similarly enjoying the moment, except from John's perspective. Happy that he finally found someone after feeling so alone for so long.

"Seems like a pretty good theory to me." Sam says softly, resting her head on John's chest, wishing they could fall asleep in each other's arms.

John rocks his head back and forth while making a thinking face, contemplating her remark while the others chuckle before approaching the couple.

"Yeah I guess it does." He replies softly, before continuing "Soon you'll be doing this to. Don't worry I won't push you too hard."

"This may sound strange, but I kind of look forward to it. I may finally feel like I get to have an effect on this world." She says, the others still unable to hear her despite getting closer with each slow step.

"Yeah?" John remarks, squeezing his girlfriend gently.

"Yeah...plus I get to be with you more and that's an appealing idea." She replies, the others finally in earshot and bursting into laughter with John upon hearing the end of her sentence.

John doesn't say anything more, deciding to keep laughing with his girlfriend and friends instead; saying something would likely ruin the moment.

“Come on you two, it’s almost dinner time.” Elizabeth eventually says trying to move the conversation along before it gets any later or colder.

“I guess it is, isn’t it?” John says calmly as he takes a moment to check the watch on his right wrist, “We shouldn’t keep chef O’Neal waiting too long since he was kind enough to cook a private dinner for us.”

“Private dinner? What for?” Elizabeth asks, just as confused as her boyfriend.

“Sorry, we forgot to mention. O’Neal is cooking the squadron a private dinner to celebrate your engagement.” Sam says turning to the surprised, young adults.

Elizabeth gasps with excitement as her fiancé places his hand over his mouth in an effort not to scream. A moment later she jumps at Sam and John, hugging them both before spinning around with an excited expression and kissing her fiancé. Jeremy just stands there, not knowing what to say or do except hug his lover as tightly as he can.

“Happy engagement you two.” Josiah says, shaking both of their hands firmly before his wife does the same.

“Congratulations.” She says happily as Elizabeth and Jeremy continue standing there in utter shock.

“How...when...why?” Elizabeth stutters, wondering how her commander was able to organize such a thing without her noticing.

“I haven’t taught you all of my tricks yet Elizabeth.” John replies almost sarcastically making Elizabeth slightly annoyed, in a joking sort of way.

“You son of a bitch.” Jeremy says kindly, still dumbfounded by the gesture being presented to him.

“Do you kiss your fiancé with that mouth cause if so, you really need to wash it out.” Sam jokes, forcing all present to laugh as they walk towards the restaurant where Clara and Neil are now waiting.

Date: Wednesday, December 9th, 2020

Time: 2125hrs SST

Location: Midway Base, Former US Minor Outlying Island, Pacific Ocean

Temperature: 27 Degrees Fahrenheit

“Boom.”

“Wolf Base, this is Wolf One. Target is destroyed, proceeding to evac point. Going radio silent.” John says after the mock warhead has been destroyed.

“Roger that Wolf One. Report back in a few hours.” Elizabeth replies, as the radio signal disappears from the television screen and she lets out a slight yawn as the beginning stages of exhaustion take hold.

“Simulation seven is complete.” A computerized voice calls out over the squadrons headsets and everyone breathes a tired sigh of relief.

“Do you want to call it a day commander? It’s getting pretty late.” Jeremy asks as John, Clara and Neil catch their breath; Sam eagerly awaiting his answer.

John takes a moment to spit into the dirt in front of him as an equally worn out Neil and Clara glance in his direction.

"Yeah, let's call it. We'll do a run through at zero seven hundred in the morning, just before breakfast." He finally says after thinking the situation over.

"Roger commander. Make your weapons safe and we'll shut everything down in here." Elizabeth says, releasing yet another yawn in the process.

"Roger Wolf Base, see you in a few minutes." John replies as soreness overtakes his tired joints, causing him a brief yet severe amount of pain.

"Any advice for tomorrow commander?" Clara asks curiously.

"Not that I can think of at the moment." He replies, wincing as he sits back down on the rock behind him after unloading his rifle.

John's remark is honest and true, the result of the last two run throughs of the ground assault being flawless in their execution. They have the bruises to show for it too, with bright red marks and scratches covering any exposed skin.

The three of them soon move to the armory, placing everything but their sidearms in their designated lockers and wiping the pooling sweat from their faces. All of them are going to need a shower before falling asleep later this evening. Tiny blood spots dot each of their towels as they toss them into a nearby trash can. The now veteran team, shrugs off the sight, choosing to not let the scratches bother them as they don't have to look their best for the next few days. Upon exiting the armory, they make sure their sidearms are secure in the holsters on their right thighs. They meet up one last time with Elizabeth, Jeremy and Sam, whose parents went to their house after the private dinner; wanting to get an early night before continuing their initiation tomorrow.

"You three look like shit." Jeremy says, getting a good look at his friends.

John, Neil and Clara only laugh in response as Sam wraps herself in John's arms, both trying to keep warm and signal to him that she wants to get to bed. Both caused by the fact she had a little too much wine at dinner and is certainly buzzed if not slightly drunk at the moment.

"How are you feeling commander?" Elizabeth asks, shattering the brief moment of silence as John slowly runs his right hand up and down Sam's arm in an effort to keep her warm.

"Two perfect runs is a start, but we need to make sure we nail this down. Overall though, I am pleased." He replies, his emotions having finally calmed down for his earlier annoyance at the mission changing so dramatically and so quickly; it's as if it's becoming the easier mission to pull off.

"Just make sure all three of you come back in one piece." Jeremy adds as a slight pang of dread passes through his thoughts, remembering that it was only two missions ago when Vladimir died.

"We will, don't worry." Clara says knowing John doesn't want to make promises he might not be able to keep.

Another small moment of silence falls over the six friends as Sam begins to shiver slightly in John's arms; she still hasn't gotten used to the colder temperatures like the rest of the squadron has.

"Alright, let me get her inside before she freezes. We'll meet at zero six forty-five to stage for the next run through, everyone is dismissed until then." John says noticing his girlfriend's plight.

"Roger, thank you commander." Everyone says in some form or another before they split off to go to their respective base homes.

"Thanks." Sam says quietly, not wanting to let go of her personal heat source.

"No problem sweetie." Her boyfriend says lightly as they walk towards his home.

A few minutes later, they walk through the front door of the one-story house and Sam is finally able to let go of John, allowing him to head for the master bathroom to peel off his sweat soaked clothes. She changes into her light blue pajamas and slides under the heavy comforter just as he turns the hot water in the shower. Neither of them are speaking, not that they'd need to; they are simply enjoying each other's company and desperate to get some rest. John winces slightly as the hot water rolls down his bruised and scarred skin as all of the tension of the last few hours is released in one big lump and his muscles relax once more.

Sam stays awake despite laying down, wanting to cuddle with her boyfriend before both of them get a well-deserved night's sleep. The heavy comforter is not making it easy however, keeping her body at the absolute perfect temperature for sleeping while providing its own form of hug. In fact, it soon becomes apparent that the only thing keeping her awake is the light that's illuminating the bedroom.

Several minutes pass before John finally turns off the shower and begins to dry off; no blood this time. The scratches have healed and the dirt that was on his skin has been dutifully whisked down the drain. He grabs grey flannel pajama pants, undergarments and white tee shirt from the countertop, putting them on before tossing his combat clothes in the hamper underneath the same counter. He sighs, turning the light off before opening the door and heading back into the bedroom; the clock on the nightstand revealing that it's already 2200hrs; ten o'clock.

"I'm surprised you're still awake." He says looking down at his girlfriend's still open eyes as she smiles at him.

"Me too." She replies, adjusting herself to keep him in her sightline as he moves to the other side of the bed and turns off the light.

The room goes almost completely dark with the only illumination coming from the base lights and stars peering through the window.

"How are you feeling?" She asks as he slides underneath the comforter and she rolls into his arms; her face looking right at his.

"A little sore, but I'm alright." John says quietly as he closes his eyes and makes himself comfortable as he proceeds to snuggle with his girlfriend, her nose touching his briefly causing her to chuckle.

She messes with her boyfriend's still damp hair, smiling the entire time as John just let's it happen, not minding one bit.

"I put you through so much and yet here you are." She remarks softly, tears almost coming to her eyes as she continues to smile.

"Well..." John finally says quietly, "I'm stubborn." His eyes are still closed.

"Yeah... you are." Sam agrees, chuckling again as her smile grows wider and tears begin to roll gently down her cheeks.

"Yeah." John chuckles a moment later, his voice trailing off as he begins to drift off to sleep; his eyes are still closed.

"John?"

"Hmm?"

"I…" Sam pauses, her emotions getting the better of her and forcing her to take a breath, "I love you."

This, the second time he's heard those three words from Sam, carries just as much weight as the first, if not more. His heart begins to pound in his chest, despite keeping the same steady beat.

"I love you too." He replies, taking a breath as a small tear rolls down his cheek with Sam seeing it instantly.

She pulls herself closer to him, holding him as tightly as she possibly can without breaking him and buries her head as deeply into his chest as possible. She cries, not out of sadness or fear, but out of joy of hearing that phrase from John.

"I know… I know." He says as he finally opens his eyes ever so slightly; his words ringing true in more ways than one and more than Sam will ever understand.

He turns slightly and kisses Sam gently on the cheek in an effort to help her calm down and get to sleep. Before he completely pulls away from the gesture however, Sam turns as well and kisses him square on the lips in an emotional release that lasts for the next five minutes. After the first kiss ends, the second begins almost instantly, a pattern that continues for the next half hour that the two lovers don't even notice ticking by despite needing to rest. When their lips finally part for the last time, they can't help but smile as they look into each other's eyes before drifting off to sleep in each other's arms. The ocean waves providing the perfect soundtrack for the rest of the night.

Date: Thursday, December 10th, 2020

Time: 0745hrs SST

Location: Midway Base, Former US Minor Outlying Island, Pacific Ocean

Temperature: 28 Degrees Fahrenheit

"Have the Chinese continued with the evacuation?" John asks, everyone instinctively knowing why as he, Clara and Neil all cool off after their first run through of the day.

"Yes the evacuation is proceeding as scheduled and there is no indication that the North Koreans know we have changed our mission plan. In fact, it seems they have delayed the launch until sometime Sunday." Rob replies.

"Alright, keep me posted. We're going to get breakfast so make sure your team takes a break Rob; I need intelligence and not zombies." The commander replies, allowing his squadron a brief moment of relaxation; Rob manages a slight chuckle at the remark.

"I'll be sure to let them know. Enjoy breakfast commander." Rob replies calmly before the television screen goes dark and everyone takes a collective breath as Sam takes her boyfriend's right hand.

"You heard the man, let's eat." She says kindly to the rest of the squadron who don't need to be told twice.

She noticed that John was almost too tired to speak, having yawned mere moments earlier while zoning out slightly after Rob's image had faded from the television. He whispers "thank you" as the still slightly groggy squadron turns and heads out the door, arm in arm with their respective significant others.

Their last run through was their best one yet, with everything going quickly and smoothly despite the massive change in where the enemy soldiers were placed. John still isn't satisfied; however, everything needs to be done perfectly multiple times for John to be satisfied.

Breakfast provides a welcome break from the constant mental and physical exhaustion of the training scenarios. Although, with a mission beginning in less than two days, the brief respite is only momentary and all through breakfast, John, Clara and Neil are constantly distracted by every little mission detail running through their minds. The result being that they barely touch the breakfast that's in front of them, much to the dismay of their squad mates.

"You need to eat." Elizabeth persists finally deciding to act after watching them play with their food.

They acknowledge the remark though don't directly respond, mainly as a result of not having the energy to do so.

"John? What's the matter?" Sam whispers so only he can hear as Neil and Clara try to motivate each other to eat by being cute.

John sighs.

"I usually get like this before a mission. I'm so focused on the task at hand that I can't focus on anything else, including food. I'm just surprised that Neil and Clara are experiencing it as well."

Sam hangs on every word of John's response as he continues to stare off into space, looking for clues as to how to get him to eat. However, his explanation makes perfect sense to her, making the task that much harder. She wraps her right arm around his back and places her head on his shoulder.

"Liza is right though; you need to eat." She says gently; it's the only thing she can think of to say, hoping it helps despite knowing that it likely won't.

John sighs again, knowing Sam is right and that she's trying to help in any way possible.

"I know sweetie, I know." he says softly, leaning his head on hers as he manages to get a piece of the eggs benedict on to his fork.

John barely manages to get the fork full of egg into his mouth, just as Neil and Clara begin scarfing down their scrambled egg breakfast; their appetites finally returning to them. Sam quickly finishes her breakfast, now knowing that there's no way John is going to be able to finish his on his own. Quickly clearing her plate, she gently takes the fork out of John's hand and proceeds to careful feed him as he continues to lean on her shoulder. The other squadron members simply look on, resisting the urge to chuckle now that they've finished their breakfasts.

"Thanks." John whispers, kissing Sam on the cheek before she feeds him another forkful of eggs benedict.

"You're welcome. Feeling better?" She replies, as John finally has the strength to take the fork from her and feed himself.

"Yeah, a little." He says softly; Sam kissing his cheek once he finishes the second serving of eggs benedict with two more servings present on his plate.

Sam continues to lean on John's shoulder with her arm around his back while he steadily continues to eat. The squads reaction going from one of humor to that of being happy for their commander and his girlfriend. A refreshing sight to be sure and one that they hope to become used to as time wears on.

Chapter Eighteen

Date: Thursday, December 10th, 2020

Time: 1645hrs SST

Location: Midway Base, Former US Minor Outlying Island, Pacific Ocean

Temperature: 30 Degrees Fahrenheit

The run throughs have all gone off without a hitch, finally convincing John that he, Neil and Clara are ready to do the mission without hesitation. A state that all special forces strive to achieve and that was ingrained in the initiative from day one; when all else fails, your instincts won't.

Once again, John, Neil and Clara's bodies are battered, bruised and scratched to no end and all of them are at risk of overheating despite the fact that they've been removing layers throughout the day in an effort to keep cool. Additionally, they have gone through at least three gallons of water and Gatorade through the course of their training, in addition to the massive meal they had for lunch. Sam has been in and out of the intelligence center, completing bits and pieces of her own initiation with her parents though being allowed to step away thanks to her relationship with John. No one bats an eyelid at this, both due to a lack of caring and not wanting to bring up the potential nepotism. Especially in front of the commander they have come to respect and admire over the last several months.

Elizabeth and Jeremy have only taken one break, immediately after lunch, in order to check in with the bases doctor about the health of their pregnancy. Naturally, Elizabeth didn't want to go, thinking the whole affair was a waste of time. Jeremy finally convinced her to go after getting her to realize that it was what was best for the baby. The whole exchange was amusing to John, even though it meant that he had very little communication with the intelligence center during the run through immediately following lunch. He also noted that the massive meal he and his squad mates had, did slow the mission down by about six minutes.

"Do you want to do one more run through before we put together a final briefing for tomorrow morning?" Rob asks over the radio as John finishes yet another bottle of water on the practice range.

"If you think we can fit it in before mass and dinner tonight." John replies taking a deep breath before speaking.

His words cause Sam to look in Elizabeth's direction, wondering what John meant as she knows they haven't scheduled Elizabeth and Jeremy's wedding yet. Elizabeth returns Sam's confused expression with a glance that tells Sam that she will explain once the business taking place is complete. An entire conversation is had without a single word being said and almost no one noticing.

"We can fit it in, though you may have to apologize to the good lord above for going to church in sweaty combat gear." Rob replies as Clara laughs while Neil and John process what he said with a smile.

"Alright, roger that Rob. I'm sure of all the things I've done, he'll at least forgive me for that." John finally replies as he performs a quick weapons check.

Everyone repositions and resets, making sure everything is ready to go for the last run through of the day.

"Before every mission, we hold a small service. Ranging from a quick prayer to a full mass. All in an effort to put everyone's mind at ease. It is a Christian service though all faiths are welcome to attend."

Elizabeth explains as the personnel around her and Sam quickly reset the targets and compile everything based on the latest intelligence.

"That's a nice sentiment." Sam replies, remembering that it's been awhile since she was last in a church of any kind, even for a wedding.

"We like to think so and it does help, though it can be hard to tell from time to time." Elizabeth responds as her fiancé places his hand on her shoulder.

"I meant to ask; how did your appointment go?" Sam asks kindly.

"It went well, though they can't see much at this point. We'll know more in a few months." Elizabeth replies after glancing in Jeremy's direction just as he is handed a piece of paper for his opinion.

Sam doesn't say another word instead opting to gently hold Elizabeth's arm and smiling as Elizabeth places her right hand over her own. A moment later she heads over to her headset, places it on her head and gently presses the talk button.

"How are you feeling John?" She asks kindly, before releasing the button just as gently as she pressed it.

"Better than this morning. How are you holding up?" He replies quickly and bluntly, though his tone is neither dismissive nor mean.

"That's good to hear, and I'm doing alright, though there seems to be a ton of paperwork that I need to read and sign." Sam replies, simply happy that she gets to hear her boyfriend's voice, having been unable to see him for the majority of the day.

"Yeah, unfortunately there's nothing I can do about that. It's mainly the legal side of making you exempt from all laws in any country. I've read every document in full and I can honestly tell you just to sign them and get it over with." He replies chuckling, mainly at the fact that the lawyers had to get involved somehow in order to get their multi-thousand-dollar paychecks.

John isn't exaggerating, he was directly involved in the approval process for the paperwork and had the final say on whether or not it was used or if needed to be rewritten. He had wished the paperwork didn't need to be there, but that wasn't a legal option and would have made the initiative a terrorist organization in the eyes of the world's governments.

"I'll be sure to remember that when I meet with the lawyers again." Sam chuckles, still slightly amazed at how much influence John has had on the structure of this fledgling organization, "Do you want me to get you anything? A snack or drink?"

"Thanks for the offer sweetheart but I am good for the time being. You may want to make sure your parents aren't pulling their hair out though, given the experience you had with the paperwork." John replies kindly just as the mission resets in his eye protection.

Sam chuckles at her boyfriend's remark, knowing that he is probably right when it comes to her parents.

"Okay, be safe out there John." She says softly, wanting to add another sentence though feeling that it's not the right time or place.

"I will be sweetie. See you in a little bit at church." John replies, seemingly sensing, though understanding Sam's hesitation before a countdown appears on the lens of his eye protection.

With this last exchange, everyone settles down in their respective places as Sam heads for the base's school, specifically built to teach it's students the skills necessary to perform any non-combat job the initiative has. Sam manages to enter the modern structure just as the last mission run though kicks off, with the distant sound of gunfire starting soon thereafter.

Moving swiftly to one of the two elevators in the center of the main lobby, Sam waves to the receptionist at the front desk, who has gotten used to seeing the young woman over the course of the day, though is still friendly with her greeting. Riding the elevator to the third of four floors, Sam moves quickly to one of the eight conference rooms that is across the hallway from the elevators and four classrooms. Children are in each of the classrooms, wrapping up various programming and coding lessons before class ends in ten minutes. Most are just ten years old though their behavior and obedience is second only to their parents, with many already possessing the skills of normal twelfth graders. Despite being too young to fully understand most adult concepts, they can easily tell that a mission is about to take place and constantly worry about those who regularly go into combat.

"Hey." Sam says quietly entering the conference room where her parents and an initiative lawyer are located; all three smile upon hearing her voice and seeing her enter the room.

"We're maybe halfway through the paperwork. Any chance your boyfriend could help speed this up?" Her mother asks with a chuckle as the lawyer smiles at her remark, having heard similar statements before.

"Well he did say to just sign it and not worry about reading it." Sam replies taking a seat, peaking the dark-skinned lawyers curiosity.

"If you don't mind me asking miss. Who is your boyfriend and how would he know that?" The lawyer asks with a smooth tone in his voice as Josiah takes a quick drink; making sure to swallow it before his daughter forces him to spit it out.

"Well my boyfriend is commander Hilderbrand and that is all you need to determine his authority." Sam says a confident smile.

The lawyer chuckles, honestly not expecting that response from the young woman as everyone in the room shares in a moment of laughter before calming down.

"Well, I can't exactly argue with our commanders stance. He did approve the forms and certainly knows what's in them." The lawyer begins his voice staying as smooth as it did earlier as he recognizes he is no longer needed, "I'll leave these here for you to sign, simply drop them off downstairs."

"Thank you Mr. Young. Have a good evening." Josiah says warmly before shaking his hand and his wife does the same.

Mr. Young then leaves the room, taking his briefcase with him and waving to Sam as he passes through the door; soon disappearing as he enters the elevator.

"That's the first time we've heard you call him that." Abigail says to Sam, still smiling as she quickly signs her name before passing the paper to her husband; both of them still taking a moment to glance over everything on the paper.

"Refer to John as what? Commander?" Sam asks innocently, clearly in a more joking mood than she usually is.

"No, not as that. As your boyfriend you silly goose." Her mother replies, pushing her arm slightly, joining in on the joking tone taken by her daughter.

Sam pauses for a moment, knowing that she's referred to John as such before now but then realizing that she's never said it around her parents. The whole process causes her to blush slightly, a moment her parents take full advantage of in order to tease her and chuckle.

"Well... he is..." Sam finally says confidently as the teasing subsides and she is finally able to catch her breath.

"We know Sam, we know." Josiah says softly, his tone subtlety indicated his approval of this fact as Abigail nods in agreement though the gesture goes unnoticed by Sam.

"Speaking of your boyfriend, how is he holding up? He and the others seem to be training pretty hard." Abigail asks, as if every member of the squadron is part of their small family.

"He's doing alright, this is almost normal for him. For all of them. So they would probably tell you not to worry." Sam replies, the smile on her face going from wide and excited to small and thoughtful as she tries to hide her own worry.

"You're still worried though, aren't you?" Her dad asks, easily picking up on his daughters subtle change in emotion.

Sam nods, still trying to keep the happy facade on her face as dread begins filling the back of her mind.

"It's ok to worry; it's a natural part of being in love with someone, but so is trust. A trust that they will come back to you, no matter what, and from what I've heard over the last few days, John is definitely coming back to you." Abigail says softly, placing her hand on her daughter's knee in an effort to reassure her.

Sam is slightly surprised, when this whole thing kicked off her mother was the reluctant parent, wanting Sam to take things slow with John and the initiative. Now she seems fully committed to the cause, especially when it comes to her relationship. The signal from her husband almost two days ago only served to help that fact. A fact that Sam has yet to pick up on fully, though she has certainly noticed the shift in her mother's attitude.

"It's all going to be okay Sam." Josiah says quietly and warmly, backing up his wife's sentiment.

"I hope so." She finally replies quietly, doing her best to believe her parents, and by association her boyfriend, but she can't help but worry that something unforeseen is going to happen.

"We know so." Abigail says, her tone staying as warm as possible in an effort to reassure her daughter and it at least returns a smile to her face.

The family continues filling out paperwork, going at a swifter pace than Abigail and Josiah were with the lawyer. A bell rings, letting the students out of class right at five o'clock. Some kindly wave to Sam and her parents, though most are too preoccupied with each other, and wanting dinner, to notice they're there.

Date: Thursday, December 10th, 2020

Time: 1745hrs SST

Location: Midway Base, Former US Minor Outlying Island, Pacific Ocean

Temperature: 29 Degrees Fahrenheit

A crowd has begun to gather around the entrance of Midway base's church, all waiting for the pastor to arrive and the service to begin. Most have just finished their respective shifts at various base facilities, including the intelligence center and base restaurant. There are only a few children present with their parents; with school having just been let out, most families are sitting down to dinner instead of attending the service. Despite this however, there will likely be at least one thousand personnel at tonight's mass, mainly thanks to the popularity of the initiatives command squadron.

When the doors are finally opened by an altar boy and altar girl, there is an organized rush as people try to find their way to their preferred seating area in one of the three columns of pews. None, however, sit in the front row of the center column, that row is specifically reserved for members of the command squadron and their guests. No signs mark this policy, yet everyone respects it out of respect for their commander and his squad mates.

The command squadron arrives at the same time, with Clara, Neil and John still sweating profusely in their combat clothes as a result of the recent completion of the final mission run through. Sam and her parents soon join them with handshakes and hugs being exchanged outside the church. Their sidearms are clearly present on their thighs though everyone continues to act as if everything is normal, mainly because it is when combat personnel are on base.

"When was the last time you were even at church?" Sam asks John as a part of the mingling conversation.

"Honestly, I don't really remember. I've only gone a few times after my parents funeral." John replies, the subject affecting him less than it use to, even when compared to a year ago.

"I didn't even know you were that religious. It seems rather odd for a government organization." Abigail says curiously, wanting to learn a little more about the initiative's policies.

“Thankfully none of the initiatives policies were based on any sort of religious writing and we don’t require anyone to attend the service. Most people do out of a need for a spiritual connection. In fact, some see it as the closest thing we have to psychiatric services.” Elizabeth replies taking over the conversation as John helps Sam put on his black hoodie that Elizabeth handed him earlier.

Abigail finds the answer rather interesting and can sense John’s fingerprints are all over the policies, just like they were with the paperwork. Before she can inquire further however, the pastor of the base’s church appears in the doorway. His long white and gold robes keeping his red-brown skin warm, though standing in the heated church doesn’t hurt either.

“The good Lord says one will catch a cold should they stay outside in this weather.” He says, his thick Hispanic accent differentiating his voice from those around them.

“Father Francesco, delivering divine wisdom as usual I see.” John replies jokingly, shaking the forty-year-old man’s hand, a gesture shared by the rest of thc squadron.

“It’s good to see your sense of humor hasn’t diminished John.” Pastor Francesco says, slightly surprising Sam and her parents as most, if not all, of the other base personnel have only referred to him as commander.

“Likewise father, I would like to introduce Samantha Adams and her parents, Josiah and Abigail. They’re a part of the initiative now, so you’ll probably be seeing them a lot more.” John continues as the three he mentioned shake Pastor Francesco’s hand in sequence.

A short exchange of “nice to meet you” follows John’s greeting as everyone begins slowly moving towards the door.

“Well, mass is going to be starting soon so you should take your seats.” Father Francesco says after quickly checking his watch.

“Alright, see you in there, father.” John says softly, shaking the pastors hand a final time before leading the squadron into the classic looking church.

Countless murals dot the nearly twenty-five-foot-tall ceiling along with multiple stained-glass windows depicting numerous saints and notable religious figures. The pews are constructed from deeply colored and worn oak boards, having been saved from three old churches: one in Pennsylvania and two in Montana. The marble altar at the head of the church is a simple design, though it is covered with an ornate white, lace altar cloth; a single gold cup is sitting in the center of the altar itself.

The squadron takes their seats at the front of the middle column of pews, with Sam’s parents on the right end, followed by, Sam, John, Elizabeth, Jeremy, Clara and then Neil on the other end. All sit down, almost in unison, as Sam and her parents take in the sights around them while controlling their amazement that no one is really bothering them, just kind of accepting their presence as normal.

At eighteen hundred hours exactly, the doors to the church are closed and the altar boy and altar girl lead Father Francesco to the altar as the processional hymn plays over the speaker system. Everyone stands when the song start’s playing, standing straight ahead before the altar. John chuckles slightly, catching the attention of Sam as he briefly looks down before returning his gaze to the altar.

“What’s on your mind?” Sam whispers curiously.

“It’s nothing.” John whispers back, continuing to smile as Father Francesco passes his peripheral vision on his left.

Sam, rightly, doesn't buy John's answer one bit, knowing that his thought will likely come to light sooner rather than later.

Father Francesco approaches the altar as the altar boy kneels on the left and the altar girl kneels on the right, after placing the ceremonial staffs in their respective holders at the edge of the platform supporting the altar. The processional hymn ends, and the congregation remains standing, waiting on the pastor to allow them to sit.

"Please be seated." He says after clearing his throat, his voice clearly heard over the church's sound system.

The entire congregation sits down as once, keeping as quiet as they can while waiting for Father Francesco to speak once more.

"We have gathered here this evening to ask for the Lord's blessing, not only for the safe resolution of the coming conflict, but for the safe return of those going into harm's way. While we ask this blessing, I ask that you join me in celebration and congratulations for the engagement of Elizabeth Foster and Jeremy Kingsman and their healthy pregnancy." The humble pastor begins, pausing at the end to allow the large hall to erupt in cheers and applause.

Elizabeth and Jeremy instantly snap to look in John's direction, who only smiles in response as the two of them stand and wave to the crowd, blushing from the embarrassment of the moment. The crowd calms down once more as the young couple sits back down in their pew with Father Francesco continuing the sermon.

"Psalm chapter twenty-seven, verse one states. *The Lord is my light and my salvation - whom shall I fear? The Lord is the stronghold of my life - of whom shall I be afraid?* We may have many adversaries in our efforts, as in life, but we mustn't be afraid. For so long as we walk with the Lord, he shall walk with us and let us pray for his mercy and forgiveness, not only for us but for those who challenge us in life." He continues, his smooth voice only taking a break to take a breath.

As Father Francesco continues with the introductory lecture, Sam gets her boyfriend's attention by gently taking hold of his right hand; still curious as to what he was thinking earlier.

"What's up?" He asks quietly, holding her hand gently while still looking up at Father Francesco.

"What were you thinking earlier?" Sam says quietly and insistently.

John chuckles slightly, not surprised that Sam is still hung up on his earlier remark.

"You'll find out when it's time." He whispers after taking a short moment.

Sam playfully leans against him, keeping hold of his hand and nudging his arm while making a cute face, all in an effort to get him to spill the beans now. He remains stubbornly silent however, as he transfers the hold on Sam's hand to his left and places his right arm around her. An embrace that she graciously accepts as the two of them continue to watch and listen to Pastor Francesco's sermon, who smiles upon seeing the sight.

Date: Thursday, December 10th, 2020

Time: 2003hrs SST

Location: Midway Base, Former US Minor Outlying Island, Pacific Ocean

Temperature: 27 Degrees Fahrenheit

Dinner has just ended and everyone heading to their on base homes, including Neil, Clara, Jeremy and Elizabeth. In fact, it doesn't take long for the only people present in the restaurant to be the bartender, one waiter, John, Sam and her parents. It's not entirely silent however, as someone put five dollars in the jukebox, allowing it to play for at least the next hour.

"Tired sweetie?" John asks as Sam closes her eyes and rests her head on his chest while he wraps his left arm around her and leans back against booth wall behind them; Sam's parents look on at the comforting sight, having just finished their crab cakes and corn.

"A little." Sam replies, she's not buzzed or drunk, just tired.

"Okay... we'll head out in a moment." He says softly, pulling her a little closer to make her more comfortable; carefully reaching for his Pepsi to finish it.

John is slightly surprised that Sam is evening willing to do this in front of her parents, thinking she would be embarrassed like Elizabeth and Jeremy were earlier in the church. He doesn't dwell on this thought however, instead enjoying the moment himself, happy to share this time with Sam.

"You two are so cute together." Abigail says gently, unable to contain her remarks any longer.

John and Sam smile, the comment finally getting both of them to blush slightly and convincing Josiah to chuckle.

"Kind of reminds me of how we were all those years ago." He remanences to his wife.

"A little, though we weren't that cute given the fashion trends when we were dating." His wife replies, getting all four of them to laugh.

Sam, however, doesn't last much longer and soon falls asleep in her boyfriend's arms; a fact he realizes by moving her slightly and quietly saying her name.

"I better get her to bed." John says after checking his watch and lifting Sam into his arms, barely straining to hold her weight.

"Okay. Have a good night John." Abigail says shaking his hand then her husband does the same before adding his own comments.

"Don't ever feel like you're not better than her previous boyfriend, John. You're miles better than he ever was." Josiah says patting John on the shoulder.

"That means a lot Mr. Adams, thank you." John responds quietly before wishing Josiah and Abigail a goodnight and walking out into the cool crisp air towards his on base home.

A short while later, the couple is fast asleep in each other's arms; cuddled up under the thick warm comforter. An early night allowing them a welcome moment of calm before the chaos of the coming mission.

Chapter Nineteen

Date: Friday, December 11th, 2020

Time: 0920hrs SST

Location: Midway Base, Former US Minor Outlying Island, Pacific Ocean

Temperature: 28 Degrees Fahrenheit

John stands at the edge of the beach, enjoying the comfort and relative warmth provided by a long sleeve grey tee-shirt, black hoodie, dark blue jeans and boots, while also enjoying the morning view of the Pacific Ocean. Sam is still in his on base house sleeping; he wants her to rest even though he couldn't sleep anymore, his body simply wouldn't let him.

"When will you allow yourself to sleep before a mission." Elizabeth asks, John doesn't turn around.

It's only Elizabeth, Jeremy is still at the house getting breakfast ready for his fiancé.

"Probably never Liza, you know that." John says eventually, still not turning around as he doesn't want to take his eyes off of the view in front of him.

"I do and that's what worries me." She replies, approaching John from the right and placing her hand on his shoulder as she looks out at the same view, "You have someone to fight for now. Someone who needs you." She finishes, not taking her eyes off of the ocean.

"I know." John says simply.

"I must admit it scares me given what you did to Richard before his death." Elizabeth continues, squinting slightly as a bird catches her eye.

"Well, you did say I have someone to fight for." He replies.

Elizabeth rocks her head back and forth, agreeing with Johns remark which also confirms to her that he will do anything to make sure he returns to Sam.

"I wanted to ask you something, though I know this may not be a good time." Elizabeth starts, revealing the real reason why she is here.

"There's no such thing anymore Liza, so just ask. I don't mind." He assures her, chuckling as he speaks; Elizabeth chuckles as well, taking a moment to look down at the dirt, playing with it slightly with her right sneaker.

"That's certainly true." She continues almost in a whisper, "Would be alright if Jeremy and I got married after this mission is complete? I know it's so soon, but it just feels li-." John interrupts.

"You don't have to explain. Of course you can have the wedding after this mission." He says in an almost father like in tone, as he finally turns to look at his second in command.

Elizabeth's eyes go wide, and a massive smile befalls her tried, young face; struggling to not scream with joy as she jumps and hugs her commander upon hearing the news. John returns the hug and pats Elizabeth on the back, knowing that she won't be the only one happy to hear the news. She smiles as she ends the embrace and runs towards her house; hair blowing in the wind as she randomly turns around to look back at John. It's the happiest he's seen her since the proposal a few days ago, bringing a smile to his face as a result; a rarity before a mission.

Taking the slight hint provided by his second in command, John heads back to his home; taking great care to open and close the front door as quietly as possible. He doesn't want to wake Samantha up if he doesn't have too, knowing that she likely won't be able to sleep for the duration of the mission.

He heads to the kitchen and begins making two servings of scrambled eggs with cheese as well as a decent helping of bacon. Waiting for the eggs to cook, he takes a moment to read through the latest intelligence briefing that has been emailed to him. It doesn't take him long to notice that there isn't anything new that he needs to worry about.

With the bacon done, John refocuses on making sure the eggs finish to his and Sam's liking. A task that is hardly a challenge for the experienced young adult and soon the eggs are plated, soon joined by five pieces of perfectly cooked bacon. With breakfast is cooked, he places the frying pans and spatula in the sink and grabs the orange juice from the refrigerator. With practiced ease, he pours the orange juice into two, thick, short glasses, getting precisely the same amount in each before replacing the juice in the fridge.

Satisfied with his handy work, he places the two plates, two glasses and silverware on a small maple tray and quietly heads for the master bedroom. He's grateful, yet surprised that cooking didn't wake Samantha up, as it had during several of their sleepovers before today, though he's not going to complain as it allows him the opportunity to surprise her.

Silently opening and closing the bedroom door, he finds Sam wearing her light blue pajamas and sleeping in the exact same position he left her in two hours ago. He carefully sets the tray on the nightstand and sits down at the edge of the queen-sized platform bed, debating whether or not he should wake her. He checks his watch; it's barely nine forty-five in the morning.

"Sam? Sweetie? It's time to wake up." He says gently, softly nudging his sleeping girlfriend's shoulder.

Sam moans slightly as she turns, clearly not wanting to wake up immediately despite the smell of eggs and bacon now filling the room. John chuckles before trying again.

"Sweetheart, it's time to get up. You're breakfast is getting cold." He says just as gently and softly as before, once again softly nudging his tired girlfriend.

Again, she moans; opening her eyes slightly to see her boyfriend above her.

"Breakfast?" She asks slowly and sheepishly.

"Yeah, breakfast." John replies, wiping Sam's black hair out of her face.

Sam smiles, stretching her arms and sitting up against the headboard before kissing him on the cheek. She then slides her bare feet out from under the comforter and shuffles across the bed to sit next to him and fall into his arms. It's only now that she sees the small wooden tray on the nightstand, gasping slightly at the gesture as John hands her one of the plates and a fork.

"I... I don't know what to say." She says, struggling to process just how nice John is being, given that no boyfriend has ever treated her this nicely.

“Then don’t say anything sweetie, just eat.” He replies with a soft smile as he uses his right arm to hug her before she takes a bite.

Sam does just that, taking a careful bite of the eggs and soon realizing that they are the best scrambled eggs she’s ever had, earning John a second glance, her eyes as wide as ever.

John smiles as he grabs the other plate from the nightstand, as if he knows exactly what Sam is thinking right now. It brings him genuine joy to see Sam as happy as she is, lifting both of their spirits in a way they’ve both needed for a while. He hands her one of the glasses of orange juice as she sets the plate in her lap and finishes chewing the first half of the serving of eggs. She chuckles and shakes her head before taking a sip from the cup.

“My father was completely right last night. You are the best boyfriend I’ve ever had.” She says just as she puts the glass to her lips, only taking a sip once she finishes her sentence.

“Is that so?” John asks, walking an extremely fine line between being playful and curious as he finishes his second piece of bacon.

“Definitely.” She replies, leaning against his shoulder.

John smiles again, though sighs slightly.

“All I do is try Sam... because you’re worth it to me... and you always have been.” He says eventually, taking a moment to think of what he was going to say.

“Well, you certainly succeed John.” She replies cutely, his words giving new meaning to everything he’s done for her over the last eleven years.

John smiles as the two lovers sit at the edge of the bed to finish their breakfast; Sam instinctively knowing why John is already dressed and not caring one bit. Both of them trust each other so completely that they don't have to worry about what the other is doing or thinking. A state of being that both of them have rapidly grown to appreciate.

Date: Friday, December 11th, 2020

Time: 1113hrs SST

Location: Midway Base, Former US Minor Outlying Island, Pacific Ocean

Temperature: 30 Degrees Fahrenheit

John, Elizabeth and Neil are pouring over the latest satellite photos of the North Korean missile base. Jeremy and Clara are in the armory, cleaning everyone's weapons. Sam has met up with her parents and the three of them are participating in a video call with Rob regarding the history of the initiative and its core principals. All three of them easily pick up on John's influence as Rob walks them through each piece of material and answers any questions that they have.

A quick and stern mood has fallen across the entire base; equipment is readied, intelligence is finalized, jets are fueled, and everyone is doing their duty completely and totally. No one wants this mission to fail or be the one to let the mission down. Normal base activities have continued, in earnest, however; with the restaurant is cooking out hot meals as usual, children are still learning in the school's classrooms, and their teachers do their utmost to keep the peace. Everyone knows what is about to happen, but their lives continue as normal.

"What do you make of this?" John asks Elizabeth handing her a picture of the missile bases runway, which tunnels through a nearby mountain.

"Two Mig-21s. Usually I would say they aren't a threat, but a lumbering transport plan would be an easy target." Elizabeth responds after taking a moment.

"Think the jamming equipment on our C-17's will be enough?" John asks, not out of a lack of knowledge but out of wanting his second in command's opinion.

"It should be, but I will get back to you on that." She replies, wanting to be absolutely sure of her answer.

John appreciates the effort she's putting in to make sure she gets the answer right, especially since he doesn't want to be blown out of the sky. He's impressed at how well she is able to keep the excitement of her upcoming wedding out of her mind; something that she may not have been able to do a couple of months ago.

Meanwhile, Rob is wrapping things up with Sam and her family, having gone over their roles in extreme detail to ensure they have no questions regarding what they'll be doing. Sam, having officially been assigned the vacant role of Wolf six, will be John's spotter and fly his spare plane once her training is complete. Her parents have been assigned the role of squadron advisors; a role that Rob currently fulfills on his own. Their primary task is to provide support and development for the six members of Wolf Squadron.

The explanation is more for legal reasons than anything as Sam and her parents had largely known what they were going to be doing before today. They don't mind receiving the explanation as it allows them to process the coming mission while pretending to pay attention to Rob.

"Are there any questions?" Rob finally asks, noticing that Sam and her family are barely paying attention.

"Only one I guess." Sam's mother starts, catching her daughters attention, "How intense will Sam's training be?"

Rob pauses, having expected the question.

"The best way I can describe the training is this. It combines the skills of Seal Team Six and British Commandos, with those of an ace fighter pilot and tactician." He replies, giving as much information as he can without scaring the family.

Sam's mother glances in her direction with a look of "are you sure about this?" plastered across her face; Sam simply replies with a slight nod. She's determined to be a part of what John has formed and kept together with his own two hands. Josiah simply goes along with the whole thing, having guessed that the level of training was pretty steep from the way squadron has been carrying themselves.

The tension on the base is only increasing as the countdown to the start of the mission continues. Sam even notices some of the students squirming in their seats as they struggle to pay attention to the days networking lesson. The teachers are doing what they can to reassure them that everything will be alright, though it is relatively ineffective. They're feeling the same thing their students are.

Date: Friday, December 11th, 2020

Time: 1341hrs SST

Location: Midway Base, Former US Minor Outlying Island, Pacific Ocean

Temperature: 30 Degrees Fahrenheit

Lunch was briefly interrupted by a snow squall whiting out the entire base, the first snowfall of the season. The inclement weather does little to slow down preparations for the mission, with only fifteen minutes being needed to clear the snow off the runway and to de-ice the transport plane. Everyone is focused on the task at hand, trying to make sure every detail is perfect.

Sam had been hoping to see her boyfriend during lunch, having not seen him since their breakfast in bed earlier this morning. However, he had to eat so quickly that he was out of the restaurant before she had even left the school with her parents. She understands how busy he is going to be today and was happy to have lunch with her parents once again. Clara and Jeremy were also able to join them, albeit briefly, which helped to take the growing weight off of Sam's shoulders.

Date: Friday, December 11th, 2020

Time: 1637hrs SST

Location: Midway Base, Former US Minor Outlying Island, Pacific Ocean

Temperature: 29 Degrees Fahrenheit

"Everything is set commander." Neil reports over the radio after giving all of their gear one last inspection while John takes one last look at the relevant intel in the Intelligence Center.

Clara, Elizabeth and Jeremy are all trying to enjoy some last-minute rest in their respective homes, even though there is barely an hour and a half left before the mission takes off.

"Roger that Neil, get some rest and I'll see you in an hour." John replies before sighing and placing his face in his hands, trying to stay awake.

"You should rest to commander." Rob says, his voice surprising John slightly though he doesn't jump before turning to face the Intelligence Center's main screen.

"You know that won't happen." He replies solemnly, desperately wanting to spend this last hour and a half with his girlfriend.

"I'm not so sure." Rob replies sarcastically, having instantly picked up on John's hesitation and causing him to chuckle.

"Alright, I'll be in touch at seventeen thirty hours." John finally relents knowing that Sam likely wants to see him just as much as he is longing to see her.

"Roger that commander. I'll keep an eye on things until then." He replies with the screen powering down immediately after as John turns for the door.

Flurries are still falling but they are not forecast to accumulate more than a slight coating on top of the snow that has already fallen. The cold air is also ensuring that any snow that hasn't been removed, will stick around for a while, making John's walk to his front door just a little trickier, though not impossible. He carefully opens the door and wipes his boots on the floor mat before being nearly tackled to the ground as Sam practically throws herself at him.

"I missed you too." He says softly, tightly wrapping his arms around her as he regains his footing.

"I made you dinner. It's not much but I tried." Sam says, her voice muffled by John's sweatshirt.

John glances in the direction of the kitchen, seeing two bowls of tomato soup as well as two plates with perfectly cooked grilled cheese on them. He's impressed, it's a meal he hadn't taught her how to make though she's done so perfectly and without help.

"It looks perfect sweetie. You did well." He says reassuringly, sensing Sam's lack of confidence.

"I did?" She asks, confirming John's thoughts and causing him to sigh unnoticeably.

"You did." He eventually says as the young couple head for the kitchen island.

Sitting down, they proceed to eat in silence, enjoying each other's company as the food fills their empty stomachs. A short time into the meal, John grabs two bottles of Coke Cola from the nearby refrigerator, handing one to Sam before he sits back down next to her. John allows himself to fully embrace this time; time that he would usually spend by himself to think about the coming mission. Now he has someone to spend it with and to give his mind a respite from the ever-increasing amount of danger he has to put himself in. This ideal is only furthered when he and Sam transfer to the couch after finishing dinner. Sam leans against her boyfriend and closes her eyes as she makes herself comfortable while he drapes his arms gently around her.

Date: Friday, December 11th, 2020

Time: 1730hrs SST

Location: Midway Base, Former US Minor Outlying Island, Pacific Ocean

Temperature: 29 Degrees Fahrenheit

"The North Koreans are still continuing as if we're heading to Hong Kong. There's no sign that they've picked up on the change in plans." Rob says as Elizabeth and Jeremy look down at the map on the table.

John, Clara and Neil are suiting up in their combat gear and checking the oxygen systems they're going to need in order to survive the jump from forty thousand feet. Clara and Neil's gear is largely similar, not only to each other but to that worn by United States Seal Teams; John's gear, however, is vastly different. Going with a sleek philosophy, his light grey plate carrier is completely devoid of any obstructions, save for a small backpack attached to its back. With nothing on the plate carrier, he has mounted a MOLLE panel on each thigh. On the left panel, he has two, double magazine pouches and on the right is the holster for his 1911 with an extra magazine pouch mounted next to it.

The panels hook on to his belt and around his thighs, while his belt is hooked to the plate carrier, transferring the whole load to his shoulders and keeping everything where it should be. The sleekness of his setup, perfectly captures John's less is more philosophy when it comes to combat, only allowing him to carry seventy-five rounds of rifle and fourteen rounds of handgun ammunition. With such a limited supply, it's a good thing that John rarely misses, a thought that doesn't even enter his mind as he loads and secures four, fifteen round magazines in the magazine pouches. The fifth and final one is loaded into his eleven-pound rifle.

“Looks like things are still on track commander. The C-17 is warming up as we speak.” Elizabeth says.

“Roger that Elizabeth. We’re almost set here.” John responds, the exchange functioning as a radio check as well as a status report.

“Copy that commander. Be advised there is another snow squall moving in. You’ll probably have to fly through it on takeoff.” Elizabeth continues after being handed a weather report by her boyfriend; Rob is handed the same thing in the Kestrels CIC.

“Wonderful.” John says sarcastically as he secures his 1911 in its holster, thankful that he had a relatively light dinner.

“Nothing like a bit of turbulence to start things off.” Neil states.

“Always something isn’t it.” Clara adds.

“Always Clara, always. Wolf Squadron be advised, the Chinese Government has just completed the evacuation of Hong Kong. They will hold the perimeter until we tell them not to.” Rob chimes in as Elizabeth takes a quick drink.

“Well that’s some good news at least. How are the markets holding up?” John asks, having a quick guess in the back of his mind.

“They aren’t. Multiple governments have already suspended trading until further notice to minimize the damage.” Jeremy joins in while looking at the report.

“Well it’s good to know that some governments are at least slightly capable of being decisive in an emergency.” Neil quips.

“It involved money, so of course they acted decisively.” John remarks, almost disgusted.

A short time later, the three squadron members make their way out into the cold as the sun slips below the horizon. The only thing keeping them warm are their black, flannel lined combat clothes. Upon arriving at the aircraft, the young adults place their gear against the sides of the plane, setting everything down that isn't attached to their person. They gather and synchronize their watches, making sure they are set to the same exact time down to the second; it's seventeen forty-five hours, fifteen minutes until the mission officially starts.

"You better come back." A familiar voice says from behind the group.

It's Sam who has spent the last few minutes changing into beige sweater dress, placing it over the tee-shirt and jeans she's had on most of the day. John turns and walks towards her, down to the edge of the loading ramp of the C-17.

"You know I'm going to." He says smiling.

"I know, I just felt the need to remind you." She replies, swaying back and forth and using her foot to play with the snow as she glances downward.

"I figured." John says smiling and placing his hands on his hips.

Sam chuckles, causing her boyfriend to do the same as the crew of the transport plane finish making their pre-flight checks.

Suddenly, Sam lunges forward, gently grabbing John's head with her hands and lifts her right foot in the air as she kisses him. He returns the gesture, wrapping his hands around her and leaning into the kiss. The young lovers smile when they finally part and John notices Sam's parents behind her. Taking her hand, he walks over to them. Knowing he can make it back in time before the mission starts.

"Make sure she gets some sleep while I'm gone." He says thoughtfully as the two parents smile at them.

"We'll try though I think that is going to be hard to accomplish." Abigail says, her daughter blushing as she speaks.

"Be careful John and we'll see you soon." Josiah says, knowing there isn't a whole lot he can offer the young man besides his support.

"Likewise Mr. Adams." John replies, shaking Josiah's hand as he reluctantly releases Sam's.

"Be safe." Sam says before kissing her boyfriend one more time before whispering, "I love you." as she hugs him gently.

"I love you too." He whispers, returning the hug before parting from his girlfriend and turning for the transport plane.

Neil and Clara are about to say something regarding the scene when John shuts them down.

"Not a word you two." He says sternly, leaving them gasping for breath.

"Bu... but..." Clara finally manages but John holds up his left index finger as he secures his gear, shutting her down once more.

The access ramp on the C-17 closes and the four jet engines roar into life as the three young adults sit by a heating vent in the cargo hold. The massive plane shutters as the pilots begin guiding it along the slick taxiway towards the runway. The jet wash clearing out any snow and forcing anyone outside to take cover to wait out the manmade snowstorm. All is quiet as everyone completes exactly what they need to before the plane is in the air. It reaches the end of the runway, facing west for the easiest and most direct takeoff possible, the snow squall looming in the distance.

Neil checks his watch, eighteen hundred hours exactly, and the pilots firewall the four throttles. The plane lumbers down the runway before lifting gently in the air; everyone settling in for one of the squadrons longest missions.

Chapter Twenty

Date: Saturday December 12, 2020

Time: 2256hrs KST

Location: 40,000 ft above Wonsan, North Korea

Temperature: 19 Degrees Fahrenheit

"Remember your timings, you don't want to keep Special Forces Squad Three waiting." Elizabeth says, the radio crackling to life.

"That won't be a problem." John replies, checking his oxygen mask as he puts it on, along with his parachute.

Everything is totally secured for the jump as the light by the rear door continues to show red.

"Three minutes to target." The pilots call out.

Sam, reluctantly went to bed two hours ago, electing to spend the night at John's house rather than her parents. While she does feel lonely not having John there, she hoped that being in his home will help her achieve some form of sleep. Her parents promise to make sure she got some form of sleep is one of the few things comforting John at the moment.

"Satellite feed confirms that the North Koreans know something's there, but they don't know what it is." Rob calls out.

"Roger, we're getting some turbulence up here but haven't encountered any resistance." John replies, keeping his breaths short and deep, slowing his heartbeat to just fifty beats per minute.

"One minute to target." The pilot states.

It's difficult for them to tell the difference between solid ground and ocean as it all seems to blend together in the biting cold air below. John takes a deep breath, grateful for the flannel lining in his combat clothes, with the nineteen-degree air feeling more like negative ten degrees with the wind chill. The light next to them begins flashing a steady half second pulse, letting the squadron know that there is thirty seconds until the jump. John positions himself between Clara and Neil, turning around so that his back is to the sky. The light continues to blink, John's heart almost exactly in line with every other flash. Then. It turns green.

Neil and Clara dive out of the back of the airplane, while John back flips out. While stylish, the move ensures that there is adequate space between the squad mates and that they don't get ensnared in each other's parachutes. All three of them keep a close eye on the altimeter displayed in their goggles as it rapidly ticks lower and lower.

Having dropped off their cargo, the C-17s pilots guide the massive plane downward and back out over the ocean, making a bee line for Japan. It manages to escape North Korean airspace with no shots even being fired at it, forcing the North Koreans to think that they were seeing a false alarm.

A short time later, the three young adults pull the rip chords on their parachutes, rapidly decreasing their rate of descent as the black parachutes unfurl.

"Three chutes." Clara calls out over the radio though her voice is almost a whisper.

Everyone in the Intelligence Center breathes a collective sigh of relief. The relief is only short lived however, as everyone slowly remembers that the landing was the easiest part of the mission. There's still a long night ahead of everyone as the pending battle gets ready to kick off. Immediately upon landing in fact, Neil is forced to take out a small squadron of North Korean troops who happened to be walking through the area; their weapons were still slung over their shoulders. Despite this, the squadron is exactly on time as they regroup behind the abandoned building and catch their breath.

Date: Saturday, December 12th, 2020

Time: 0310hrs SST

Location: Midway Base, Former US Minor Outlying Island, Pacific Ocean

Temperature: 25 Degrees Fahrenheit

Sam hasn't been able to sleep ever since arriving at John's house; despite the things around her reminding her of him and bringing her some level of comfort, she simply can't get over the fact that he is not there. Almost in tears and dreading the thought of being alone for another moment, she decides to head outside, wrapping John's grey sweatshirt over her light blue pajamas and putting on her sneakers. Almost in a daze, she tiredly stumbles towards the church, who's lights are constantly illuminated for anyone on the base to see. Sam is drawn to the structure, not entirely knowing why or even trying to move towards a different building.

Upon entering the church, Sam subconsciously moves towards the same seat she sat in just over a day ago. She isn't looking around her as she moves to the very front pew in the center column, not noticing Father Francesco lighting a few candles throughout his church. He notices the young woman sitting there, seeming lost in an emotionally confused sea.

“May I?” He asks Sam calmly, after placing the lighter he was using in the pocket of his robes, next to the cellphone that he discreetly texted Elizabeth on mere moments ago.

Sam only nods, still in a daze and barely recognizing the Pastor.

“Can’t sleep?” He asks in a friendly tone, his sensitive nature clearly coming through.

Sam sighs, nodding, completely unable to speak.

“It’s hard, waiting for those you love to come back to you.” He continues, almost as if he has had this exact same conversation before.

“Too hard.” Sam finally whispers.

“What did John tell you before he took off?” Father Francesco asks, thankful to get Sam speaking.

“That he was coming back.” Sam murmurs, barely holding back tears.

“He tends to keep his promises doesn’t he?” The priest continues, his questions specifically designed to keep her talking.

“Yeah he does.” She chuckles, the tears she’s been holding back finally rolling down her cheeks.

If she wasn’t emotional, Sam would be realizing that the person who Father Francesco had this same conversation with was John himself, nearly five months.

"He does. Trust in him as you trust in God and everything will work out." The pastor says, getting Sam to chuckle again through the tears.

"I'm sorry to say father, but I've never been really religious." She says still chuckling, though slowing her tears slightly.

"That's funny, neither is John. Both of you are a lot alike in so many ways." Francesco says realizing the similarities for the first time.

At last, it's curiosity that finally helps Sam fight against her tears, wondering just how similar her and John are in the eyes of those around them.

"How are we alike?" She asks, her voice not choking up like before.

"Well you are both greatly concerned for each other, you both appear to like the same food, and you even dress similarly." Francesco says yawning.

Sam thinks the pastors words over, studying them carefully in her mind before deciding for herself how incredibly true they are.

"If it's any reassurance. I can guarantee, that despite being focused on the mission, John is thinking about you right now. You are always with him and I think it's safe to say that he is always with you." Francesco says softly.

"It does help." Sam replies quietly as a warm feeling passes through her body.

"Good, now go and get some sleep." The pastor replies as Elizabeth arrives at the back of the church with Sam snapping around in her seat to see her.

Sam only smiles, giving the tired pastor the only thank you he needs as he waves to Elizabeth while Sam gets up and walks over to her.

"Let's get you back in bed." She says kindly before leading Sam back out into the cold air, the two of them slipping around slightly on the thin layer of ice.

Once they enter John's house, Elizabeth guides Sam to bedroom and stays well past the time she falls asleep.

Date: Saturday, December 12th, 2020

Time: 2330hrs KST

Location: Missile Base, Wonsan, North Korea

Temperature: 19 Degrees Fahrenheit

"I'm halfway through my ammo. How about you?" Neil asks his girlfriend as he goes through a reload while John lays down a wall of precise and deadly fire.

"Same. We're almost there thankfully so I think we'll have enough." She replies after laying down a burst of suppressive fire.

The increased radiation from the warhead is clearly displayed, marking a building about one hundred yards away, exactly where they thought it would be. Adding to the continued ease of the mission is the confusion on the part of the North Koreans; they simply don't realize where the attack is coming from.

"You're still on schedule, so don't any risks." Jeremy says, having taken over for Elizabeth, who still has not returned from making sure Sam is asleep.

“Roger that Jeremy.” John says, breathing heavily as he reloads his rifle, having gone through the second of his five magazines.

A few minutes later, the squad leader and his two squad mates have lined up on the door as a lull in the gunfire calms things down. It’s all going as it did during the training runs and that’s when everything comes to a screeching halt.

John stumbles out of the way as Clara proceeds to kill the first three Russian soldiers and Neil kills another two. John comes in and kills another four... with his sidearm, his rifle slung in front of him.

“Shit.” He curses to himself as an incredible amount of pain rushes through his body, emanating from the back of his left shoulder, with his blood slowly dripping to the floor.

“Wolf One, this is Wolf Base, what’s going on?” Rob asks frantically, noticing the change in John’s tone as Elizabeth returns.

“One second Wolf Base.” Clara says instinctively, doing her best to keep Rob silent as they deal with the evolving situation.

The silence is almost unbearable.

“Just get a bandage on it for now. There’s no exit wound.” John says angrily as Clara does exactly as she’s told; the pain causing him to punch a nearby wall in frustration.

He takes a moment to calm down before radioing the Intelligence Center.

“Wolf Base, this.... aggh... this is Wolf One... I took a round to the left shoulder... Can continue with mission.” He says fighting through the pain.

One of the Russian soldiers Clara killed, had managed to fire a shot through the door just as John was kicking it in. The bullet burying itself in John's left shoulder bone and leaving his arm partially limp. Everyone struggles to process the news, knowing there is nothing they can do and yet wanting to help any way.

"Roger Wolf One, proceed as scheduled." Elizabeth says breaking the uncomfortable silence.

"Roger Wolf Base." John spits as they set to work removing the nuclear detonator and setting the demolition charges.

Having only killed about a third of the Russian soldiers that were supposed to be present, Neil keeps a close watch for any sign of movement outside the building. Though the lack of any light is making the task even trickier.

"Charges are set." Clara says softly as John's wound begins to bleed through the bandage Clara placed on his shoulder.

Neil carefully places the nuclear detonator in his own backpack, its own shielding protecting everyone from a lethal amount of radiation.

A second later, the room erupts in gunfire from the North, South and West, chipping away at the concrete walls and shattering the glass windows. The three young adults reactively hit the floor, knowing they can't stay there for long. Making their way out of the eastern door and crawling along the snow-covered ground, they are able to take cover behind another building. A second later, Clara sets off the charges with the wireless detonator in her hand.

The massive explosion is bolstered by the warheads own explosives, causing the fireball and shockwave to quadruple in size. It blows apart the soldiers surrounding the building, which itself was reduced to ash. Rubble from the building they're hiding behind pelts John, Clara and Neil. The cinder block cutting and bruising their bodies as the building practically falls on their heads. Collecting themselves, they wipe off any debris they can and proceed in an easterly direction, the gunfire having finally stopped as the remaining North Koreans regroup and try to figure out what happened.

"This is Wolf One, we are proceeding to the evac point." John says, gasping for breath as a streak of blood rolls down his face from a gash the crosses his left eye from his forehead to his cheek, luckily missing the eye itself.

The message is heard by all in the Intelligence Center, who are still processing what happened, having seen it unfold on the live map.

"Ro... Roger wolf one." Elizabeth says stuttering in amazement and abject horror.

"We're... we're all... pretty beat up here." Clara adds, blood rolling down her cheek from her own open wounds, which are shared by her boyfriend.

All of them are limping and barely making the pace they need to make it to the evacuation point in time.

"Roger Wolf Four, medical personnel have already joined Special Forces Squadron Three." Jeremy says being as reassuring as he can, keeping a close eye on the vital signs being transmitted back to the Intelligence Center.

Elizabeth debates whether or not she should wake Samantha and give her the news, despite having just made sure she got to sleep. The thought makes her sick to her stomach, as if she wakes her up now then she might not fully understand what's happened but on the flip side if she doesn't, she's going to have to tell her later which could make things worse. She looks to her fiancé for guidance, he gives her a reassuring look that tells her, she should stay for the time being.

Neil throws up, having accidentally swallowed too much blood with the taste being instantly rejected by his body. Clara helps support him as John drags himself to lead them through the mountain pass towards the nearby river, avoiding any buildings and people along the way.

Date: Sunday, December 13th, 2020

Time: 0220hrs KST

Location: Wonsan, North Korea

Temperature: 20 Degrees Fahrenheit

No one has been able to sleep or catch a break as John, Neil and Clara made their way to the evacuation point, which they reached with barely ten minutes to spare. All three of them have collapsed on the snow-covered bank of the river, careful to make sure they are obscured from view in case anyone comes looking for them after seeing the obvious blood trail.

Barely any communication has been shared between the squadron and the Intelligence Center, with only a couple of replies from John or Clara making their way to the ears of those gathered. Now, the squadron has fallen completely silent, pain overtaking their bodies as they struggle to stay conscious from the massive amount of blood they've lost. They don't even hear the sound of the approaching Osprey as it finds a safe place to land, sandwiching John, Clara and Neil between itself and the river in an effort to protect them from any approaching threats.

"John?" Elizabeth calls out, trying to let the squadron know that the Osprey has landed.

There is no response. All she can see is their three bodies being placed onto stretchers and carried into the gunship before it takes off and heads for Japan. It's unknown if they are even conscious as they are given I.V. fluids by the medics.

Chapter Twenty-One

Date: Sunday, December 13th, 2020/ Saturday, December 12th, 2020

Time: 0430hrs JST/ 0830hrs SST

Location: Toyama Airport, Toyama, Japan

Temperature: 38 Degrees Fahrenheit

"They're alive, try and hold on to that." The lead medic says over the radio as the tired personnel in the Intelligence Center hang on every word.

"Roger Lieutenant. Doctors will meet the plane once you land in nine hours." Robs says, taking over so that Jeremy and Elizabeth don't have to talk.

The news is hitting Elizabeth especially hard, knowing just how close they came to losing three of their friends, so soon after the loss of Vladimir. It likely would have caused a ripple effect down the chain of command that the initiative would not have recovered from. She just can't bring herself to speak.

"Roger Colonel." The medic replies before the transmission is shut off.

"Try and rest if you can. I'll make sure you are woken up when the plane lands." Rob finally says, breaking the silence, though not expecting any form of response from the two young adults.

"How do we tell her?" Elizabeth asks, catching Rob slightly off guard.

"I don't know I'm afraid, though I don't recommend hiding it from her." He replies, giving the best advice he can.

Elizabeth only nods as she and her fiancé walk out the door while Rob sets to work, keeping a watchful eye on the return flight.

The cold air bites at Elizabeth and Jeremy's skin as Jeremy keeps his arm wrapped around his tired fiancé as they head for John's house. They quickly debate whether or not they should wake up Sam's parents to tell them what happened as well, deciding to send a messenger to wake them.

"Sorry about the hour, but we think it would be best to have you here." Jeremy says as they arrive on John's front porch.

"No worries." Josiah says as Elizabeth thanks the messenger and sends him to bed; Abigail yawns as they enter the silent house.

Doing their best to make as little noise as possible, they proceed to turn on as many lights as they can in the living room while Elizabeth heads into the master bedroom. Carefully sitting down on John's side of the bed, she gently nudges Sam in an effort to wake her; wanting to wake her up as gently as possible.

"Sam I need you to get up." She says calmly, her tone similar to the one used by John nearly twenty hours prior.

Sam tosses and turns slightly though does wake up quicker than she did earlier, having only gotten to sleep a couple hours ago.

"What's the matter Liza?" She asks, turning on a nearby light before sitting up against the headboard.

"Come to the living room." Elizabeth continues unable to hide the slight hint of sadness in her voice as Sam wraps a blanket around herself to keep warm.

Leading her out of the room, Elizabeth has Sam sit down next to her mother; her tiredness lessening the surprise of seeing her parents there while Elizabeth makes herself comfortable in Jeremy's arms. Elizabeth sighs after hoping her fiancé would speak for her, but this has to come from her and no one else.

"Sam... something happened on the mission to North Korea." Elizabeth starts, trying her best to remain calm as Sam hangs on every word, sensing what's coming and grabbing her mother's hand.

"Almost everything went to plan, and it was a success, but the explosion caused by the warhead was larger than expected and completely destroyed the building John, Clara and Neil were hiding behind..." Elizabeth has to pause, her wavering voice allowing tears to fill her eyes. "All of them were severely injured by falling debris... John had also been shot in the shoulder..."

"How bad are they?" Sam asks, shaking as her mother pulls her closer.

"I don't know how else to say this..." Elizabeth chokes, unable to keep her emotions in check, "They're unconscious Sam. Due to the blood loss, they're unconscious."

As soon as the sentence leaves Elizabeth's mouth, it levels Sam like a freight train; forcing her to feel uncomfortably numb as tears begin rolling down her cheeks. Her parents appear to take the news a little better, though this is due to their need to be a point of stability for their now sobbing daughter. Abigail pulls her even closer as Elizabeth sets her hand on her leg, trying to provide some level of comfort. Not long after, Sam completely pulls away from her mother and falls into Elizabeth's arms.

Elizabeth and Jeremy glance at each other, easily figuring out that there is no chance of them getting Sam to sleep until the transport plane arrives. They feel for her, understanding the immense amount of emotional pain she is experiencing. The tears rolling down her cheeks turn into rivers as she holds Elizabeth, tighter and tighter.

Date: Saturday, December 12th, 2020

Time: 1730hrs SST

Location: Midway Base, Former US Minor Outlying Island, Pacific Ocean

Temperature: 30 Degrees Fahrenheit

The transport plane lands, the international date line playing havoc with the crews sense of time. Their minds are obviously elsewhere however, as they taxi to one of Midway Bases hangers and lower the cargo ramp to the cool air below. Medical personnel from the base swarm the aircraft, the whole scene resembling that of an emergency room during a mass casualty event. Elizabeth holds Sam back as much as she can, knowing that she will only get in the way as the three lifeless young adults are carried into the medical center. She can't hold her back forever though and Sam manages to break away from Elizabeth's grip and runs alongside her boyfriend as he is wheeled towards the operating room; an oxygen mask being placed over his battered and bloody face.

"John. I'm here, John... Can you hear me?" She says frantically, some of his blood staining the left sleeve of her pajamas.

"He can't sweetheart, I need you to back up." One of the nurse's says sternly but kindly, gently pushing Sam to one side and holding her back as the stretcher is wheeled into the operating room.

Sam is lead to a nearby observation room where she is able to watch the surgery unfold, however, the curtain hanging on the glass separating the rooms is closed on Elizabeth's orders. She knows how damaging it could be for Sam to watch the procedure, especially if something goes wrong. Sam is furious at first though she comes to understand why Elizabeth did what she did as she sits down on the couch behind her, where Elizabeth joins her. A short while later, Jeremy arrives with the base's lead doctor; a shorter, Indian woman who he refers to as Doctor Koothrappali.

"Give it to us straight doctor." Sam says, almost demanding the action of her, though she takes it in stride, having been warned about Sam's mood.

"As you know, they've all lost a tremendous amount of blood, however, their vital signs are good, considering. John will be out of surgery in about an hour. They just needed to go in to retrieve this." The doctor says calmly taking a small vile out of her lab coat pocket, containing the bullet that the surgeon pulled out of John's shoulder.

"When can we see them?" Elizabeth asks as the doctor hands the vile to Samantha, momentarily distracting her.

"Neil and Clara have already been placed into a recovery room, but they need to rest. They'll wake up on their own in a couple of hours if they aren't disturbed. John likely won't wake up until tomorrow at the earliest. All of them are going to be in pain despite the morphine drip we're giving them. They're not out of the woods yet, but the worst is over." The doctor replies calmly and precisely as Samantha hands the vile back to her.

"Thank you doctor. Keep us posted." Elizabeth replies, shaking the doctors hand before Samantha does the same.

The doctor leaves the room to keep an eye on the rest of the medical center's operations as Sam, Jeremy and Elizabeth sit back down on two of the couches in the clearly hospital like room.

“So they’re going to be alright?” Sam asks, her tired voice almost a whisper.

“We’ll see, but most likely.” Jeremy says, trying to keep Sam’s hopes in check while not snuffing them out completely.

Sam seems to understand this as she slowly begins to doze off to sleep in the comfortable embrace of the couch she is currently laying on. Elizabeth quickly recognizes what’s happening and gently drapes a blanket over the tired young woman. Both of them are glad that Sam is able to rest and eventually doze off to sleep themselves.

Date: Saturday, December 12th, 2020

Time: 1930hrs SST

Location: Midway Base, Former US Minor Outlying Island, Pacific Ocean

Temperature: 28 Degrees Fahrenheit

Neil tosses from side to side as the pain courses through his body, unable to get comfortable in his hospital bed. He soon notices a soothing effect taking the edge of the still present pain, allowing him to relax just a little bit. Clara takes his left hand gently, avoiding the I.V. line in the back of his hand, while making sure her own hand doesn’t get tangled in her own I.V. line. Both of them are covered in bandages and have been changed into warm yet light, dark blue pajamas.

“It’s okay, we’re home.” She says softly, repeating the statement in an effort to calm her boyfriend down.

She gently strokes his fingers, hoping that it somehow lets him know that she’s there and that everything is now okay. In the back of her mind however, she worries about John, who she hasn't seen since the three of them were airlifted out of North Korea. She knows that he suffered roughly the same injuries as she did, but neither her nor Neil had been shot before sustaining those injuries.

Neil soon opens his eyes, unable to keep them closed any longer, and gazes up at his girlfriend; easily making out the features of her face in the dark room. He smiles, grateful to see that she's okay despite the pain he is currently experiencing; she returns the same smile before they gently kiss.

"We basically had a building fall on our heads didn't we?" Neil manages to ask quietly, slowly regaining his voice.

"Yeah, we did." Clara says, wanting to kiss Neil even more.

"That's a first." He remarks, chuckling only slightly due to the pain.

"Shut up." Clara says in a playful whisper before pressing her lips against his; she doesn't want to talk anymore; she just wants to kiss him.

Not that Neil minds, he was simply trying to make small talk though he definitely enjoys the kissing a lot more. A nurse pokes her head in the door, wanting to check Neil and Clara's vital signs though instantly deciding to not disturb the young couple, who don't even notice that she opened the door. The painkillers being fed into their I.V. lines, finally begin to take hold, easing their battered bodies into a restful state.

Date: Saturday, December 12th, 2020

Time: 2015hrs SST

Location: Midway Base, Former US Minor Outlying Island, Pacific Ocean

Temperature: 27 Degrees Fahrenheit

Jeremy, Elizabeth and Sam all sit quietly in Neil and Clara's room with the heater being the only thing that makes any sort of noise. Clara has managed to crawl into Neil's bed with him and the two hold each other gently as the entire group waits impatiently for any news regarding John. The nurse from earlier came in with Jeremy, Elizabeth and Sam and got the vital readings she needed; luckily for the young couple, she didn't embarrass them by bringing up what she witnessed earlier. There is a soft knock on the door before Doctor Koothrappali enters calmly, everyone looking in her direction.

"Glad to see you're both up." She says with a soft, almost motherly tone.

"How's John doing?" Sam asks instantly.

Elizabeth places her hand on her shoulder to help keep her calm.

"He's resting. His shoulder only needed stitches once the bullet was removed, but we had to give him additional oxygen because of the procedure. This means no missions for any of you for at least the next week." Koothrappali says calmly, though knowing that it's not likely they will follow her orders.

Samantha attempts to stand though Elizabeth keeps her in her seat by exerting a slight pressure on her shoulder; smiling to reassure her when she snaps around.

"When will we be able to see him?" Elizabeth asks calmly, her tone reassuring Sam that everything will be ok.

"If you want to, you can, but I will warn you, he won't be awake for a while." The doctor replies softly, wishing she had better news.

"Thank you doctor." Elizabeth says before dismissing her to her duties and pulling Sam back into her arms, "He's going to be okay."

"Yeah." She replies in a barely audible voice.

No one else speaks, it simply doesn't feel right for them too as a heavy cloud continues to hang over the squadron as snow begins falling outside. The storm is forecast to last most of the night and the following day and will likely dump six inches of snow on the ground before dissipating.

There's another knock on the door, a messenger with a note from the Intelligence Center. Elizabeth reads it before handing the piece of paper to Jeremy, who passes it around the room as Elizabeth kindly dismisses the young messenger.

"I guess we can take a break like the doctor wants." Neil says, unable to hide his gratitude as he throws the piece of paper at a nearby trash can. missing hopelessly five feet to the left.

"Hopefully, assuming nothing else comes up." Elizabeth sighs.

Date: Saturday, December 12th, 2020

Time: 2234hrs SST

Location: Midway Base, Former US Minor Outlying Island, Pacific Ocean

Temperature: 26 Degrees Fahrenheit

Josiah walks out of Neil and Clara's hospital room after making sure the squadron was comfortable. He also wanted to be sure his daughter was doing alright given what's happened, but she was already asleep when he walked in. Returning to the waiting area, he meets up with his wife and proceeds to give a rundown of how everyone is doing.

"That's too much, that's way too much." She says looking down at the ground, placing her head in her hand.

"That very well might be, but they signed up for this and are handling it about as well as can be expected." Her husband replies, carefully straddling the line between being reassuring and agreeing with his wife.

Before Abigail can reply, Doctor Koothrappali catches their attention with a short wave and a tired smile.

"Pardon me, Mr. and Mrs. Adams, but someone wants to see you." She says quietly.

Shock easily falls across their faces as their deductive reasoning kicks in and they realize just who wants to talk to them. Their thoughts only confirmed when they reach the door to John's recovery room.

Gently opening the door, they find the worn out, battered and bloody twenty-one-year-old lying in his hospital bed with his left arm in a sling and an intelligence report in his right hand. His bandaged and scarred face only illuminated by the reading lamp on the nightstand. He has been changed into the same dark blue pajamas that Neil and Clara and has a thick grey comforter pulled up to his chest, covering most of his body.

"Thank you doctor. You can clock off early tonight." John says kindly, his voice hoarse from the breathing tube he needed during the surgery.

"Yes commander, have a good night." She responds before leaving the room and closing the door behind her as Sam's parents stand there with their mouths nearly hitting the floor.

"The North Koreans seem to think the warhead detonated while the Russians were inserting the nuclear detonator... because a concentrated attack wouldn't have caused so much damage. I guess that means we did our jobs." He says, clearly still in a tremendous amount of pain despite the morphine drip attached to the I.V line in the back of his left hand.

"I guess so." Sam's father replies as he and his wife move to the foot of the bed.

"Thankfully the Americans seem to think along a similar line and the Chinese have begun allowing people back into the evacuation zone." John continues flipping the paper over.

"Seems like everything is going back to normal." Abigail says after taking a breath and noticing what time it is.

"As normal as it can be." He replies, wincing in pain as it finally begins getting to him, "How are the others holding up?"

"Pretty tired honestly. Neil and Clara are in rough shape, but they're going to be okay." Josiah says, placing his hands in his pockets as his wife sits down on the couch behind him.

John chuckles, wincing in pain once more.

"I figured. Still is nice to ask. I'm guessing Sam is taking this pretty hard?" He continues, a pained smile crossing his face.

Josiah nods as John carefully sets the intelligence report on the nightstand and leans back into the pillows supporting his shoulders and head.

"I am sorry about that. We had hoped the charges would merely disperse the warhead, not set it off." He says solemnly.

"She'll be alright once she knows you're awake." Her father states, leading John down a logical path.

"Yeah that's true." He coughs.

"Want me to get her?" He asks gently as John closes his eyes.

John nods with what little strength he can muster as Abigail walks over to him, helping him press the button that increases the morphine dose for a few seconds.

Josiah swiftly leaves the room, staying quiet as he enters Neil and Clara's hospital room. Barely making a sound, he lifts his tired twenty-one-year-old daughter into his arms and carries her gently out of the room. She moans slightly, subconsciously noticing that she is no longer lying on something solid.

"It's ok, I have a surprise for you." Josiah says gently as he silently closes the door of the room once more.

His reassuring words allow her to close her eyes once more, much like they would when she was younger.

Reentering John's room, Abigail gently helps him shift to the left side of the hospital bed as Josiah brings their daughter around to the right. He gently sets her down and helps her lean into John's free right arm. He manages to wrap his arm around Sam's shoulders and back as her mother pulls the comforter over both of them. Sam moans again, clearly on the verge of waking up completely if they continue moving her like they have been.

"Hey Sam." John says quietly, making sure they're both comfortable as her parents sit down on the couch, turning off the light.

John doesn't have to speak twice. Upon hearing his voice, Sam begins crying into his shirt. He kisses her forehead and holds her as tight as he can with only one, sore arm.

"Shh, it's okay. I'm okay." He whispers, doing what he can to calm her down.

Sam continues whimpering, but her tears slowly begin to abate as she clutches John's shirt with her right hand as he kisses her forehead a second time.

"It's alright." John continues, the exhaustion caused by the morphine finally taking hold.

Sam's cries continue to calm down though she continues to have a practical death grip on John's shirt.

"I love you Sam and I always will. No matter what." He says, closing his eyes after kissing her forehead for a third time.

"I love you too... Forever... and always." Sam whispers, releasing the grip on John's shirt as both of them drift off to sleep.

Chapter Twenty-Two

Date: Sunday, December 13th, 2020

Time: 0714hrs SST

Location: Midway Base, Former US Minor Outlying Island, Pacific Ocean

Temperature: 26 Degrees Fahrenheit

Elizabeth slowly begins to wake up, pushing her now messy hair out of her face and rubbing her eyes. Her muscles ache with stiffness as she carefully stretches so as not to wake her still sleeping fiancé. It doesn't take her long to notice that Sam is no longer in the room. In a tired daze, she pushes herself up from the couch and silently heads for the door, opening it slowly and carefully. Once the door is closed, she quietly makes her way down the hallway, seemingly drawn to John's room as she crosses her arms in an effort to keep warm.

The medical centers heating system is struggling slightly to keep the whole space warm thanks to the continuing snowstorm outside. The severe weather shutting down most of the base and giving all non-essential personnel a welcome and much needed break.

Finally arriving at John's room, Elizabeth briefly considers knocking before entering though she hesitates, realizing the hour and that no one is likely awake in the closed room in front of her. After debating with herself for a moment, she decisively and quietly turns the handle and eases the door open. Finding a touching scene that nearly makes her audibly gasp, if not for covering her mouth with her hand.

Sam is still cuddled in John's arm, her head gently placed underneath his as her parents sleep soundly on the couch in front of them. She slowly approaches, making every effort to make as little noise as possible, when a whispering voice causes her blood to run cold.

"You're going to have to be quieter than that, if you want me to sleep."

Elizabeth freezes, not knowing if she should reply or even if she recognizes the voice due to the incredibly low volume.

"It's alright Liza, I was already awake when you entered." The voice continues as Elizabeth finally notices that the person speaking is John, who still has his eyes closed and head tilted comfortably above his girlfriends.

"It's good to see you're alright." She whispers in return, gently moving to the chair next to the nightstand.

John silently chuckles, allowing himself a tired smile though keeping his eyes closed. Elizabeth smiles, grateful to see that the mission hasn't dampened her commanders spirits one bit and that he is not letting his injuries get to him, though the morphine drip is certainly helping as are the cuddles.

"I'm still pretty sore though." John eventually says, his eyes remaining closed and his body remaining still.

"Yeah, I'm pretty sure Neil and Clara would say the same."

"I'm sure they would."

"We're all just glad you guys came back, largely in one piece." Elizabeth says, doing her best to keep her voice low after hearing Sam moan.

"You should know by now Liza, that's going to take more than a bullet and a building to put me down for good." John replies, managing to turn the morbid thought into a decently funny joke as Elizabeth chuckles once more.

"Yeah I know." She says, unable to contain her smile as John does the same, finally opening his eyes.

Before either of the tired young adults can continue speaking, Sam begins whimpering once more, her tears rolling down her cheeks and on to John's arm and shirt.

"Hey... it's okay... Let it out sweetie, let it out." John says calmly, pulling her closer and rubbing her side.

Elizabeth places her hand on Sam's shoulder, assisting John as he only has the use of one arm. Neither of them want her to hold her emotions in; they would only fester and re-emerge later on.

"It's okay Sam, it's okay to cry." Elizabeth says as John kisses her slightly warm forehead, slightly annoyed that he has to keep his left arm in the sling.

Tears continue falling from Sam's eyes as John sighs, he's seen her like this a handful of times.

"She's having a nightmare." John whispers to Elizabeth, who nods in response as John continues gently rubbing Sam's side.

He gently kisses her on the lips in an effort to get her attention and wake her as gently as he can. It begins to work as multiple soft kisses lessen Samantha's tears and she slowly begins to open her own eyes, though her body remains still.

"There we go." John whispers, a wide smile falling across his face as he looks into Sam's dazed eyes.

Elizabeth leans back in her chair allowing John to kiss Sam one more time, this one being much longer than the others.

"I'm glad to see you." He continues gently, his words causing Sam to smile.

"I'm glad to see you too." Sam replies quietly, quickly forgetting the nightmare she just had as she gazes into John's eyes.

Elizabeth continues to look on, not wanting to disturb the couple as they quietly wake up while the morning wears on.

Date: Sunday, December 13th, 2020

Time: 0748hrs SST

Location: Midway Base, Former US Minor Outlying Island, Pacific Ocean

Temperature: 28 Degrees Fahrenheit

Sam's parents woke up about fifteen minutes ago, slightly startled to see Elizabeth in the room, though instantly welcoming her as they said good morning to their daughter. However, Neil, Clara and Jeremy are still sound asleep in the other hospital room, not that anyone minds.

"How'd you sleep?" Abigail asks her daughter gently, breaking the silence.

"Pretty good." Sam replies smiling back, keeping her eyes partially closed as she gently adjusts the blanket that's covering her and her boyfriend.

She's already forgotten about the nightmare that caused her to wake up in the first place, something that John and Elizabeth are happy to see and not going to remind her of anytime soon.

"How about you?" Josiah asks directing his comment to John, who only smiles.

There is a soft knock on the door before it opens revealing Doctor Koothrappali, gently holding a clipboard in her experienced hands.

"Mornin' Doc." John says slipping into a southern accent; his eyes closed.

Sam remains curled up in John's right arm, making sure everyone sees that she is perfectly comfortable right where she is.

"Good morning Mr. Hilderbrand. I'm glad to see that you're awake and hope you remember that I am not just here for emergencies." She replies, carefully checking his vital signs and taking his blood pressure from his slung left arm.

"Yes mother." John replies in a joking tone that gets the doctor to laugh, having heard the remark from multiple members of the squadron.

"All things considered; you're doing well commander. Though I am definitely going to say you're grounded for at least the next week. After that, you're going to have to take it easy, so you don't reopen the wound." She says after writing the readings down on the clipboard as John opens his eyes.

"I'll certainly try Doc." He says, not even trying to hide the sarcasm.

"I'm sure you will." She replies, doing the same as everyone in the room begins to laugh, including Sam, who continues to keep her eyes closed.

"Don't worry, I'll make sure he does." A soft, tired voice says, muffled slightly by John's shirt and chest.

"Will you now?" John asks her quietly, chuckling as he looks down into Sam's eyes, transfixed by their beauty.

Sam only nods in response with a wide smile across her face causing Elizabeth and her parents to laugh as John kisses her gently on the forehead.

"Looks like you've been told commander." Doctor Koothrappali says, beaming as she experiences the same joy as those in the room.

"Yeah, looks like I have." John replies calmly, finally turning back to look at Doctor Koothrappali, "Thanks Doctor, go get some breakfast before it gets cold."

"Thank you commander, I'll be in around eleven hundred hours unless something comes up." She replies, heading out the door.

All of them have been so used to the breakneck pace of having to execute mission after mission, as well as solving crisis after crisis, that they don't know what it's like to have nothing to do. A messenger brings the morning intelligence update, but it doesn't share any new information; all is quiet for the time being.

"Speaking of breakfast, does anyone want anything?" Josiah finally asks the room, breaking the short period of silence.

"I could go for some French toast." Elizabeth says after taking a moment.

"Same." Sam jumps in.

"How about you John?" Josiah asks as his wife begins collecting their things.

"Thanks but I think if I eat something right now, I'll puke." He says, remembering what happened the first time he was shot.

"Understandable, we'll get the order in and freshen up while it's cooking." Abigail says, handing her husband his coat which he promptly puts on.

"Sounds like a plan. Thanks for doing this." John says, carefully shaking each of their hands while having Sam move as little as possible.

"Thanks." Sam adds.

Her parents then leave the room and the brief moments of activity, calm back down to a steady and unsure silence, though this time John has the perfect topic to keep the three of them from growing uncomfortable.

"So, have you and Jeremy picked a day yet?" He asks Elizabeth, snapping her out of the slight trace she was in.

"Uhh...umm... not really. We haven't talked about it with everything going on." She replies, slightly confused at first as she almost forgot what she had asked John a couple of days ago.

"Why not Christmas Eve?" Sam suggests, starting to sit up more and allowing John to regain the feeling in his arm, though he still keeps it around her as she readjusts the comforter.

Elizabeth takes a moment to think, slowly realizing just how close to Christmas they are and just how perfect a Christmas wedding would be.

"That... that could work." She says, almost desperate to present the idea to her fiancé, though not for his approval, mainly to tell him that it's happening.

"Eleven days to plan and organize a wedding... should be doable." John thinks aloud.

"It won't be too much trouble will it?" Elizabeth asks, knowing the tactical situation could change at any possible moment.

"None at all Liza, though I don't know how much I, Neil or Clara will be able to help over the next week given the shape we're in." He says calmly.

"I hope the staff is willing to pick up the slack. I know it's not their area of expertise." Elizabeth says, her tone making sure that her comment is well received by both her commander and Samantha.

"Honestly, I think they would welcome it. It'd be a nice change of pace for them when compared to their usual work." John says gently scratching Sam's back as she tries and fails to scratch an itch because she can't reach it.

"When what is compared to their work?" A voice asks jokingly from the doorway.

"Glad to see you're up sweetie." Elizabeth says as her fiancé enters the room, clearly in need of a shower.

"Likewise honey." He responds still processing the fact that his commander is fully conscious.

"Don't look so shocked Jeremy, you haven't even heard what we've decided yet." John says shaking his hand.

"What do you mean John?" He asks, clearly confused as he sits down next to his fiancé and she leans into his arms, smiling.

"Well, we decided that you and Elizabeth are going to get married on Christmas Eve." He says softly, and Jeremy's eyes grow wider and wider.

"Do we have enough time t-... I mean... can we..." He stutters, unable to speak.

"Breathe Jeremy, it'll all work out." John says reassuring his stunned friend.

Jeremy doesn't reply, instead choosing to sit there and smile as his fiancé playfully kisses his cheek.

"Should we make sure Neil and Clara aren't alone when they wake up?" Sam suggests calmly, realizing that everyone who was in their room is now in John's.

John only nods and Sam, Elizabeth and Jeremy proceed to help him out of his bed. Making sure that John's I.V. line doesn't come out of his left hand and doesn't get tangled around his body as Sam pushes it along next to the two of them. The group moves slowly as John steadily regains his balance and strength in his legs as a dull pain causes him to wince with every step. Sam is briefly concerned when she notices but John does his best to reassure her that the pain is nothing to worry about though he does accept her assistance in holding himself upright.

Jeremy and Elizabeth walk slowly behind them, hand in hand, so completely overtaken by both each other and their upcoming wedding.

Date: Sunday, December 13th, 2020

Time: 1610hrs FKST

Location: UNS - Dallas off the coast of Stanley, Falkland Islands

Temperature: 30 Degrees Fahrenheit

Captain Xi has just laid down in his quarters as the Dallas floats quietly next to the Andromeda. Tomorrow they're going to make way for the Panama Canal with the rest of the fleet in order to regroup, rearm and resupply at Midway Base. His crew has enjoyed the last few days in the Falklands, taking full advantage of the much-needed time off. Some of them are still at their posts however, keeping an ear out for any possible threats that could approach the fleet. The Captain's phone rings, slightly waking him though he calmly answers.

"Conn, this is Sonar." Turke says on the other end of the line.

"Go ahead Turke." He replies quietly, knowing that if someone is calling him at this time it likely isn't good.

"Sir I am picking up something in the high frequency band. It's faint and far away but definitely man made." Turke replies, his voice unwavering.

"Alright, I'll be right there." Xi says reluctantly, hoping that the noise is nothing he needs to worry about.

Carefully getting out of his bunk, the Captain throws on his uniform and makes his way to the bridge as the rest of the crew arrives back on board. Arriving at Turke's sonar station, he puts on the spare headset to listen to the noise that he has noted in the submarine's system.

"How far away is this?" He asks Turke after a few seconds.

"Thirty thousand yards and closing at forty-two knots." Turke replies, taking a moment to double check the reading.

Captain Xi lowers his head, there is only one thing that goes that quickly and makes that noise.

"Cast off the lines, alert the fleet, there's a torpedo in the water." He shouts over the submarines intercom system, followed swiftly by the action stations alarm.

Everyone on board snaps to their battle stations as the crew of the Andromeda cuts the lines holding the cruiser to the submarine. Admiral Anderson orders a defensive formation as the Dallas dives to two hundred feet below the waves. The cruisers, Andromeda and Helena, and the destroyers, Samuel B. Roberts and Johnston, instantly surround the Kestrel and Georgia with a defense box lead by the two destroyers. The torpedo is twenty thousand yards away when the Dallas is able to identify it as a Mark 42 ADCAP, launched at least forty thousand yards from the fleet, though they can't seem to locate what launched it.

"Get me something Turke." Captain Xi says, having moved to the center of the bridge, plotting a course to intercept the torpedo with noise makers.

"Trying sir." The sonar operator replies doing what he can to not panic, peering into the dark sea through his waterfall display.

Admiral Anderson is soon joined by Rob on the bridge of the Kestrel as they turn into the wind and prepare to launch two anti-submarine S-3 Vikings in order to assist the Dallas in the search for their hidden attacker. The torpedo is ten thousand yards away.

"What's the latest Rob?" Anderson asks, making sure there isn't anything he needs to know at this very moment.

"Nothing and that's the problem." He replies, frantically searching through the latest intelligence reports from the Andromeda as well as Midway base.

As he searches the reports, he sends a message to Midway Base's Intelligence Center, informing them of the surprise attack. The torpedo picks up on the first noise maker dropped by the Dallas, latching onto it like a dog attacking a bone. The fact that the torpedo stays latched onto the noise maker, instantly tells the fleet that there is no one guiding the torpedo, a lucky break. When it finds the first noise maker, it tries to go into countermeasure homing, but suddenly runs out of fuel and sinks to the bottom of the Atlantic Ocean. The fleet breathes a tentative sigh of relief but remains at action stations as the crew of the Dallas tries to pick up any trace of the submarine that launched the torpedo.

"Conn Sonar. Contact bearing zero three zero, classified Sierra one. Contact identified as United States Seawolf Class. Range is five zero thousand yards and opening." Turke finally calls out as he picks up a faint sound signature.

The submarine's location is pinpointed on the tactical map in the bridges and CIC's of all the ships in the fleet and the two S-3 Viking's are guided in to drop sonar buoys on top of the lone American submarine. The drop goes as planned and soon the sub is boxed in and unable to escape the grasp of the initiative's naval forces.

Four torpedo's are soon dropped in the water and heading for the Seawolf as its crew tries to work out what to do. Unfortunately for them, there is nothing they can do, and all four torpedoes hit home, ripping the unfortunate submarine to pieces before it sinks to the bottom of the Atlantic. The fleet stands down, once the solemn news is confirmed by Turke on board the Dallas.

"I'm sure John is going to love this." Rob says taking a breath, though only receiving a glancing look from the battle-hardened Admiral.

Within the span of a couple of weeks, the initiative has shot down an American stealth fighter and sunk one of the United States Navy's most advanced submarines. The facts being presented aren't making a comfortable picture, especially since the United States was one of the key players in the initiative forming in the first place.

Date: Sunday, December 13th, 2020

Time: 0830hrs SST

Location: Midway Base, Former US Minor Outlying Island, Pacific Ocean

Temperature: 29 Degrees Fahrenheit

"What the actual fuck!?" John exclaims nearly chucking his phone to Japan upon hearing the news.

"Just get to the damn canal and back to base." He continues barely calming down before hanging up and tossing the phone to Jeremy who puts it on a nearby table.

Everyone in the medical center heard the outburst and is reluctant to even go near the emotional commander as he strains against the sling holding his left arm.

"Come here John, you need to relax." Sam says, sitting on Clara's bed as she is still lying with Neil in his.

She's the only one who dares to speak and is thankful her parents were out of earshot for the outburst. Having been called to the Intelligence Center a few minutes ago, around the same time one of the nurses removed the I.V. from John's left hand.

John debates the words of his girlfriend as his blood slowly comes back down from a boil. Eventually, he gently sits down next to her; the tension in his body slowly being released as she wraps her left arm around him, and he wraps his right arm around her. The calming sensation brought on by the half hug, bringing John's blood pressure under control and relieving the remaining tension in his back. Everyone understands his frustration, they just wish they weren't around when he expresses it so abruptly and bluntly.

"You alright commander?" Elizabeth finally asks gently, noticing the change in John's mood.

"Yeah... I'm better." He replies, a statement that likely would not have been said barely a couple of months ago.

"Good to hear." Neil says with a tired smile, still holding Clara in his arms as they lay comfortably in his bed.

John smiles, glad that he was able to quickly dissipate his anger. A feat that he knows he would not have been able to accomplish on his own.

"Do you have an idea of what you want your wedding to look like?" Clara asks, moving the conversation along.

The question catches Jeremy and Elizabeth slightly off guard, betraying the fact that they haven't given it too much thought since the proposal in the Falklands.

"I'm not sure... I was thinking more of a modern feel... I don't know though... sweetie?" Elizabeth says, hoping Jeremy will be able to bail her out of having to completely answer the question.

"I would agree..." He says tepidly, clearly not wanting to commit to too much at this stage in the process, "Though I like the idea of incorporating Christmas somehow."

"What about some traditional elements? I always kind of wanted a dress with a lot of lace and a long train." Elizabeth interjects as more and more ideas begin to take shape in her mind.

"It's ok you two, we have some time." John says gently, having picked up on the unsure nature of his friends comments, "Besides, it's not like you don't have help or anything."

Elizabeth laughs as everyone else smiles, both due to the truth of John's statement, and out of happiness at how involved John is allowing himself to be. They know that he could be dragged away at any moment, despite his injury, but he usually would actively avoid conversations such as these when the initiative first started. He's finally lightening up and it's all thanks to Sam.

Chapter Twenty-Three

Date: Monday, December 14th, 2020

Time: 1232hrs SST

Location: Midway Base, Former US Minor Outlying Island, Pacific Ocean

Temperature: 31 Degrees Fahrenheit

Most of the last twenty-four hours have been a frantic mix of figuring out why the United States launched a torpedo at the initiatives fleet and how they're going to pull off Elizabeth and Jeremy's dream wedding in ten days. The entire base has come together in a massive effort to pull the whole event off, even the children are making decorations and writing cards for the event.

Neil and Clara have been fully discharged from the medical center, though can't help as much as they would like. John, much to his frustration, still has his left arm in a sling, rendering him physically useless when it comes to the wedding preparations. To keep their commander from becoming too frustrated with the situation and to keep his mind busy, Sam, Jeremy and Elizabeth keep him heavily involved in the planning stage of the wedding.

John appreciates the gesture though he also feels a certain amount of regret when he gets dragged away to receive another intelligence report or update from the fleet as they head for the Panama Canal. Everyone is on edge, waiting for the inevitable response from the United States; whose government has already pulled back the Truman and Ford battle groups from the Sea of Japan. The latest tactical intelligence supports the fact that their path back to the United States will take them within striking distance of Midway Base; a prospect that has raised the young commander's blood pressure.

"How much time do we have?" Rob asks him as he looks down at the latest report in the Intelligence Center as Sam looks on from the doorway, still tired from the beginning of her training this morning.

John adjusts the massively uncomfortable sling that is continuing to dig into his neck, forcing him to consider violating Doctor's orders; it wouldn't be the first time.

"I say a week to nine days at most, depending on whether or not these storms slow them down." He replies, finally making up his mind with regards to the sling around his arm as he unbuckles the strap holding it to his body.

Sam doesn't protest, knowing how much the sling annoys her boyfriend and instead decides to help him remove it as gently as possible.

"That's cutting it awfully close, even if we travel at maximum speed." Rob replies simply.

"Well it's the hand we've been dealt Rob so there's not much we can do about it." The commander replies, gently stretching his arm until he can't move it any longer, as Sam throws the sling in the trash.

"Roger that commander, enjoy lunch." Rob says ending the call.

"Come, everyone's waiting." Sam says, gently taking his right hand and leading him out of the room.

"How was your first day?" John asks as they exit into the cool, crisp air, the sun peeking through the early afternoon cloud cover.

"Tiring, it's been awhile since I've had a workout that intense." She remarks.

“I hate to say it, but it’s only going to get more intense.” He chuckles.

“I’m sure it will, but that’s okay, because I have you.” She says, hugging him tightly as he kisses her on her forehead.

“Yeah you do.” He replies softly as they reach the restaurant, welcoming the blast of warm air that engulfs them when they open the door.

They are immediately greeted by Sam’s parents, who have quickly grown accustomed to their new jobs in the initiative. They lead the couple to the squadrons usual table where the rest of the squadron is already seated. With everyone present, the waiter takes their order and the squadron settles in to enjoy the break.

“How are things coming with the wedding?” Sam asks Elizabeth as an appetizer of garlic bread is brought to the table.

“Well we have color scheme picked out as well as the menu, but not much else.” She replies, taking a piece of garlic bread before passing it down the table.

“It’s a start at least.” Sam responds smiling.

“Yeah, it just seems like there is so much to get done.” Elizabeth continues with a slight laugh.

“It is a lot, but it’s worth it.” Abigail interjects, overhearing the conversation from her seat next to her daughter.

Elizabeth’s appreciates Abigail’s remark; it brings her a certain level of calm having someone who has planned a wedding before there to help with the whole process. Another thing that’s been helping has been the lack of worry about how much the wedding is going to cost, with the UN giving the initiative an almost unlimited budget to work with. This clause helpfully covers weddings as they are good for the initiatives morale and the UN figured they were bound to take place at some point.

"Do you think the United States would be willing to attack us? Even after supplying us with most of our firepower?" Jeremy asks, sharing the same concern that John is currently experiencing.

"Yes I do. I think they know we were the ones who shot down their stealth fighter and they are definitely aware that we destroyed one of their three Seawolf class submarines." John replies, taking a quick drink.

"So in a week, we might have two carrier battle groups to deal with." Jeremy replies trying to get a complete grasp on the situation.

"Yep. Just another day at the office." John says jokingly.

"Seems like it." Jeremy says calmly, gently taking a drink from the beer in front of him.

The lunch continues in characteristically joyful fashion, helping the entire squadron keep their minds off of the impending confrontation. Despite this however, John is glad that they are planning Elizabeth and Jeremy's wedding. It gives him and the entire initiative something to look forward to after the confrontation with the Americans. Almost as if someone, somewhere, is trying to subtly tell them that everything is going to be okay. Even this feeling can't change the fact that the squadron is going to have to go back to the United States and address the repeated attacks on the initiative.

"Clara, Sam, Mrs. Adams, would you want to help me pick out a wedding dress this evening?" Elizabeth asks near the end of their allotted lunch time.

“Absolutely!!” Sam yells with enough excitement to make everyone turn and look in her direction.

“Sure thing.” Clara adds after being dragged into a group hug with Elizabeth by the still extremely excited Sam as the rest of the squadron looks on and laughs at the whole scene.

Date: Monday, December 14th, 2020

Time: 1747hrs SST

Location: Midway Base, Former US Minor Outlying Island, Pacific Ocean

Temperature: 29 Degrees Fahrenheit

Sam, her mother, Clara and Elizabeth have been looking at dresses on a massive screen, all of which are available in Elizabeth’s size and being presented by the initiative designer. The young woman finally happy to be presenting something other than new designs for uniforms and simple utilitarian clothing, both of which are a severe waste of her talents. This, however, is what’s she has been waiting for; to design and present a dress for one of the members of the initiative’s star squadron and she couldn’t be more excited if she tried.

“What about this one?” She asks, wiping the blonde hair out her eyes, not even noticing that Elizabeth has been struggling to pick a dress for the last forty-five minutes.

An elegant, long sleeved wedding gown that’s covered in lace and floral accents appears on the screen before the women, which is also reflective so Elizabeth can imagine how she would look in the dress.

"Almost seems like it's too much. I don't know." Elizabeth states, clearly struggling.

"You sure? I think it fits your style perfectly Liza." Clara says studying the dress closely, almost as if she is picking out a dress for herself.

"We could always set this one aside for you to try on." The designer suggests.

Elizabeth takes a moment to consider the suggestion while examining the dress further; noticing that Sam has remained rather quiet as she sits on a nearby bench.

"Yeah let's do that." She eventually says as the designer makes a quick note on tablet, "Give us a minute Martha." She says quietly, holding up her left index finger before approaching Sam.

It takes her several seconds to realize what Elizabeth has said and even longer to notice that the soon to be bride is sitting next to her.

"Everything alright?" Elizabeth asks her, placing her hand gently on her lap.

"Yeah... sorry... just memories... Richard and I would sometimes talk about getting married and... this whole thing just kind of reminded me of that... I was so excited because... because I was hoping this would help me forget the whole thing but... I'm sorry if I haven't been much help." Sam replies, reluctant to share what she's been feeling but it comes out in a massive wave once she starts talking.

"It's okay Sam, no need to apologize." Elizabeth starts, hugging the emotional twenty-one-year-old, "The only thing that will likely help you forget those conversations is talking about it with John."

"Talk to John about getting married?" Sam says with a chuckling gasp; gently wiping the single tear from her left cheek, "How would I even start a conversation like that? Is that even appropriate?"

Sam's mother hangs back, already knowing more than her daughter does regarding the answer to her question. Elizabeth sighs, completely understanding where Sam is coming from, chuckling at the thought.

"I know it seems daunting but give it a shot. As you know, he has human moments from time to time." Elizabeth says reassuringly.

"True." She says simply, still trying to figure out how to approach the subject, and trying to hide this fact from Elizabeth so she can still have a good time this evening.

Unluckily for Sam, Elizabeth sees right through her facade, having been taught the same technique by the same person.

"How about we pick out your wedding dress? Maybe that will get you to believe me a bit more." She recommends kindly yet conveying that she will not accept no for an answer.

"Uh... uhm..." Sam barely utters before Elizabeth takes her by the arm and drags her in front of the screen, much to the amusement of Martha, Clara and her mother.

"Martha, I want you to show a few dresses to Sam. I'll try on the three we set aside later." Elizabeth says quickly, the excitement of the situation overtaking her body; an excitement that also begins to overtake Martha and the still sore Clara.

Clara winces, sitting down on the now vacant bench to prevent the pain from overtaking her. She adjusts the bandages and checks the various stitches scattered around her young body, making sure they are still intact from the brief outburst. Martha quickly begins showing various pictures of wedding dresses, but only one captures Sam's attention, completely and totally.

Date: Monday, December 14th, 2020

Time: 2153hrs SST

Location: Midway Base, Former US Minor Outlying Island, Pacific Ocean

Temperature: 25 Degrees Fahrenheit

Sam enters John's house, having spent the last few hours looking at dresses for Elizabeth and, surprisingly, for herself as well. She had noticed the living room light was on, bringing her a certain level of warmth and comfort knowing that John was relaxing rather than working. She smiles as she finds him sitting on the couch with the television on, his eyes closed.

"Sweetheart... I'm home." She whispers, wrapping her arms around him from behind the couch and kissing his cheek.

She's careful to avoid his left shoulder, not wanting to cause him any pain.

"Hey sweetie." He says softly, placing his right hand on her right arm while keeping his eyes closed, "How was dress shopping?"

"It went well, Liza was finally able to pick a dress after looking at a couple hundred of them." She replies, climbing over the back of the couch and making herself comfortable in John's arms, who quietly chuckles.

“That sounds like Liza.” He says, recalling all the times he went clothes shopping with her and Jeremy and realizing that Sam wasn’t much better.

“Yeah.” She smiles, happy to be curled up in her boyfriend’s arms, though Elizabeth’s earlier remark hangs on her mind, “Can I ask you something?”

“What’s up?”

Sam begins speaking on instinct rather than thinking, hoping that it will make things easier.

“Do you think we should get married?”

John considers the question, his tiredness mitigating the shock of hearing the word “married” come out of his girlfriend’s mouth. Though, it also brings him a level of comfort and excitement to hear her even consider the concept with him.

“Well... do you want to?” He quietly asks, barely knowing what words are coming out of his mouth, though managing to deliver them with complete compassion and without giving away the fact that her parents already know.

Sam slowly realizes what John has asked as tiredness begins to overtake her body, rendering her momentarily unable to process John’s question. A thought runs through her mind at this exact moment, remembering what Elizabeth had told her before they started looking at dresses for her.

“Yeah... someday.” She whispers, closing her eyes as John’s arms begin to feel more like a blanket.

John smiles, finally opening his eyes for the first time since Sam walked through the door.

"Me too." He gently whispers in Sam's ear before reaching for the television remote and turning off the television.

He carefully adjusts Sam in his arms to get her facing towards him as he carefully lifts her into the air, despite the incredible amount of pain the maneuver is causing him. Sam instinctively, wraps her arms around him, careful to avoid his injured shoulder. John gently carries her to the bedroom, turning off the living room light as he walks by the switch, navigating to the bed on pure memory and limited vision. The two of them change in silence before cuddling up to each other under the massive comforter once more. Happy to be doing so in something other than a hospital bed, which they both agreed, wasn't the easiest or most comfortable thing to do. It doesn't take long for the couple to drift off to sleep, floating in each other's embrace, having both gotten the answers they needed.

Date: Thursday, December 17th, 2020

Time: 0934hrs SST

Location: Midway Base, Former US Minor Outlying Island, Pacific Ocean

Temperature: 28 Degrees Fahrenheit

Clara and Neil look on as Sam works her way through the same obstacle course they navigated at least a hundred times during training. They're impressed by how easily she is able to navigate her way through it, with only John being able to pick it up quicker.

Over the last couple of days, Elizabeth and Jeremy's wedding has begun to take shape, with Elizabeth's dress and Jeremy's suit having been chosen. They're also supposed to pick the playlist for the wedding by lunchtime today.

"Take a break Sam, you've already done three runs this morning. No need to show off." Neil says, calling the sweating young adult over to him and his girlfriend.

She breathes heavy once reaching them in order to catch her breath as quickly as possible, thankfully able to keep down her small breakfast.

"We don't need you to get hurt out there." Clara remarks as Sam takes a quick drink of water before letting the bottle fall to the ground, trying to make her lungs as large as possible by putting her hands on her head.

"With us and Elizabeth grounded, the only people capable of putting up a fight are yourself and Jeremy; and the only one stupid enough to, is your boy-." Neil says, getting cut off by a swift punch to the gut; the only part of his body without any bandages covering it.

"Don't ever call my boyfriend stupid." Sam says placing her hands back on her head as Clara gasps and then laughs at the sight of her own boyfriend crumpling to the ground.

"Ok... noted... ow... that hurt." Neil says barely able to speak through the pain before Clara helps him up.

"You are definitely John's girlfriend." Clara says gently brushing the snow and dirt off of her boyfriend.

"I'll say." He says, not surprised that he got punched for his earlier comment.

Speaking of the still injured commander, he is back in the Intelligence Center, receiving an update on the whereabouts of the

American fleet; they are projected to enter the winter storms by the end of the day. The United Nations fleet is still making best speed back to the island, but whether or not they make it in time largely depends on how strong the winter storm is.

The whole situation is plotted out on the table for John to see and process, though he knows there is nothing he can do. His fighter doesn't have the range to strike the battle groups and even if it did, he's in no condition to fly, let alone into a winter storm. All he can do is stay at the base and monitor the situation as it unfolds, all the while helping his close friends plan their perfect wedding.

Chapter Twenty-Four

Date: Saturday, December 19th, 2020

Time: 1121hrs SST

Location: Midway Base, Former US Minor Outlying Island, Pacific Ocean

Temperature: 28 Degrees Fahrenheit

The tension has been building, as the American fleet draws closer and closer. So much so that even the not insubstantial amount of joy brought by the planning of Elizabeth and Jeremy's wedding can overshadow what is looming over the horizon. In two days the American's will arrive just right around noon and the options are looking increasingly grim.

The impending conflict weighs heavily on the young commander; despite having to disarm a nuke during the last mission, the thought of having to face off against the United States Navy has him shaking. Sam's soft embrace and warm kisses are the only thing that is able to break through the dread he is feeling.

"I want to apologize for being tense over the last few days." He says looking out over the base from the massive fourth floor conference room where he has just finished briefing his commanders before Sam entered the room.

"Don't apologize. I understand." She says softly, gently running her hands over his shoulders.

"You shouldn't have too." He says quietly, bowing his head slightly.

"Do you want an ibuprofen?" She asks feeling his boiling hot forehead for the first time that day.

"Yeah, thanks." He says as she takes a small container out of her pocket and handing both it and a water bottle to her tired boyfriend; he takes the medicine without hesitation and hands the bottle back to her.

Sam sets the bottle on the table behind her before returning to her boyfriend, wrapping her arms around him and leaving him no choice but to wrap his arms around her.

"You need to relax." She says hopefully.

"I wish I could sweetheart, I wish I could." He replies quietly.

"I know." She starts before wondering about the rest of the day, "Are we going to be able to do dinner tonight?"

"Of course sweetie. I may have meetings all day today, but I will always make time for you." He replies calmly, the warmth in his voice finally managing to overcome the stress of the situation.

"That's good to hear." She replies, closing her eyes and leaning against John in an effort to get him to come back to his house.

"Tired?" He asks, noticing what Sam is trying to do.

"Maybe." She replies, her tone holding both truth and sarcasm effortlessly.

John chuckles, appreciating her tone though feeling a pang of dread as well, as he knows he can't take a nap with her right now.

"Unfortunately, I have to work Sam." He says, disappointed in his own inability to be with her when she wants him to be.

"It's okay." She says, still smiling before kissing him on the lips, knowing that she was reaching a bit and wanting him to stay happy, "It's okay."

John wishes the kiss would never end; the act returning a level of comfort to his body, much like the fact that they have been sleeping together ever since their relationship started. In fact, their relationship has been so naturally formed that the short amount of time it took them to go from hugging to making out simply felt right to both of them. Afterall, they've known each other for so long that everything has just felt right.

When they finally part, it doesn't take long for a call waiting screen to show up on the glass projector screen causing the couple to sigh as John gently touches the answer button.

"Go ahead Rob." He says placing his hands on his hips.

"Good morning commander, I hope I'm not interrupting anything." Rob replies as he appears on the screen.

"I would rephrase your statement, if I were you, but that's neither here nor there. What do you need?" John replies sarcastically.

"My apologies commander. I just wanted to let you know that our fleet is projected to arrive an hour before the US battle group." Rob says quickly, wanting to move the conversation along before John's temper flares up again.

"That is good news Rob, I'm glad to hear it." John says simply, the news providing him some semblance of relief.

"I thought you might, though the crews of our ships are slightly upset that their shore leave was cut short." Rob continues, beginning to run through the bulleted list in front of him.

"They'll get over it once they get back. Speaking of, when you arrive I want you to split the two squadrons and send the Georgia's battle group twenty miles to the south. The Americans might not fall for it, but it's worth a shot." John says running through his list of topics and forcing Rob to throw his list in the trash can next to him; much to the amusement of Admiral Anderson who is just off screen.

"Are you sure that splitting our forces is ideal commander?" Rob asks, wanting to know his commanders thinking.

"I'm hoping it will divide their attention long enough that we can destroy a few support ships and make them question whether or not they actually want to attack us." He says without hesitation.

"Sound thinking commander." Rob says knowing the alternative is the Americans potentially wiping out the entire fleet at once.

"I would hope so because I just thought of it." John replies causing Rob to almost spit out the water he just drank, "Relax, I thought through it last night."

"I would certainly hope so." He yells as he walks off screen to grab a towel, with Admiral Anderson replacing him in the camera's view as John chuckles.

"How are you holding up Admiral?" He says composing himself.

"Just fine commander, yourself?" He replies, an experienced smile falling across his face.

"I'd doing a lot better if the Americans didn't object to Jeremy and Elizabeth getting married." John quips, briefly searching through an intelligence report on a tablet before handing it to Sam.

"Now that's rather unsporting of them." Anderson replies with a slight chuckle and an air of confidence.

"I would say." Sam interjects, placing the tablet next the bottle of water.

"We'll just have to teach them some manners then won't we." Anderson continues playing into the humor of the whole situation.

"Yes we will Admiral, yes we will." John says before moving on through his list of topics with the Admiral and Rob, all the while, keeping Sam in the room.

Date: Saturday, December 19th, 2020

Time: 1921hrs SST

Location: Midway Base, Former US Minor Outlying Island, Pacific Ocean

Temperature: 27 Degrees Fahrenheit

The entire squadron has now gathered in the fourth-floor conference room, including Sam's parents and Martha the designer. In an effort to take everyone's minds off of the mission, it was decided to have a meeting about what still needs to be done with regards to Jeremy and Elizabeth's wedding. Thankfully, being at Midway Base has its perks in this area, as does being in the initiative.

"So the color scheme and style, the dress, the grooms outfit, the menu, the playlist and the venue have all been sorted out." Martha begins as images of all the items appear on the projected screen behind her; everything except the wedding dress.

"That leaves..." Abigail says prompting further discussion.

"The bridesmaid dresses, we decided on those an hour ago." Elizabeth says, an image of the long pink gowns appearing on the screen.

"You don't need to worry about the "save the dates" or "RSVP's. Everyone who would attend is either already here or on their way." Sam adds, grateful to be talking about something other than the American fleet.

"You also don't have to worry about the cost." John adds, which would be substantial at this point.

"That just leaves..." Martha says crossing things off of the list on her own tablet, "picking the maid of honor, best man, bridesmaids, groomsmen as well as the schedule, passages and vows that will be read during the ceremony."

"Geez. One thing down and two more take its place." Jeremy says, starting to become overwhelmed by the experience of wedding planning.

"It seems like it but you're almost there. One more round of decisions and you're done." Neil chimes in with his calm, dulcet tones, easing the tension.

"Hard to believe we're five days away honey." Elizabeth says now taking her fiancé's hand, as the two of them smile before kissing gently and blushing.

"Yeah that's true." He smiles after the kiss, pulling Elizabeth into his arms.

"Alright everyone, I hate to end this meeting early, but I need you to grab a bite to eat and head to bed. Unfortunately we have a situation to deal with and I need everyone rested. The first briefing will occur at zero nine hundred tomorrow morning." John says wrapping up the meeting after checking his watch.

"Roger that commander." Clara says, not thinking twice as Martha begins shutting down the presentation and projector screen.

"Stay here a second Martha." John whispers so that only she can hear as everyone leaves the room; Sam initially pauses before he reassures her that he'll catch up.

Once everyone has left the room, John gives the signal to the young designer that it's safe to speak.

"What's on your mind commander?" She asks tepidly, not used to speaking with John alone, let alone face to face.

"I don't really know how else to put this, but Liza doesn't have a father to walk her down the aisle." John begins, deciding the best course of action is to say things bluntly; the news causes Martha to draw short of breath.

"I had no idea." She says sitting down.

"No one does so please keep it to yourself." John says with Martha nodding immediately after the sentence leaves his mouth, "I need your help to steer Jeremy away from asking me to be his best man. I ask this because I know Elizabeth is going to ask me to walk her down the aisle and I don't want to disappoint Jeremy by having to tell him no." He says sitting down in a chair across from the designer in an effort to lessen the intimidation she is feeling.

"I understand commander." Martha replies obediently, nodding her head rapidly, though it doesn't keep her from extending her remarks, "I will do my best to make sure he doesn't ask you."

"Thank you Martha. I expect nothing less." He replies calmly, shaking her hand, though his tone betrays the fact that there is something more he wants to say.

"Is there something else on your mind commander?" She asks still sitting as John heads for the door.

"If... if it's not too stupid to ask... how did your husband propose to you?" He replies scratching the back of his head, unsure if he should even be asking such a question.

"Well, he took me to our favorite restaurant. Nothing fancy, just a diner kind of a place. When the cheesecake came out for desert, there was a small red box on top of it." She replies, slightly taken aback by the question though more than willing to elaborate, "Why do you ask?"

"That's classified Martha sorry." John says with a slight smirk, almost taking pride in the fact that he can keep certain details from her, though he knows her powers of deduction will figure out who he's dating.

"I'm sure it is commander. Have a goodnight." She says, smirking in return; John's prediction immediately coming true.

"You too Martha."

John turns and heads for the elevator, placing his hands in his pockets after pressing the button for the first floor. Stepping out onto the ground floor, he meets up with Sam who had been waiting for him while the others returned to their homes for a home cooked meal with their significant others.

"What was the hold up?" She asks taking his left hand gently to prevent from pulling on the stitches that are still in his shoulder, despite the amount of bandages around his body decreasing over the last few days.

"Nothing, it was nothing." He replies, though his guard is down, and Sam can easily see through his little white lie.

"Sure it was." She says, poking him and teasing him as they make their way across the base.

“Yeah, yeah, you’ll find out when the time is right.” He responds, returning the teasing in kind before wrapping his arms around his girlfriend and spinning her around.

“You’re perfect.” He says stopping the spin and pulling Sam into his arms as he once again gazes into her eyes.

Sam begins to blush and tear up, having never been called that word, by anyone, ever before. She begins to turn away to hide the tears, but she is stopped by John gently placing his right hand against her cheek. She shakes her head slightly, tears falling gently down her cheeks as she struggles to decide whether to be sad or happy before being both at the same time, only confusing her further.

“You’ve always been perfect Sam.” John says, feeling her apprehension as he wipes the tears from her cheeks and she looks back into his eyes, still reluctant to accept what he’s telling her.

“No... no I’m not.” Her voice is barely audible as she once again turns away from her boyfriend, the memories of her previous relationship beginning to overwhelm her.

John shakes his head, not accepting her description of herself.

“No... I’m sure... you’re definitely perfect.” He says calmly, tears of happiness flowing from his eyes as he brushes his hair away from the scar running down his face.

Sam looks back to his eyes, then looks away again, fighting to accept what is being said to her when finally... she turns back one last time. She looks into her boyfriend’s eyes and knows what he’s said is true. She throws her arms around him, forcing him to stagger back as he catches her, tears soaking his shirt. He rubs her back gently, just letting her get her emotions out and calm down on her own time.

“Thank... you... John... Thank you.” She finally says, her voice once again muffled by John’s shirt and her tears.

“You’re welcome Sam, and remember, it’s true, it’s all true.” He replies quietly, getting Sam to bury her face further into his chest.

The couple soon moves inside John’s house, after getting too cold despite being in each other’s arms. They begin cooking together as if they’ve been married for the last decade, sharing multiple cute and playful moments throughout the night including sharing each other’s food as they sit on the couch watching television. In what feels like no time at all, they are laying down in bed together and falling asleep in each other’s arms.

Date: Sunday, December 20th, 2020

Time: 0835hrs SST

Location: Midway Base, Former US Minor Outlying Island, Pacific Ocean

Temperature: 26 Degrees Fahrenheit

“Neil, Clara, are you going to be up to flying today?” John asks as soon as they enter the intelligence center; Jeremy, Elizabeth and Sam’s parents have yet to arrive.

“So long as it doesn’t involve any combat maneuvers and you don’t tell Doctor Koothrappali.” Neil answers after confirming things with his girlfriend.

“Don’t worry, she’s already yelled at me for it. We’re going to be starting combat air patrols today and I am going to need you to take the second CAP after I take Sam up on her first training flight." John continues.

"You sure about that?" Clara asks, simply double checking,

"Like I said Clara, Doctor Koothrappali has already yelled at me at length this morning. I'll have two fighters from red squadron with me." He says annoyed though going along with Clara's question, alleviating any concern she might have.

"Roger that commander." She says as Josiah and Abigail enter the intelligence center.

Jeremy and Elizabeth arrive a short time later having made a stop at the medical center for check up on their baby. It's a healthy pregnancy so far and everyone is hoping that it stays that way.

The screen at the front of the room springs into life with Rob and Admiral Anderson appearing after having their morning coffee in the Kestrels CIC. The minutes tick by until it's time for the briefing to start and John gathers everyone around the table, pulling up a map of the area before clearing his throat.

"Alright, here's what we know so far. The United States has been getting increasingly more aggressive over the last couple of weeks, starting when we had to shoot down one of their raptors. It is assumed this prompted the attempted sinking of our fleet off the coast of the Falkland Islands. This resulted in the sinking of one of their Seawolf class submarines. Now they have made their next move and two carrier strike groups are closing in on our base from the west. They have not made any offensive actions and they haven't tried to make contact through the United Nations. The prelude to this was our mission into North Korea which resulted in the successful destruction of a stolen Russian Nuclear Warhead, the detonator of which was safely dismantled and destroyed earlier this week." John says only stopping to take a quick drink of water to soothe his dry throat.

"Each carrier brings with it a cruiser, two destroyers and a supply ship, for a total of ten ships and at least one hundred and eighty aircraft in two carrier air wings. Compare that with our own battlegroup containing one carrier, one battleship, one submarine, two cruisers and two destroyers and you will realize we have two thirds as many ships and half as many aircraft. We have been trying to contact the American chain of command, but our calls have remained unanswered." He finishes taking another drink of water as Rob takes over the briefing.

"Starting today at twelve hundred hours, we will begin four-hour Combat Air Patrols around Midway Base, beginning with the aircraft already at the base and then supplemented by the Kestrel's strike wing at midnight. At that time, the Georgia battlegroup will split off from the main task force and approach from the south. This is in an effort to lure the American's in a false sense of security. Should shots be fired, we will respond by knocking out their support ships and destroyers with the combined firepower of the carrier strike wing and Georgia's main battery." Rob says, everything he says playing out on the table in front of the squadron, as he too takes a quick break for a drink of water.

"The hope is at this point the Admiral in charge of the American fleet will either retreat to Hawaii or be willing to talk. Opening a dialogue with American chain of command so we can figure out what is going on." Abigail says, picking up the briefing with the ease of a relay runner grabbing a baton, "If not, then we will continue to attack the carriers until they are either wiped out or surrender."

"No matter which option the American's go with, the entire battle is forecast to take most of the day, and we will only be able to sleep once the fighting is over. So enjoy what sleep you can get tonight.

All base activities have been cancelled and everyone is advised to stay in a blast resistant shelter until the fighting stops. While we don't think the American's will attack the base once they see the Kestrel and Georgia, we don't want to take the risk." John finishes, wrapping the briefing up as neatly as a bow on a tightly wrapped Christmas present.

"It looks like we actually stand a chance." Neil says quietly to himself; only his girlfriend hears him and gently takes his hand.

"Any questions?" John asks calmly, everyone shaking their heads in response, "Alright, enjoy the rest while you can, we go to action stations at twelve hundred hours today."

"Roger commander." Everyone says in some form or another before leaving the intelligence center, wishing they could have more time off.

Date: Sunday, December 20th, 2020

Time: 1145hrs SST

Location: Midway Base, Former US Minor Outlying Island, Pacific Ocean

Temperature: 30 Degrees Fahrenheit

John helps to strap Sam into the rear seat of his Phantom as two F/A - 18E Super Hornets roar into life behind them. John has already completed the necessary preflight checks and briefed Sam on what they are going to be doing during their four hours in the air. Even so, Sam is still apprehensive about the whole thing given that she has slept every time she's been in John's plane.

"Alright, you're all set to go." John says after making sure the straps on Sam's helmet are tight around her chin.

"Are you sure about this John? I mean, I've never piloted a plane before." She says hesitantly, though knowing that they are well past the point of no return.

"You'll be fine Sam; I won't let you do anything that will put us at risk." John says warmly, bringing comfort to his girlfriend as he straps into the front seat of the massive fighter, pulling his helmet over his head before calling out, "Red One, Red Two, this is Wolf One requesting a comm check."

"Wolf One this Red One, we are reading you loud and clear." The lead F/A - 18E replies, holding short of the runway as the two engines on John's plane shutter into life, shaking it as Sam catches her breath.

"Roger that Red One. Be advised we aren't expecting any American fighters yet as we are at the limit of their range though keep an eye out just in case." John says glad to hear the older squadron leaders voice as he taxi's his fighter to just behind the two super hornets.

"Roger that Wolf One, we're hoping things stay quiet for now." The squadron leader replies before taxiing onto the runway and requesting permission to takeoff.

Permission is granted and soon the two naval fighters are rocketing down the runway and into the sky. Sam's heart rate doubles as John maneuvers the massive fighter onto the runway. Yes, she's flown with him before, but this is different, this time she is going to take the controls of the fighter and it terrifies her. She wishes there was a simulator at the base, but no such luck is bestowed upon the young woman.

The F-4E's engines roar to life once more, shaking the plane violently as Sam is shoved back in her seat. She can barely move as the massive fighter slips the surly bonds of earth and takes to the sky. John throttles the engines back and forms up with the two red squadron fighters, taking the lead as they climb to twenty thousand feet above the island below them. Sam relaxes, her earlier worry completely set aside as the floating sensation of flight completely overpowers her senses.

"Alright, Red One, Red Two, four hours on the clock and a member to train. Let's settle in." John says calmly over the radio; pain still present in his left shoulder.

Date: Sunday, December 20th, 2020

Time: 1345hrs SST

Location: 20,000 ft over Midway Base

Temperature: 28 Degrees Fahrenheit

"Okay Sam, I want you to take the stick in front of you and pull back gently until we're in a climb." John says, taking his hand off of the control column between his legs though keeping his left hand on the throttle to maintain airspeed.

"Okay, like this?" Sam replies having to sike herself up to take control of the vintage plane.

The fighter slowly begins to rise higher in the sky, followed closely by the two super hornets.

"Good Sam, good. Now push forward on the stick until the plane levels out." John continues, taking it slow with his girlfriend though encouraged by her talent.

Sam does as she's told, pushing forward on the stick and finding it a little more difficult to do as she begins to go weightless, being held in place by the straps attached to the seat. The fighter obediently responds, slowly leveling out now after reaching twenty-five thousand feet.

"That seems easy." Sam exclaims, sitting back in her seat as John takes control once more, something catching his eye on the radar screen in front of him.

"Well, climbing and leveling off is a simple move, just wait until I have you doing barrel rolls." John says, his attention now transfixed by two blips at the very edge of his radars range: popping in and out of view.

"Wolf one are you seeing this?" Red two calls out, as John leads the formation in the direction of the unidentified blips.

"Yeah I'm seeing it Red two." John responds, his eyes now outside the cockpit, looking for any sign of the two contacts; a glint, a vapor trail, something, anything.

"I'm not liking this commander, should we pull back?" Red one asks, his nerves getting the better of him, as the two blips disappear from radar.

"Let's maintain the CAP, Red One. I think they're just feeling us out." John says calmly, turning the formation back on to the designated path.

"Roger commander." Red One replies, still uneasy about the situation.

"Everything okay?" Sam asks, unable to fully understand what's happened.

"For now Sam, for now." John replies, trying to make himself comfortable in his seat, but only succeeding in causing himself more pain thanks to his shoulder.

"Okay." Sam says quietly to herself, settling in for the rest of the flight.

The uneasy feeling continues to grow across the base as the minutes steadily tick by. Any thought of Jeremy and Elizabeth's wedding has completely vanished.

Chapter Twenty-Five

Date: Monday, December 21st, 2020

Time: 0730hrs SST

Location: Midway Base, Former US Minor Outlying Island, Pacific Ocean

Temperature: 26 Degrees Fahrenheit

The Kestrel's fighter wing is finishing up its second Combat Air Patrol as John and Sam begin to wake up, thanks to the blinding light of the sun rise coming in their bedroom window. Neither one of them wants to get up, but daylight beckons it so and thus, John slowly crawls out of bed, sitting at its edge as he stretches his tired and sore arms.

"Don't go." Sam says playful from under the comforter, looking up at her boyfriend with barely open eyes and a smile as she places her hand on his back.

John chuckles, turning to face her before taking her left hand with his right. They both know what has to happen today, but it doesn't make them wish for more time together any less.

"Sleep well?" He asks quietly, placing his left hand on her cheek as he's transfixed by her beauty.

"I always sleep well with you." She replies, holding the hand John has placed on her cheek, keeping a calm smile firmly fixed on her face as she gazes up at him.

"That's good." John says quietly as she uses his arms to hug him.

She's careful to avoid undue stress on John's injured shoulder, knowing the pain the patrols caused him once he landed at midnight and came to bed around one in the morning. He even had to take an ibuprofen just to be able to fall asleep, and yet, he's more worried about how Sam slept. Sam is still constantly amazed by his inexhaustible capability to show her compassion and love in a manner that she never felt she deserved to experience. He had always been kind, had always been nice, even while she was in her other relationship, but the last couple of weeks have shown her that was just the beginning.

"Be careful today. Okay? I need you to come back to me." She says softly, refusing to let go of John until he replies, not that he minds.

"I will." He says, the two words being the only ones he needs to say.

"Good, you better." She replies simply, finally releasing the hug and allowing him to head to the master bathroom in order to get the day started.

As warm steam fills the small bathroom, John carefully takes off his pajamas and carefully removes the only bandage now present on his heavily scarred body. The move reveals the mostly healed wound on the back of his shoulder; the stitches holding it together having finally dissolved during the night though he still needs to be careful. Stepping carefully into the shower, the warm water overtakes his body; open wounds stinging as sore muscles relax, followed by a dull numbness washing over him.

The warm water also brings a welcome respite from the continual cold of the base. This allows the young commander to breathe clearer and forget the near constant threat posed by the world itself. However, all too soon, John has to return to reality and turn off the still warm shower water, drying off using one of the two nearby towels. He pulls on his undergarment as well as a pair of jeans before grabbing a green tee-shirt and heading back into the bedroom where Sam is waiting with a fresh bandage for his shoulder wound. He can't put the bandage on by himself, a fact that both frustrates him and endears Sam to him even more.

"This might hurt slightly." She says as he presents his back to her and she begins the delicate process of applying the bandage.

"You always say that and yet it's somehow never true." John replies as he feels Sam's practiced and gentle touch working its way around his left shoulder.

He's right, Sam is so gentle when applying the bandage that he needn't worry about any sort of pain being caused while she applies the bandage. Upon finishing however, she hesitates, getting a look at all of the scars covering John's back and arms, amazed that he isn't in more pain. She begins to move around to John's front when she is stopped instantly by him gently holding her head and kissing her; knowing what she is looking at and hoping to distract her. Although, it doesn't stop her from getting a closer look at the scar on the left side of his face. It's hid itself well over the last week, but they both know that it will always be there.

"What is it sweetie?" John asks after his lips part from his girlfriend, placing the tee shirt in his hand on the bed next to him.

"Nothing..." She says reluctantly though she can't help but smile before saying, "I do find that scar kind of hot."

John laughs, getting her to laugh in the same instant before he wraps his arms around her and pulls her down on top of him as he lies back on the bed. The two continue to laugh for several minutes as John tries to put the tee shirt on but is continually blocked from doing so. They enjoy the playful moment as much as they can, but soon they both know that they have to get ready. She finally allows him to sit up, helping him put the shirt on and hugging him one last time.

"Have a good day sweetie." John says quietly, holding on to the hug as long as possible.

"You too." She replies before releasing the hug and kissing him once more.

He then grabs his 1911, still in its thigh holster from the previous day, rigs it on his thigh once again. Every adult is going to have a weapon on them today, standard procedure when a threat is so close to the base. Everyone's on a knife edge but is leaning on their training and remaining calm.

Date: Monday, December 21st, 2020

Time: 1100hrs SST

Location: Midway Base, Former US Minor Outlying Island, Pacific Ocean

Temperature: 28 Degrees Fahrenheit

"Has the American fleet made contact?" Jeremy asks, the frantic pace of the Intelligence Center overtaking everyone as the live map updates with the locations of both fleets.

"No, they haven't. They don't even have a Combat Air Patrol in the air." Rob replies, his voice coming through over Jeremy's headset, so they can clearly communicate in the controlled chaos of the Intelligence Center.

"Strange, I would have expected something by now." Clara says, having just entered and put on a headset of her own.

"I would have too. We'll just have to be careful." John says, on final approach with Neil from the CAP; the Kestrels pilots are being briefed.

"Roger that commander. We have a V-22 ready for both of you. Special Forces squadron three is already on board." Elizabeth says studying the map closely as it is continually updated by radar and sonar data.

"Excellent Liza." John says quickly as his fighter touches down on the runway behind Neil's SU-33.

The two pilots taxi to their usual location on the base's ramp, barely fifty yards away from the Osprey as the ten men and women of Special Forces Squadron Three begin loading their equipment. John and Neil jump out of their fighters and head over to the battle-hardened squadron; the same squadron that pulled them out of North Korea while they were unconscious.

"How are you doing commander?" The leader of the squadron says as he places his pack on the Osprey, his beard holding more hair than is on John's head.

"Feeling better than I did when you last saw me Commander Rothberg. Thank you for dragging our asses out of there." John replies shaking his hand, knowing he doesn't have long.

"I would imagine so and just doing our jobs sir." The squad leader replies humbly.

"Still, it's greatly appreciated commander. Have your men been briefed?" John continues, turning to the rest of the squadron.

"Yep and they're ready to go sir." He replies calmly, as if landing a special forces squad on a U.S. carrier is just another day at the office.

"Excellent. We're going to get changed and you'll be the first to know when it's time to go." John says, completely focused on the task at hand.

"Roger that commander." The leader responds calmly before shaking John and Neil's hands and they head for the armory.

Clara begins trying to contact the American Admiral on board CVN - 80, USS Gerald R. Ford, using all known military channels as well as several civilian ones. Her calls initially go unanswered, increasing the tension in the Intelligence Center to an almost fever pitch when finally...

"This is Admiral Perkins, to whom am I speaking?" An elderly voice, even older than Admiral Anderson, calmly calls out over the radio.

"Admiral Perkins, this is Wolf Four of Wolf Squadron with the United Nations. Your fleet is sailing rather close to our base. Please state your intentions." Clara responds, returning the Admirals calm confidence as those present breathe a sigh of relief.

There is a brief pause.

"Wolf Four... our intentions..." The Admiral is hesitating, clearly shaken from having received a radio message from the initiative, acting on orders he doesn't agree with, "We have been ordered to bomb the base."

"Take a breath commander, an Osprey will arrive on your flight deck in ten minutes. Please hold your fire and we will handle things from there." Clara replies calmly as the whole picture becomes clearer.

"Roger Wolf Four." The Admiral says calmly.

"Good thing we were able to encrypt that frequency." Rob says to himself though everyone hears him.

“You said it, not me.” Elizabeth says quickly sending a messenger to the armory, “It looks like someone in the American government isn’t happy.”

“I guess we’re going to find out.” Her boyfriend says as the messenger leaves the room.

It doesn’t take long for the messenger to reach the armory, entering it and breathing heavily as he hands the handwritten note to Neil, who quickly passes it to John after he has his plate carrier and MOLLE panels affixed to his body. He also dismisses the messenger back to the Intelligence Center, ordering him to take it easy and walk.

“We have an audience. That’s a start.” Neil says as John places the note in his pocket and begins loading magazines into the magazine pouches on his legs.

“That it is Neil, but there are a lot of people in that fleet and I am sure there’s at least one that doesn’t like the fact that their Admiral is willing to talk with us.” John responds, keeping his expectations realistic.

“True, though this explains why they haven’t launched a CAP since yesterday.” Neil replies, finishing loading his own magazines and double checking his weapon.

“It does.” John says simply, checking his rifle and making sure there is a round loaded in the chamber, “Shall we see what doth trouble’s the Admirals mind?”

“Roger that commander.” Neil smiles, appreciating John’s joke as the two young adults leave the armory.

A few minutes later, the twin engines on the Osprey roar to life and lift it gracefully into the air. The Kestrel’s fighter wing is back in the air with another four fighter CAP that forms up with the slow lumbering transport.

"Wolf One to Wolf Base, we are five minutes out from the carrier. Have not encountered any resistance enroute." John says over the radio.

"This is Wolf Base, roger that Wolf One, all is quiet on our end. There is no sign that the American Government knows of the conversation we had with the Admiral." Elizabeth responds.

"That's good to hear. Keep an eye on Congress and the President, it might be Christmas break but that doesn't mean they aren't up to something." John replies before heading back from the cockpit to join his men in the cargo hold.

A short while later, the massive American Fleet comes into view below them and the United Nations pilots make contact the Ford's air boss who gives them permission to land on the cleared mid-section of the ship. The Osprey shutters as it transfers from horizontal to vertical flight and lowers gently onto the flight deck.

"Remember, do not fire unless fired upon." The commander of the third Special Forces squadron reminds his men as John and Neil head for the exit ramp, weapons slung in front of them.

The ramp begins to lower, and the cold windy air of the Ford's flight deck fills the small transport plane. The ramp hits the deck with a thud and soon the young commander leads his men into the light, finding they are surrounded by a squad of marines. Behind the marines stands the Admiral, wearing his combat uniform over his battle hardened, fifty-year-old body.

"At ease gentleman." John says calmly, noticing the marines twitching nervously in front of him; some of them are younger than he is.

The Admiral approaches, despite the brief protests of his aids, walking gently through the half circle of marines and standing before John.

"Admiral Perkins, United States Seventh Fleet." He says calmly extending his hand.

"Commander John Hilderbrand, United Nations." John replies emotionless as he extends his right hand.

The two shake, firmly as military leaders do, before the Admiral disperses the marine squadron behind him.

"I hope you don't mind the entourage Admiral, standard procedure when I can't bring the full squadron along." John says motioning to the Special Forces squad standing behind him.

"I understand." The Admiral replies, before motioning towards the control tower, "Let's get inside before we freeze, we have a lot to talk about."

"Lead the way, Admiral." John says simply as the twelve adults follow the Admiral into the control tower and down into the bowels of the ship: the rest of the squadron is monitoring the situation from the Intelligence Center.

"This almost seems too easy." Elizabeth whispers to Clara, wishing they could see where the squad was going.

John doesn't share such reservations however, confidently following the Admiral into the Ford's CIC as multiple sailors stand and salute the Admiral. Upon arriving, the thirteen men and women gather around a backlit table, a relic when compared to the televised tables the initiative uses.

“Immediately following the explosion near Wonsan, we were ordered back to the San Diego. We weren’t told why, but we were told to take a route that went as close as possible to your base. A day later, we were told that on our way past we were to launch two waves of strike fighters and destroy as much of the base as we could in as little time as possible.” The Admiral begins, showing John the communication logs spread out on the table before them.

“So why didn’t you?” John asks calmly, reading the logs over before handing them to Neil.

“We’re not at war with you commander. We have no reason to attack you.” The Admiral replies just as calmly.

“I wouldn’t be so sure about that Admiral. We sunk one of your subs and shot down an F-22.” John says with a slight chuckle.

“Those we were acts of provocation by my superiors; acts that us at the theatre level don’t understand nor agree with.” Admiral Perkins replies urgently.

“Disobeying orders to save your fleet, I admire that Admiral. Who sent the orders?” He says patting the admiral on the shoulder.

“They’re supposedly coming from the Secretary of the Navy at the Pentagon, but I don’t think he is the one actually sending them. He used to be one of us, in command of the Lincoln during the second gulf war.” The Admiral continues, doing his best to vouch for his superior officer.

“I believe you Admiral, but that means these orders are coming from higher up the chain than the Secretary of the Navy.” John continues, reassuring the Admiral.

"There aren't many people further up the chain." He replies, running through the extensively short list in his head.

"On that Admiral, we certainly agree." John says, glad to finally be able to piece things together, but certainly not enjoying what he's been told.

Before the Admiral can speak, one of the marines from earlier enters the CIC, sidearm drawn and leveled at John's head.

"You are under ar-." He begins to speak but is suddenly cut off by a loud and piercing bang as his body slumps to the floor followed by John holstering his 1911.

Everyone stands in stunned silence as they recover from the sudden and deafening noise, trying to make sure their eardrums haven't burst. John and Neil calmly return to looking the audio logs over on the table. Two more marines rush the room and drag their now dead comrade's body away as the Admiral turns back to the table. Those in the Intelligence Center return to work after staring at John's vital signs on the screen at the front of the room.

"My apologies commander." He says not entirely knowing what to say.

"Not to worry Admiral, I had a feeling he was going to try something given that he had his finger on the trigger of his carbine when I arrived." The calm commander replies.

"Do you think anyone else will try the same thing?"

"Most likely, but we're not going to be on board much longer."

"What do you want us to do?" The Admiral asks, clearly struggling to understand who he should be listening too.

"You'll continue to San Diego, as planned, and report that you were able to inflict substantial damage to our base. Meanwhile, we'll head to D.C. and sort things out from there." The young commander replies, speaking slowly so that those in the Intelligence Center can hear him clearly over the radio.

Neil glances at his commander, wondering if that's the best idea but he doesn't question his commander, not now and not in front of the Americans.

"That's a pretty risky plan commander, if you don't mind me saying." The Admiral says still struggling to process what he's been told.

"I know it is, but it's what we've got. I'll work out the details over the next couple of days." John replies, wrapping things up and motioning for one of the Special Forces Soldiers to take pictures of the documents for evidence.

"Okay, I'll trust you commander and I wish you the best of luck." The Admiral finishes, finally calming his nerves.

"Thank you Admiral. Is there anything you want me to mention when I pay your government a visit?" John asks kindly shaking his hand once more as the Special Forces squadron heads for the door.

"If you could, remind them that they serve the people and don't rule over them." He replies, grateful to have his thoughts delivered to his government without causing a conflict of interest or a congressional investigation.

"I'll be sure to relay that. Have a safe voyage Admiral." John replies before heading for the door himself.

"So much for not having to deal with time zones." Neil says sarcastically as they reboard the Osprey with the flight deck crew looking on in stunned silence, having just been told the fate of the misfortunate Marine.

"I know, but it's what we have to do. I hope Elizabeth and Jeremy haven't planned their honeymoon." His commander says as the ramp raises once more.

The engines soon spool into life, the Osprey takes off vertically from the Ford's flight deck as the Admiral orders best speed to the engines and a course for San Diego. His men are unsure if they should shoot the Osprey down or let it be, sensing that retribution would be swift from the United Nations carrier and battleship, both of which have just come in radar range of the Ford.

"Admiral allow the Americans to pass. We have work to do." John calls out over the radio.

"Roger that commander. I'm glad we didn't have to use more force than necessary." He replies, spreading the message swiftly throughout both battlegroups.

"As I am Admiral. Allow your men two weeks shore leave for the Christmas and New Year's break." John replies, getting a surprised look from the leader of Special Forces Squadron Three as well as Neil.

"That is greatly appreciated commander, thank you." Anderson says the cheers from his men clearly audible over the radio.

"Does that include us, sir?" Commander Rothberg asks curiously as Neil regains his composure.

"Yes it does commander." He replies simply, a small smirk crossing his face as the American battlegroup grows smaller in the window.

Everyone smiles, happy to be granted a break from the constant training and fighting of the last couple of months. Elizabeth smiles as cheers erupt from the Intelligence Center. However the squadron knows they won't receive much of a break, with a wedding to finalize and a trip to plan.

Chapter Twenty-Six

Date: Monday, December 21st, 2020

Time: 2014hrs SST

Location: Midway Base, Former US Minor Outlying Island, Pacific Ocean

Temperature: 25 Degrees Fahrenheit

Music is blasting from the restaurant as Elizabeth's bridal shower begins amidst the celebration of the announcement of the Christmas break. Everyone is getting drunk, everyone that is, except for John, who has not left the Intelligence Center since returning from the Ford. He had planned on joining the party about forty-five minutes ago, but he got caught up in monitoring the activities of the United States Government.

"Commander, your absence is becoming quite conspicuous." Clara says from the doorway; he had been expecting Sam.

"I know Clara, just trying to make sure things are set for our trip on Saturday." He replies, turning carefully as his left shoulder has begun to hurt again.

"It's not going to kill you to have some fun you know." She continues, the sarcasm ever present in her voice as she knows he's right.

"Fine, I'll take a break for the night." He says, taking a couple of seconds to think things over before finally shutting down the screen and table, walking towards Clara before pausing briefly, "She's outside isn't she."

Clara nods, though smiles, once again happy that her commander has someone to look out for him. John sighs and then smiles; he had figured Sam would be waiting for him and likely has been for the last few minutes. The pair of young adults walk outside, and sure enough there is Sam, all bundled up in a thick, light blue winter coat.

"Took you long enough." She says, wrapping her arms around John's body as he puts his right arm around her; all in an effort to stay warm.

"Sorry sweetie, I had business to take care of." He replies, earning a glance over the shoulder from Clara as she leads them towards the restaurant.

She holds him tighter upon hearing this remark, understanding where he is coming from, but wishing it wasn't true; it's almost Christmas after all.

"I'm cold." She says quietly, desperately wanting to change the subject in order to keep John's mind off of work for longer than a few minutes.

"Aww, I can tell." John says keeping her close to him as they steadily make their way towards the restaurant.

"You two are too cute." Clara whispers to herself, smiling, the warmth provided by John and Sam's love for each other helping her keep warm in the cold air.

Barely two minutes later, the trio enters the restaurant and are instantly overtaken by the buildings heating system and lively atmosphere. The music being played is a mix of rock and country hits from the last couple of decades and everyone is dancing or at least having a good time, especially happy couple. They've already had three glasses of white wine and a glass of champagne, each, and were about to pour a fourth round when John, Sam and Clara entered.

Instantly, Neil brings his girlfriend on to the dance floor where the two begin jumping around with several of the bases personnel as John and Sam look on. They soon find Admiral Anderson sitting by the bar next to the squadron's mechanic Pops. Realizing that neither man has been properly introduced to Sam, John leads her to them after they remove their coats and place them on a nearby coat rack.

"Admiral, Pops, there is someone I'd like you to meet." He says excitedly, catching Sam pleasantly by surprise as she is handed a glass of wine by the bartender, "This is Samantha Adams, she'll be taking over the role of Wolf Six."

"It's a pleasure to meet you, Sam." Admiral Anderson starts, gently shaking Sam's free right hand before allowing Pops to do the same.

"Likewise, I've heard a lot about the both of you." Sam replies kindly as John once again puts his arm around her accepting a Pepsi from the bartender.

"Only good things I hope." Pops says, throwing a wink in John's direction.

"You have nothing to worry about Pops." John says after taking a sip, the simple motion causing him considerable pain, while Sam leans against his shoulder.

"So what do you think of our little group here Ms. Adams?" Anderson asks, putting down his beer on the bar top behind him.

"I think we're doing a job that needs to be done and no one else is willing or able to do it." She replies simply, realizing she hadn't really given it much thought.

"I certainly agree." He replies warmly as John maintains the smile on his face though grows increasingly uncomfortable in the large crowd of people, "From what I've read and heard you seem to have adjusted well to your new life."

"It was definitely a shock, but John made it as easy as possible which helped." She says, snapping him out the slight trance he had fallen into.

"That's certainly good to hear and nice to know our commander has a more human side to him." Anderson says with a chuckle as John takes another quick drink; Sam smiles, thinking of everything John has done for her.

"Don't say that too loudly Admiral, I don't need everyone knowing." He says with a chuckle.

"I understand commander." Anderson replies kindly, letting out a small, barely noticeable yawn.

"How's your plane working for you commander?" Pops asks finally remembering the question he wanted to ask John.

"Purring like a kitten as usual Pops. You should be proud; you've trained the mechanics well." John replies yawning slightly and desperate to slip into his bed.

Unluckily for the young commander, the conversation continues well into the night as he and Sam catch Pops and the Admiral up on everything that has happened in their lives since Sam joined the Initiative. Elizabeth's bridal shower continues in earnest, with cake, ice cream, stories and dances being shared by all well into the night. Eventually, people begin filing out and heading to their homes in groups of two, three and four; some hooking up for the night, others going home with their significant others.

"Congratulations, both of you." John says to Elizabeth and Jeremy once the crowd has subsided and only the squadron and restaurant staff remain.

"Thank you John." Elizabeth says, clearly drunk, much like her fiancé.

"Have a goodnight commander." Jeremy adds, as both of them say the same to Sam before she and John head for the door.

They're tired but happy with how the day turned out, hoping that they can have more days like this, more often. Though, they know that isn't likely in their line of work, but at least they'll face whatever is coming, together. A fact they both smile at as they walk towards John's house, gently holding hands as they've done all night.

Date: Tuesday, December 22nd, 2020

Time: 0630hrs SST

Location: Midway Base, Former US Minor Outlying Island, Pacific Ocean

Temperature: 25 Degrees Fahrenheit

Jeremy and Elizabeth slowly begin to wake up, their alarm blaring on the nightstand next to their bed. Neither of them want to wake up, it's too early, but turning off the alarm does little to help them to get back to sleep. Soon, Jeremy heads downstairs to begin cooking breakfast as his fiancé heads into the master bathroom to shower and start her day.

Her stomach has grown slightly since her pregnancy was discovered a few weeks ago, it's barely noticeable so no one has said anything. She welcomes the warm water as it eases her awake more effectively than the sharp noise of the alarm clock. Though it doesn't completely alleviate her tiredness, thanks to the hour. Luckily for her, her fiancé is feeling the exact same way as he puts four pieces of bread in the toaster and sets them to lightly toast.

Bacon is already in the oven and he waits patiently for it to be done before starting to fry the eggs. It's a typical breakfast, he's made multiple times before today, though his continued tiredness forces him to slow down and take his time with every step. He turns on the news, a habit formed long ago, and waits patiently for Elizabeth to finish getting ready.

Some of the news coverage is of Presidents upcoming New Year's Address, though most of the coverage is the news anchors complaining that he managed to be elected for a second term. The whole situation makes Jeremy chuckle as he's heard it all before and knows they won't let up until he is forced to leave office in four years' time.

"Maybe this is just a vanity exercise." He thinks to himself as the timer on the oven runs out and beeps to let him know the bacon is done.

He hears the water running to the shower in the upstairs master bathroom turn off, instantly knowing that he has timed things perfectly with the toast finishing right as he sets the bacon down on the glass stove top on top of the oven. After plating the toast, he is able to quickly fry the eggs, using a burner not occupied by the bacon tray, finishing them just as he hears Elizabeth walking gently down the stairs. Still wearing her pajamas from the night before.

“I thought John was kidding when he said we could have the day off.” Jeremy remarks, vaguely remembering something John told him the night before.

“He wasn’t” Elizabeth replies cutely, sitting down at the kitchen island across from her soon to be husband before briefly pulling out her phone, “He even texted us this morning to remind us of what he said.”

“Guess he knew we were drunk last night.” He says with a chuckle as he begins plating the eggs.

“Well we weren’t exactly trying to hide it.” Elizabeth replies, giggling as she remembers how she felt the night before as he plates the bacon.

“That’s certainly true.” Jeremy smiles, gently pushing Elizabeth’s plate towards her and handing her a fork as she returns the smile.

“I’m so happy I get to spend the rest of my life with you.” She says, placing her hand on Jeremy’s once it’s close enough to her.

“Likewise my love.” He replies, leaning across the island and kissing her.

It takes them minutes for them to part, good practice for two days from now, as they sit comfortably across from each other. They chuckle, all the while enjoying each other’s company as they’re both glad to make their life together official.

Date: Tuesday, December 22nd, 2020

Time: 0807hrs SST

Location: Midway Base, Former US Minor Outlying Island, Pacific Ocean

Temperature: 27 Degrees Fahrenheit

"How do you think Liza and Jeremy slept?" Sam asks as her and John cuddle on the sofa in front of the television in his living room, still in their pajamas and having finished breakfast about an hour ago.

"I'm sure they slept well, though I can imagine they're both getting butterflies with their wedding being so soon." John replies, his attention focused on his beautiful girlfriend as she subconsciously continues to watch the news.

"Have you ever thought about what it would be like to be married John?" She asks diverting her attention to her boyfriend as he takes a quick glance at the television before looking back to her.

He sighs, briefly looking away.

"I used too, but I haven't given it much thought recently." He replies, masterfully hiding the half truth behind the real emotions of having to see the love of his life with someone else.

"Same." Sam says, catching him slightly off guard and forcing him to take a second to formulate a response to her simple, yet emotional statement.

"I'm sure we'll start planning ours someday." He says, a half smile falling across his face as he kisses her on the top of her head.

"Me too." She replies, smiling and snuggling just that little bit closer to him.

John breathes an unnoticeable sigh of relief, glad his was able to keep what he is planning to do, hidden from Sam. In fact, the only people who truly know what he is going to do are her father and mother and even they don't know every detail.

This thought is fleeting however, as John settles back in to enjoy the late start, at least for him, and quickly checks his watch to make sure that he doesn't have to leave quite yet. He wants to spend as much time as possible with his girlfriend before having to go to work, despite the pain it's causing him.

Date: Tuesday, December 22nd, 2020

Time: 1012hrs SST

Location: Midway Base, Former US Minor Outlying Island, Pacific Ocean

Temperature: 27 Degrees Fahrenheit

Clara and Neil have been up the longest, waking up and going on a run by six in the morning, while getting their showers and having breakfast by seven. Despite having the day off, they decided to go to the Intelligence Center to keep an eye on the American Fleet, currently four hundred miles away. Like John, both of them have had their bandages removed from their visibly scarred bodies.

"Looks like the Admiral was true to his word." Clara says, looking over communications intercepted by the Andromeda.

"He was surprisingly cooperative when we talked to him. Nervous, though I wouldn't say he was intimidated." Neil says, carefully recalling yesterday's mission as he hugs Clara from behind.

“Shame John had to shoot that marine though, I’m sure it didn’t help settle the mood.” She replies, finally turning to face him, wrapping her arms around him.

“It didn’t though I think it kept the other marines from trying something. All of them seemed on edge when we landed.” He says, wincing in pain as she squeezes slightly too hard.

“Sorry.” Clara says, releasing the pressure upon seeing her boyfriend’s pain, resting her head gently on his chest before asking, “How have you been feeling?”

“Better, how about you?” He says quietly.

“Same though I’m still sore when we wake up in the morning.” Clara replies, closing her eyes and almost wishing they were still asleep.

“Well, I’ve been told that can happen when a building falls on top of you.” Neil chuckles, making light of the situation and earning a chuckle from Clara.

Neither one of them notice the door to the room being opened and subsequently closed until the person clears their throat.

“Rob... sorry we didn’t see you there.” Clara says, turning rapidly to see the middle-aged squadron advisor.

“It’s alright Clara, I just came to remind you that John gave you the day off. He would probably be upset if he found out you were working instead of relaxing.” He replies, chuckling at the fact that the two young adults are acting like he’s just caught them doing something they shouldn’t be.

“Yeah you’re right.” Neil says, feeling guilty as he chuckles to cover it up.

Rob only raises an eyebrow in response before Clara and Neil head out of the room and back to their house in order to do just that. It's been awhile since they were able to completely and totally relax. Though this isn't likely to be the case for long, there's a wedding and a Presidential visit to plan after all.

Date: Tuesday, December 22nd, 2020

Time: 1655hrs SST

Location: Midway Base, Former US Minor Outlying Island, Pacific Ocean

Temperature: 26 Degrees Fahrenheit

Preparations for the wedding are in full swing as John and Sam are busy hanging decorations in the church, hoping that the others are following their orders to stay home and relax. Josiah and Abigail are there as well, helping to ensure that everything is perfect for the big day. Father Francesco is helping as well, making up for the lack in manpower as a lot of the base's personnel have stayed home; perfectly following their commanders orders.

Multiple white and gold banners are hung throughout the large church, as are multiple mistletoe plants and wreaths. The altar has been dressed in a white and floral gold cloth and the reserved seating signs are white with gold letters. All is designed to perfectly match the soon to be married couple's chosen color scheme, including the plates, silverware and, naturally, the bride and groom's outfits.

John is glad to be doing such grunt work, it's a great change of pace for the constantly working commander and he welcomes the time he gets to spend with his own significant other and her parents. It also begins to pull memories out of the back of his mind, memories that were long thought lost by the commander. Memories of how he and Sam would plan their own imaginary wedding when they were younger. Mainly as a joke to occupy their time while their parents were busy cooking dinner. Now though, helping with Elizabeth's and Jeremy's wedding has helped him to remember every little detail from their childhood.

"Whatcha thinking about honey?" Sam asks softly, handing him another wreath to hang as she notices his smile.

John chuckles, quickly and expertly hanging the wreath and climbing down the short ladder he's standing on.

"You'll find out... some day." He says mysteriously, quickly giving her a hug before moving the ladder to the next location as Elizabeth enters the church, greeting Sam's parents before heading towards John and Sam.

"Hey Sam, could I borrow John for a moment?" She asks gently, the slight nervousness in her voice barely noticeable to the novice squadron member.

"Of course Liza." Sam replies before walking over to her parents; both of whom have been keeping a favorable eye on their daughter and her boyfriend.

"I thought I told you that you had the day off." He says, carefully setting the ladder up and preparing another wreath to be hung.

"You did, but you know how well I listen sometimes." Elizabeth replies smirking and turning her head as she places her arms behind her back, "There is something I want to ask you though... A favor, if that's okay?"

"Anything for you sister." John replies kindly, referencing the familial bond the two have shared for quite some time.

Elizabeth staggers slightly, glad that John is willing to do this for her but unsure of how to ask the favor itself. John patiently gives her all the time she needs, his calming smile bringing her some level of comfort and relief.

"Could you... would you b... would you be willing to walk me down the aisle? I asked Jeremy if it would be okay and he said it would be." She finally asks as memories of her father flood her heart; her voice so quiet that even John can barely hear it but hear it he does.

John smiles and bows his head, briefly glancing to the sky as he not only thought this would happen, but is grateful that he doesn't have to tell Jeremy no.

"I would be honored Elizabeth." He states, not wanting to say another word.

"Thank you!" Elizabeth exclaims, eyes filled with tears as she nearly knocks John over as she wraps her arms around the back of his neck and is lifted into the air by the strength of his back.

"You're welcome." He replies softly, gently returning the hug as Sam and her parents look on with smiles on their faces.

A few moments later, Elizabeth finally releases her grip and drops back down to the floor, walking away radiating happiness as she continually looks back towards John with a smile on her face. She does the same with Sam after giving her a hug on her way out of the church. Sam smiles and hugs her boyfriend upon rejoining him, knowing what his answer meant for Elizabeth and sensing that there was no way he would say no. She notices Father Francesco smiling by the altar, having witnessed the whole scene from his perch. Everyone seems to be truly happy for the first time since Sam joined the initiative, though with everything going on, it's easy to see why.

Date: Wednesday, December 23rd, 2020

Time: 1534hrs SST

Location: Midway Base, Former US Minor Outlying Island, Pacific Ocean

Temperature: 30 Degrees Fahrenheit

Jeremy and Elizabeth were separated from each other at the squadron's lunch around noon; they won't see each other again until tomorrow at fourteen hundred hours. The whole squadron is pitching in to make sure this is the case, with Elizabeth staying with John and Sam, while Jeremy is staying at Neil and Clara's house. Josiah and Abigail are also keeping Elizabeth's dress under wraps in their home while Rob and Admiral Anderson coordinate any relevant intelligence and makes sure it gets to John if it needs to be acted on.

Everyone is excited for the big day, though none more so than the happy couple; if they could, they would move the wedding to this very moment. John and Sam have even had their hands full trying to keep Elizabeth occupied and from running out the front door towards the church. Thankfully, she had a lot to eat at lunch has just fallen asleep on the couch while watching the news with her squad mates, making John and Sam's job, just that little easier.

"She's going to be so happy tomorrow." Sam says as she and John look on from the kitchen island, turning the television volume down to a background level.

"Yeah. She's also going to be up all night tonight agonizing about everything." John says after taking a sip of Coke Cola, having been distracted by a particularly in-depth special report on the United States President's upcoming address.

"She might not be the only one." Sam says sarcastically having noticed her boyfriends distracted glance and tone.

"Sorry." He replies quietly, realizing what she knows and bowing his head slightly as she places her arm on his back.

"It's ok, I know you have a lot on your plate." She says reassuringly.

"When don't I?" He chuckles rubbing his face with his hands after Sam's hug ends, going a long way to keep the tired commander from being overwhelmed.

"I know." Sam responds, continuing to be as supportive as possible as she refills John's glass and leans gently against his back, "How's your shoulder?"

"Better that it has been. It's nice to be able to use it again." He replies, taking note of the fact that it hasn't been hurting for the last couple of days.

"That's good to know."

Sam begins gently massaging John's shoulders, something he's needed to have done for the last few years let alone days.

"How does that feel?" She asks after a few minutes, with John practically falling asleep in her arms.

“Pretty great actually, thanks.” He says feeling more relaxed than he ever has before, his eyes closed as he leans back against his girlfriend’s chest.

“I can tell.” Sam says, having felt the tension leave her boyfriend’s shoulders.

After a while, she stops, realizing that she won’t be able to make John any less tense and proceeds to drape her arms across his chest. Bending over, she gently kisses him with her head upside down in relation to his. They smile, though little does Sam know, John has something planned that will make her happy for the rest of her life.

Chapter Twenty-Seven

Date: Thursday, December 24th, 2020

Time: 0734hrs SST

Location: Midway Base, Former US Minor Outlying Island, Pacific Ocean

Temperature: 25 Degrees Fahrenheit

A light snow is falling across Midway Base as all personnel begin to wake up, excited for the big day ahead. Most of the base has a light dusting covering every surface, with another two inches forecast to fall by the time the wedding begins. It was task keeping the couple in their respective houses for the entire night and even more so this morning as Neil and Clara had to lock their front door to keep Jeremy from heading to the church too soon. John and Sam had a similar problem though they we were able to distract the young bride to be by having her help them decorate John's home and Christmas tree. Now they stand back, admiring their handy work.

"It's been awhile since I've had a tree to decorate." John says, his arm gently around Sam's shoulders; he hasn't put a tree up since his parents passed away.

"Now you have one." Sam says softly, leaning against him as Elizabeth takes a step back to admire the seven-foot-tall fake tree.

"Shame you don't have any stockings to hang on the fireplace." Elizabeth comments, knowing that it would complete the scene.

"Yeah, I didn't think to grab them from my Pennsylvania house." John says with a sigh.

“That’s okay, it still looks great.” Sam says rubbing John’s back, feeling she needs to keep the mood light and happy though that’s hardly the case.

“Yeah, it does.” He replies, happy at the thought that he finally gets to spend a major holiday with Sam, having never been able to before now.

A warm fire is burning in the fireplace, filling the house with a light, warm heat that gives the home’s heating system a welcome break. It also provides a welcome surprise for Martha as she and her small design team are welcomed into the home to help Elizabeth get ready for the wedding. Her team also brings the bridesmaid dresses for Sam and Clara, as well bright white flats with gold accents for both young women. Both dresses are exactly the same; being bright pink, sleeveless, long gowns with shiny gold stitching and a gold floral pattern around the waist. John clears the coat rack on the wall so Martha can hang the dresses, preventing them from wrinkling as Martha’s team works on the young bride’s hair.

“I’m going to be amazed if I have any hair left after today.” Elizabeth says with a chuckle as she tries to remain as still as possible for the stylist.

“Honestly, I’m surprised Jeremy isn’t already bald.” John smirks, doing what he can to keep the mood light just like his girlfriend was earlier.

“Don’t make me laugh.” Elizabeth replies with an annoyed tone as she struggles to remain still for the stylist who only smiles as she concentrates on the task of turning Elizabeth’s hair from being understatedly plain to beautifully curled.

Sam can't help but laugh at the whole scene, knowing that she and Clara will have to experience the same thing soon. There is another light knock on the door which Sam swiftly answers, finding her parents on the other side. They're both carefully handling Elizabeth's wedding dress, so it doesn't fall into the snow nor gets wrinkled. The snow beings falling a little faster as Sam gently closes the door behind her parents, noticing the ground is now covered by an inch of snow. John helps to make sure there is enough room on the coat rack to spread the dress out to its full length with everyone taking care when they step over and around it. Elizabeth gets slightly annoyed as she is unable to see the dress from where she is seated near the kitchen.

"It's ok, my dear, you'll see it soon enough." Martha reassures the young bride as Sam and John gather around on the nearby couch with Sam's parents

"But I want to see it now." She says being more sarcastic and joking.

"Can't say I blame her, it's a beautiful dress." Sam whispers so only John and her parents hear her, all of whom smile as John gently plays with her hair as he holds her left hand with his own.

"Yeah, it kind of reminds me of yours Abi." Josiah says softly.

"You're right." She says, remembering her dress after getting distracted.

John chuckles, while he would certainly admit that the dress looks beautiful, he doesn't really have anything to compare it to. He begins to think about how Sam might look in one, but this thought is only fleeting as there is a final knock on the door that he answers.

"Hey Clara." He says welcoming her in out of the cold as Sam jumps up from the couch to give her a hug.

"Hey guys, how's our bride to be doing?" Clara replies joyfully, eventually hugging absolutely everyone in the room, including Elizabeth.

"Not sure honestly. I kind of feel like I am going to puke." Elizabeth chuckles as Clara releases her embrace.

"I've heard that's normal and will get better once the champagne is opened." She says, nearly laughing before she heads to the third couch.

One question soon falls on everyone's mind as they sit down, though only Sam is curious and brave enough to ask it.

"How is Jeremy holding up?" She asks, nearly napping against John's chest, using his arms as a makeshift blanket.

"He's doing okay, though John may want to head over as he was just starting his second Scotch when I left." The tired squadron member replies.

"I guess that's our cue Mr. Adams." John says as Sam reluctantly sits up, allowing him to stand and grab his sweatshirt and coat.

"I guess so." He says smiling, reaching for his heavy winter coat and realizing just how quickly the day is going.

The two men leave the house, heading towards Clara and Neil's dwelling with a calm sense of purpose as the women settle in for the whirlwind of preparations that is about to befall them.

"And... we're done." The hair stylist says excitedly as she steps aside to show Elizabeth's hair to Sam, Clara and Abigail; it is simply gorgeous.

"I want to see." Elizabeth says as the others immediately and happily begin complimenting her on the style she chose as well as the stylist on a job well done.

The stylist quickly digs through her bag of products and tools, shifting things around to find the tool she is looking for, a small round mirror with a simple round handle. She quickly hands it to the ever more beautiful bride to be and stands back to receive her reaction, hoping that it's a happy one. Elizabeth examines her hair closely, for what feels like forever.

"I... I love it. Thank you so much." She finally says, a smile falling across her face as she hugs the stylist, something catching her eye in the corner of the mirror.

Her pupils go wide, and her mouth practically drops to the floor as she slowly turns around, handing the mirror back to the hair stylist. Everyone knows what she's caught sight off and simply steps back, remaining silent as they admire the bride who has just seen her dress in person for the first time.

The elegant, long sleeved wedding gown is now beautifully appointed with white lace and the floral accents have been done in gold stitching, a modification that Elizabeth requested when she picked the dress. The strappy, white pair of medium height heels are present as well, having had gold floral accents added to them by Martha's design team. Everyone is simply taking in the moment as Elizabeth gently strokes and holds different parts of the dress delicately in her hands; completely overcome by the sight.

Meanwhile, across the base, Jeremy is nearly going into a full-blown panic attack as the wedding draws closer, pacing back and forth as John tries to calm him down. Neil and Josiah stay out of the way, letting John do what he needs to as he talks to Jeremy in the upstairs bedroom. No voices are being raised as the two friends talk, it isn't necessary, instead John is simply allowing Jeremy to get his emotions out and heard by a listening ear.

"I just... I just... I don't know... Is it too soon? Is it the right time?" Jeremy says flailing his hands and arms in a frustrated manner, while John sits on the bed.

"Yes." He says simply.

"What?" Jeremy asks confused.

"Yes." John repeats calmly, flopping back onto the bed, crossing his arms and closing his eyes, "Yes, it's too soon but it's also the right time. Most people get married in their late twenties or thirties, but most people don't do what we do."

Jeremy considers his commanders words as he stops pacing for the moment and place his hands on the tuxedo pants covered hips.

"So you're saying?..." Jeremy eventually stutters.

"Look I may not know a ton about love or weddings, but I do know this. It felt right when you proposed, and it feels right now. You're just nervous because this is about the happiest day of your life and you don't want anything to ruin it." John says sitting up, opening his eyes and patting the groom on the shoulder before using him as support to stand up, "Now, you need to finish getting dressed, you'll be a married man in just over four hours. When you're done there is someone I want you to meet."

Jeremy nods before John leaves the room, heading back downstairs to rejoin Neil and Josiah. There is a light knock on the door before the ensuing conversation gets too involved and Neil opens it delicately, so he doesn't ruin his own grey and white tuxedo. Walking through the door is Rob with a four-legged friend, a black labradoodle named Marley who promptly shakes off the snow covering her fur.

"How are you doing Marley?" Neil asks, crouching down to pet the welcoming dog as Rob closes the door behind him.

Josiah gives John a confused glance as Rob reaches down and removes the leash from Marley's collar as she grateful accepts Neil's affections.

"We found her wandering the streets of London the night after a long training mission with the British SAS. Personnel here at the base have been taking care of her ever since. Elizabeth and Jeremy needed a ring bearer today, so it was decided to have Marley fill the role." John replies calmly, bending down as Marley runs over to him; it's been three months since he, or any squadron member, has seen the dog.

Josiah nods, understanding the circumstances perfectly as he too kneels down to pet the attention seeking dog. She looks to be about two years old and is weighing in at around thirty pounds. More often than not she can be found in the base's school, providing comfort to the students whose parents are sent to the numerous fronts the initiative is forced to fight on. With a lot of them returning when the fleet arrived earlier in the week, Rob had taken Marley to his home in order to give her some private time before being called to duty for Jeremy and Elizabeth's wedding.

As the small group moves to the three couches in Jeremy and Elizabeth's living room, John's phone buzzes with a message from Sam; Neil's does as well as he receives a message from Clara.

"I guess the bride liked her dress." Neil chuckles, passing his phone to Josiah as John puts his back in his pocket and gets Marley to jump up on the couch.

"That certainly seems to be the case." Josiah says, smiling at the picture of Elizabeth being fitted into her dress.

"Speaking of... What are you going to wear John?" Neil asks noticing that he isn't wearing a grey tuxedo like himself, Rob and Josiah and is instead still in a sweatshirt and jeans.

"I'm pretty sure that regulations say you have to wear your dress uniform." Rob says thinking aloud as John turns on the television, keeping the volume low.

"Yeah, I know it does." John says seemingly dreading the thought of having to wear the dress blue uniform that's been collecting dust in his closet.

"Have you ever worn that thing?" Neil asks, smiling and chuckling, trying and failing to think of a time where he's seen John in the uniform.

"Once and only once. I was forced to wear it when I accepted the position of Initiative Commander six months ago." John says recalling the one concession he had to make when accepting the position.

"I remember. You practically ripped it off once the secret ceremony in front of the security council had finished." Rob says, looking around for something to drink before Neil points to the refrigerator in the kitchen.

"Yeah. As soon as I was out of the room I was back in a tee shirt and jeans with my forty-five on my thigh." John laughs remembering the stunned reactions of multiple guards as he and Rob walked out of the United Nations Headquarters.

"Is there even a picture of the ceremony? I don't recall seeing one in our archives." Neil comments, having done what Sam did and gone through all of the initiatives files when he joined.

"No there isn't, I requested that it be kept under wraps and that no photos be taken. The only record of it is the signed copy of the initiatives doctrine and bylaws that has my signature affixed to it as well as the signatures of all nations present." John replies, leaning back and closing his eyes as Rob returns to the couch with a bottle of Miller Light as an opening door is heard from upstairs.

Neil nods, knowing not to question his commanders reasoning for keeping the ceremony as secret as possible as Jeremy carefully walks down the stairs, black tuxedo providing the perfect contrast to the grey versions worn by Josiah and Neil. John checks his watch, two hours to go until the wedding ceremony begins.

"You look good Jeremy." Neil says, standing to greet the young groom at the bottom of the staircase.

Josiah and John do the same as Marley jumps off of the couch and runs over to Jeremy in order to get, and receive, his attention. He grants the dogs request though is careful to not get too much slobber and dog fur on his freshly pressed and fitted tuxedo.

"Does anyone have something stiff to drink?" Jeremy asks needing something to flush out the last remnants of nervousness from his body.

"I have something that may hit the spot." Neil replies, heading over to one of the lesser used kitchen cabinets and pulling out a glass bottle containing a dark liquid, "I found this while we were in England a few weeks ago, it's a Ben Nevis twenty-one-year-old single malt scotch. It was bottled in twenty twelve and put in a cask back in nineteen ninety."

Jeremy gasps in shock at the high-end bottle of scotch, having been wanting to try it for years, though only being able to once joining the initiative made him immune from any laws of any nation. Gently taking the bottle from Neil, he examines it closely, feeling the heavy yet not unwieldy weight in his hands.

John gently sets four, small, heavy glasses on the kitchen island as the four men gather around. Jeremy opens the bottle and carefully pours equal portions into each glass before capping it again and setting it on the counter.

Jeremy takes a breath, "Thank you, everyone. Here's to marriage." He says softly raising the glass in front of him; the others do the same.

"To marriage." They all say in unison before finishing their glasses of scotch in one collective gulp, setting the glasses down as the stinging in their mouths intensifies then subsides.

"Yeah I think that hit the spot." Neil says, enjoying the feeling the scotch is pushing through his body.

"I agree." Josiah responds, finding a drinking glass and filling it with water.

John has a similar reaction though doesn't say anything, his mind is once again distracted by thinking beyond his friend's wedding and wondering what he is going to do over the coming days. The scotch effectively bringing the thoughts to the forefront of the young commanders mind in a way his usual alcoholic drink of choice never could. He is able to quickly suppress them however, not only for the sake of the wedding but for his own as well; today is a day of celebration, not work.

"Alright, it's time to get you to church." He says calmly, double checking the time once more, "Remember, no seeing Elizabeth until she's walking down the aisle." He finishes patting the groom sternly on the shoulder.

"Roger that commander." Jeremy replies before Neil turns off the television and the four men and dog head for the door, leaving John an hour and a half to get changed.

Date: Thursday, December 24th, 2020

Time: 1315hrs SST

Location: Midway Base, Former US Minor Outlying Island, Pacific Ocean

Temperature: 27 Degrees Fahrenheit

The falling snow shows no signs of letting up as John carefully attaches his rank medal to the chest of his pressed and ironed dress uniform. The blue uniform with gold accents are similar to a marine's dress uniform, though much fancier in design and vastly different in color scheme. John is the only one with a uniform like this, not just in the initiative, but in the world. Accompanying the uniform is a golden saber with a simple, yet decorative hilt and long, thin, golden blade.

He takes a breath, looking at himself in the mirror hanging on the closet door, making sure the uniform is perfectly fit and placed where it should be on his body. He hates having to wear it, it makes him feel too much like a ruler rather than the fair commander he has turned into. Elizabeth, Clara and Sam headed to the church once John arrived back at the house, as did Martha and her design team, leaving John alone to prepare and collect his thoughts.

Stretching the muscles in his back and shoulders, he tries to relax, feeling happier with each passing moment as the wedding approaches. All of the details are final and in place, the groomsmen and bridesmaids are all ready and the entire base is prepared to throw a massive party afterwards. For once in the last six months there is a situation that doesn't require him to really do much of anything. All he has to do is walk Elizabeth down the aisle and help marry her to her best friend. His only wish is that the coming mission to Washington D.C. wasn't looming over his head. Overshadowing not only the wedding, but the fact that it is Christmas as well.

He once again manages to push that mission to the back of his mind, determined to enjoy the next couple of days. Glancing back towards headboard of his bed, he peers into the dark corner of one cubby holes on the right-hand side. He smiles; nothing is overtly visible, though he knows that something special is located in the dark corner. Chuckling to himself, he straightens the dress uniform one last time before heading out of the room and towards the church. The snow now two inches deep and almost covering the toes his dress black boots.

Many of the bases personnel are lingering outside, playing in the snow with their friends and children. Thankfully distracted enough that most don't notice their commander; though some do, greeting and saluting him as he passes. He returns the gesture with a small smile and quick salute of his own, managing to make a younger child's day as it is the first time he recognizes John. Multiple snowmen have popped up around the base and everyone is getting the Christmas spirit, with several of the lights visible on the fronts of their homes. John even hears carolers off in the distance, practicing for their performance at the reception.

Upon entering the church, he finds even more people present as he welcomes the warm air present inside the massive structure. All of them are going about their business and waiting for the ceremony to begin, allowing John to slip through the crowd, only being noticed a handful of times. He's looking for a few very specific people as the minutes slowly tick by, finding them in one of the church's wings.

"You made it; we were beginning to worry that Rob would have to be your stand in." Clara remarks as John approaches her, Sam, Elizabeth and Neil.

"Yeah, yeah, you all know I wouldn't miss this for the world. You look beautiful Elizabeth." John says gracefully as he greets everyone before gently hugging the young bride as she tries to keep from happily crying.

"Thank you John." She says blushing as the commander releases his hug and takes his own girlfriend into his arms after she finishes examining his uniform.

"You need to wear this more often." She whispers to him as she rests her back against his chest, making sure her dress isn't showing too much.

"Yeah sorry sweetie that's not happening. This is rather uncomfortable to wear." John whispers back, getting disappointed yet understanding smile in response as people begin taking their seats.

"I wonder if Jeremy is as nervous as I am." Elizabeth says, making light conversation as John checks his watch and Neil gets Father Francesco's attention.

“I can guarantee you that he is.” Neil says quickly as the pastor walks over to the small crowd and is soon joined by Josiah and Abigail; the only one not present is Jeremy who is hiding in the pastor’s office.

“I second that, he’s been wanting the ceremony to start for the last fifteen minutes.” Father Francesco joins in, hearing what Neil said as he approached.

“Well, he has to wait a little longer.” Sam says checking her own watch before she reaches back and takes gentle hold of John’s right hand.

“Still, we should probably make sure that he doesn’t melt.” Neil says motioning for some of the group to head to the Pastor’s office, most do, saying various forms “good luck” to the bride as she, John and Sam hang back.

“How are you feeling?” John asks turning to Elizabeth, who hasn’t been able to sit down ever since putting on her dress.

“Honestly, I wouldn’t mind if we started a little early.” She replies, chuckling slightly and shuffling the large bouquet of white and gold roses in her hands.

John smiles, knowing the love that Elizabeth and Jeremy hold for each other and he can easily imagine how joyful the reception is going to be after the ceremony.

“It must feel like a dream, all of… this?” Sam says lightly, briefly looking around her at the beautifully decorated church.

“It honestly does. I would say pinch me, but I don’t want to ruin the dress.” She laughs, nearly going lightheaded as she draws a deep breath.

"Steady now, I don't need you falling on your way to the altar." John chuckles, reaching out to support the young bride as his girlfriend does the same.

"Sorry." She says playfully and with a chuckle, adjusting her hair as she regains her balance despite the heels she's wearing, "I guess we better get in position." She continues, her gaze looking more beautiful by the moment.

"I guess so." John says kissing Sam on the forehead before she heads off to join the others while John and Elizabeth make their way to the back of the church.

They meet the honor guard who will process before them but after the bridesmaids and groomsmen. It's made up of members of Special Forces Squadron three, the same men and women who have supported the squadron while their numbers have been reduced. They salute the bride and their commander as they pass, formally extending their congratulations with a firm handshake. Their uniforms are similar to the one begin worn by their commander but they're not nearly as decorative and are rather plain in nature.

John is careful to keep Elizabeth hidden from view, seeing Jeremy walk to the altar with Father Francesco as a hush falls over the crowd. Sam, Clara, Neil and Rob all line up in front of the honor guard with Neil pairing with Clara and Rob pairing with Sam. There's no best man or maid of honor, it was deemed too difficult to pick either one given how Elizabeth and Jeremy feel about each of their friends.

"I wanted to thank you John. For everything. For all of the support you've given to me, and Jeremy. Better than any brother I could have hoped for." Elizabeth whispers as she and John make final adjustments to their outfits.

“All I do is try Elizabeth.” He says simply, allowing himself to smile as he looks into her eyes.

“I know, but you’ve succeeded and more than you will ever realize.” She replies, smiling as well, “Soon, that’ll be you down by the altar.”

“We’ll see.”

“No, you’ll see.”

John chuckles, trying to not simultaneously cry and laugh as it wouldn’t be appropriate with the church falling silent.

“Maybe.” He says, almost whispering as he takes Elizabeth’s veil gently in his hands, “What do you say? How about we make you a married woman?”

“That would be great.” Elizabeth smiles, as John drapes the veil in front of her face, taking his arm as the traditional wedding processional begins to play.

The two take a collective breath as the bridesmaids and groomsmen move towards the altar, carefully followed by the honor guard who will take flanking positions upon reaching it. A single, joyful tear rolls down Elizabeth’s cheek and falls to the floor as everyone turns to face her. She can barely breathe but can’t help but smile as she and John step forward. He’s guiding her to her new life; a life where she is finally with the person she’s meant to be with for the rest of time.

Date: Thursday, December 24th, 2020

Time: 1707hrs SST

Location: Midway Base, Former US Minor Outlying Island, Pacific Ocean

Temperature: 26 Degrees Fahrenheit

The music is practically blasting the roof off of the restaurant as everyone is happily dancing, shaking the building to its foundation. The newly married couple as already had their first dance together and is now partaking in the fun being had by all after changing out of their wedding clothes and into long sleeve tee shirts and jeans. No one complains about the informal move, it's their wedding after all and they can do what they want. Everyone is getting drunk and eating whatever is put in front of them, a party in the truest sense of the word. Well almost everyone, John, Sam, and her parents are keeping alcohol out of their systems, simply wanting to enjoy the afternoon and evening while not regretting it tomorrow. Clara and Neil, however, are fully embracing the fact that they are going to be suffering from hangovers on Christmas morning.

"What are your plans for tomorrow?" Sam's mother asks her as she takes a drink from her boyfriend's glass of Pepsi and leans against his now plain clothed body; he didn't want to spend more time than needed in his dress uniform.

"Not sure, I think we were going to play it by ear." Sam replies gently, barely remembering that tomorrow is Christmas Day.

"Not surprising, I think everyone is going to want to sleep in thanks to the party." Her father says, releasing the first yawn of the evening.

"Yeah, that's true." His daughter says, closing her eyes as John takes a drink from the same glass of Pepsi, not minding that there is a little less soda in it.

Abigail, glances at her husband, admiring the scene before them and how in love John and Sam are with each other. So much so that it's rivaling the love shown between Elizabeth and Jeremy during their wedding, even now. Josiah notices the young commander's mind is elsewhere, though it's not the coming visit to the United States that seems to be distracting him. No, it's something else as he carefully holds Sam's left hand, her ring finger in particular, with his own. Sam doesn't even notice the small gesture as she continues to hold a conversation with her mother though it's barely audible to the two men as they slowly gain each other's attention. Locking eyes in a moment that seems to move in slow motion.

Josiah asks John a question using only his eyes and seemingly on instinct, the young commander gives a slight one nod response, though it's enough for a smile to fall across the tired fathers face.

Date: Friday, December 25th, 2020

Time: 0013hrs SST

Location: Midway Base, Former US Minor Outlying Island, Pacific Ocean

Temperature: 24 Degrees Fahrenheit

Sam and John finally arrive at his home after the party went entirely too late and many of those present, including Neil and Clara, had to be carried back to their own houses. Sam carefully kicks off her flats, thankful they weren't heels and heads to the bedroom where John has already changed into a white tee shirt and grey flannel pajama pants.

“I’m going to get a fire going again, should help us sleep.” He says softly, noting the fact that both of them are tired though neither of them want to go to bed, glancing back from the doorway as Sam begins slipping out of her dress.

“That sounds wonderful.” She replies, smiling at the thought of cuddling on the couch with her boyfriend as a warm fire burns away the night.

John smiles, slipping something from the cubby on the headboard into his pocket and walking into the living room, grabbing an old newspaper and lighter on his way to the fireplace. Butterflies begin filling his stomach, as he carefully sets three logs in the fireplace, the newspaper underneath and carefully reaches in with the now lit lighter. It doesn’t take long for the dry newspaper to light and even less time for the small flame to expand and engulf the dry pine wood.

Warmth begins filling the room as John sets the lighter on the mantle and keeps the lights on a dim setting as he silently walks into the kitchen. The fire grows as does the butterfly feeling in John’s stomach, who is now preparing a mug of hot chocolate with Baileys for his cold girlfriend. A small consolation for her having to wear the bridesmaid dress and flats for the entire night. He debates taking a shot of Baileys himself in order to calm his nerves, but decides against it, instead welcoming the nerves like an old friend.

Sam emerges from the bedroom wearing her typical blue pajamas and carefully positions herself on the couch with a light, white blanket to keep her bare feet warm until the fire is able to eliminate the cool air from the room. John smiles upon seeing her, in a way, looking the most beautiful she ever has in his eyes despite the gorgeous dress she was wearing earlier this evening. With the hot chocolate finished, he carefully lifts the almost full mug and gently carries it over to her. She grasps it with both hands while he sits down and makes himself comfortable behind her.

"Did you put something in this?" She asks curiously, leaning back against his chest after taking a brief sip from the still warm mug.

"Just hot chocolate and Baileys, nothing more." He replies kindly, debating whether or not to turn on the television but deciding against it.

"I can't believe I haven't tried this before. It's so good. Thank you." She says, pressing the side of her face into John's chest and closing her eyes, still holding the hot chocolate with both hands in order to keep warm.

"You're welcome sweetheart and Merry Christmas." He gently whispers, placing his right arm around her stomach and strokes her hair with his left.

Sam smiles though it's only fleeting as she remembers something.

"I forgot to get you something for Christmas." She says, her eyes watering, trying to sit up but John stops her by pressing lightly down her stomach.

"Shh, it's okay, you don't need to get me anything." He says softly, keeping the pressure light in order to help her calm down.

"But... you've always been so nice too... so kind." She says, still disappointed.

"You're enough sweetheart, you're all I need for Christmas." He responds, now gently hugging her as she sets the mug on the coffee table.

"You sure?" Sam responds quietly, almost on the verge of tears as the warmth from John's body and the fire begins washing over her.

"I'm sure Sam. I'm sure." He says, the butterfly feeling in his stomach becoming almost unbearable, if there was ever a time, it's now; no other moment would feel this perfect, "I did get you something, though there is something I need to ask you first."

"What is it sweetie?" Sam says lightly, finally sitting up and kneeling on the couch, now facing her boyfriend as she struggles to hold back the tears in her eyes.

John pauses, moving his right hand down to his pocket without Sam noticing, her eyes transfixed on her boyfriend. He removes a small, wooden box made of purple heart from his pocket, engraved on one side of it are the words "*I need to ask*".

"What do you need to ask?" Sam asks, not annoyed but curious.

"Wi..." John stammers, losing all of the air in his lungs at once.

Sam takes his free left hand still not noticing the small box in his right as she continues gazing into his eyes.

"Will you marry me?" He finally asks, nearly choking on his words as he too begins to tear up, revealing the now open wooden box and unveiling a gold ring with one half carat diamond and two, one third carat diamonds on either side: it's beautifully simple.

Both of Sam's hands instantly cover her mouth in a desperate attempt to hold in any amount of air in her lungs. She takes a deep breath, letting go of what was holding the tears in her eyes and allowing them to flow down her cheeks. The whole scene playing out in a matter of seconds.

“Yes... For all... of my life... yes.” She finally whispers repeating the word over and over again, “Yes... yes... yes...”

John gasps, carefully removing the ring from the box and placing it on Sam’s left ring finger before wrapping his arms around her as she does around him in the same moment. Everything melts away from the couple, as the warmth of the fire overtakes the room and their hearts as two become one.

Chapter Twenty-Eight

Date: Friday, December 25th, 2020

Time: 0957hrs SST

Location: Midway Base, Former US Minor Outlying Island, Pacific Ocean

Temperature: 26 Degrees Fahrenheit

Josiah and Abigail settle in on their couch, after feeding breakfast to Neil, Clara, and the newlyweds, all of whom are slowly recovering from their respective hangovers; a result from the heavy drinking they all partook in the night before. John and Sam have yet to make an appearance this morning and their absence has become rather conspicuous as time continued to move on.

"I wonder where those two are?" Clara asks, quickly checking her phone for any messages from the couple, seeing none.

"Maybe John decided to sleep in for once." Jeremy says, wincing slightly as the rising sun peeks through the windows and blinds his eyes.

"You just worry about yourselves. It's Christmas, the one time a year you seem to have off. They don't need a reason if they're going to be late." Abigail says interrupting the group as she sets another round of orange juice on the coffee table while Josiah begins putting the dirty dishes in the dishwasher.

He laughs upon hearing his wife, they've only ever had one child but now it seems like they've adopted at least five more. It's refreshing to see his wife be such a motherly figure again, even if it is only for a short time while the squadron recovers. He does wonder what is taking Sam and John so long to get there, checking his phone for any messages from the couple, seeing none, just like Clara. Soon there is a light knock on the door, which Abigail answers though everyone's hopes are dashed when Rob walks in and not their commander and his significant other.

"Merry Christmas everyone and congratulations to the newlyweds." He says kindly, holding a bag in his hand as Abigail closes the door behind him, briefly giving everyone a view of the snow melting in the direct sunlight of the morning.

"Thanks Rob." Elizabeth says with a tired, headache fueled smile, her left hand firmly holding on to her husband's right, "What'd you bring?"

"A bottle of your favorite, when you're up for it." He replies, pulling a bottle of bespoke red wine out of the holiday themed bag and handing it carefully to Jeremy's wife for the two of them to examine.

"Thank you so much Rob." She says giving the middle-aged man a hug after which Jeremy shakes his hand while Josiah hangs his coat near the door.

"You're welcome." Rob states, making himself comfortable on the only empty couch in the room, where Abigail joins him as Josiah starts the dishwasher.

Once again everyone's thoughts turn back to the still missing John and Sam, though they finally get some semblance of an answer when Rob's phone rings with a text from John. He promptly reads the message aloud for all to hear.

"Commander Hilderbrand requests that everyone stop by the base's school for a preliminary briefing on the mission to the United States." Rob says almost reluctant to speak, worried that his commander has forgotten that it's Christmas.

Everyone sighs before Elizabeth stands up.

"Well, commanders orders, I guess we need to get going." She says clearly not happy about the fact they have to work.

"So much for having off." Abigail mutters to herself as everyone reaches for their coats.

"I'm sure he has a good reason." Josiah reassures her, helping her with her coat as the seven of them head towards the school.

Carefully navigating over the melting snow and ice, they make light of the situation by throwing snowballs at each other and generally acting like a bunch of children. The joy of the moment is short lived however, as it doesn't take them long to arrive at the school and make their way up to the fourth-floor conference room as the commander looks on, gently holding Sam's left hand.

"You ready?" He asks, now looking out over the base and towards the Kestrel anchored offshore, the sun glaring across his black tee shirt and blue jeans.

"I am, my love." She returns, smiling and thankful she wore a warm green long sleeve shirt in addition to her tan cargo pants.

John smiles, gently keeping hold her left hand and feeling the ring around her finger as the two turn to face the now arriving elevator. Placing his right hand in his pocket, the elevators door opens swiftly yet controllably across from the conference table and the seven individuals soon line up in front of them shivering as they attempt to warm up using the buildings heating system.

"Good morning, I hope all of you slept well last night and I want to personally wish each of you, a Merry Christmas." He begins, his tone completely different than the tone he uses when a briefing is about to start; it's friendlier, calmer, catching the entire squadron off guard, even Rob.

"You as well commander." Elizabeth says, hesitant to speak.

"Now as you know, I called you here to talk about our coming visit to the United States, but there is something I need to discuss with you first." He continues, removing his hand from Sam's and crossing his arms.

It takes a short while for everyone to pick up on what John has just revealed to them but once they notice, they can't unsee it.

"Sam? Is that?" Clara asks curiously, noticing the ring on her left hand.

Sam nods, smirking as she too crosses her arms though keeping her left hand perfectly visible to everyone in the room as they gasp for breath. Josiah takes his wife in his arms and the two smile, happy for their daughter and soon to be son in law. The rest of the squadron, aghast at the sight, struggle to breathe, let alone talk.

"Well I'll be damned." Jeremy says, finally able to sputter the short sentence though needing to catch his breath immediately after, hugging Elizabeth as he speaks.

"When the fuck did this happen?" Neil says, not even noticing his foul language, though Rob certainly does.

"Language." He says as Neil briefly covers his mouth before regaining his composure.

"My apologies commander." Neil says as Clara hugs him and chuckles at his sudden realization.

“It’s alright.” He says confidently, placing his right arm around his fiancé, both of them blushing.

There is another pause while everyone continues to process the sight in front of them. Their commander, seemingly the loneliest bastard on the face of the planet, now has a fiancé who loves him as much as he loves her. Throwing caution to the wind, the four squadron members across the table, jump and slide over said table and begin congratulating the now engaged couple. Sam’s parents and Rob take the longer route, unable to perform the athletic feat of the younger squadron members.

“Let me see.” Sam’s mother says calmly upon reaching reach the group of young adults; her daughter extends her left hand, obliging the request.

“It’s beautiful.” Elizabeth remarks, completely taken aback by the whole situation.

“Stunning I’d say.” Clara adds.

“I second both statements!” Abigail exclaims.

The men are busy congratulating their commander on the engagement, though he is much humbler about the whole thing than Jeremy was with his engagement to Elizabeth. His temperament at work and nothing more. It may not look like it, but he is thrilled to finally be engaged to Sam; it just feels right.

“Alright, give them some space.” Rob says noticing that they’re both becoming slightly overcrowded and overwhelmed.

The squadron obliges as John and Sam glance into each other’s eyes before briefly kissing for the second time as an engaged couple, while everyone else sits down around the conference table. Following the kiss, Sam and John continue looking into each other’s eyes, chuckling at each other after the gaze lasts slightly too long. Everyone present joins in as the couple leans against the glass wall of the room, relaxing as they once again fall into each other's arms.

“So what’s next commander?” Rob asks, knowing that the coming mission is on his mind.

“Well, we’re going to take our private plane to D.C. with our combat gear. Everyone is going this time as we might have to fight through the secret service, metro police and national guard in order to get to the White House. Once there, then the real show starts.” John says, easily slipping into briefing mode though is reluctant to do so, “We’ll worry about the details tomorrow. Right now I do want everyone to relax; it is Christmas after all.”

“Roger that commander.” Rob replies calmly, much to the relief of everyone in the room as they’re still trying to work off their hangovers from the night before despite the joy present on their faces.

“Have a good day everyone, you’re dismissed.” John says kindly, allowing everyone to get up; congratulating the couple as they leave.

“So it finally happened huh?” Abigail says, the only people left in the room are her husband, daughter and, eventual son in law.

Sam nods as her fiancé smiles, putting his arm around her as she buries her blushing face against his chest. It’s clear to her parents that this is the happiest she has ever been in her life.

“Just look at you two... so perfect.” Her mother continues, unendingly happy.

“I don’t think I even need to remind you to take care of her. Right John?” Josiah says the smile on his face just as wide as those on his daughters and wife’s.

"No, you don't Mr. Adams." John laughs, "We'll join you for dinner tonight."

"Excellent, I want to hear all about the proposal." Abigail says, ecstatic that she gets to cook a holiday dinner after all.

"Don't worry, you will." Her daughter replies, having expected the statement.

With that, her parents head for the elevator, seemingly floating as they head back to the first floor and subsequently to their home.

"You had them all worried that they weren't going to have the day off." Sam whispers, chuckling at her fiancé's sneakiness.

"Well I had to get them in one spot somehow." He says, chuckling as well, still overcome by the events that transpired overnight.

"Shut up." She replies before kissing him a third time, longer this time.

He returns the gesture in kind, having completely fallen for Sam and wanting this feeling last forever.

"Merry Christmas, my fiancé." He says softly finally parting his lips from Sam's, though the two remain close.

"Merry Christmas, my fiancé." She replies, kissing him yet again.

Date: Friday, December 25th, 2020

Time: 1925hrs SST

Location: Midway Base, Former US Minor Outlying Island, Pacific Ocean

Temperature: 25 Degrees Fahrenheit

Sam parents have managed to put together a veritable Christmas feast for the squadron. There's turkey, ham, ribs, stuffing, corn, salad, and dinner rolls all spread out on top of the massive table. Candles are thrown in to add to the ambiance of the Christmas meal. The lights are kept low as the squadron, Rob, and Sam's parents begin passing the various dishes to each other, filling their plates to their heart's content. A fire is brilliantly burning in the fireplace with three stockings hanging from it, shifting slightly due to the slight draft caused by the fire. In the background, Christmas carols play a soft volume from the homes sound system, further adding to the ambiance of the meal.

"Thank you for cooking Mr. and Mrs. Adams. Everything is amazing." Neil says thankful for the full holiday meal.

"You're welcome Neil. It's been a while since we had to cook a meal this large." She replies smiling.

Each couple is sitting next to one another, teasing one another relentlessly throughout the meal.

"What the hell?" John says as his phone begins to ring, "Shit, I have to take this." He continues, heading outside, answering the phone as he does.

Everyone briefly glances in Robs direction before looking confused at each other, wondering what was so important to interrupt Christmas dinner. Sam quickly decides to find out and heads for the door in order to check on her fiancé.

"I understand Chief Logan. Wish your family a Merry Christmas for me." She hears before he hangs up the phone, muttering "So much for Christmas spirit."

"What is it honey?" Sam asks, gently announcing her presence as her fiancé does the reluctantly smart thing and puts his phone back in his pocket.

"The FBI has seized all property belonging to initiative, specifically Wolf Squadron. Everyone's houses, vehicles, you name it, have all been seized in a secret, paperwork, raid. Midway base is officially our home now." He replies solemnly, forcing Sam to gasp as she approaches and hugs him.

"When did this happen?" She says, speaking on instinct.

"About an hour ago."

"It's okay." She says, taking John slightly by surprise as he glances down at her, "Home for me is where you are."

"Same." He whispers as they finally head back for the door to rejoin the bountiful feast currently in progress.

While the squadron is slightly taken aback by the news, all of them take the same line of thinking that Sam has. They have a home with each other no matter where that is. The news is soon a distant memory as the night wears on, gifts are exchanged, and everyone settles in for their first holiday evening off in months.

Date: Saturday, December 26th, 2020

Time: 0630hrs SST

Location: Midway Base, Former US Minor Outlying Island, Pacific Ocean

Temperature: 25 Degrees Fahrenheit

John is already in the Intelligence Center when Sam arrives, both in their standard black tee shirts and jeans. They've both been up since five o'clock this morning when John's alarm went off. The rest of the squadron woke up around the same time though they have yet to make their way to the Intelligence Center, needing more time to wake up after last night's massive meal.

"I guess this means our break is over." Sam remarks, hugging John from behind as he begins pulling together the intelligence files regarding the address.

"Unfortunately. I don't think we will get another for a little while." John replies, placing his left hand on hers, feeling the engagement ring on her finger.

"It's okay, we'll just have to take a longer one for our wedding." She chuckles, kissing him on the cheek.

"I guess so." John says simply, returning the kiss on her forehead.

A simple, yet cute moment for the couple as they transition back to intelligence gathering along with the rest of the bases personnel, some of whom are returning to their posts after waking from their food induced sleep. The snow of the previous day is almost completely gone from the bases paved surfaces though certainly present on the sand and grass. Several of the snowmen have survived for the most part, though it is likely that they will be gone before the end of the day.

"Let's take a break, I have something for you." John says after a few minutes.

Sam is confused as John leads her out of the building and towards the armory; not knowing what John is talking about, though welcoming the break all the same. Walking into the armory, John leads his fiancé back to his personal weapons safe, where his custom designated marksman's rifle is kept, as is his 1911 when it isn't located on his thigh. John carefully enters the pin code on the pin pad and pulls the heavy safe door open, blocking the view of what's inside with his body.

"I built this for you in between training runs for the North Korean mission. Since wolf six's role is being my spotter, I figured you needed a rifle and well... here it is." He says pulling out what appears to be an AR fifteen with a twenty-inch barrel, magpul handguard, pistol grip and adjustable stock; it's chambered in 5.56 NATO and is topped with a four and a half to eighteen by forty-millimeter scope.

The rifle is effectively a lighter and slightly smaller version of John's, a fact Sam immediately notices upon gently taking the rifle from his hands and placing it against her shoulder. It feels perfectly suited to her body, it's not too heavy and not too long, it's practically perfect for her.

"You'll also need this." John says, handing her a black thigh holster; cradled in it is a Ruger Security-9, the same one she shot Richard with.

"Don't you need it?" She asks gently, holding both weapons at her side as John closes his safe.

"I use my forty-five more often than not, so I won't miss it." He replies, barely glancing back at her before moving a few feet to the right.

He stops in front of an empty safe and presses the nine button four times before pulling the door open and a smell, similar to the new car smell, wafts into their noses.

"This is yours; I know it's a little empty, but it'll fill up over time." John says his voice kind and light.

"You're too kind." She says, placing the rifle and handgun carefully in the safe before turning to him.

"You're my fiancé." He says, his unexpected response elisteding a slight laugh from Sam as she closes the door behind her, not breaking eye contact with John.

"That's true." She says softly before hugging him.

"Let's head back. We don't need the others to arrive and wonder where we are." He says after a few long moments, before taking her left hand once more.

They head out the door and back towards the intelligence center, the brief walk barely allowing the cold to affect their bodies.

Date: Saturday, December 26th, 2020

Time: 1535hrs SST

Location: Midway Base, Former US Minor Outlying Island, Pacific Ocean

Temperature: 34 Degrees Fahrenheit

"Alright, we know the speech is taking place on Monday evening at twenty hours eastern and is set to be only a half an hour in length." Clara begins with the entire squadron gathered around the table, while Rob and Sam's parents make their way to the Kestrel to brief Admiral Anderson.

“Which means the President is likely saving the big announcements for the State of the Union.” Jeremy adds as the bullet points begin appearing on the table before them, including a timeline.

“What’s security looking like?” John asks, already knowing the answer but wanting it confirmed.

“Secret Service and Metro Police units have been placed around the White House.” Elizabeth replies, the positions illuminating as red dots on the digital map, “No armor but plenty of small arms.”

“Proposed routes?” John asks continuing the train of thought he started with his last question.

“The shortest route will be to approach from the west. We would enter through the west wing.” Neil says, as the designated street is illuminated in red.

“What assets do we even have in the area?” Jeremy asks as John takes a drink from the water bottle in front of him.

“Nothing. Not unless we bring the C-17 with us.” Elizabeth replies after checking the squadrons database and crossing off assets located in Pennsylvania.

“Let’s plan on that. What can we bring with us?” John says, effortlessly rejoining the conversation.

“Armor wise, nothing. Our one Bradley is down for repairs after the mechanics blew the engine during testing. Which leaves two Humvees, a black hawk and our performance vehicles.” Neil says taking over for Elizabeth as she too takes a drink.

“Performance vehicles?” Sam asks curiously, remembering the invoice for them in the initiatives files.

“The United Nations let us buy three cars just in case we needed to blend in on a mission. A Humvee is a more than a little conspicuous rolling down a residential street.” Clara replies, making a note to have the three cars loaded on to the C-17 by tomorrow morning.

“Do we want to try the peaceful option first?” John asks, keeping the conversation from getting sidetracked.

“Our UN IDs will get us in, but I doubt it’d work for long.” Jeremy says, using the experience of the last few days to guess at what is going to happen.

“I say we give it a shot; we’ll have a limited ammunition supply any way.” Neil’s adds, the rest of the squadron agreeing with him.

“I agree, though we should be mentally prepared just in case.” John decides, practically cementing the idea in stone.

“Roger that commander.” Elizabeth says quietly, sensing what’s coming next.

“Elizabeth, are you up for this?” John continues with a regretful sigh.

She nods.

“Jeremy?” He says, more so asking for reassurance than permission.

He nods, not hesitating, even for a second, as he answers.

John sighs again, still regretting that he has to ask them to go on this mission, but what choice does he have? This mission has the clear potential to go either extremely well or extremely poorly and the best chance of success comes if all six of them tackle it together.

“Alright, you all have studying to do this evening. Special Forces Squadron Three will be providing cover for our planes and equipment while the mission takes place. Wheels up is zero seven hundred tomorrow morning and we’ll be wheels on the ground at twenty-three hundred hours local time. I’ll take care of informing Rob and Mr. and Mrs. Adams. Rest up, you’re going to need it.” John says, the commanding tone returning to his voice once more.

“Roger commander.” Everyone says, regretting that they have to go back to work so soon.

As they leave the room, the joyful fallout from the discovery of John and Sam’s engagement seemingly becomes a distant memory. A brief increase in the clouds block the sun, shrouding the base in shade for what feels like hours despite only being a few minutes.

Date: Saturday, December 26th, 2020

Time: 2147hrs SST

Location: Midway Base, Former US Minor Outlying Island, Pacific Ocean

Temperature: 24 Degrees Fahrenheit

“Sorry about the accelerated timeline commander. Intel reports said that if we flew in at the last minute, there would be a substantial anti-air threat.” John says as Special Forces Squadron three gets their gear in order.

“Not to worry commander. We’re just glad this is happening now and not over Christmas.” The squad leader replies, zipping up his pack after double checking its contents.

"Yeah, I'm glad I didn't have to explain that one to your significant others." John chuckles placing his hand on his hips as he catches sight of Sam conversing with the squad in front of him.

"If that happened, you would've had to find a new special forces squad." The squad leader replies candidly.

"Well that's comforting." John says, grateful to see his fiancé bonding with the special forces squadron.

"You sure I'm not allowed to drive your mustang sir?" The squad leaders asks, finally satisfied that his things are in order.

"Next time commander." John smiles shaking his hand, knowing that he has his own preparations to deal with.

"Roger that. Remember you're a lucky man." He replies glancing back in Sam's direction.

"How could I forget?" John smiles.

Date: Sunday, December 27th, 2020

Time: 0630hrs SST

Location: Midway Base, Former US Minor Outlying Island, Pacific Ocean

Temperature: 25 Degrees Fahrenheit

"You sure you're not hungry."

"I'm sure sweetheart, plus anything I eat right now is liable to make a second appearance."

"Alright if you're sure."

"It's a long flight, bring some snacks just in case."

"Ten hours in the air, I'm going to need a nap for something that long."

"Well it's a good thing that the beds are comfortable."

"I know, my parents told me all about it."

"Did they now?"

"They sure did. Hopefully you'll join me for at least a couple of hours."

"I will if I can sweetheart, make sure you have everything okay?"

"Okay... I love you John."

"I love you too Sam."

Date: Sunday, December 27th, 2020

Time: 0730hrs SST

Location: Midway Base, Former US Minor Outlying Island, Pacific Ocean

Temperature: 26 Degrees Fahrenheit

"Alright everyone, we have a plan, let's stick to it." John says to the screen as the squadrons private plane continues climbing to its cruising altitude; C-17 following close behind.

"Roger that John, good luck." Sam's parents say kindly, wishing the squadron didn't have to leave so soon but knowing there isn't another option.

"Give 'em hell commander." Rob says before the feed shuts down and John sits back in his chair, debating whether or not he should join the rest of the squadron in catching up on some sleep during the flight.

There's nothing more that he could be doing after all, all of the planning and briefing is already complete and there's no sign that the Americans have noticed the mission going ahead. The young commander briefly reflects on the events of the last few weeks, a dull soreness washing over his body as he contemplates the speed with which events have taken place. He wishes they would slow down, but in a way, he's glad that they haven't.

"You should get some sleep. Sam won't until you do." A soft, gentle voice says from behind him.

"Okay." John says, his mind made up, "Will you and Neil be alright keeping watch?"

"Of course." Clara replies, her and Neil approaching carefully.

"Wake me should anything come up." John says, patting their shoulders.

"Roger the commander." Clara replies quietly as she and Neil take up their station and he heads back to his bedroom which has been combined with Vladimir's old room in order to make a massive room like the other two.

Softly opening the door he finds his fiancé laying on the bed, curled up in the thick white comforter. He sits down next to her and gently sets his right hand on her stomach; she softly moans, knowing that he's there. Sliding under the comforter, he carefully guides his arms around her body and softly pulls her close to him.

"Comfortable?" He whispers, as Sam sets her arms on his.

"Now I am." She smiles, keeping her eyes closed.

Date: Sunday, December 27th, 2020

Time: 2302hrs EST

Location: Ronald Reagan Washington National Airport, Washington D.C.

Temperature: 30 Degrees Fahrenheit

"Everything is ready to go commander." The squad leader says over the radio as the cargo planes crew begins unloading the three vehicles.

"Alright, we'll head to a hotel for the night, make sure you keep as much as you can out of view. Cover the markings if you need to." John says placing his weapons in the trunk of his mustang; a red with black stripes, 2020 GT350.

"Roger that, be safe commander." He replies shaking his hand before gathering his own squadron for the long day ahead.

"Are you going to be able to keep up in that thing?" Elizabeth jokes as she and Jeremy squeeze their equipment into a black C8 Corvette; Neil and Clara have a similar vehicle.

"Are you?" John replies simply, sliding into the driver's seat of the Mustang and carefully closing the door as Sam does the same in the passenger seat.

The car's five-point two-liter V8 engine roars to life drowning out the engines of the two corvette's next to them.

"I never knew you could drive a manual." Sam comments as John puts the car in gear and begins slowly navigating the convoy towards the airport exit.

"Yep; it's not as hard as you might think." He says, firmly concentrating on the road in front of him as they join the normal flow of traffic, which is thankfully light given the hour.

Sam chuckles as John lets the engine sing, briefly accelerating to fifty miles an hour before slowing back down and allowing the others to catch up. It's a good thing that there is no ice on the roads, they've been well treated with salt and it hasn't snowed in a few days. The group settles down, not wanting to attract too much attention to themselves before they have too. Elizabeth and Jeremy laugh, making the most of the time spent in the budget supercar while cruising around the streets of Washington D.C. The drive soon comes to an end however, as the group arrives at the Hampton Inn, northwest of the White House.

Parking in the underground parking garage, they are soon heading to their rooms on the third floor; barely anyone gets in their way or even notices them. The rooms are decidedly low end when compared to what the squadron is used too, though they don't mind. Anything higher end would have drawn too much attention and may have blown their cover before they even landed in the United States. Everything is falling into place, with the squadron unable to sleep thanks to the rest gained on the flight to the Capitol.

Date: Monday, December 28th, 2020

Time: 0830hrs EST

Location: Hampton Inn, Washington D.C.

Temperature: 32 Degrees Fahrenheit

After not sleeping much during the night, most of the squadron has elected to sleep in with Neil and Clara being the only members awake at this hour. They were the only ones who got some sleep during the night thanks to the watch they kept on the plane. Just as they are now, keeping a watchful eye on any intel that comes their way.

"Looks like our strategy worked. The CIA and FBI don't think we're here." Clara says passing a piece of paper to her boyfriend.

"I'm surprised they haven't put out a bolo on us." He replies.

"Well they only knew what was owned by the squadron not who is in it, so I'm guessing they don't even know who their looking for." Clara says, glad that her former countries intelligence agencies are taking their time with the situation.

"They may find out soon. It depends on how much of a spectacle John plans on putting on at the White House." He says, slightly hoping that his commander takes the entire half hour that the President had blocked out.

"True." Clara replies, hoping for the same thing as her boyfriend.

Date: Monday, December 28th, 2020

Time: 1923hrs EST

Location: Hampton Inn Parking Garage, Washington D.C.

Temperature: 29 Degrees Fahrenheit

"Everyone have everything?" John asks the group, finalizing his gear.

"All good here commander."

"All set."

"Locked and loaded."

"Good to go."

"I'm ready."

"Alright, mission timer starts in five minutes. Remember to keep an eye on your tactical maps, they'll show you exactly where potentially hostile contacts are. We'll make our way through the West Wing until we reach the Oval Office. From there, we're going to have to wing it." John begins, placing his hearing protection over his ears and turning on the communications link with Midway Base.

"Wolf One this is Wolf Base, communications check when you're ready." Rob says from the Intelligence Center, Sam's parents are present as well.

"Roger Wolf Base, this Wolf One, reading you loud and clear." John replies as everyone else follows the same procedure in sequence.

"Wolf squadron, we are reading all of you loud and clear. Vital signs are looking good and everything seems to be on track. Mission will start in three minutes." Rob replies after everyone performs their respective radio checks.

"Roger that Wolf Base, we seem to be all set on our end." John says, helping his fiancé adjust her plate carrier, her gear setup being almost exactly the same as his, the only difference being that she can carry six magazines instead of four.

Sam is clearly still adjusting to her gear and her nerves are beginning to show on her face.

"Everything is going to be alright. Just follow my lead." He whispers getting her to smile, though it does little to ease her fears about her first mission.

"Two minutes." Rob calls out over the radio.

"Yes, thank you mother, I know how to tell time." John quips both annoyed and amused, the whole squadron laughs as do Sam's parents back at the base.

John takes an unsteady breath. Truth is, he is nervous about this mission too; going up against the only superpower left in the world is not something he ever thought he would have to do. He's glad that he has his friends here with him, otherwise the stress of it all might just be too much to bear.

"Alright, it's time. See everyone at the White House." John finally says, checking his watch as it clicks over to nineteen hundred thirty hours.

"See you there commander." The squadron replies in unison, swiftly entering their vehicles.

The three vehicles start, filling the garage with the echoes of three V8 engines. Turning left and joining the flow of traffic, the squadron keeps their actions subdued; not wanting to draw attention to themselves as they split into several different directions. Just in case someone is watching.

"You're tense." Sam says breaking the silence having noticed John's silent and purposeful breath.

"Yeah." He replies simply, as they pass the Treasury Department.

“Any way I can help?” Sam asks becoming concerned and placing her left hand on top of John’s right.

“Not really.” He sighs, struggling to come up with something else to say.

Sam takes a moment as they stop at a red light, preparing to turn right and pass the south lawn.

“What are you going to do?” She asks, trying to keep John talking.

“That’s up to the secret service and the President. The peaceful option can work, if they want it to but...” His voice trailing off as the light turns green.

“But?”

“But they ordered two carriers to bomb our base, so they may not be interested in the peaceful option.”

“I see.”

The couple passes the south lawn, traffic moving slowly as everyone tries to get a look while John finally take a deep breath.

Date: Monday, December 28th, 2020

Time: 2000hrs EST

Location: The White House, Washington D.C.

Temperature: 29 Degrees Fahrenheit

“My fellow Americans, good evening. I hope you had a Merry Christmas.”

Pop... pop pop pop...

"As we look forward to the New Year, I want to take a moment and reflect on what kind of year it has been."

Pop pop... pop... BANG...

The cameras are still rolling, and the President's mic is still hot.

"What the hell is... who's there? What do you mean... don't you know I'm in charge here!" The President exclaims, arguing with the lead agent on his security detail.

"Mr. President, I need to get you t-" The agent begins before slumping to the floor with a bullet in his back.

The room falls silent, cameras still rolling as everyone looks towards the hallway entrance of the oval office, uneasy about what is going to happen next. A slow clapping sound is then heard as John purposefully enters the room.

"Tell me Mr. President. Do you feel in charge?" He states, smirking as his squad mates enter the room behind him, preventing the television crew from cutting the camera feed.

"Who are you?" The President asks, sitting down behind his desk.

"Commander John Hilderbrand, United Nations." John replies, his voice being picked up by the President's microphone while the camera remains zoomed in on the President's face.

"Commander John Hilderbrand." The President repeats quietly, recognizing the name.

“Yes sir, and you have some explaining to do.” John replies, sitting in a chair on the right-hand side of the desk, just out of camera shot.

“Watch this.” Clara whispers to Sam, feeling what is about to come.

“What do you mean commander?” The President asks, trying to play dumb.

“Oh Mr. President, surely you know about the incident involving one of your stealth fighters or the sinking of one of your submarines. All acts of self-defense I might add.” John says, chuckling throughout his sentence as the President looks on, sweating, “Let’s not beat this around the bush Mr. President, you’ve ordered our destruction, multiple times, and I’m not entirely happy about it.”

The President gulps, more nervous than when he was re-elected.

“Do you have anything to say for yourself, Mr. President? No? That’s okay, I figured as much from one of the Initiatives biggest supporters. The ships are working out well by the way, thanks for asking.” John continues, the menacing tone of his voice mixing with a humorous one.

“What do you want, Commander?” The President finally whispers.

“What do I want Mr. President?” John laughs, “What I want is for you and all of congress to resign before the start of the New Year or none of you will live to see it. Before that happens, however, I want congress to be called into emergency session and for three bills to be signed into law.”

“Three?” The President asks, choking.

"Bill one will set term limits on congress, a maximum of two should do nicely. Bill two will ban all lobbying by corporations, because well I just hate them. That leaves bill three, which will ban any form of political party." John states, calming down slightly, only slightly.

"Why those three?" The President replies, trying to follow the logic.

"Because all of you have become too complacent. You feel like you rule over your citizens and dictate to them as if they're a bunch of peasants. I am simply putting the power back in their hands, something that this government should champion Mr. President. That's what made this country great after all." John says, an underlying growl forming in his voice.

The President remains silent, contemplating his options.

"Don't push me Mr. President. Try and wipe out the initiative again and I'll make sure this spot becomes a crater." John finishes, standing up and leaving the room with his squad mates as he collects his thoughts and the live feed is finally shut off.

Walking past the bodies of multiple secret service agents, several staffers look at the squadron. Feeling unemployed as they watch the young men and women leave the building.

"Still nervous?" Sam asks John as they get back in the Mustang.

"Nope." He states definitely, smiling at his fiancé as they head for the airport.

Date: Friday, January 22nd, 2021

Time: 1200hrs EST

Location: White House, Washington D.C.

Temperature: 25 Degrees Fahrenheit

A cold snap has caused a massive amount of snow to fall outside the oval office as the newly elected president looks out over the south lawn before the soft sound of footsteps catch his attention. He turns to face the lobby where a young man and woman stand before him, wearing black sweatshirts, red tee shirts, and blue jeans with handguns on their right thighs.

"I was expecting a visit from you, eventually." The calm, older, black man says unphased by who is standing before him, "How are you doing commander?"

"We're fine Mr. President, thanks." John replies calmly, more relaxed than the last time he was a few weeks ago; Sam remains silent.

"That's good to hear. Your message seems to have had far reaching implications." He continues holding up a folder as the couple continues to stand at the entrance of the room.

"Yes sir, I guess it did." John replies, raising his hand slightly, subliminally letting the President know that he doesn't need to see the report.

"I'm assuming you're not here for a social visit." The president continues, sitting down behind the resolute desk.

"I'm here to wish you luck Mr. President and to tell you that my speech was just the beginning, it's up to you to keep this going." John says calmly.

"I understand." The president says simply, finally calming down.

"Just remember, you may not be my primary concern right now, but I do have my eyes on you." John says, keeping his tone light.

"I understand commander, I won't let you down." The president says, a small smile falling across his face.

"I know." John replies before he and Sam leave the room, leaving the President continue his day without further interruptions.

Walking out of the same entrance they came through just under a month ago, they get in the mustang and are soon heading for I-95 northbound. The snow is still being cleared away as they make their way up the on ramp, carefully handling the mustangs power in the less than ideal conditions.

"That didn't take as long as I expected." Sam remarks, knowing the drive to Scranton is a long one.

"The new President knows what needs to be done. I just hope he and the new congress learn from the previous administrations mistakes." John replies gently.

"Makes you wonder what's next."

"There's always something, I'm just glad I get to face it with you."

"Me too."

Sam wraps her arm around John's, gently clasping his right hand with her left. Leaning against his shoulder, it becomes clear that she's tired though not exhausted like she was when she joined the initiative.

"I'll always love you John."

"I'll always love you too Sam."

She closes her eyes, promising herself that she'll enjoy the weekend in Scranton with her fiancé before resuming her flight training on Monday. Her first solo flight from Scranton to Midway.

Epilogue

Date: Monday, June 21st, 2021

Time: 1830hrs DST

Location: Seven Springs Fin & Feather Lodge, Champion, Pa

Temperature: 78 Degrees Fahrenheit

Sam's father and mother look out over two ponds from the screened in, front porch of the main cabin. A swan is gentling floating around, unfazed by the staff moving the white chairs with light blue cushions from the ceremony to the reception tables. The tables are already set with light blue and Ivory tablecloths, white silverware and white plates, both with gold accents. Another small team of staff is quickly setting up the makeshift dance floor, lighting, and buffet line for the reception.

Sam's mother is wearing a simple, ankle length, sleeveless, light blue dress with white heels, complementing her light blue eyes. Meanwhile, her father is wearing a simple button up shirt, blue jeans and black formal shoes. He certainly wishes he could change, on account of the heat, however, the wedding photos have been postponed slightly due to a phone call the groom received. He uses a small hand towel to quickly dry his sweating forehead and moves his hand through his bright grey hair in a last-ditch effort to keep it from frizzing.

The proud parents take a look at reception present given to them after the ceremony had finished; a necklace made out of black paracord, a 6.5 Grendel shell casing, and a 5.56 NATO shell casing. Turning the casings in their hands, they find their names carved into each of the casings, *Josiah* and *Abigail Adams*.

"Sorry about the wait mom and dad. Sometimes the world can't wait even for a wedding." A shy yet kind voice says behind them, causing them to turn; it's their only daughter Sam; black hair pulled back into beautiful, braided ponytail.

She is wearing an ivory ankle length dress with lace floral accents covering it and extending down the full length, lace sleeves. Around her waist is a small blue belt and she is wearing ivory, closed toe, sandals with a low, almost two-inch heel with thin straps and a floral back; both accessories are covered in small pearl accents. She's holding a small bouquet of light blue flowers and is wearing a small wreath of the same flowers around the top of her head with a short lace veil draped over her braided hair.

She also has two rings on the ring finger on her left hand. The first ring is the engagement ring John proposed with six months ago. The second ring, closest to her palm, is a simple, thin gold wedding band with ten tiny diamonds around half of its circumference. Engraved on the inside of the first ring are the words *Forever & Always*, while the wedding band is engraved with the days date; June 21st, 2021. Two ivory, pearl bracelets and an ivory pearl necklace complete the stunning yet simple outfit for the beautiful young woman.

"It's alright sweetheart, we understand." Her mother replies giving her still nervous daughter a gentle hug.

"We may not have tactical experience, but if you and your husband need us, just say the word and we'll be there." Her father continues softly as he too gives his daughter a gentle hug.

"We'll keep that in mind." Sam replies trying to keep herself from choking up and chuckling at the same time, "Thank you for everything."

The wedding guests; mainly Rob, Pops, Admiral Anderson, and some of the initiatives staff; begin making their way to reception tables in preparation for the buffet dinner.

Elizabeth comes through the doorway, wearing the same color dress and shoes as Sam's mother. The subtle sound of her footsteps causing Sam to turn around and the two squad mates embrace after sharing a brief gaze.

"He should be out in a minute, the German Prime Minister had too much beer at a state dinner last night and insulted the queen of England." Elizabeth says softly.

"When's he going to learn not to do that? I swear." Sam says moving the conversation along, "How are you and Jeremy holding up? With the baby on the way?"

"We're doing alright, though Jeremy isn't letting me touch any alcohol." Elizabeth says as Sam's father chuckles; he did the same thing to Sam's mother.

Upon hearing his name, Elizabeth's husband walks out of the cabin and onto the porch, wearing a similar outfit to Sam's Father. The same goes for Neil as he and his girlfriend appear a second after Jeremy does. Clara is wearing the same outfit as Sam's mother and Elizabeth. A number of soft embraces are quickly shared by all present as they wait for Sam's husband to come out of the cabin.

The guests begin getting pictures with one another and sharing pleasantries in addition to champagne. One of the two photographers begins taking candid pictures of the squadron members and Sam's parents. They indulge him with a collective smile as the photographer continues snapping away with his camera. Hundreds of pictures, all for one album that only the happy couple will be able to possess; only a select few will be given to their friends and family.

"My apologies everyone, Prime Minister Marshall is now recovering from his hangover and will apologize for his remarks tomorrow morning." A tired, yet strong voice says from inside the cabin; the soft sound of footsteps can be heard as everyone on the porch quiets down.

John, wearing a white button up shirt with the sleeves rolled up, blue jeans and black boots, makes his way through the doorway onto the porch. There is a skinny, brushed gold wedding band on his left ring finger; like Sam's wedding band, it is also engraved with today's date. Marley, the black labradoodle scurries past him trying to receive as much attention as possible.

"I'm sure we'll read about it tomorrow." Sam's father says shaking his new son-in-law's hand after petting Marley on the head.

"Yeah, it'll be in the morning news dump." John chuckles, "Thank you for helping organize this, and, well, for letting me marry Sam in the first place."

"It's an honor, John." Josiah replies, finally letting go of John's hand and allowing his wife to hug the young man.

John sighs with wide smile on his face as he turns to his wife, barely able to contain his emotions for the third time today.

"I know I've said this a lot today, but you look stunning Sam. You really do." He says, bowing his head slightly and holding her hands with his own after she hands the bouquet to Clara.

She smiles, looking up into his eyes and raising her right foot slightly, she brushes some of the hair from his face. She chuckles causing John to do so as well; she can barely believe all this is happening either. No one is talking, though everyone is smiling as the photographer continues to take pictures from different angles.

Sam shyly glances away for a brief moment before standing on her toes and kissing John softly on his lips while gently holding his head. She wipes her thumb over her husband's mouth as he continues to smile and gently kisses him one more time, as if there is no one else around. The second kiss continues while the two lovers fully embrace each other as the couples around them lean on one another. When the kiss ends, John and Sam gaze into each other's eyes, still blissfully ignoring that the squad and Sam's parents are still standing around them. They're both lost in each other's embrace.

"Alright, you two love birds, you don't want Pops eating all the food, do you?" Elizabeth says glancing over her shoulder at the reception, as Clara hands the bouquet back to Sam.

John and Sam chuckle before being led out the door, arm in arm, by their squad mates and Sam's parents. The photographer is still capturing every moment and every detail as the four couples walk over to the reception. Everyone present greets them and soon the sun begins to set as everyone takes part in the barbeque feast being served at the buffet tables.

Dessert is served just as the last rays of sunlight fade behind the trees and mountains; combinations of various ice creams, cupcakes and normal cake is spread out along the buffet line. Sam and John stand around their own table as everyone gathers around them before getting their own dessert. The couples wedding cake is relatively simple; two ivory colored tiers with light blue banding around the bases and few gold lace embellishments. After cutting the cake, Sam playfully shoves her piece into John's face who returns the gesture in kind. They never wanted anything too fancy; a philosophy that has guided the whole ceremony from the planning stages. The joyful couple only wanted something simple and low stress, that would allow them to relax for the first time in months.

Finally, the dancing begins after dessert is finished and the LED lights illuminate the dance floor. John and Sam are the first to dance, to a song called *Lost in this Moment*, by Big and Rich. It's an appropriate choice as their friends and family seemingly melt away, giving them a public moment all to themselves.

"Hard to believe you never imagined this would happen." Sam whispers.

"Now, I can't imagine it any other way." He replies quietly, kissing his now wife on the cheek.

"I wouldn't want it any other way." She says, returning the kiss.

"I wouldn't either." John replies simply and with a smile, though not wanting to spend much time talking as it may taint the moment.

The two pause for a long second before kissing for one long, tender moment just as the song is coming to an end. Their friends and family come back into view as their lips part with an applause erupting while the song falls silent. The couple stands there, holding each other gently as Sam rests her head on her husband's chest. Both of them are tired enough that they could fall asleep right then and there; then... John's phone rings...

www.ingramcontent.com/pod-product-compliance
Lightning Source LLC
Chambersburg PA
CBHW020943310726
48980CB00001B/37

* 9 7 8 0 5 7 8 2 2 8 3 3 4 *